Irons kissed h hen you kiss back."

She could feel ingling. The tender skin was abraded where his mustache had prickled. He was a rough, crude man. But his hard-muscled body called to her own, exciting her, warming her. She lifted her arms and put them around his neck.

"That's right, baby." He found her mouth again, gentle this time, assuaging the hurt.

She shivered. The kiss stepped up the tempo of her heart and started a trembling in her belly.

When he finally drew back, the mock anger on his face had been replaced by a dazed look.

Unconsciously seductive, she lowered her eyelids to hide the passion he had aroused. . . .

"*Wild Texas Heart* is boldly sensual, riveting, a truly compelling, passionate and memorable romance."

Kathe Robin, *Romantic Times*

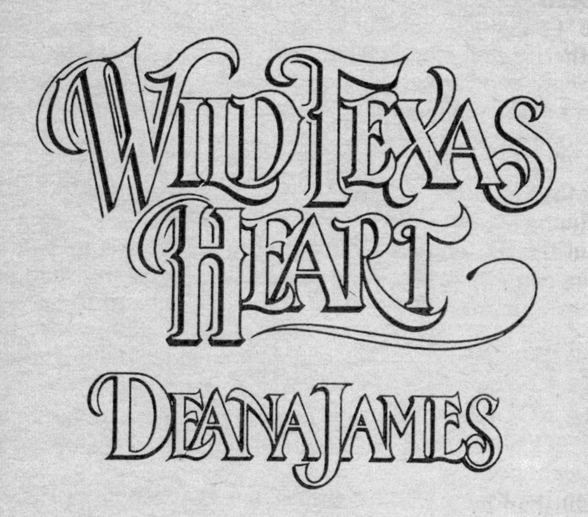

ZEBRA BOOKS
KENSINGTON PUBLISHING CORP.

ZEBRA BOOKS

are published by

Kensington Publishing Corp.
475 Park Avenue South
New York, NY 10016

First printing: November, 1990

Printed in the United States of America

For you,
Rachel Andrea,
with the world waiting for your hand—

Acknowledgment

Thanks to Reed S. Pace, old-time oil man from Gladewater, Texas. When he was just a youth, Reed began work in the oil fields of Burkburnett as a tool dresser on a cable-tool rig. He worked for Humble Oil and later for Magnolia, which became Mobil Oil. He worked near Laredo, at Del Rio, at Crystal City, and at all the fields in East Texas around Longview, Gladewater, and Kilgore. His memories and enthusiasm for the early days of the industry were a source of inspiration and enlightenment to me.

Chapter 1

The hooded figure tossed the rope over the limb.

Fan screamed in terror and struggled, but the tough hands clamped her arms too tightly for her to break free. She screamed again when another pair of masked figures hustled a third forward.

Like hobgoblins they seemed to swim in the thick fog that laced the darkness with thigh-deep swathes. Holes had been hacked out of lengths of heavy unbleached domestic cotton creating ragged black circles through which neither mouths nor eyes showed. Lengths of clothesline rope gathered the hoods loosely around their necks.

Breckenridge's face was dead white; his nightshirt, ripped at the neck, hung off one muscular shoulder. His throat worked convulsively.

Fan looked frantically around her. She screamed again. Surely, someone would hear her and come to their aid. How far had they come? Somewhere close there must be a house. A barn. Something.

The hangman widened the loop at the end of the stiff Manila rope and flipped it over the captive's head. The two men staggered as the man, his arms bound behind his back, flung himself from side to side seeking escape.

"No! For mercy's sake!" Fan shrieked.

"We told you, Breckenridge." The voice was muffled through the heavy cotton. "Sell out and move on. You didn't pay any attention."

"He'll go," Fan screamed. "I swear, he'll go."

"Shut yer mouth." The man holding her snarled in her ear. "Yer gonna be swingin' with 'im if y' don't keep quiet."

"Tell them you'll go." The sleeve of her nightdress ripped off in the man's hand as she managed to pull one arm loose. "Listen to me! *Tell them!* He'll go. Oh, please . . ."

The captive's mouth worked. His lips opened.

The man yanked the knot tight across the Adam's apple.

Another man snubbed the end of the rope around the thick tree trunk. "Gimme a hand here," he called to his fellows.

One of the two abandoned his captive.

Fan screamed again. Her fingernails raked at the eyes of the man who held her. The heavy cotton protected his face, but her fingers caught in the makeshift holes and the mask was torn askew, blinding him.

"Here now." His growl was muffled. "Cut that out!"

Fan's nightdress ripped from her shoulder and split to the waist in back as she twisted and fought.

Seizing his chance, the captive swung round kicking his captor in the thigh. Handicapped by bound hands, he nevertheless ducked his head and rammed his shoulder into the hangman's bulging belly.

"Goddamn! He's loose."

"Naw, he ain't!"

The man who had snubbed the rope gave a fearful yank. It jerked the victim upright.

"Heave!"

The body swung free. Bare feet jerked and kicked for the earth. Toes stabbed downward, frantically searching for something to bear the weight.

Fan screamed again. With primordial strength she flung herself against the man who held her. Perhaps she was too strong for him, perhaps he no longer needed to hold her so tightly. For whatever reason, she was able to wrench from his grasp. She dashed across the intervening space and threw her arms around the jerking knees. Hugging them against her chest, she tried to lift the too-heavy body.

Slight of form, she still managed to take some of the weight off the rope.

Breckenridge sucked air into his lungs even as the men on the rope pulled him higher. One of them laughed. "Lookee that, wouldja? She's sure stronger'n she looks."

Breasts crushed by his knees, Fan could not even draw a breath. Her laboring heart sent pains like knives stabbing through her chest. Black spots swirled in her vision. Her ankles collapsed, she listed to the side.

The hangman climbed to his feet. Clumsily, he adjusted the hood, shrugged his heavy shoulders, then tore the sobbing woman away from the victim's knees.

Fan fell backward, landing hard on the tip of her spine. With a cry she pushed herself up, and sprang on him, clawing at the eyeholes of the mask.

He caught her wrists in both hands, then twisted them down together and closed his fist around them both. Deliberately, he struck her with the hand he had freed. Her head snapped back on her slender neck. She cried out in pain.

He struck her again, doubling up his fist and slamming it into the side of her temple. At the instant he struck, he let go. The force of the blow sent her slender body spinning. She crashed into the bole of the tree.

The breath whooshed from her lungs. Through failing sight she stared at the shadowy scene.

With deadly determination he turned back to the jerking, swinging body. "Ready, boys!" he called.

The hooded figures on the end of the rope braced themselves.

"No—o—o—o . . ." The cry was only a painful moan.

The executioner lapped his burly arms around the man's twitching legs. Jumping high, he kicked his heels out from under himself and dropped. His full weight came down on Breckenridge's lower body.

The neck snapped like a dead branch.

The hangman's knees scraped the ground. He let go of the corpse and climbed to his feet. Stepping back, he surveyed his handiwork. Dusting his hands, he motioned to the two holding the rope. "Tie it off."

"Hey! This here's a new rope."

"Tie it off!"

Obediently, they looped it around the tree and made it fast.

The fourth man stooped over Fan's body. "She's still breathin'."

"Finish her," said the hangman succinctly.

Instantly, the man stepped back, shaking his head. "Not me."

The hangman stripped off his mask. "You do what you're told."

"Not my style," the other amended quickly.

"Damn it. You was paid."

The other two joined him. "A hundred dollars. That's all we got paid for this. We didn't settle for two."

"Listen here . . ."

Still arguing, they drifted back into the fog that came

seeping back into the clearing beneath the tree. The new rope creaked eerily as the body turned slowly.

The hangman took a step toward the small bundle crumpled at the foot of the tree. Saddle leather squeaked as his companions mounted. One called to him, the voice sounding hollow out of the smothering fog. "Let's beat it."

He hesitated. Killing a man was nothing. But killing a woman could mean trouble. Twenty-five dollars apiece was too little to run the risk. He could hear the stamping of the horses. His companions had started moving away.

"Come on," one called.

He shrugged. He had hit her pretty hard. Probably cracked her skull. Even if she lived, she would never be able to identify them. He mounted his horse and spurred it after his fellows. The thunder of their hooves died away.

Irons studied the scene beneath the water oak with merciless detachment. Except for the huddled figure on the ground, he would have ridden on with no more than a curious glance.

While he was deciding whether to climb down and investigate, the tired gelding shifted from one hip to the other and blew a roller through its nose.

The homely noise communicated itself to the body on the ground. It shuddered, then whimpered.

A woman! Irons raised his dark eyebrows. Still he did not swing down from his horse and dash to her side. Women were trouble. Doubtless she had witnessed a horrible scene. Probably she had been raped. In another minute she would become hysterical. Hysterical women would say anything. She might accuse him. Even if she did not, her relatives might assume that the person who came hauling her in would have had something to do with what had happened here.

Better to ride on, he decided, than risk the chance of involvement. At the next town, he would report the hanging and send help out. Until then she probably would stay right where she was.

The woman stirred. Her bare leg, its skin startlingly white, slid across the rough ground. As Irons gaped, she pushed herself up on one elbow. Her eyes met his. They were strange pale eyes, an odd golden color, their lids swollen and blotched, their black lashes spiky from tears. The bruises on her cheek and temple were reddish purple, painful to see. In the center of her temple was a crescent-shaped cut. She stared at him blankly.

A sudden gust of cold wind stirred the torn ruffle of the heavy cotton nightdress. It also set the body to swinging.

The woman caught the movement out of the corner of her eye. Slowly, as if her neck hurt, she turned her head. The corpse's bare feet, black with coagulated blood, the toes strutted grotesquely inward, swayed only inches from her face.

Here it comes! he thought, and hunched his shoulders.

She did not move, did not flinch. But tears, silent and huge, gushed from the corners of her eyes. She stared up and up the swinging, elongated body, and the tears splashed down onto the bosom of her nightdress.

Irons felt a momentary painful twisting in his gut. He blinked, mildly surprised. The feeling was a stranger to him. Perhaps the silence of the tears unaccompanied by any hysteria, was what got to him. He swung down off his horse and approached her.

She heard the crunch of earth beneath his heavy

brogans. Her eyes turned to him. They were no longer blank and dull. Terror and frantic pleading spoke through the bright tears. *Help me! Please, help me!*

The power of those eyes made him suck in his breath and hesitate fractionally between steps.

The woman looked again at the corpse swinging above her, its neck grotesquely elongated. Instinctively, she lifted her hand to her own neck. At that moment she became conscious that not only her throat but her entire shoulder and the mound of her breast were bare.

Irons saw her drop her eyes to her bosom, saw the scarlet blush rise. As he watched, practicality blunted the horror. A chill breeze gusted at that very moment. The ruffle of the nightdress stirred and fluttered. With shaking fingers she gathered it and pulled the rest of the gown across her shoulder. Fumbling, blinking rapidly through the tears that kept falling, she tried to fasten the garment together.

The effort met with scant success. Her violent struggles had shredded the waist of her gown, ripping it away almost completely in back and leaving her right shoulder and breast bare. Fearful of his reaction to her nudity, she pulled up her knees to her chest.

Irons did a quick about-face and returned to his horse. From his saddlebag he pulled one of his own shirts, rough blue chambray, heavy and durable. He brought it to her. "Here."

"Thank you," she whispered.

"It's not much."

"I . . . I'm grateful." Slowly, as if her shoulders hurt, she maneuvered it around and slipped her arms into it. He should have helped her, but he could only stare at her chest. Her breast was a small perfect cone peaked with dusky rose nipple erect and hard in the cold air.

He cleared his throat and let his stare move lower. Dark bruises stood out harshly on the white skin of her ribs and at her waist. As he had suspected, she had been handled roughly. Probably raped.

"Look the other way." Her voice quivered with embarrassment.

He ducked his head, then shifted his eyes to the wet gray landscape.

At last the garment was decently buttoned. She looked up at him. "All right."

Silently, he held out his hands. She reached to take them, then drew back, fingers clenched.

With a grimace he jerked them back. What woman could keep from flinching at the sight of his hands. He thrust them into the pockets of his slicker. "Can you ride?"

"I've ridden since I was two," she muttered. She held up her hands with steady determination. "I'll be happy to take the hand you were offering."

He stood like a statue as she closed her fingers over his and pulled herself upward. As if she were discovering how to use her body anew, she struggled until she got her feet under her. The deep ruffle of the tattered nightdress drooped in scallops that fell over her bare feet and trailed on the ground.

"Pet's about done in." He nodded toward the rawboned sorrel. "She can't carry us both. You'll have to sit the saddle alone."

"What about him?" she asked instantly.

"Best leave him just as he is. I'll take you to the nearest town and send back for him."

"Leave him hanging?" Her face twisted until he thought she might cry again.

"Be better." He slipped his hand under her elbow to guide her toward the horse.

"Oh, no."

"Nothing can get to him up there on the end of that rope," came the practical reminder.

A distinct green tinted the pallor round her mouth. "G—get to him?"

"Don't think about it."

Even as he spoke, she twisted aside, staggered a few steps, and vomited. He rolled his eyes skyward, then followed. Putting a hand around her, he splayed it over her stomach while with the other he held her forehead. Sweat dampened his hand. He could feel the flat belly convulse. Then she went limp.

"Women!" With a groan of disgust, he swung her up into his arms. They were more trouble than they were worth. No question about that. He looked around him wearily. They never pulled their weight, especially when a man was caught with one in the big middle of nowhere.

Again he was tempted to leave her underneath the tree. He could cover her with his slicker. A stronger gust of cold wind rattled the dry leaves still clinging to the branches. A drop of rain hit him. And then another.

Damn! Bad luck! Now he was up a stump. If he left her, she would be sure to tell her relatives that he had been here. She might even get him confused with whoever had done the job.

The rain began to strike her in the face. She flinched, then twisted and moaned. A couple more huge drops splatted her cheek and nose. She opened her eyes. Her head was tipped backward on the slender stem of her neck. He saw her throat work.

A couple more long strides and he was beside his horse. "Spread your legs," he instructed coarsely. "I'll lift you right into the saddle. We need to get a move on. We're gonna get wet."

The drops were falling faster now. The front of the blue chambray shirt and the bottom of the nightgown were wet. As he tilted her into the saddle, the gown rode up thigh high exposing her bare legs. Shivering violently, she clasped stiff white fingers around the horn.

Suddenly, the heavens seemed to open up. The heavy downpour, coming on a slant, beat down her heavy tangle of black hair to trailing ropes. It soaked the shoulders of the shirt and the gown beneath. To the east thunder warned of heavier squalls on the way.

She swayed forward in the saddle.

He shot her a quick look, but her eyes were closed. Her lips moved. Was she praying? He quickly looked away. Prayer was a waste of breath. He hated to look at anybody praying. The sight made him angry. He hated futile gestures, and nothing was so futile as prayer. Cold water streamed off the dip in his hat brim like water poured from a pitcher. "Come on, Pet." He wrapped his hand around the mare's ear and called to her. "Let's get the hell outa here."

One mile. Two. The rain continued to fall steadily, but the wind switched around until it was blowing due south. The woman hunched over the saddle. Her hands clasped around the horn; her teeth sank into her bottom lip. Her eyes were closed.

A third mile. Then through the gloom he spotted a rectangular shape. He shook her shoulder and pointed. "Look! A roof!"

She did not open her eyes, did not respond in any way.

He guided the stumbling mare toward it. It was

nothing but a stock feeder, a roof with three sides and a long rick. The ground was bare and wet, but at least it was a shelter against the rain and wind.

He led the mare under it.

Fan opened her eyes when the icy rain no longer beat on her head, then closed them again. Her head ached so badly that at first she could not see. She was so cold that she was beyond shivering. Pain, weakness, shock—all blasted her.

Nevertheless, an indomitable instinct to survive directed her mind deep into the center of her body where a tiny shadow of warmth beat. Her consciousness sought that shadow, that single lick of flame, and left the outer shell of her body as untenable.

Irons unbuckled the cheek strap and pulled the bit from the sorrel's mouth. Immediately, the famished mare tore a switch of hay from between the slats and began to chew. Giving her a pat, Irons lifted a whole bale from storage in the back and spread it over the wet ground.

His bedroll followed from behind the saddle. The tarp went down first, then the blankets. He put his hand on the woman's elbow. "Let's get you into this."

She did not move. The shirt was sopping and icy. He transferred his hand to her bare knee. The skin was so cold, it shocked him. She was too cold. He looked into her face. Her teeth did not even chatter. Yet her lips were bluish purple.

With a curse, he pulled her down from the saddle. She was stiff, unable to move her limbs or straighten her back. She slumped over his arm. He looked down at the damp blankets. While not actually wet, they were not warm. A fire was impossible. Everything for miles around was soaked.

He groaned again. He should have ridden on.

Rolling her over on his arm, he stripped off the sodden shirt and nightgown and stuffed her nude in between the blankets. She lay deadlike while he stripped off his own outer clothing. Spreading the slicker over the top of the blankets, he climbed in beside her.

Her skin was so cold it made him shiver. His teeth began to chatter. He clenched them so tight that his jaw began to ache. "You are one cold woman," he murmured against her wet hair as he maneuvered her limp body into a cradle made by his torso and thighs. "Never could stand a cold woman myself." He pushed her wet hair back from her face. "Don't have much use for any woman, but I sure do hate a cold one. Freeze a man's . . ."

She moaned faintly as his hands moved her about.

He broke off his speech. No sense in shocking her if she were half conscious. As a matter of pure fact, the press of her smooth body had not frozen him at all. The curve of her bottom pressed into his belly. His member, turgid from the cold blasts, remained stiff as he began to warm. He shifted uncomfortably.

She lay cradled with the curve of her neck fitted over his upper arm. He ran one hand down her side. Her skin was so cold; her breathing, so faint. He let out his breath in a sigh of despair. She was probably dying of exposure. And he had nothing to help her—only thin blankets to shield her from the cold wet air. With every slow breath she exhaled, the heat was flying from her body. His own body pressed against hers could not warm her fast enough.

He slipped his arm out from under her head. It rolled limply to the side. Her face, presented in profile, was dead white. He had to bring the blood back to that white skin. He sat up. His brown hands, the scar tissue horribly mottled, hung over her for an instant.

She had flinched at the sight of them. Now she had no choice. He had no choice. He began to rub her shoulders. Vigorously, roughly, he massaged the white skin, bloodless except for the bruises where hard hands had gripped her. He rubbed until a faint color began to appear. Her chest came next. He took a deep breath. Her firm breasts yielded and moved beneath his hands. Her nipples were pinched into tight buds by the cold, false signs of arousal, while their aureoles looked shrunken and pale.

Still, he felt himself grow warm. An ache began in his groin. He set his teeth to endure the feel of her bottom against his bare thigh.

She groaned again.

His hands halted their massage, then went on. Down over her bruised rib cage, across her belly and onto the top of her thighs, he moved. His scarred fingers slid into the black curls, startling in contrast to the white almost translucent skin. He could feel the warmth there, feel the tiny knot of nerves that nestled in it. At least she was not quite dead.

Did her eyelids flicker? Were her cheeks faintly flushed? A violent shudder ran through him as he slipped his arm under her thighs. Swiftly, he turned her over, his own face hot.

Her bare back stretched before him. Her shoulder blade was terribly bruised as was her left side. Still he did not spare them. Sweeping the damp hair aside, he began to rub her spine and shoulder blades.

He rubbed until a healthy flush spread over her torso. The bruises looked worse than ever as the increased circulation brought more coagulated blood to the skin. Breathing a fervent curse at the men who had abused her, he covered her with his shirt and bent her leg back at the knee. Her delicate foot was shrunken and blue with cold.

At least three men must have done the deed—two to hang the man and one to hold her. He lifted one slender wrist. No rope burns encircled it. They had not needed to tie her. She had stood no chance against them.

She moaned again. Her eyelids flickered. The black lashes swept up, then down again.

He tucked her foot back beneath the blankets and slid down beside her to take her back in his arms.

She went willingly enough until she opened her eyes. Only inches from his own, they stared at him, puzzled. Her lips framed the question.

"Don't be afraid. I'll take care of you. Everything's going to be all right."

She looked over his shoulder at the falling rain. Her forehead creased in a frown. Her first words escaped on a breath. "What happened?"

He felt her body begin to shiver. Roughly tender, he drew her head down to his shoulder. "Cuddle up to me and don't worry about anything. You and I both need to sleep."

"Where are we?"

"In a stock feeder."

She accepted this information and moved her hands up his body until they lay palms open against his chest. Her legs moved, sliding along his until she had cupped her cold feet over the back of his calf.

He swallowed hard. The position brought her in contact with the rest of him, now aching with need. He clenched his teeth against his own desires. She was no stranger to a man's body.

Something was not quite right about her attitude. She did not know him, had never seen him before. The ripped clothing, the bruises on her skin, the flood of tears at the sight of the dead body, all led him to believe that she had suffered a hideous shock. Yet she seemed unaware of it.

Thunder rumbled in the distance. The rain struck the wall with renewed force. The woman in his arms snuggled closer to him. Tentatively, almost unbelieving of his luck, he slid his hand down to cover her breast.

She sighed. And wriggled closer to him.

One dark eyebrow rose. A sly grin spread his mouth beneath the black mustache. Had he ever been wrong about her being cold! He tightened his arm across her back. "Well, hello, baby."

Rolling her nipple between his thumb and third finger, he lifted his head and fitted his mouth to hers. His tongue slid between her lips in a long kiss.

She moaned and tilted her hips up to him.

"You want it?" He drew back his head and stared into her eyes. His whisper was incredulous. "You really want it?!"

Her golden eyes searched his face. "Yes."

He could hear the faint note of uncertainty. Before she could change her mind, he rolled her onto her back and raised himself on his elbows above her. His kiss was long. His tongue played along the silken surfaces inside her mouth as his rough hands squeezed her breasts and rolled the nipples beneath his thumbs.

She arched her throat and gasped for breath. Again the tilt of her hips. This time more demanding.

"Let me in, baby," he whispered as he left her mouth to move down her throat.

"Wh—what?"

"Let me in," he repeated, finding the nipple and biting it.

"Oh!"

"Come on," he whispered, pressing himself impatiently between her thighs.

She shuddered. Her hands pushed against his shoulders.

"Come on," he demanded, a little louder. He sucked her nipple into his mouth. "Baby, don't go cold on me now."

Her hands slid over his shoulders and drew his head down against her. She spread her legs, and he slid into her warm, melting sheath.

Chapter 2

"Well, hello, baby!"

Had someone actually said those words? To her? Icy fog crept back into her mind, threatening to suffocate her. She opened her eyes. At least, she imagined that her eyes were open, but she could see nothing. Nothing at all.

Warmth. She needed warmth. She was so cold. She sent messages to her legs and arms to move, but a weak shudder of her torso was all she could manage. She was tired too. Sleepy. Sleepier than she was cold. She could not feel her feet nor her hands.

"Let me in, baby."

What was he talking about?

Her heart began to beat again. Blood began to run through her veins. Her breasts tightened, and a sweet ache began somewhere between her legs.

She opened her eyes again. A dark silhouette filled her vision. A man. Who? What was happening? Her body began to assert its desires in a manner that left her gasping.

She could feel her hands. They were resting on a man's shoulders. But whose? She pushed gently, then a bit harder.

His mouth. She felt a shock of pleasure. His mouth was at her breast. Her nipple tingled. Nerves jumped and skittered. Her skin prickled and warmed.

". . . don't go cold . . ."

Cold. She was cold. No. Not cold. Not cold at all. The deep voice mesmerized her. Hot weakness loosened her thighs. Hard fingers pushed between them, parted her. She took a deep breath of anticipation. The heavy thickness slid into her, filling her, driving the breath from her lungs in a soft exhalation.

He waited as her anticipation built. She clutched at his back as aroused senses clamored for release. Still he waited. A sweet agony. She tightened her own muscles, urging him, begging him. At some deep level she craved his hardness and strength, wanted to draw his warmth and life more deeply inside her.

She heard a deep chuckle, that swiftly changed to a groan. The man pushed deeper into her, then pulled back, to drive forward again. And again.

Yes! That was what she wanted. What she had to have. The rhythm, the effort of their joining made a light sweat break out on her body. Delicious warmth pervaded every limb. She was cold no longer. Experimentally, she opened her eyes.

A man's face hung above her. Her eyes widened. She realized that she stared into the face of a stranger.

Even as her mouth opened to scream, his shudder of fulfillment began. He plunged against her, lifting her hips off the blankets. He pushed himself up, his arms at full stretch, his back arched like a bow, a groan of delight and deliverance rising from his throat.

Her own body skidded to a halt. The flush of excitement drained from her cheeks. Uttering a cry of panic and disgust, she began to lever herself backward. What had happened to her? What was she doing here beneath a stranger? Where was she?

Her violent movements lasted less than a minute. Pain exploded in her head, making her cry out. Likewise, her left arm refused to function properly. As she fell back, half in, half out of the blankets, more pain blossomed in her shoulder and all along the length of her arm.

The man sat back on his knees, hands resting on his thighs. He was breathing hard, his stormy eyes looking at her in amazement.

She stared into his face, trying without success to recognize him, trying desperately to call his name. At that moment her mind was a complete blank. She could not think of a single human being. Her eyes slid down his hairy chest to the nest of black hair between his heavily muscled thighs. His manhood, glistening, still half . . .

Shuddering violently, she covered her eyes. Tears squeezed between her fingers.

She heard him move, heard the rustle of clothing, felt the movement of the air as he stood up.

After a minute, he said, "It's all right now. I'm decent."

She shook her head refusing to look at him.

"All right," he said, his voice sounded amused. "Suit yourself. But at least get back under the covers. After all the time and effort I went to get you warmed up, the least you can do is try to stay that way."

She shook her head again, wrapping her arms around her. She was cold, but she would not climb back between those blankets where he had . . . where they had . . .

She told him so.

He laughed. "Well, if that's the way you feel. But I can sure look my fill at you so long as you're out in the open, 'nekkid' and all."

Her eyes flew open. While they had been closed, he

had dressed completely and now stood rolling a cigarette. When he finished, he licked it, twisted it, and stuck it between his lips. While he fished a match from his pocket, he stared at her, his gray eyes taking in every curve of her shivering body.

Hastily, she slid back under the covers and pulled them high over her chest and shoulders.

He grinned as he struck the match on the rough wood of the hayrick and held it to the tip of the cigarette. He inhaled deeply to get it started, then exhaled a long blue breath of smoke. "Figured you'd get back under the covers after you thought about it a few minutes."

"Where are my clothes?"

He pointed laconically to the nightdress spread over the top of the rick. Its torn ruffle trailed in the dirt.

She stared at it as if she had never seen it before, then turned back to him. "I don't believe you. Where are my clothes?"

"That's all you were wearing when I found you, baby."

"It—it couldn't have been." She passed a trembling hand over her eyes. Her head had begun to pound with renewed vigor. "I know . . ." She felt the nausea rise in her throat. Hastily, she squirmed over on her side leaning out over the side of the makeshift bed.

He rolled his eyes heavenward. "Women! Are you going to be sick?"

She swallowed heavily. Then managed a tiny shake of her head. "I don't think so."

He dropped down on his knees beside her and slipped the blanket up where it had fallen off her bare shoulder. "Don't worry," he counseled. "You had a real bad time last night. You need sleep."

"What happened?" she whimpered. "What happened? I can't remember anything."

His dark eyes searched her pale face. "Now don't worry about that," he advised. His forehead wrinkled in thought. "You don't have anything to worry about. When you want up, I'll tell you what happened. Till then, just go to sleep."

"What about you?"

"I'll just sit down here and smoke a cigarette and then I'll see about rustling us up something to eat. I'm so hungry my belly button's shaking hands with my backbone."

At the mention of food, she shuddered. Nausea returned with claws to add to her distress. Her face contorted. She clutched at her belly in helpless panic.

He shook his head. "Here now. That's enough. Settle down. I'm liable to pitch you right out in the cold if you make a mess in those blankets. They're all we've got."

The authority in his tone steadied her. Obediently she lay back, her face pale as death except for the hideous bruises. He adjusted the covers around her throat with a nod of satisfaction.

Turning to his saddlebags, Irons pulled a sugar sack from them. Seating himself on the bedroll, he opened the parcel and found a couple of strips of jerky and a package of dried apples. "Here you go."

She shook her head dumbly. She was too sick to eat.

He pushed a slice of apple at her. "Eat a bite," he ordered in his authoritative tone. "It'll make you feel better."

"I don't think so," she whispered.

"Sure," he insisted. "You passed the low point early this morning. It's uphill from now on."

She looked at him drearily, thinking that uphill sounded too high for her to climb. Still she took a small bite of the apple he proffered. It was moist and chewy, its natural sweetness seeping into the corners of her dry mouth, stimulating her tastebuds. She took another bite.

"See, I told you," he grinned. His mouth spread beneath his mustache revealing strong, even teeth. He pushed the jerky into her hand. "Now take a bite of that and I'll give you something that'll make you smile."

She did as she was bid while he rose and went back to Pet's side. The mare was dozing now, having eaten her fill. He loosened the girth and pulled a second shirt from the saddlebag. Juggling it expertly, he unrolled it until he had in his hand a flat pint bottle. His smile even wider, he returned to the blanket.

He caught the cork between his teeth and extracted it with a twist. Gallantly, he offered his companion the first sip. "Here."

"Whiskey?"

"Right. Don't worry. It won't make you blind. I bought it off a fellow north of here. He swears he's got a hundred satisfied customers."

She hesitated. Her head was pounding so hard, she could barely think. Did she drink whiskey? She could not remember. He shoved it into her hand. With no protest she turned the bottle up.

Once in her mouth, she held it on her tongue allowing the fumes to rise. When it slid down her throat she was prepared. Though it burned, it was pleasurable. She welcomed its warmth.

He watched her narrowly. She was no stranger to whiskey neat. He accepted the bottle as she handed it back and toasted her. "Sure does the trick, doesn't it?"

"Yes, it does," she agreed hoarsely.

"Now eat your jerky and we'll get back under the covers."

"No."

"Yes."

She looked at him coldly. "I don't share my bed with strangers."

His grin changed to nasty. "Well, we sure ain't been introduced, baby, but you sure had me fooled, throwing it up to me like you did."

She paled. The jerky dropped from her shaking fingers. "I didn't know who you were or what I was doing. I didn't even know what was going on. I must have been crazy."

He shrugged. "Maybe you didn't know who I was, but you sure did know what you were doing." He took another drink of whiskey. "And you sure weren't crazy. Just natural as can be."

She covered her face to keep out the sight of his mocking grin.

He mocked her scornfully. "That's the trouble with women. They act like they just can't get enough and then when it's over, they start singing a different tune, lying their heads off."

She lowered her hands. The eyes that stared at him were the saddest, the most hopeless he had ever seen. Her voice was a hoarse-pained whisper. "If I'm lying, I don't know it."

Neither spoke for a moment. His voice when it came was noncommittal. "Relax. I promise I won't bother you anymore."

Obedient in despair, she clutched the blankets at her chin.

He tucked the jerky into her hand and patted her shoulder.

She heard him moving around, then steeled herself as he lifted the corner of the blankets and slid in beside her. For a moment she lay stiff as a poker, but he patted her hip familiarly and then gathered her in against him.

"Relax," he advised again. "I'm not going to do anything to you. Just imagine you're sleeping with your brother."

For long minutes after his remark while his warm breath blew in her ear and his even breathing lulled and relaxed her, she wondered whether or not she had a brother.

"Care to tell me where you live?"

She closed her eyes in anguish. Then opened them and looked around her. Nothing looked familiar. The trees, the road, the house and barn set back from it on the left—none of it rang a bell.

"I . . . My head hurts so badly I can hardly see," she muttered.

"Looks like we might be getting close to civilization," he suggested. "I expect we're just a mile or so from Waldrow." He looked at her closely as he said the name.

"Waldrow?"

"Of course, you might be from somewhere else," he said after a pause. "It's just a rag town. Maybe from Batson," he emphasized the name.

She stared upward at the dark pines. "I don't think so."

He put his hand on her thigh. Startled, she looked down from the back of the rangy sorrel. "Care to tell me your name?"

She shook her head gingerly. "I've been trying to remember, but to tell the truth . . ." Her voice quavered. ". . . I can't remember anything."

"Swell."

"I'm sorry." She rode in silence for a minute. "What's your name?"

"It's Irons," he told her shortly.

"Irons?" She knew she had never heard that name before. Her lips formed the word a second time, and a third.

"Do you remember how I found you?" he asked suddenly.

She shuddered. He had given her his slicker since the rain had stopped and the pale blue Texas sun was pushing feebly through the clouds. The heavy garment moved as she shrugged. "Not really."

"You don't remember . . . er . . . anything about last night."

She blushed. "I remember what you did to me."

He brushed past that without a flicker of emotion. "Nothing before that."

She shook her head. "What happened? Where did you find me?"

"Under a tree."

She remembered the torn nightdress. "A tree. Did you"—she swallowed hard—"kidnap me?"

He shot her a murderous look. "Damn woman. Just like I thought. You're going to try to hang that on me."

"What?"

"Just keep your mouth shut. I'm sorry I brought it up."

"What? Brought what up?"

"Nothing."

She leaned forward over the horse's neck. In her anguish her voice rose to a panting cry. "For mercy's sake, tell me. Tell me something. I can't remember anything."

He swung around, his face very close to hers, his black brows drawn together in a scowl. At that minute a buggy came round the turn in the road ahead. "Will you shut your mouth?" he grated. "We've got company. And you'd sure as hell better not try to hang that thing on me."

To his surprise she straightened up. Her hands clasped over the pommel. She waited stiffly as it came on.

Its black top glistened with moisture. Its occupants looked curiously at the duo. What they saw was a man, by his dress a roustabout, and a woman, enveloped in a yellow slicker, her black hair streaming over her shoulders.

Irons stared blackly at them.

They drove on never slowing the horse.

"What?" she demanded. "What am I supposed to try to hang on you?"

"If you don't remember . . ."

"If you tell me, I'll most likely remember."

"The hanging."

"Hanging!?"

"Sure you don't remember," he accused.

"No. No, I don't." Her face became abnormally pale.

"Look," he sneered. "All I want to do is get you into Waldrow and turn you over to somebody else. You're just like every other woman I've ever known. More trouble than you're worth. I didn't have anything to do with what happened back there. And I'll be damned if I'll take the rap for it. All I did was play Good Samaritan." He began to walk the horse faster than before. He threw a last command over his shoulder as if it were an invective. "Don't you dare faint on me."

She swayed back in the saddle. "I promise I won't faint," she whispered more as a pledge to herself than to her escort.

They rounded the bend in the road. The first tents appeared nestled beneath the shadows of the pines.

"Is that Waldrow?" she asked.

"Yep. Should be. Unless they've thrown up another rag town between here and there."

"Rag town?"

He looked up at her disgustedly. "Tent city. Camp town. Boomersville. What do you want to call it?"

She did not answer. Instead she was sitting straighter in the saddle, staring beyond the tents and through the trees. A frame of bare wood rose among them. Nearly fifty feet in the air it towered above the rig floor. Horizontal beams and cross beams were hooked to the huge frame. And in the center of it, encircled and protected like the heart within the rib cage, the drill moved rhythmically up and down.

"It's an oil well," she said unnecessarily.

He looked at it critically, noting the solitude of the derrick. "Maybe so. Maybe not," he said laconically. "Not much action around it. Probably some wildcatter's pipe dream."

The horse stumbled over a clod in the rutted dirt road, exacerbating her headache by the sudden jolt. She uttered a moan of pain and slumped back in the saddle.

He glanced up at her and shook his head. Women took a lot of looking after. "Almost there," he consoled her. "I'll find you someplace to lie down before I go looking for someone who'll know you."

"Thank you." The words slid from between tight-clenched teeth.

On the edge of Waldrow, he swung up on Pet's back behind the woman. He preferred to ride in for the simple reason that the main street was so deep with mud that it would have been over the tops of his brogans. As they rode past the first tent, a little boy and girl scrambled up from among the pine needles at the base of a huge trunk. Barefooted in the thick black gumbo, they ran in through the open flaps of the canvas tent, tracking the mud in onto the slab floors.

A woman's disgusted snarl and a couple of sharp slaps drove them out again, but Pet had already moved on past the scene.

Irons reined to a halt before a story-and-a-half building with a hotel sign propped on its porch roof. The woman in the saddle in front of him stared doubtfully at the place. It had once probably been a farmhouse, now its shape had been distorted by ramshackle wings added on either side. "Is this all there is?" she asked worriedly.

"Ol' man Rice hasn't gotten around to building a hotel out here yet," he sneered.

He heeled Pet sideways so he could step down on the hay and gravel spread in front of the porch steps. "You stay put," he told her. "I'll see about getting a room."

She nodded gratefully and shifted in the saddle. The bare leather even at the mare's slow pace was rubbing the insides of her thighs and undersides of her buttocks raw.

Across the sea of mud stood a saloon made out of sawmill slabs and roofed with palmetto. She stared at it, her face twisting with the pain throbbing in her brain. Had she ever seen it before? The rest of the street was comprised of several large tents and a barn that had been turned into a general store, its sign hanging below the hay doors. Nothing looked familiar.

The sun had burned away the morning clouds and now burned down on the top of her head and her bare feet and legs hanging out from beneath the slicker. She felt dizzy and sick. Hopelessly, she closed her eyes against the pain.

"Come on," Irons called to her from the porch step. "They've got a room on the second floor."

She tried to move, tried to swing her leg over the horn. Her muscles would not work. She looked at him piteously.

His mouth twitched under his mustache; then he came down the steps. "Just let go and fall off," he advised with a touch of weary disgust. "I'll catch you."

His tone awakened a spark of pride. Her teeth sank into her lower lip. Sliding her hand under her thigh, she literally lifted her leg over the horn. At the same time she freed her foot from the stirrup and slid down. The edge of the slicker and her gown caught on the horn. By the time her feet touched the ground, both legs to the top of her thighs and one hip were naked to the world.

She cried out in anguished embarrassment.

Irons shook his head, a grin twisting up the corners of his mouth. In the light of day, her legs were long and shapely. The graceful curve of her buttock invited him forward, his hand cupped automatically.

Across the street from the saloon came a noisy whistle and several catcalls. A couple of men lounged out and stood grinning, their beer bottles in their hands. "Say, lady," one called. "How about if I give you a hand?"

She twisted in the trap her garments had made for her. The hem of the slicker was anchored firmly around the horn. Her face went pale an instant before turning bright red.

The other gawker slapped his hands on his thighs and gave a whoop of delight as her desperate struggle pulled the slicker and nightgown waist high.

Their jibing irritated Irons. A couple of swift strides put him between her and the saloon. Roughly, he twitched the garments free. "I told you to just let go," he snarled in her ear.

"Maybe you could use some help, buddy?" came the leering voice behind.

"Much obliged," Irons grinned over the dark head, now buried in his shirt front. "I think I can handle this myself."

"Good luck to you."

"Please," she whispered. "Please get me inside."

He swept her up and mounted the steps. Once in the dark, cool interior, he did not stop but mounted the narrow stairs. Four doors faced a short barren hall. One stood open. A sharp-nosed woman with a Gibson girl hairdo and a tight-drawn mouth waited beside it, key in hand. "This is a decent house," she declared at the sight of the naked legs and trailing nightgown. "If you want to do that, there's a house for it in the old barn out back."

"Ma'am, I don't want to do anything," Irons assured her. "I found this woman on the road. I just want to put her down so she can get a little rest until someone can contact her folks."

His burden raised her head from his chest and stared hopefully at the hotel keeper.

The other stared back. "You're not from anywhere close around here, are you?"

"I thought I might be. I just can't remember."

"Got hit on the head," Irons explained.

The woman shrugged uncaring. "Well, all right. But the room is seventy-five cents a day for two."

"You didn't tell me that," he argued.

"You didn't tell me you were going to carry a woman in."

"How much for the week with meals?"

"Twelve dollars."

"Twelve dollars!"

"This is a decent place," the woman repeated. She closed her hand over the key and pulled it back.

"All right," he acceded wearily. He dropped his chin to rest it on the top of the disordered black head. "Take the key."

His burden held out her hand.

The proprietress surrendered the article and stepped aside. "Leave the door open, if you're not married," she cautioned as she started down the stairs.

Irons carried the woman into the room and stood her beside the bed. "Can you undress yourself?" he asked.

She glanced at the open door.

With a mild curse he closed it. "Now."

She started to undo the tabs on the slicker, but her fingers fumbled so badly that he pushed her hands aside and opened them himself with quick efficiency.

She stared at the wrinkled shirt beneath and the skirt of the torn nightdress, gray with rain and soil. "I've ruined your shirt."

"Don't worry about that." He pulled the covers back. "Climb in."

"I . . . all right."

When she was lying down and covered to the chin despite the closeness of the room, he pulled off his hat and raked a scarred hand through his hair. For the first time she noticed that it was gray. Thick and wavy as a young man's, it was nevertheless steel gray, like his eyes.

She searched his face again for some idea of his age. His deeply tanned skin stretched firmly across the sculptured bones. He did not look like an old man.

He replaced his hat quickly under her scrutiny. "I'm going to leave you for a while and find out who's the law around here. Bound to be something about the hanging."

"The woman didn't recognize me," she reminded him.

"She wouldn't have recognized her own mother if she couldn't turn a buck over it." He stared down at the tired little face. "What's your name?" he asked.

She opened her mouth. Then shook her head. Tears welled in her eyes.

"It's okay." He patted her hand. "I was just checking. Figured you might just blurt it right out before you thought."

"Don't you believe me?"

"Oh, I believe you all right. You haven't looked at yourself in the mirror. You took a knock on the side of the head that looks like it could have killed you."

"My head hurts," she agreed.

"It should." He raked his fingers through his hair again and put his hat back on. "I'll be leaving you now, Jane."

"Jane?"

"Got to call you something. Otherwise it's going to be, 'Hey you.' "

She smiled a little shakily. "All right. Jane it is."

When he left, she threw back the covers and eased herself up. She was dizzy, her stomach grumbled loudly, but his comment about her appearance had stirred her curiosity. Leaning against the mattress, she made her way to the end of the bed and then around the foot. A small washstand with a bowl and pitcher and a good-size mirror was the room's only other piece of furniture. Teetering with every step, she approached.

The mirror was crazed and smoky, but a reflection appeared in it. She stared appalled. The face was scarcely recognizable as a woman's. In fact, it was scarcely recognizable as a face. She put out a trembling hand. It too appeared. Her fingertips touched the fingertips in the glass.

The image was hers. Her eyes were sunken and hollow with dark bruised circles beneath them. One was almost closed by a huge swelling knot on her left temple, a crescent-shaped scab crusted on top of it. Her mouth was likewise swollen, her lips cracked and peeling. Her hair was a witch's snarl of tangles, starting out from her head in tufts and drabbling down over the bosom of the wrinkled chambray shirt.

A tiny sound escaped her. What had happened to her? Who had mistreated her so that she looked like this?

Never taking her eyes from the image in the mirror, she unbuttoned the shirt. The shredded gown made her wince. Slowly, she plucked it open. More livid bruises contrasted with her white skin. How could she have sustained such a beating and lived?

She shook her head. With the movement the pounding in her head increased tenfold. Blackness closed in over her vision.

She sank to the floor in a dead faint.

Chapter 3

"Sheriff!" The sharp-faced woman laughed incredulously. Without seeming to move, she pulled a Colt .45 from under the table she had positioned to use for a desk.

Irons dropped back a step, hands raised before the ominous black bore pointed straight at his face.

"Meet Sheriff Colt. He's the only law we've got around here. He won the election by a landslide. We weren't even a town six months ago."

Irons edged a couple of feet to the left, but the gun sight followed him remorselessly.

She grinned maliciously. "Know why this place is called Waldrow?"

He shook his head.

" 'Cause Old Man Waldrow owned all the land around here. This is his house. That's his barn out back there." She gave a jerk of her head. "It's been turned into a bawdy house."

"What happened to him?"

She shrugged her shoulders dislodging the tatty shawl, but the gun did not move. "Dead. Some toughs from Standard Oil came by. He ran 'em off the place with a shotgun. Next day he's dead. But they've got signed leases."

Irons felt the screen door at his back. "Much obliged for the information, ma'am." He lowered his hands. "I'll just ask around at a couple of other places."

"Well, good luck," the woman sneered. The gun vanished beneath the table. Irons curbed the impulse to duck down to find where she kept it. "Nobody here knows nothing about nobody. People come and they go." She hitched the shawl back onto her shoulder with a sniff. "If you wanta know what I think, I think she didn't look much like anybody'd be missing her."

"Well, I'll ask around anyway. Somebody's bound to know something." Irons tipped his hat and backed out the door. The skin itched between his shoulder blades as he hurried down the steps.

Jane opened her eyes to the sight of gray dustballs under the washstand. She closed them, at the same time drawing a deep breath. Beneath her cheek the floor felt gritty. Muddy boots had stood where she now lay.

She shuddered at the thought of what might be beneath her cheek. Head aching and dizzy, she pushed herself up on one elbow. Her left eye began to water, and she lifted her hand to wipe at it.

The sight of the grimy paw stopped her. It was filthy. Black dirt filled every crevice in her knuckles. The same dirt also showed beneath her torn and jagged fingernails.

She looked down the length of her body. From beneath the wrinkled muddy shirt trailed a length of muddy material that had been once a ruffle. Irish crochet an inch wide trimmed it.

Curiously, she examined it. Irish crochet, indeed.

Expensive stuff. Though filthy and gray its quality was unmistakable. She was not poor. The realization gave her a lift. She pulled her knees under her and shifted her body so she could pull herself up by the chest of drawers.

Ignoring the horror in the mirror, she looked around hopefully. Water. Water would make it right. She could wash herself at least. And she was so thirsty. Her throat felt like a desert. She swallowed experimentally and shuddered at the taste in her mouth.

The pitcher was empty. She stared around her then down at herself in dismay. Irons had taken his slicker. She had no clothing except the torn gown and the wrinkled shirt. What if she opened the door and met a strange man? Or a drunk? Like the two across the street. The thought of them filled her with inordinate fear. They might grab hold of her and beat her.

Suddenly, a fist came out of the fog at her. She could not dodge. Her wrists were being crushed in a powerful grip. A blow struck the side of her head. Pain rocketed through her head. Dark figures rose round her. One swayed back and forth far taller than the rest.

She clapped her hands over her mouth, barely stifling a shriek. In a flash the images disappeared.

Terrified by her thoughts, she could feel a cold sweat break out on her body. Tears started in her eyes and her hands began to shake.

Her plight would have to get much more desperate before she could bring herself to leave the room. The trap of a moment ago now became a haven. With a moan, she staggered toward the bed. She almost made it before the black fog rolled up into her vision again.

* * *

In the middle of the afternoon, Irons knocked on the door. He waited a moment and then let himself in. The woman lay on her face beside the bed, her arm outstretched.

He shook his head in irritation. What was she doing down there? He had told her to rest. Scooping her up without ceremony, he dumped her on the bed. He was certainly getting his share of exercise hauling her around.

He crossed to the washstand, removed his hat, and lifted the empty pitcher. It brought him up short. He glanced at the still figure guiltily. He should have thought about getting her some water at least. He had taken care of his horse and his own needs but had had no care for her.

He scowled. She was not his responsibility. He could walk away anytime. Anytime he wanted he could call up his rule about women and get rid of her.

He could do it anytime, he assured the image in the mirror. He ran his hand across his cheek and chin. He needed a shave and a bath. He moved so he could see the reflection of the still form. He might as well get enough water for the two of them while he was getting it.

"Bathroom at the back," the woman at the desk told him. "It costs a quarter extra."

Irons shot her a malevolent look. "I'm already paying seventy-five cents a day for a fifty-cent room."

"Nothin's free around here."

"Except Old Man Waldrow's house," he reminded her sourly.

"He's not using it anymore, and I kept it for the old bastard for fifteen years. I figure I'm entitled." She hesitated, then relented grandly. "You can use two towels."

The bathtub was an enormous affair with claw feet and silver fixtures. Its rim rose nearly three feet off the floor. The water that flowed from them looked clear; but as the white porcelain began to fill, it showed itself to be the color of very weak tea.

Jane sat on a little camp stool beside the tub, her hands clenched together between her thighs. The problems of getting in and out of the tub grew more obvious as the stained water rose.

Irons came in at that moment carrying a huge copper kettle. Steam rose from the spout as he emptied its contents back and forth the length of the tub. Then he turned off the water and set the kettle down. "You first."

Jane rose to her feet. "I don't think I want a bath," she murmured. "I think I'll just use a cloth."

He stared at her. "Listen, baby. We're going to be sleeping in the same bed tonight. I'm going to be clean. And I expect you to be clean too."

"I'll be clean."

He rolled his eyes to the ceiling again. "What's the matter now?" he growled. "I'll leave you alone if that's what's bothering you. Don't you want a bath?"

She hung her head. "I want a bath. I want one badly. I just don't think I can get in and out of the tub. I can't . . ."

"Is that all that's bothering you?" He bent and lifted the edge of the shirt and gown together. In a quick motion he pulled them over her head.

Her hands flew to her naked body ineffectually trying to shield herself. "For heaven's sake!"

He scooped her up. "In you go."

"Oo—o—o—oh!"

He set her down feet first, then supported her to ease into it. Her whole body trembled. "Easy now," he said soothingly. "Easy now. Just settle down."

The bath was only lukewarm. She scarcely felt it rising over her buttocks to her waist, gently lapping the undersides of her breasts.

When he released her, she huddled forward, ducking her breasts under the water, crossing her arms tight around her knees. "I . . . Thank you for helping me."

He did not answer. Instead, he rolled his sleeves up to his elbows and put one knee on the stool. "I'll wash your back."

Awkwardly, she shot a glance over her shoulder. "Oh, you don't have to. Oh, please, you don't have to bother."

He lathered the soap into the washrag and began to rub.

She stiffened instantly, straightening out of her tight ball, arching her back in pain.

Their eyes met. "Looks like bruises under the dirt," he remarked, lightening his touch.

She let her head sink forward again. Heat, so hot she could feel the blush, rose in her face. She could not believe a man whom she had only known for twenty-four hours was giving her a bath. Her teeth began to chatter.

His hand cupped her shoulder. "Settle down," he said. "Don't get so excited. Talk to me. Come on."

She made a strangled sound, then the words came out nearly choked with embarrassment. "How did you get your name?"

The water splashed. Then he started on her left shoulder. "Irons?"

"Yes. Irons."

"I gave it to myself."

"Is that all of it?"

"It's enough."

"Is it your real name?"

"Yes. I gave it to myself. It's real."

"First or last."

"Only." He turned his attention to the right shoulder. "I don't have a last name. The name they gave me in the orphanage doesn't count. This is the name I earned for myself. Tilt your head back."

She obeyed him. The warm water weakened her. Hunger weakened her. The throbbing headache weakened her. And his rhythmic gentle touch weakened her most of all. Her arms fell away from their tight grip on her knees. Her head lolled on her shoulder. She persisted in their conversation as a way to hang onto consciousness. "It's not like a real name," she murmured as his hand moved down her arm. "How did you earn it?"

"Spanish-American War. I packed in a load of guns, sidearms and ammunition for some boys. They were pretty damn glad to see their shootin' irons." He chuckled, but the note carried no humor.

"You mean your name means 'guns.' "

"That's right." He moved the cloth around to her belly.

She caught at his hands. "I can do that myself."

"Just relax," he told her a little hoarsely. "I've already started. Tip your head up."

The long unblemished column of her throat sloped down to breasts that gleamed with moisture. Her nipples stood out taut, beaded with droplets of water. Where the bruises stood out on the white skin he passed the cloth with gentle care.

He shifted his weight, feeling himself tighten. Concentrating fiercely on the job at hand, he gathered her long hair in his hands and guided her head back until her scalp was under water. Supporting her neck with one hand, he ran his fingers through her hair, combing it over and over again in the water, combing the tangles and snarls out, combing the dirt from it, rinsing it, until it flowed free like silk around her in a heavy black cloud.

Her eyes remained closed during the entire operation. Her lashes, like black fans, spread on the satin skin turned up to the light. Her lips parted slightly.

He could not help himself. He bent and put his own lips to hers.

She stiffened but did not struggle. She found she could not had she wanted to. Heaviness and a rising heat began in her loins.

As he drew back from the kiss, he shifted her upward in the water so her back was supported by the cold porcelain slope. Water and long black hair streamed over her breast.

The washcloth slid down the inside of one thigh and up the other. She opened her eyes. He dropped the washcloth and retraced that path with his fingertips, lingering in the nest of black curls. Her hands clenched then released in the water.

He rose and eyed the bathtub appraisingly. "Be right back, baby," he said huskily. "Stay right where you are."

She waited, her hands floating weightlessly in the water, her head tipped back.

He returned with another steaming kettle. The water warmed instantly around her feet where it was too deep to be uncomfortable. "Now," he murmured. "Let's see if we can make this work."

She stared wide-eyed as he stripped. For the second time she saw him in the light of day, but this time she could not turn her eyes away.

His body was hard and lean, muscular through the shoulders and arms, but narrow at the waist and hips. Every muscle was clearly defined beneath the sprinkling of black hair on his thighs and calves. A fine mat of black hair curled on his chest and arrowed down past his navel to spread again in a tangle. His manhood jutted out from it, dark and thick with desire.

She swallowed, trying to alleviate a sudden acute tightness in her throat.

He carefully stepped into the tub, pushing her knees wide and up to receive him between them.

"I don't think . . ." she began nervously.

"Let's not worry about thinking, baby," he interrupted. "Let's just make this work."

"But . . ."

One hand closed over her mound, his thumb seeking and finding the nub of pleasure while with the other hand, he pushed her knees upward, easing them toward her chest.

"Wait. I don't . . . Ooooh!" Her eyes closed as acutely pleasurable sensations raced through her and the heaviness and heat increased.

"Is it good, baby?"

"Y-yes." She sucked in her breath so hard that her chest heaved.

"You're sure you don't want me to stop?"

"No. No. Don't stop."

He worked his way forward in the tub until his knees were tight against her buttocks, then swayed forward to kiss her breast. Instead of a gentle kiss, he bit her. She opened her eyes, gasping at the pain, writhing.

The motion served to lift her onto his thighs. Hands spread across the tops of her hipbones, he guided her onto him.

"I'll be damned," he whispered incredulously as he rocked back, lifting her out of the water. "I didn't think this was going to work."

She slid down even farther until she rested against

his belly. Shuddering with ecstasy, she clasped his shoulders.

"Move for me," he whispered. "Come on, baby. Move for me."

She swayed her hips back and then brought them forward.

"That's right. Good. Oh, God. That's right."

She raised herself. The tip of her breast brushed against his face. With a growl he snapped at it, catching it in his teeth with mock fury. She shivered, her whole body tensing in anticipation of pain.

The shiver transmitted itself to him. He groaned, his breath warming the nipple. "God, you're good, baby." One hand cupped her buttock pulling her back down, holding her against him, holding her mound throbbing, wet, hot, against the root of him, holding her still.

The torment was exquisite. Hot desire curled and writhed at the base of her belly, curled and writhed for release. "I can't stand this," she cried. "I really can't. Please. Oh, please."

Still he held her. Both hands clasped her buttocks, pressed her harder into him. "It's great, isn't it, baby?"

"No. Yes. No. I can't stand this. Please. Please." Her sheath contracted and released, squeezing him, begging him even as her voice begged him.

He gasped, then groaned, his teeth clenched beneath his mustache. His jaw tight. "You beg so nice. Pretty baby."

"No. No more. I can't stand this." She writhed her upper body, pushed against his shoulders, trying to escape the heat coursing through her veins.

"Wait, baby. Wait. Let it build."

"No." Her hair lashed round her shoulders, drops

of water spattering the walls, whipping about his shoulders as well. "No. Please. I . . . Please."

"Wait, baby." He set his teeth, his shaft throbbing inside her, throbbing.

Her sheath clutched him, tugged at him, urged him even as he held her outer body immobile.

Finally, he could bear no more. "Now," he groaned. He pulled her buttocks back with his hands, pulled half out of her, then rammed himself upward as he brought her back.

She cried out and went rocketing into unimaginable pleasure just before her climax drew off the last reserves of her strength.

When his own release came, he found he held her unconscious in his arms. Cradling her limp body, he turned his face to the ceiling to suck in great lungfuls of air.

For several minutes he sat while the bathwater cooled and the tops of his feet were bruised from their combined weights resting on them and pressing them into the bathtub. At last, he heaved a deep sigh and hoisted himself up holding her in his arms.

"Damn, baby," he sighed as he stepped over the edge of the tub. "I'm forever and a day hauling you around."

He stretched her out on the floor, a towel rolled beneath her head, while he hastily bathed. Then with quick efficient movements he donned his clothes.

She was already awakening as he stood over her drying himself vigorously. As she sat up, shivering with chill, he hunkered down in front of her and began to towel her dry. "What's your name?" he barked suddenly. "Tell me."

Her mouth opened. For just an instant, knowledge brightened her eyes. Then the spark flickered out; the memory evaporated. The steel trap snapped to again. She shook her head. Her face tired and sad.

He patted her shoulder reassuringly. "I'll keep trying," he said. "I promise you that. One day, I'll catch you. Till then, up you go, Jane."

He pulled her gently to her feet and slipped her arms through his clean shirt. "Now." He stepped to the door and looked out into the hall. Satisfied that he could make the stairs with a good chance of their being unobserved, he turned back and held out his arms. "Hop in the saddle, baby."

She did not hesitate but came to him and locked her arms around his neck.

He swept her knees up with his left arm. His right twisted the handle of the door. "We're getting good at this," he declared as he mounted the stairs.

"What did you do about the body?" she asked.

They were seated on the bed where she was devouring the tin plate of beans, beefsteak, and cornbread that he had carried up from the dining room below.

"I asked around. No one that I talked to had heard of any man and woman missing. Of course, they probably wouldn't have told me if they had. My guess is that you and whoever that man was, your husband maybe . . ." He looked pointedly at her left hand where a faint indentation showed at the base of her third finger. "Looks like you lost a ring."

She rubbed the spot. "I can't remember."

He shrugged. "Maybe you made somebody mad at you. Maybe you had a piece of land that somebody wanted to drill on. Maybe your husband wouldn't lease it. Stuff like that happens all the time. Maybe they didn't mean to kill him. Maybe just scare hell out of him."

In the back of her head she heard the words. *"Sell out and move on."*

Irons watched the color drain from her face. "What is it?"

She rubbed her forehead with the tips of her fingers. "I don't know. I seemed to hear words just then. Then they were gone. I can't remember anything like that. I can't even remember the hanging. I don't know whether I was there or not. But I must have been. I was lying under his feet."

She shuddered and set the plate aside.

He put it back on her lap. "Eat it. It's costing me twelve dollars a week."

Flashing him a guilty look, she picked up the fork again. "What about the man?" she asked again after a time.

"Nobody's talking. I figured out pretty quick that I was getting nowhere. There's no sheriff." He shrugged. "The best I could do was pay a kid roughneck fifty cents to ride over to the closest town—that's Batson—and tell their sheriff where to find the body."

"The closest town," she said hopefully.

"It's south of here. I was north of town when I found you. If they were going to hang somebody, they wouldn't take him around a whole settlement to do it. Besides, Batson's no place to be from."

She frowned. "It's booming itself, isn't it?"

He nodded. "Right you are. How'd you remember that?"

"I remember most things. I can remember about clothes and food and all sorts of things. I can remember how to do things. I'm not a halfwit. I just can't remember my name."

"Or the name of any of your family," he reminded her.

"Or the name of any of my family," she agreed sadly.

"It'll come," Irons counseled.

"What did he look like?"

He raised one black brow and regarded her thoughtfully. "You don't want to know."

This time she did set the plate aside and lie back on the bed. "I can't remember." She pressed the heels of her hands to her temples and squeezed, as if she could squeeze the words out. The only thing that squeezed out were two tears from beneath her closed eyelids.

Irons set the plate on the floor and reached over for her. "Here, now. Quit that. It won't do any good."

"But what if I'm never able to remember anything again? What if my mind gets worse and worse? What if I become an idiot?" Her voice rose hysterically.

"Now just calm down, baby." He held her tight thinking that he was getting into this deeper than he had intended. "You're not going to become an idiot. You're just like a soldier who's had a big gun, maybe a cannon, go off too close to his head. He gets kind of shocked. For a while he doesn't know anything. Can't hear anything, can't feel anything. He just wanders around in a daze. Then a little bit at a time, it starts to come back. Finally, it all comes back."

She looked at him with hope in her eyes. Then it died. "I wasn't near a big gun."

"Hell, baby, you're so much littler and weaker than a soldier, just a little gun would make you go crazy."

"So I am crazy."

"No. For God's sake. Don't put words in my mouth. Listen, baby. You're going to be all right. I promise you."

She nodded slowly, then lay back exhausted on the bed. The pain in her head seemed to have abated somewhat after the food. She began to feel drowsy.

The room had grown dark while they talked. He could hear the saloon across the street getting louder and louder. He stirred restively.

"Do you want to go over to the saloon?" she asked, her voice husky. "I'm not afraid to stay here alone, if you do. I'm about to go to sleep anyway."

"Are you sure, baby? Are you real sure?"

"I'm real sure." She made a little joke imitating the intonation of his voice.

He patted her hip familiarly. "Then I'll just take a little stroll and wet my whistle. There's bound to be a foreman or two over there that I can tie in with. Maybe start to work tomorrow."

She was turned on her side, her eyes open wide. The moon came through the window, casting enough light to see her white face. "I hope you find what you want."

He strode toward the door, looked back, then came back. "Don't worry about anything, Jane, baby. I'll be back." He dropped a kiss on her temple and pulled the covers higher up on her shoulder.

He pulled himself out of bed the next morning hung over. "I don't like to talk in the morning," he moaned as she asked him for the second time how he was feeling.

"I'm sorry." She subsided back onto the covers, her lips tight.

He pulled on his shoes and stumbled to the door. "Just let me get down and get a couple of cups of coffee down me, and I'll be right as rain."

When he returned, she asked, "Did you get a job?"

He looked affronted. "Didn't I say I'd get one? I'm the new rigger on the Boomin' Bessie, Number Ten."

"Congratulations." She hesitated. "I'll be happy to

do your laundry and cook for you, if you'll just get me some clothes."

"What're you talking about?"

"I'm saying that I'll work for my keep."

He scowled heavily. "There's no need for you to do that."

"Of course I need to. That's what women do for the men who support them." She rose and came gingerly around the end of the bed. Her head still ached, but the pain was a shadow of its former self.

"You can't even walk across the floor."

She waved her hand rather than shake her head and take the chance on increasing the pain. "I can. I'm fine. I've been walking around and around the room while you were out. I'm getting my strength back. The swelling has almost gone." She looked at herself in the mirror. "I know I'm not good to look at but . . ."

He took her arm and guided her back to sit on the bed. "Hold it right there. You're just fine. But you don't need to work."

"I do. And we need to move out of this hotel. You can't afford twelve dollars a week. We can move into a tent like those over behind the saloon."

He caught her hands and clasped them together between his own. "Listen, Jane," he growled. "Forget that stuff. I'm not going to take you into a tent with me."

"I don't mind," she insisted. "I really don't mind."

He tilted up her face. His eyes were gray steel, his jaw set. "Listen," he said again. "I don't care whether you do or not. I'm not taking you on. Do you understand what I'm saying? Women are trouble. I've got a rule about them. I won't have one hanging around my neck."

If he had hit her, he could not have hurt her more. Her face turned white.

He flushed but kept on doggedly. "If I moved you into a tent with me, it'd be permanent like. Neither one of us need that. So just forget about it. I'm asking everywhere I go. Somewhere somebody's looking for you. He'll find you in just a few more days. And then you and I'll part company." With that he turned and hurried from the room, closing the door hard behind him.

In the silence of the room, the woman called Jane drew her knees up to her chest and wrapped her arms tightly around them.

Chapter 4

"Here you go, baby." Irons tossed a parcel onto the bed at her feet.

She looked at it in some surprise. "What's this?"

"It's what you've been begging for the last couple of days."

"Clothes?"

"Yeah."

His answer instantly galvanized her into action. "Oh, thank you. Thank you." She scrambled around on the bed twisting the sheet which had been carefully draped across her bare feet and legs. Eagerly, she lifted the paper-wrapped parcel and felt the thickness and the weight of it. She looked at him suspiciously. "This feels like a lot."

He shrugged offhandedly. A commotion in the street drew him to stroll to the window. He raised it and leaned out, tossing a terse command over his shoulder. "Just open it."

She untied the string and pulled apart the brown paper. The dress, neatly folded inside, was simple blue chambray, but nothing except the material was simple. Her eyes were instantly drawn to the shirtfront bosom, richly and delicately embroidered with lazy daisies and

French knots. She held it up with a cry of pleasure. "Why this is beautiful! Where did it come from?"

He turned away from the window. "I traded for it."

"Traded? What?"

"Your nightgown."

She looked incredulous. "Tell the truth."

He strolled back to the foot of the bed, his thumbs hooked in his belt loops. A smile twitched the corners of his mouth beneath his mustache. "Honest Injun. There's this woman over in one of the tents by the rig. She does all sorts of sewing. Got a sewing machine and everything. I heard about her from her husband. She was looking to make some money."

"You paid a lot of money for this, Irons," she accused.

Shaking his head and grinning beneath his black mustache, he rocked back on his heels.

She let the dress fall back on the bed and crossed her arms over her bosom. Her sigh was eloquent of her distress. "Oh, I can't stand this. I'm so beholden to you. I'll never be able to pay you back. How could you go and pay a lot of money for a dress like this?"

"I didn't, Jane. I swear." He could no longer conceal his grin. "I traded your old nightgown."

"My nightgown? Come on. It was torn. And filthy."

"That's what I thought. But then I thought about that lace." He took a deep breath swelling his chest a little.

She started to speak, but he continued eagerly.

"That woman that I took it to. She liked to have had a fit over that lace. You know what it was? Irish crochet."

"Yes, I knew," she said softly.

He looked a little disappointed. "You knew that? Bet you didn't know that she'd want the material in the gown too?"

"But it was torn and filthy."

"She said it was raw silk."

The woman he called Jane stared at him incredulously. Silently, she lay back on the bed, the new dress spread across her. Its skirt covered her bare legs down to her ankles. Her eyes were bleak. When she spoke, her voice quavered close to tears. "Who am I, Irons?"

He gave a grunt of disgust. Instead of being proud of his clever trading, she was back to fretting and worrying again. He frowned heavily. "Now cut that out. That's just like a woman to be worried about something that'll all come out in the wash anyway."

She did not raise her head. Her eyes were bleak; her face, sad.

With an exaggerated sigh, he sat down on the other side of the bed and patted her hand with easy familiarity. In the three days they had lived together in the hotel room, she had had to accept ordinarily shocking behavior as normal.

On the first day she had huddled under the covers making herself as small as possible when he stretched out beside her. On the second when she had jerked the covers over herself, he had jerked them back off again. Women were silly things, he told her irritably. Just sitting around in his big shirt that fitted her like a tent was not going to upset him. "Stop squawking and ducking every time I come in."

So she had driven her modesty deep inside her and presented him a calm face whenever he entered either to bring her food or to rest and sleep himself. The only place to sit in the tiny room was the bed. He had to sit down beside her to put on his clothes and to take them off. Now he sat down to talk to her.

Awkwardly, he patted her hand in an uncustomary gesture of comfort. "I know you're worried about what you can't remember," he said. "That's why I got this dress. So you can get out of this hotel room.'' He studied her critically. ''You're beginning to look pretty good. The swelling above your eye's gone down and your face looks okay.''

''Thanks.'' She smiled a little grimly at his left-handed compliment.

''You know what I mean.'' He grinned, then sobered. ''I figure once you get out and look around, see people again, you'll see something that looks familiar, and right away it'll all start coming back to you.''

She shook her head. ''Do you really think so?'' She rearranged the skirt of the dress, then smoothed out a crease. ''It's just so awful. You can't imagine.''

He shook his head. ''I guess not.''

''It's like living in a kind of prison. Except the walls don't seem to be there at first glance. I've been trying to remember, trying to trick myself. I start thinking about how to do something, like cleaning house. I see myself put on an apron. Then I get out the broom and carpet sweeper, feather duster and polishing cloths. I start into the parlor of my home. And suddenly I can't remember it. I can't remember anything.'' Her voice quavered hysterically. ''Not a single thing!''

''Easy. Easy.'' He patted her hand again.

''Not a single thing,'' she repeated softly. She made a snubbing sound as she drew in her breath.

''It'll come,'' he promised.

She nodded. ''If you say so.'' With a violent movement, she pushed herself off the bed. Her hands rose to unbutton the shirt she wore, then halted. ''Turn your back.''

He grinned. ''Why?''

''I just want you to.''

He leaned back against the iron bedstead, his smile toothy, his fingers laced across his chest. ''I don't want to. I got these things for you. I want to see you put them on. She put some drawers and stuff like that in the package too.''

Her skin pinkened as she lifted the dress in front of her as if covering her nudity. ''I can't.''

He scowled. His black brows drew together in a sharp line. ''You tell me if I'm wrong, but haven't I seen you naked as the day you were born?''

''Yes.''

''Who washed you from head to toe and dried you off, I'd like to know?''

''You.''

''Who's hauled you up and down stairs like the Queen of England herself?''

''You, Irons.''

''Then why all the fuss about putting on drawers and a dress in front of me?''

''It just doesn't seem right. A woman shouldn't get dressed in front of any man except her husband.''

His voice was a dry leaf rustling. ''Who's to say you've got a husband anymore?''

She paled. ''That man might not have been my husband.''

''And you might not have been married.''

Her color came back with a rush. ''I . . . I wasn't a virgin.''

At the memory of their shared passion, he grinned lecherously and recrossed his legs on the bed. ''You sure weren't, baby.''

''Irons! I might be someone's wife. I shouldn't be doing anything in front of you that would h—hurt him.''

He rolled his eyes heavenward. ''You think you wandering around the countryside naked in my company isn't going to h—hurt him?''

She could feel the tears prickling at her eyes. ''I wasn't naked.''

"Damn near."

"And I wasn't wandering."

"You were just getting ready to get up and wander off when I happened to ride by."

Tears spilled over onto her cheeks. She hung her head miserably. "Please, Irons. Stop it."

"Oh, for God's sake." He rolled onto his side making the bedsprings creak violently. "Now get dressed. I want my shirt back."

At the mention of his taking back his possessions, she went cold. If he took his shirt back, would he walk out of the room and leave her? Her hands clenched in the soft chambray. Then she dropped the clothing on the bed and hurried around to his side. There she knelt on one knee, her eyes level with his own. "Please don't be mad. Please. I'm sorry."

His hand clamped tight around the back of his neck; his ear was fairly nailed to his forearm. His mouth was drawn tight; the black mustache bristled. "I'm not mad."

She could feel the ice water coursing sluggishly through her veins. Her heart pounded with the effort to draw breath. "I'm so scared."

"Scared." He relaxed slightly. "What's there to be scared of?"

She threw a glance over her shoulder at the open window. Street sounds continued to waft in on the cold wet breeze from another norther. Drunken laughter. Shouts. The badly tuned piano thumped and tinkled. Horses' hooves and wagon wheels made sucking sounds as they passed through the quagmire that was the street. Her voice, when she spoke, seemed out of place among them. "I don't know who or where I am."

"I know that. You do too. I've told you, you'll be all right."

"But when? How long?"

He relaxed slightly. His shoulder lifted offhandedly. "Not too long. Nothing to worry about."

"But I do worry. I'm scared to death." She stood up, clasping her hands tight in front of her.

"Of what, for God's sake." He too sat up and dropped his feet onto the floor with a thud.

She winced at the sound. Her hand rose to the crescent-shaped cut on her temple, still the center of a violent purple bruise. "I . . . I'm afraid."

"Why?"

"Because you're all I've got. And I'm afraid you'll leave me." Her lungs felt as if her ribs were constricting them. She tried to draw a deep breath, but her heart was beating so hard that all she could do was pant. She tried to read the expression on his face. Had she said the wrong thing?

"Now where'd you get an idea like that?"

"You told me you didn't want to move into a tent because you didn't want me hanging onto you."

"Well, that's true." He pushed himself up on his elbow. "But I didn't mean I was going to desert you. You oughtta know that."

"No, I don't," she gasped. "That is, I'm afraid."

"So afraid you've done what I've asked you to do," he said slowly.

"Please don't be angry. That's all I ask. I'll put on the clothes."

"Listen, baby, what kind of a guy do you think I am? You don't need to worry that I'm going to take off just because some little thing doesn't go my way." Even as he spoke, he could feel a flush of anger rising in his face. The really great time they had spent together in bed the past few days had been because she was afraid to refuse him. He had been thinking he was something special to her, and instead she was really paying for her bed and board like a sick whore. He felt insulted and somehow used, even though she was the one who had given the use of her body.

His lip curled in disgust. Trust a woman to get things screwed up. He had just been trying to make her feel good. He stood and strode to the window, to lean out and look down. "Get dressed," he threw over her shoulder. "I won't watch you."

Feeling awkward and unhappy, she pulled on the drawers and chemise. The underwear was soft and thin from many washings. Probably the seamstress had thrown it in for free. Still just the feel of familiar clothing gave her a little more confidence. The skirt billowed over her head and dropped to her ankles. She buttoned the waist front and stood with hands clasped in the center of the room.

"I'm ready." She still had no shoes nor stockings, but the effect was wonderful. "I'm dressed."

He turned back from the window, a sour expression on his face.

"How does it look?"

"Looks fine." He barely glanced at her. "It would have looked just fine if I could have seen you put it on."

Her face crumpled, then she brightened determinedly. "I think you did a marvelous job of arranging for it. It fits really well. Are you sure it truly didn't cost you anything?"

He strolled back across the room to run his hand appraisingly down the sleeve. "Not a thing. You bought it for yourself."

Her smile did not falter. "But you picked it out and went to all that trouble. I won't forget that. I'm just so glad that it didn't cost any money. When I recover my memory, I'm going to owe you so much as it is."

He dropped his hand away. "Yeah. I'm thinking

about that too. How about taking a walk? The day's still young."

She nodded slowly, then lifted her skirt. "Is there any place where I can get a pair of shoes?"

He stared down at the bare white feet, then slapped his forehead. "Shoes. I should have thought." The exaggerated gesture served to dispel the last of his irritation. "There's a tent store down the street two doors. I'll bet they'll have shoes."

"They'll probably cost a fortune."

"Don't worry," he advised her. "I'm keeping a page on you."

"Good."

He led her to the door and held out his arms. "Hop aboard."

She smiled tremulously and put her arms around his neck.

The next morning after Irons left for the Boomin' Bessie, Jane presented herself to the landlady. "There must be something that I can do to earn part of the rent."

"You married to that big bruiser?" came the accusing question.

Jane clasped her right hand over her left. "No," she whispered.

"None of my business if you were or weren't. Just I wouldn't let a fella beat up on me if he wasn't my husband."

Jane touched her hand to the side of her face where fading blues, purples, and reds were beginning to be tinged with ugly yellow. "He didn't beat me," she insisted. "He saved me. I owe him my life. He found me—beside the road—where some men had left me for dead."

The landlady stared at her keenly. At last her mouth twitched back and forth across her teeth. "Was you raped, honey?"

"No." The woman called Jane drew back insulted, then faltered. "That is, I don't think so."

"Well, if you find out you're in a fix, Ma Baxter down the way'll knock it quick and painless. Won't hurt if you do it soon as you think you might be."

Jane could feel the color drain from her face. While she was sure she had not been raped, she might still be pregnant with Irons' child. She instinctively hugged her arms across her waist. "No. I'm not . . . 'in a fix.' "

The landlady regarded her critically, noting the protective gesture. Her mouth twitched in a cynical smile. "Tough." She studied the girl a moment longer. "You really wanta work?"

Jane dropped her hands to her sides. "Yes. Please. I'll do anything. That is, anything that's legal," she amended as the woman's eyebrow rose. "I just don't want to be a drag on him. He's been so good to me."

A quick bark of mirthless laughter followed that statement. "Sure he has, honey. But he's being a damn sight better to hisself. He's the one who's gettin' the free ride."

She could feel the bright blush rising in her throat and cheeks.

The landlady was staring at the floor in front of the table where she stationed herself most of the hours of the day. The oily mud and filth crusted on it were in places an inch thick, beaten down and tracked dry by hobnail brogans. The stairs to the second floor were likewise covered. "You wanta scrub floors upstairs and down?" the landlady asked.

Jane looked around her aghast, then carefully

schooled her expression. "The common rooms or every room?"

The woman calculated. "Just the common rooms. My boarders might not take to someone in their rooms, even to clean 'em."

Jane brushed the toe of her new shoe across the hard-crusted stuff and turned over a dry clod. "I don't mind. But I think I'll need a hoe to drag it out."

Again the mirthless bark of laughter. "A hoe, is it? Might not be a bad idea at that. I might have a hoe someplace around here. You clean this mess outa here any way you want to, and you can have two dollars off the week's bill."

"That's a lot of work for two dollars."

"Two floors—two dollars. Take it or leave it."

"How much is the bill?"

"Twelve."

She squared her shoulders. "I'll take it."

The woman gave a little squawk. "You will?" She rose from behind her desk and held out her hand. "The name's Floreine Dittman. You can call me Flo. What's your name?"

"Jane. Jane Irons. You can call me Jane." She took the proffered hand and shook it firmly. If Irons could give himself a name, so could she.

"Come on. I'll show you where the cleaning stuff's kept."

In a few minutes, Jane had removed her new dress to don Irons' shirt over her petticoat. Her expression grim she began on the second-floor landing.

"What in hell have you been doing?" Irons caught the palms of her hands and spread them with his thumbs. Her hands were red and scaly where the strong lye soap had attacked her skin.

Jane pulled her hands back and thrust them behind her. "I helped Mrs. Dittman clean house."

"Who?"

"The landlady."

"You helped her clean house. What house?"

"This house. I helped her clean this house."

He stared around him at their room. "You mean you cleaned it for her," he remarked dryly. "This place hasn't looked this good since she moved in."

Jane put on her bravest smile. "And . . . the rent for the week is only ten dollars."

"What?"

"I cleaned the floors. She knocked off the rent. Two floors—two dollars."

"Lord God Almighty." His face thunderous, he dragged her hands from behind her and inspected them again. The longer he stared, the tighter he squeezed until she squeaked.

"You're hurting me."

He let her go, and strode to the door of their room. Opening it, he stared at the bare expanse of hall and the stairs that dropped into the well below. They were clean, scrubbed until the grain of the wood shone. He turned back into the room, his brows drawn together, his mustache bristling. "How long did this take you?"

"I worked all day."

"I'll bet. Damn! Damn it to hell. Did you do the other rooms too?"

"No. Just ours and hers."

He was not taking this as she had envisioned that he would. He should be grinning, congratulating her on her resourcefulness in getting the job. He might even say that the floors looked nice. At the very least he could say that he was glad that she had got the money knocked off the rent. Instead he was acting as if she had committed a crime.

She smiled tentatively. "Don't they look nice?"

He stared at the floor as if he expected it to open and reveal the landlady. "That bitch," he growled, then raised his head. His gray eyes were cold as steel. "Now you listen to me, baby. I'll take care of you. And I'll pay the bills. Do you hear me?"

"But, Irons . . ."

"You're sick," he blazed. "You're hardly able to stand up, and you get a job scrubbing floors."

She tried to make light of it. "I thought it was the perfect job. I couldn't stand up, so I could crawl around on my knees."

His expression would have blistered paint. "What's it going to be tomorrow? Shoveling out the back-houses? I told you to stay in the room."

She set her mouth tight. She had worked so hard today. The very least he could do was to pretend that he appreciated her effort. "I can't stay in the room forever."

"You didn't have any trouble the first few days."

"That was before you got me some clothes." She felt her temper rise. He was being so unreasonable. "I wanted to help. You're working so hard. And you wouldn't have all this expense if you didn't have me hanging on to you."

"You're not hanging on to me!" he roared suddenly. "At least not very much."

She blinked at his ferocity. Then her own temper boiled over. "I'm a burden!" she shouted back. "I need to pull my own weight so you won't get tired having to support me."

"I don't mind!"

"You think women are more trouble than they're worth!"

The sentence stopped him cold. He gaped at her. "When did I ever say that?"

"Lots of times," she lowered her voice, but her breath still came hard. "Oh, maybe not in so many words. But the expression on your face was clear enough. Most of the time you don't like having me around."

He hesitated, rocked back on his heels by the shock of having what he thought were his own private opinions trotted out in public. He ran his hand around the back of his neck before he gave her a long steady look. The stormy look was suddenly replaced by a sort of tenderness. "I like having you around just fine."

She fell silent. The tone of the confrontation had changed abruptly. A new kind of tension seemed to vibrate in the air.

He hesitated, then drew in a deep breath. "I like coming back here to you. I . . . I haven't been drinking this week. Not since the night I got the job. There's never been a damn thing for me to do in these hell-holes, except drink and gamble and pick fights. I used to get beat up about two or three times a week just for the hell of it. But I've just been the once to that saloon across the street. I just don't seem to want to do that with you here."

His voice was deep and deadly serious. It soothed her tightly stretched nerves like a warm caress. She couldn't think of anything to say. After a confession like that, anything seemed inadequate. Finally, she smiled a little. "I'm glad."

He took her blistered hands and rubbed his thumbs across them again and again. He shook his head after a minute and turned them together between his own big hard palms. "I don't want you to do anything like this again. Ever. Promise?"

"I . . . all right."

"Promise."

"I promise."

"Good."

"But the money."

He opened the door and led her out into the hall. "Let's go get some of that slop that Mrs. Dittman calls food. And don't say another word about money. You've saved me all the money I'd have lost over in that saloon. Hell! I'm worth more now than I've been in ten years, because of you just sitting here."

The woman Irons called Jane slept in his arms like an exhausted child. He lay holding her, his maleness aware of her as she cuddled against him. Her breast pressed against the side of his chest. He could feel its shape as he breathed.

Last night, had she lain as she did now, he would have closed his hand over it, fondled the nipple into hard response, awakened her with kisses, parted her sweet thighs . . .

He stopped abruptly. He was a real fool. Thinking those thoughts had brought a fine sheen of perspiration to his skin. Now he had to talk fast and sternly to himself if he were to relax and get any sleep at all tonight.

He wondered about himself a little. This forebearance was foreign to him. It had kept him holding her as if she were his sister, or someone he cared about deeply. How ridiculous! She was just an unfortunate woman he had gotten himself saddled with.

He would ask around again tomorrow. Someone must know something about her. Any day now he would find out who she was. Then he would not be responsible for her much longer. He felt a little cold at that thought. His excitement over her proximity immediately receded.

Her body jumped, like that of a small child who has played too hard all day. She muttered and clutched at his shoulder. He patted her clumsily and hugged her a little tighter.

She had yawned her way through her supper. He had been about to suggest a walk when he caught her at it. Shortly thereafter, he had suggested that he had really had a hard day. As Jane and he mounted the stairs, he had looped his arm around her narrow waist and all but lifted her off her feet as they climbed together.

He grinned. He was well on his way to making a habit of hauling her around. Of course, he complained to her, but he was teasing her more than being serious. He was going to have to watch his complaints. She had taken them at face value and worked herself almost to death today.

He turned his head on the pillow. The top of her head was only an inch from his mouth. A wave of silky black hair brushed against his chin. Not bothering to examine his feelings, he kissed her.

The next morning Irons stepped into the street with a smile on his face. His parting words had been punctuated by a kiss that left Jane breathless, her face pink. Hitching his pants tighter around his lean middle, he strode off in the direction of the well.

The Boomin' Bessie was a dry hole if ever he had seen one. More than three miles from the first strike, its lease had been speculation. Now as the bit went deeper and deeper without cutting oil sand, the truth was becoming fairly obvious to the whole crew.

Irons stopped in the shadow of the big trees. He should be looking to sign on with another rig. Getting ready to jump, so to speak. After all, he had responsibilities. Jane could not wear the same dress day in and day out.

Angrily, he shrugged the thought away. He was the biggest fool in the world.

Jane would recover her memory any day now and remember that she had a husband and four or five little children. Maybe a husband, he amended, but he would be willing to bet all he owned and all he ever hoped to make that she had never had a baby. She was too tight, almost virginal. If she had a husband, he must not spend much time with her.

Damn! Here he was thinking about stuff like that when he needed to be over there at work on that rig. The time to think that was when he was walking home.

He tugged his hat harder down on his brow as a gust of cold wind threatened to lift it off. Time to go to work, he reckoned.

As he started toward the well, a man straightened from where he was lounging against the rig. A tin star flashed on his chest.

"Are you the man that reported that hanging?"

Irons halted in midstride. "Yeah."

"I'd need to talk to you, buddy. We got a real problem over at the county seat trying to figure out your story. Why don't you step over here for a spell and tell it to me to my face?"

Chapter 5

"I'm sure glad to see you, Sheriff." Irons extended his hand.

The lawman ignored it. His right thumb rested along the top of a row of .45 cartridges loaded into the belt at his waist. His fingers curled ever so slightly around the curved butt of the big revolver that matched the cartridges. His stern, tired face looked as if it had never worn a smile.

"You're the man who sent the kid with the message."

"That's right. I . . ."

"Then he's your man, Sheriff Barfield."

Irons' attention shifted to a man leaning forward from the shadow of a black phaeton. Beneath a narrow-brimmed derby, the face was thin, the eyes sunken in their sockets. The beginnings of a dark beard and mustache blurred the lines of his jaw and mouth.

The sheriff, looking more tired than ever, never took his eyes off Irons. "I'll be the judge of that Mr. Breckenridge."

"He must have been part of the gang that murdered my brother and carried off his wife. Her body still hasn't been found. Poor thing. Arrest him and he'll name the others."

Irons' mouth hardened. "I didn't kill anybody. I was just riding along minding my own business. And as for his wife. I guess she's the woman I found."

"You found her!" the man yelled. "You *murdered* her! Poor Fan. Poor Fan."

"Where's the body?" The sheriff's hand tightened over the butt of his .45. Listen, buddy . . ."

"Hold on. She's not dead," Irons interrupted.

"What!" The man in the phaeton practically shrieked the word. "Not dead?"

The sheriff turned his back to the buggy. His bloodshot eyes met Irons' in a look of silent communication. He heaved a disgusted sigh. "Maybe you'd better tell us what you found."

Irons looked from one to the other contemptuously. "I can tell you all I found in about two sentences. A dead man was swinging from a tree. A live woman was just waking up at the foot of it. I've got her back at the hotel now. And I'll sure be glad to get her off my hands." He turned toward the man in the phaeton. "She's sure going to be glad to see you. She's just about to go crazy over this deal."

"C—crazy," the man stammered. Then his mouth tightened. "You haven't got my sister-in-law. She'd have come back to Rosemeade if she'd been alive."

The sheriff nodded slowly. "Who is this woman you've got?"

"Yes, who? Who?" The man was practically hanging out of the buggy, his face red, sweat trickling down his face.

"Hell, I don't know." Irons rolled his eyes. "You tell me."

"Why don't she tell you herself?" the sheriff asked reasonably.

"That's right. Why?" the man insisted.

"Because she got beaten up." Here Irons paused, thinking fast. "She's sort of dazed."

"Oh." A short silence followed. Then the man slumped back in the carriage. "It couldn't be her."

"When I found the body, she was sure there with him," Irons declared.

Angry color rose in Breckenridge's face. The buggy whip in his hand vibrated; its tip switched wildly back and forth. "My sister-in-law would not go to a hotel with a strange man, especially a killer."

Irons hesitated again, then clamped his jaws together. Any information about Jane's loss of memory would put him on his way to the Hardin County Jail for assault and rape—if he were lucky. Despite the coolness of the day, he could feel the heat between his shoulder blades.

The sheriff turned back to Irons. "Maybe we'd better all go back to the hotel and get the straight of this story."

Irons backed away a couple of steps. "I've got a job here. I just can't take off."

The sheriff trudged wearily over to the foreman, who lounged with the rest of the crew watching the scene with interest. "All right if I take him away for a couple of hours?"

"No skin off my nose."

"But what about my job?" Irons protested, his brows drawn together.

"It'll be here when you get back," the foreman called. "If you get back."

The sheriff swung around on his boot heel. "Satisfied?"

Irons scowled. "I'll have to be."

The sheriff nodded. "Okay. Let's go back to this hotel and talk to this woman."

Inwardly Irons cursed. Now he was in for it. How many times had he told himself that women were really more trouble than they were worth. If not for Jane, he would have ridden right on by. Now he was going to lose a half-day's pay. A half day. Hell! He was about to get himself arrested and all because of her.

The sheriff swung into the saddle of a Roman-nose bay. "Mount up," he said to Irons. "The three of us'll ride together back to the hotel."

"I can't be riding around the countryside all day long," the man in the phaeton complained. His voice became more and more agitated. "I'm satisfied that you've found your man. Whoever he's got back there shacked up at the hotel can*not* be my . . . er . . . brother's wife. This must be somebody that he's picked up to try to give himself an alibi."

The sheriff gaped incredulously. "Mr. Breckenridge . . ."

"I've identified my poor brother's body. I can't stand any more of this right now." The voice was practically a shriek. The whip snaked out over the horse's back, and the phaeton clattered out of the clearing lurching from side to side as it gathered speed.

The sheriff crossed his hands over the saddle horn in weary resignation. When the black top had disappeared completely among the pines, he looked disgustedly at Irons. "You want to mount up?"

"Sure. If you're still interested."

"I've come this far. Might as well."

Irons mounted Pet and they rode out side by side. Out of sight of the Boomin' Bessie, the sheriff asked, "You want to tell me again what you found?"

"The story's not going to change. I was riding along, cold, wet, and hungry, hoping to make Waldrow in time for breakfast."

The lawman's eyes narrowed. "What were you doing out on the road at that time of the morning?"

"Got an early start," Irons sneered.

"From where?"

"North."

The sheriff's voice carried a hint of steel underneath the weariness. "This is a murder investigation, fella. You might be smarter to cooperate."

"Look. I was riding along by myself just at dawn. It's a free country. If I want to ride all night, I can."

"Get on with it."

Irons pulled his hat a little tighter down on his forehead. "I'd taken the wrong fork in the dark and was up a logging road before I knew it. Just as I was about to turn around it seemed to widen out, so I thought maybe I was right after all. Suddenly, there it was. The whole thing."

"What was?" the sheriff prompted.

"This corpse swinging from this tree in the clearing."

The sheriff waited.

Irons pulled Pet to a stop and turned in the saddle to face the lawman. "He had his nightshirt on. It was white in the dark. That's why I saw him swinging back and forth. He was dead. No question about that. His neck must have been stretched nearly a foot. And underneath his feet was this woman."

"Was she with him?"

"Had to have been. She had on a nightgown. They were probably both jerked out of bed. Hers had been torn nearly off her and she'd been beaten nearly to death."

"Anything else?"

Irons shrugged. "I didn't have any way of finding out. She sure wasn't in any condition to tell me."

The sheriff nodded. "And you took her with you?"

"I couldn't leave her lying there on the ground at the end of a logging road. A wet norther was blowing in. She'd have died of pneumonia if I hadn't taken her. She's back at the hotel right now. I put her there because I didn't have any choice."

"Sounds like you did the right thing," the older man agreed.

Pet moved from one hip to the other impatiently. The sheriff nudged his mount forward. Irons followed. "Who is she?"

"That's what we're trying to find out."

"Well, who was the man?"

"According to his brother—that dern fool that just drove off—his name's Rex Breckenridge. But here's the funny part. He ain't from around here. He's got a ranch north of here where they've found some oil." The sheriff's tone clearly implied that that piece of information explained everything.

"But he had his nightshirt on . . ."

"Sure don't make much sense to ride half the night to hang a man in somebody else's jurisdiction," the sheriff mourned.

Irons shook his head. "And carry his wife with him. Always supposing she was his wife."

"It don't make no sense at all."

"If she was his wife, then it must be his widow I've got over at the hotel."

The sheriff raised one scraggly eyebrow. "Might be. Course a man don't always sleep with his wife. Is her name Breckenridge?"

Irons did not answer immediately. The sheriff's observation had opened a new and unpleasant line of thought. Jane's own innocence was in question. Her condition left her vulnerable. He was conscious of the sheriff's scrutiny.

"What about it?" the lawman prompted.

Irons shrugged. He had no choice. "She doesn't know her name."

The lawman pulled his horse to a halt. His brows drew together in a frown. "Don't know. Or won't say."

"Doesn't know," Irons asserted hastily. He wanted to make very sure the sheriff understood that Jane was not faking.

"Has a doctor taken a look at her?"

"Around here!" Irons sneered. "There's no such animal."

The sheriff's eyes roamed along the rows of tents as they rode past them.

"What I'm saying," Irons continued, "is that I've done what I could for her. Don't blame her or me. She was almost beaten to death. When you get a look at her, remember that she looks good compared to what she did."

The sheriff digested this. "Then let's go take a look," he said mildly.

Her back straight, her chin level, Jane came down the stairs followed closely by Irons.

Hastily, the lawman removed his hat. "Ma'am."

"Sheriff . . ."

"Paschall Barfield, ma'am." Gently, he took the hand she extended.

She could feel him staring at the bruises on her face. By a dint of will she kept from raising her hand to try to cover them. He would get used to them. For now, she wanted one piece of information from him immediately. "Who am I?"

He shifted uneasily. "Well, now that's what we're trying to find out, ma'am."

"The man who was hanged was named Rex Breckenridge,'' Irons put in. Both men searched her face for some reaction, some faint flicker of recognition, but the name meant nothing. Again she resisted the temptation to hide her face.

They sat around the scarred oak table in the dining room of Mrs. Dittman's hotel. In no other room could they be private except for the tiny bedroom upstairs. The sheriff cleared his throat. ''Did that name sound familiar, ma'am?''

''Breckenridge.'' Jane said the name slowly. ''Breckenridge.'' Her eyes misted. ''It doesn't sound familiar.''

''Rex Breckenridge.'' The sheriff repeated the name. ''Take your time now and think real hard.''

''Want any coffee?'' Mrs. Dittman asked from the doorway. Her face was avid with curiosity. Her sharp nose twitched. ''I've got a pot that's hot.''

Irons scowled at her, but the sheriff looked relieved. ''That sounds real good, ma'am. I could sure use some.''

''Comin' right up.''

Jane leaned forward, her elbows on the table, her hands clasped in front of her. The swelling had gone down completely on the left side of her face. The ugly discoloration had drained into the sockets around her eyes making their unusual color more pronounced. Now they might have been bright metal, so intently were they trained on the sheriff's face. ''What was his wife's name?''

The lawman hesitated, scratched his head. ''Did he say?'' he asked Irons.

''I thought he said 'Fan.' '' Irons looked at her face. ''Does the name Fan mean anything to you?''

Her face contorted in pain. ''Fan Breckenridge. Fan Breckenridge. Fan.''

''You shouldn't have let him drive away like that,''

Irons told the sheriff. "He didn't have to leave. He wasn't all that upset. He could have come in here and identified her."

"We didn't know she needed identification," the sheriff pointed out sourly. "He insisted she was some kind of imposter." He looked at Jane. "She still could be. She's not wearing a ring."

Irons reached forward and turned Jane's hand face down on the table. He pointed to the white indentation at the base of her third finger. "She was."

Unreasonable pain flashed up Jane's arm. She winced and tried to jerk her hand away as memory seared her. A cruel hand grasped the gold band set with diamonds and twisted it off her almost breaking her finger in the process. She could hear her own scream ringing in her ears.

Irons frowned as the color drained from her face. At that moment Mrs. Dittman entered with an enamel coffeepot and a fistful of cups. Expertly she set them down on the table and pushed them toward each in turn. "Don't let me interrupt," she said. "Just go right on with whatever you're saying."

"Are you living here with this man?" the sheriff asked abruptly.

Jane's face paled, making the bruises more noticeable than ever. The tears started in her eyes. She bit her lower lip.

"That's nobody's business but ours," Irons interrupted.

But Jane raised her chin a notch. "Mr. Irons has taken care of me since he found me. He's asked and asked trying to help me find out who I was. He has been so kind."

"It's none of your business," Irons repeated savagely.

"Might be. Somehow she's mixed up in a cold-blooded murder," came the laconic observation.

His words created a little pool of silence. A muscle flickered in Irons' jaw. Uppermost in his mind was the vow that he would not go to jail for this. Partner to the vow was the belief that once inside he would never get out. His whole body tensed; he gathered his feet under him.

Then Jane carefully laid her hands side by side palm down on the table. Her golden stare riveted the sheriff. "I may be mixed up in this some way," she said. "I can't deny what I don't know. But I'll tell you one thing. And this I do know. Mr. Irons is not mixed up in this in any way. He saved my life. He's taken care of me like a baby. And it's been at his own expense."

Barfield rocked back in his chair. "Well, now that's mighty good to hear, ma'am. But that's supposin' you know what happened to you."

"Mr. Irons has never laid a finger on me," she said positively.

Irons relaxed fractionally.

Behind him, he heard Mrs. Dittman's give a snort. Fortunately, the sheriff ignored it. "Suppose you just tell me what you can remember."

"I remember waking up in the dark. I was so cold. I looked up and Mr. Irons was there sitting on his horse across the clearing from me. Then I heard a sound." Her eyes got as big as twenty-dollar gold pieces. "It was a rope creaking. There was a man's body swinging above me."

"Go on," the sheriff coaxed when she seemed about to start crying. "You're doing just fine, ma'am."

"There's nothing else I can tell you. Mr. Irons came over and picked me up and put me on his horse and led it away. It started to rain and I almost froze to death. Mr. Irons put his slicker on me and shared his blankets with me. Otherwise, I'd be dead. That's all I can remember until we got here."

"Do you think it possible that Mr. Irons might have been responsible for hanging that man?"

"Damn you." Irons' chair scraped back as he sprang to his feet. "I told you I didn't have a thing to do with that."

"No!" Jane's voice rose determinedly. "No. I don't believe that's possible."

"You don't have any idea how long you were lying there. Maybe you were knocked out for just a minute and caught him as he was about to ride away."

"Why didn't he kill me then? Why save my life and bring me here and pay for me to have a place to stay?"

The sheriff's eyes shifted to Irons, whose hard hands had clenched into tight fists. "A lot of men are funny about killing women," he observed. "They'll kill a man for the change in his pocket. Don't think anything about it. But they won't touch a woman."

"He didn't have to pick me up," she insisted.

"You'd seen him," came the instant reply. "You could identify him."

"I'd been beaten senseless. It was dark. The fog was thick. I couldn't have identified him in a million years."

"But he didn't know that."

Jane pressed her hands into the table and stood up. Her back was straight, her chin thrust forward pugnaciously. "Now you listen to me, Sheriff Barfield, Irons didn't do anything except help me. He saved my life. Since that morning, no man could ever had been nicer to a woman. He's been the most wonderful friend to me and a perfect gentleman. Don't you dare arrest him."

Set back by her sudden determination, the sheriff rose hastily. "Who said anything about arresting anybody? I'm just asking questions and trying to get to the bottom of this. Chances are the man was killed because he owned some land that someone wanted to lease."

"But Irons has just arrived, and he had to go out and get a job. He doesn't know anyone."

The sheriff looked over her head at the angry man. "I'm just doing my job," he said half apologetically. "You both stay close around here. I'll get back in touch when I know something else."

When the sound of his horse's hooves had died away, Irons helped Jane to her feet. "Ready to go back upstairs."

"Please." She turned her face into his shoulder to hide the tears.

As they left the dining room, they passed by Mrs. Dittman, who gave them a forbidding glare. "Be out by the end of the week," she said. "This is a decent hotel I'm running. Not a hideout for murderers and their doxies."

Eyes like shards of steel, Irons abandoned his charge at the foot of the stairs and turned back to the woman. Before she could move, he strode between her and the revolver she kept under the table. Fists clenched, shoulders hunched, he herded her back until she was pressed against the wall.

"You leave me alone," she warned desperately. "The sheriff knows . . ."

"That old fool doesn't know spit."

"He'll be back."

"He won't do you any good though if you keep on talking like you're talking." He doubled his fist under her chin.

Frantically, she twisted her head sideways. Her eyes were wide with terror.

He pressed his knuckles into the crepy skin on the underside of her chin. "You keep your mouth shut," he growled. "We'll stay here till we get ready to move. Hear?"

"Y—yes!" Her voice quavered and broke.

"Our money is just as good as anybody else's. Right?"

"Right. Oh, yes. Right."

"It's nobody's business what we do, so long as we pay. Isn't that so?"

"Yes."

He stepped back. Mrs. Dittman slumped against the wall. "Now we're going upstairs; but before we go, I want you to tell Jane how sorry you are that you said what you did."

The woman's face was whiter than her apron.

"You are sorry, aren't you?" he insisted.

"I'm sorry," she muttered.

"That's what I thought." He walked over to the stairs where Jane stood in fascinated silence, the tears drying on her cheeks. "Apology accepted." He put his arm around Jane's waist. "Hop aboard."

Dazedly, she put her arms around his neck, and he swept her up into his arms. "I may be late for supper, Mrs. Dittman," he called over his shoulder. "Got to try to make up these last couple of hours at the Boomin' Bessie. So save me a plate if you don't mind."

At the foot of the stairs, the woman nodded fearfully.

In the bedroom, he laid Jane on the bed. "Are you sure you don't remember the name Fan Breckenridge?"

Her head began to pound. "I don't think so. Fan Breckenridge. No, I don't remember."

"I've got a hunch it's your name. What about Rex? Do you remember anybody named Rex?"

She shook her head. Tears trickled down her cheeks.

"Hey, don't start crying. It's nothing to cry about."

"I'm not crying about not remembering. I'm crying because the sheriff acted as if he didn't believe me." She rolled over on the bed and crooked her arm under her head. "He wanted to arrest you. And he didn't believe me. You were right."

"What about?"

"You said women are more trouble than they're worth. And you're right. If you hadn't picked me up, nobody would have even known you were anywhere near that tree."

In amazement he stared down at her huddled body. He could not believe he had heard her. He sat down carefully on the bed beside her and rolled her back over and into his arms. "Jane. Now, Jane. Stop crying. Don't be upset. Don't even think that."

She shook her head. Her hand clenched at his shirt-front, then pushed away. "I'm so sorry. I'm so sorry."

He held her tighter. "Well, I'm not. I'm glad I picked you up. You're the best." He kissed the top of her head. "Why listen? The way you defended me to that sheriff, why that was great. I felt good all over."

"You're in trouble because of me."

"It was worth it to hear you say all those things. Even if they weren't true and you didn't mean half of them." He kissed the top of her head again. "Nobody's ever said anything like that about me."

"He just couldn't arrest you."

Irons realized she needed reassurance. "Listen, baby. He came here and asked questions, but he didn't get any answers for the simple reason that neither one of us knew anything to tell him."

"He'll be back."

Irons made a rude sound. "Naw. He won't be back. Hear me. *He won't be back.* Not that two-bit tinhorn. He's done his duty. He's asked questions. He doesn't have anybody else to ask. What's more, he wouldn't know what to ask if he had. He'll go back to Batson and write a report and forget about it."

"Are you sure?"

"I'm sure."

She lay still against him for a long time. He thought she had drifted off to sleep. He was just about to disengage himself and go back to his job, when she spoke. "Am I Fan Breckenridge?"

"You might be. Would you like for me to call you Fan, so you can see if the name sounds familiar?"

She shook her head. "No. Call me Jane. It's the name you gave me."

He flashed her a peculiar look. Her mouth was set in a narrow line. He patted her shoulder. "Now lie here and have a nap. Is your head aching?"

"Yes."

"It figures. I shouldn't have let him near you."

"No. It was all right. He might have arrested you."

"He might have tried." Irons kissed her on the forehead and left.

She smiled then scolded herself. Irons had threatened the landlady and defied the sheriff, and she thought he was wonderful. What kind of person did that make her?

* * *

The driller was desperate to hit some kind of oil sand and had insisted on the crew working overtime. For Irons his decision was an opportunity to make up the time he had lost, so his pay would not be shorted.

At almost full dark Irons rode back to the hotel from the Boomin' Bessie.

On the porch of the hotel, a figure stepped out of the shadows. "What did you tell the sheriff?"

Irons stared down at the man. Breckenridge was nearly half a head shorter than he was. "I told him what I knew, which wasn't much."

"You killed my brother, or you know who did."

Irons took a tight grip on his temper. "I didn't kill your brother. But I probably rescued your brother's wife. She's about to lose her mind with worry. I figure she's supposed to be dead too. She was beaten so badly that her brains are rattled. She can't remember who she is or what happened."

Breckenridge's jaw dropped open. He regarded Irons intently, trying to make out his expression in the semi-darkness. "Is that the truth?"

"Why don't you come in with me and ask her?"

"If she's with you, then I don't want to see her. My brother's wife wouldn't be with a hired killer."

"Listen, mister." Irons clenched his fists. "I'm not a hired killer. You get that straight."

Breckenridge retreated the length of the porch. "Pyote!"

A heavyset man pulled himself up over the porch railing and lumbered to Breckenridge's side. "What y' want, boss?"

"Your gun."

Fast as an old-time gunfighter's, the weapon leaped from the holster strapped to the man's hip. Its bore came up aimed for Irons' midsection. "Y' want I should shoot him?"

"No. Just keep him at a distance." Breckenridge grinned and strutted forward like a gamecock, his high-heeled cowboy boots thwacking the porch. "I'm not tall like you, Mr . . . Irons, so I have to have a bodyguard. He makes sure I get to talk uninterrupted."

"He's mighty fast," Irons agreed, "but can he shoot?"

Breckenridge moved closer. "Of course."

"With an empty gun?"

Breckenridge swung round to stare at his bodyguard. The weapon wavered. The man looked at it uncertainly.

Like lightning, Irons moved. Pushing Breckenridge before him, he literally threw the slight man against the chest of the other. His arm snaked around to wrench the pistol out of Pyote's hand. A quick flip, a twirl, and it was pointed at its owner, who had fallen back against the rail under his boss's weight.

Irons laughed mirthlessly as they both sorted themselves out and faced him. "Better get a bodyguard with sense enough to know how to use a weapon if you're going to have him point it," he suggested sarcastically.

Neither man spoke. Irons broke open the gun and shucked the shells out into the palm of his hand. Then he tossed them out into the street where the muck instantly swallowed them up.

He thrust it into the man's burly fist. "Take it back. And don't come near me again with it. Now, get!"

Breckenridge nodded curtly. "As the fellow says, Pyote, 'Get.' "

Irons strolled back into the light spilling from the open front door. "Do you want to come upstairs now and say hello to your sister-in-law?"

Breckenridge shook his head. "I don't think so. Maybe later. I need to know more about the situation."

"Then get off the porch and stop bothering a man on his way home from work."

Breckenridge tucked his head down and darted off into the night.

Chapter 6

"So. Turned up again. Just like a bad penny, ain't you, Fan?"

The woman Irons called Jane jabbed the needle through the hole of the button and into the end of her thumb. A swear word slipped out as she cocked her head to one side and looked upward trying to make out the face of the woman who was nothing more than a black silhouette between Fan and the sun.

"Oh, did you hurt your finger?" came the unsympathetic question from the flat, black figure. "Sorry, sorry, honey bunch. Better run on home to the family to kiss it and make it better."

Doubling the hurt thumb inside her other fingers, Fan put Irons' shirt aside. A trembling began deep inside her. "I . . . can't recall your name. But I suppose we have met before. And you say my name is Fan."

The woman gravitated around the rocker so the bright sun was no longer at her back. She thrust her face down level with the bruised face and bared her teeth in an exaggerated grin. "Take a real good look then, honey bunch," she sneered. Her voice had a nasal twang. "Come on and tell me you don't remember who I am."

Fan stared into the face of a stranger. Stared and stared with a growing sense of frustration. When the pain began above her eyes, she dropped her head. "I'm sorry, but I can't remember."

The woman drew back. Her grin disappeared to be replaced by an angry frown. "You're lying."

"Why would I lie?" Fan raised her head. "Do you know me?"

" 'Course I know you." The woman leaned back against the porch railing. A sharp bark of a laugh burst out of her rouged mouth. Her head tipped back on her shoulders, slipping great sausage rolls of dishwater-blond hair precariously to one side. "I wouldn't be here if I didn't."

Fan gripped the arms of the rocking chair. "Then will you please tell me who I am?"

Again came the sharp laugh. "You're Rex Breckenridge's wife."

"The wife of the man who was hanged." A shudder ran up her spine. She gripped the chair arms harder.

The woman's mouth snapped closed as if the laughter had never been. "So they tell me."

Fan blinked at the lack of emotion in the voice. "Did you know him—us—well?"

"Pretty well." A crash of broken crockery came from the saloon across the street. The blonde laughed again and swung around. Elbows on the porch rail, she squatted down trying to see inside the other building. "Quite a comedown for you, ain't it, honey bunch?" She threw a malicious look over her shoulder. "Across the street from a saloon and all."

"Where do I live?"

The woman ignored the question. Her attention

seemed fixed on trying to see the source of the commotion.

Fan tried another tack. "Were we friends?"

The woman hauled herself up and swung around. Thrusting her hands deep into the pockets of her faded cotton skirt, she stared at the figure in the rocking chair. "We weren't friends," she stated with relish. "High and mighty folks like you don't have friends like me. But you're not so high and mighty now." She smiled. "I guess you've seen your face in the mirror. That place on the side of your head looks like it's going to leave a scar." She leaned forward. "Why, I declare, Miz Breckenridge, honey bunch, looks like you've got a white hair."

Fan raised her hand self-consciously, then dropped it. She lifted her chin. "Who are you?"

"Me? You want to know me? That's rich." She jeered, and the blond sausage rolls bobbed precariously. "You're so down on your luck that you wanta know me. You're nothing now but a poor ol' widder woman."

Fan pressed her hand to her forehead. She could feel the pressure building behind her eyes. "My name . . . ?"

A stream of cursing burst from the saloon across the way. Furniture banged and glass shattered. Grinning, the woman turned her attention back across the street of mud. Rain had fallen during the night and every rut was filled with greenish-gray water. "I already told you. You name's Fan. You teched or somethin'?"

"Fan?"

"Short for Fancy. Leastways that's what I heard. Heard you come from a whole long line of rich folks. Folks with ranches and plantations—stretching all the way back to the Atlantic Ocean. Rex was really bustin' his buttons off braggin' about what kind of gal he'd married." The woman bounced up, making the roll of hair bobble forward. She pushed it back impatiently. "I wasn't much competition for someone with that kind of start."

Fancy shrank back in the chair, instinctively recoiling from the bitterness in the other woman's voice. Her hand fluttered to her temple where a pulse began to pound. "Please, Miss . . ."

"Carlton's my name. Eufemia. Ain't that a hoot? Eufemia. God! I hate it. Course Fancy's not much better, honey bunch. They must have been hard up for names for the both of us. Probably used all the good ones back up the line."

Sharp pains slashed between Fancy's eyes. She swallowed hard as her mouth began to water, a sure prelude to nausea. "You . . . You say my name is Fancy." She clutched the arm of her chair. "Fancy what?"

"Hell, I don't know. The first time I saw you, I just heard Mrs. Rex Breckenridge." The blond woman fairly flung the words at Fan's head.

The lack of compassion made Fan angry. If she were indeed a widow, she deserved a decent expression of sympathy for her loss. What possible motive could this woman have coming here to hurl taunts and insults? Through slitted eyes, Fan studied her. "Were you perhaps a friend of my husband's?"

"You catch on quick, honey bunch," Eufemia answered defiantly. Affecting a burst of raucous laughter, she caught hold of the pillar at the end of the porch rail, swung around it, and started down the steps.

"Wait." Dumbfounded that the woman would suddenly leave, Fan jumped from her chair and followed her. "Wait. Please. Tell me more. Where do I live? Where is my home?"

The blond woman gathered up her skirts and stepped without hesitation into the mud. It squelched up around her boots, already gray to the ankles. Bare knees flashing, she hurried away.

"Wait!" Fan halted on the bottom step. "Please!"

Eufemia stopped and turned half around. "You can tag along," she jeered, "but you'd have to get your feet dirty."

Fan stared at the green-gray mess in front of her, then down at the new buckle shoes that Irons had bought for her. "For heaven's sake," she called. "Where are you going in such a hurry? At least tell me where I can find you."

"Oh, I'll be around." Eufemia laughed. "See ya, honey bunch." She broke into a run, slogging away between the tents until she disappeared.

Fan pressed her fingertips to her temples and tried to force memory to come. A horrible blankness lay in her mind. She could think of nothing. For an instant she doubted the existence of the woman. Had Eufemia Carlton really appeared out of nowhere?

Was her name really Fan—no—Fancy Breckenridge? She shivered. A strange name. Something else strange was going on here. If Eufemia had recognized her, why did other people not recognize her?

She looked around her desperately. If only she had a horse, she could ride through the rows of tents looking for Eufemia. Irons ordinarily walked to work. Pet was stabled in the barn behind the boardinghouse.

Did she dare take his horse without permission? Fan caught up her skirts and took the steps two at a time.

Pet was a slow-moving mare, well past her prime. Her fastest gait, a trot, slowed immediately to an amble unless the rider kept spurs to her sides. Fan found herself increasingly impatient with the animal. What kind of horses had she been used to riding? As small pieces of the jigsaw of her life fell into place, she became more and more puzzled. Silk nightgowns and spirited mounts did not fit with personal friendships with Eufemia Carlton. Of course, Eufemia was not a friend. She had denied it flatly. Likewise, she had shown no concern about the death of Rex Breckenridge.

"Rex Breckenridge." She said the name aloud. One of Pet's ears flicked backward. "Fan Breckenridge. Fancy."

Try as she would to recall images, the same distressing darkness remained in her mind. The two names might have been the names of strangers just introduced. "Fancy Breckenridge," she whispered again. "Fancy."

Again Pet flicked back her ear, and Fan pushed the names away and concentrated on the surroundings. The paths between the tents of the rag town were no better than the street between the saloon and boardinghouse, except here she could hear the squeals and laughter of children playing rather than the curses of men and the tinkle of an out-of-tune piano.

At one tent, an eight-by-twelve, the door flap was tied open. Fan could see three children playing on the floor between the cots. From somewhere within, a sewing machine whirred, its treadle pressed by some unseen foot. Fan wondered if the woman who had made her dress lived there.

Pet stumbled. Muddy water from the ruts splashed up on Fan's pant leg. Lucky she had changed into a pair of Irons' pants. She could wash it and leave it no worse for wear. The blue chambray would have been indelibly stained.

Mud was everywhere, but no water. Not a windmill, not a well. Where the top sagged in some tents would be a water barrel to catch the run off from the frequent rains. But most people did not even have this poor cistern. How did these women keep their children and themselves clean? Where did they bathe? How could women live like this?

Abruptly, she was conscious of her own distaste, her own contempt. Who was she? What had her life been like that these feelings made her want to guide the horse away from this squalor and out into the green fields?

The tent city seemed to stretch forever. She could see no end to it, nor any pattern. Some were not even tents, but huts with slabsiding and palmetto roofs. The plywood slabs leaned inward, their corners comprised of steep triangular spaces that did not dovetail. They were like crazy card houses ready to fall at the first puff of wind.

Fan shuddered as she cast her eyes around her, searching for a glimpse of the woman called Eufemia Carlton. Already she was beginning to wonder if she should have followed. The search seemed futile.

She was just about to turn her horse around to ride back when she came upon the first derrick. A professionally lettered sign tacked to the cross timber named it the Blue Star No. 2. The sound of its engine had been in her ears for several minutes, but she had paid no attention. Now she watched as the big belts and chains turned in the draw works and the rotary table turned driving the drill deeper and deeper into the earth.

She frowned, pressing her hand against her temple. She knew what the structure was. Nothing more. Nothing here was familiar. A half-dozen men moved methodically and purposefully about on the floor of the derrick.

Pet shifted from one hip to the other and dropped her nose down to snuffle at a clump of grass grown up around a tree stump.

A man straightened from his task and stepped down. With one economical motion, he swept off his felt hat and wiped his brow, split horizontally half white and half brownish-red from exposure to the elements. "Can I help you, ma'am?"

"Why, I suppose you can." Fan blinked. "I'm sure you can. Thanks. Can you tell me where I might find Eufemia Carlton? She's a friend of mine," she added hastily.

His forehead wrinkled. Shaking his head, he called over his shoulder to the crew. "Ever hear of a gal named—what'd you say?"

"Eufemia Carlton." Fan raised her voice.

"Nope."

"Naw."

"Whaddoes she look like?"

"Blond hair, medium height." Fan paused. She could not think of a single distinguishing feature.

The men muttered among themselves, shaking their heads, shrugging. The spokesman turned back to her. "Can't say I've heard of the lady," he replied. "Anything else?"

"Rex Breckenridge."

He scratched his head and replaced his hat again with the same economy of motion. "Can't say the name's familiar. Course none of us are from around here." He stepped back.

She nodded. "What about the Boomin' Bessie, Number . . ." She paused.

"Boomin' Bessie, Number Ten," the man supplied cheerfully.

"Right."

"Just follow that path. Keep bearin' left. You'll see it when you get into a tall stand of pines. Nothin' doin' there though. It's a dry hole. They'll strike anyday."

"Thank you."

She might as well take a swing in that direction and tell Irons that she had borrowed his horse and clothing. If he became angry with her, he could have time to cool down before he got back to the boardinghouse. With that thought came a smile. She had managed a man before. She spared herself a sad thought for the late Rex Breckenridge. Nobody around here seemed to have heard of him; nobody knew him, except his brother, who had not come to see her, and Eufemia Carlton.

Had the woman been Rex's mistress? Was that why the hostility had fairly radiated from her? If so, why did she not mourn his death?

The road widened, then narrowed again. Various paths turned off to clusters of tents sitting around one, two, a half-dozen derricks. She continued to bear left, always taking that fork when she had to make a choice.

Suddenly, she realized she had made a mistake. She must retrace her steps. Either the man at the Blue Star No. 2 had given the wrong directions, or she had gotten them wrong. The road ended at a single cabin in a clearing surrounded by green pines. As part of the pastoral picture, a blue jay flashed across the clearing. From a bush beside the door, a mockingbird burst into a trill.

At odds with the bucolic solitude rose a derrick, not completed, its tower unweighted with drilling apparatus and hoisting equipment, its platform bare boards unstained by oil.

A faint uncomfortableness dragged at her memory. Dragging her eyes from the derrick, she studied the unprepossessing cabin. The grass and weeds rose around the front steps. Who had lived there? Why had it been abandoned?

Suddenly the birds stopped singing. A crackling sound came from the underbrush to the right. Unaccountably, she felt the hair rise on the back of her neck. The sound came again nearer.

With hands suddenly cold, Fan jerked Pet's head out of the new grass in the middle of the two-lane road and pulled the right rein hard back. The mare whickered in surprise and turned with ponderous slowness.

Fan felt the tears starting in her eyes. Her heart pounded. She caught her breath as the brush crackled again. A terrified glance over her shoulder showed her that the clearing was still bare. Whatever was in the brush was not stepping out of it.

Yet the noise was coming closer as a large body pushed the underbrush aside. A couple of quail shot out of the thicket less than twenty feet from her.

9"Giddy-up!" she shouted to Pet and lashed the mare across the withers with the ends of the reins. At the same time she drummed her heels on the back ribs.

The sorrel broke into a bone-jarring trot.

"Faster!" Fan lashed her again. "Faster!" she screamed in the horse's ear.

The sorrel stumbled then lumbered into a gallop. The dark pines and water oaks were on either side of the path. A cloud glided across the sun.

Fan lashed the horse again and looked back over her shoulder.

A heavy dark figure had emerged from the brush at the opening to the clearing. He stood hands on hips, the brim of his hat shading his face.

For only a second she saw him, not enough time for her to see his face, but his figure was terribly familiar. Pain lanced through her temple. The mare stumbled again, throwing Fan forward on her neck.

A roaring wind filled her ears bearing on it, the sounds of men's voices. Cold fear, drenching rain, icy blackness. Fan threw her arms around the mare's neck, urging her with voice. The blond mane switched her face and lashed across her gritted teeth.

Pet burst out onto the main road, her hooves thundering, the saddle leather creaking. Ahead Fan could see another trail and through the trees a cluster of tents. Tents meant people—people who would help her, save her.

She shot another look over her shoulder. Pet's gallop had taken them far enough away so that the entrance to the trail had disappeared. No heavyset man followed her. Fan managed to push herself back off the neck and straighten in the saddle. At that moment a team of mules pulled into the road ahead.

Exhausted and feeling a slackening in the rider's urging, Pet's gallop subsided to a trot, then to a lope, and finally to a walk. Still, Fan easily came alongside the wagon whose flatbed was loaded with a huge metal cylinder. Its wheels were already plowing deep ruts in the mud. The big mules threw their shoulders against the collars.

"Which way to Waldrow?" she called to the driver.

"Long or short?"

She would not search for the Boomin' Bessie. Let Irons be angry. She wanted to get back to Mrs. Dittman's boardinghouse. "Short."

"Go back along the trail yuh just took . . ."

"Long!"

He gaped at her, then shrugged. "Just follow this road and keep right. Can't miss it."

She shook her head unhappily. "I hope not."

"There's a man to see you, Miz Breckenridge." Mrs. Dittman's mouth was tight as if she might have bitten down on a very sour pickle.

"A man?" Fan froze in the doorway. "What does he look like?"

"What do you mean, 'what does he look like'? He's just a man. Kind of short. Nice clothes, but scruffy. Needs a shave bad."

"Is he fat?"

"No, my dear. I am not fat."

Mrs. Dittman turned. "I was getting her," she explained sourly. "I told you to wait. I don't allow anybody in my kitchen."

Fancy clutched at the door facing, her body tingling with apprehension. Slowly, slowly, she let herself relax. The man standing in the doorway was not fat, but he appeared to be in the early stages of growing a beard. In no way did he resemble the heavyset figure that had terrified her so unreasonably.

Floreine Dittman jerked her head toward the dining room. "If y'all want to talk, why don't you go in and sit down like you did when the sheriff came? I don't have to start setting up for a while."

"Fancy?" He took a hesitant step into the room and then another.

She peered at him intently, leaning forward, searching the thin features, the eyes peering out between black-fringed lids that effectively hid their color. "I . . . You have the advantage of me, sir."

The man hunched his shoulders. "I don't look familiar to you at all?"

She shook her head slowly, her eyes never leaving his face. "No."

"Perhaps if we spoke in private?" He turned an accusing stare at Mrs. Dittman.

"Fine with me," the woman said nastily.

He held out his arm to Fancy. "Perhaps if we went for a drive."

Even as she shook her head, Mrs. Dittman spoke. "Take her," she urged. "Take her and good riddance. She can't get out of here too soon. She's been carryin' on with that roughneck ever since he brought her in here. And her near naked too.''

''For heaven's sake,'' Fan protested. ''I wasn't . . .''

''Fan,'' the man interrupted sternly. ''I think you'd better come with me.''

Anger waged a war with fear for the dominant emotion. Anger won. Fan dropped her tight-clenched fists at her sides. ''Why don't both of you go into the dining room, where you may sit down and defame my character at will? For my part, I'm going up to my room to rest until Mr. Irons comes home.''

''Well, I never.'' The landlady's mouth twisted angrily.

''Fan. Behave yourself.''

''No!'' She marched past him into the hall. A quick swing around the newel post and she was halfway up the stairs before the man could get to the foot.

''Fan,'' he called plaintively. ''Please stop. I'm sorry. Don't you know me?''

''If I had known you, I would have greeted you.''

''I'm Paul.''

''Paul who?''

''Paul Breckenridge. Rex Breckenridge is—was my brother.''

''You know me?''

''Of course, I know you. I just couldn't believe that you were here in this—this dump. . . .''

Mrs. Dittman gave an outraged gasp. She screwed up her mouth in her favorite sour pickle look and folded her arms across her chest.

''So I'm your sister-in-law.'' Fan stood at the top of the stairs staring down into his upturned face.

''Of course. Please come down. We'll talk this through. I spoke hastily. In anger.''

''Why should you be angry with me? I'm the one who should be angry with you. The sheriff was here day before yesterday. Why didn't you come with him?"

He shot Mrs. Dittman a deadly look, but the housekeeper held her ground. "I didn't know it was you. That is, I didn't believe it could be you. I was sure you were dead, too, after I saw Rex. You had to be." His voice trailed away. He heaved a sigh. "Fan, please come down and let's talk this over in privacy."

"Why should I come down and go somewhere with you? I don't know you. And nobody around here ever heard of the Breckenridges. I don't think I believe any of this."

"Fan." He started up the stairs.

"No! Stay down there." She backed away hastily, hand outstretched to hold him off.

"Fan, please."

She stared at him. He looked harmless enough. Beyond his shoulder Mrs. Dittman's hand slid under the table. The housekeeper had her hand on her gun. Fan took a deep breath. "Just go into the dining room and wait for me. I'll be back as soon as I take care of myself and change clothes. As you can see I've been riding."

He hesitated. "But . . ."

"Just wait, I tell you."

He muttered into his beard, then capitulated with a smile that fell short of being reassuring. "I'll wait."

Upstairs, Fan staggered to the bed, her head throbbing painfully. Dropping down upon it, she stared around her. The man downstairs claimed to be her brother-in-law, yet she had no memory of him. He was a stranger.

Dizzily, she fell back across the mattress, staring at the brown circles in the ceiling. The shocks had come thick and fast today. Likewise, the ride on Pet had exhausted and strained her muscles. She ached all over. She did not want to talk in private to anyone.

A glance out the window told her that the day was getting on. Irons would be returning from work. But not soon enough. She feared he would not get back in time to help her. She had to face this alone.

Climbing to her feet, she stripped off Irons' clothing, bathed her face and arms, and slipped into her new dress. Her black hair lay lank upon her shoulders. Her eyes faintly sunken looked out of a face white and shadowed with strain. Leaning forward, she searched for the white hair Eufemia Carlton had commented on. The corner of her mouth lifted mirthlessly. What difference did a single hair make? What mattered was that she looked to be in her right mind.

She carefully gathered the hair back up and attached it at the top of her head in a semblance of the current style. It gave her a modicum of confidence, a bit more of the appearance of a lady. Then she pinched her cheeks and bit her lips to bring color to the surface. Tilting her head to the side, she smiled coolly. The reflection in the mirror despite the remaining discoloration from the bruise seemed to have more self-possession than the hollow-eyed witch woman who had darted into the room a quarter of an hour before.

Still she felt naked with nothing but a cotton dress and thin underthings to hide her body from the man below. Irons' saddlebags hung over the back of the room's only chair.

The gun. Pulling it out, she stared at it for a long time. An army revolver, a souvenir from his stint in the Spanish-American War, its heavy weight dragged her arm down.

Its mechanism, however, was not unknown to her. With a sort of deadly calm came a sure knowledge that she knew how to use it. Someone, somewhere had taught her how to shoot. She spun the cylinder. Every chamber was full.

On a peg on the wall hung Irons' coat. Turning up the cuffs, she thrust her arms into it and looked again at the mirror. It came down to mid-thigh and in no way resembled a lady's pelisse. But the heavy navy wool had pockets. Into the right one, she slipped the heavy Colt. She might look as if she were dressed from a poor box, but she was trembling at the prospect of the confrontation.

"Irons," she whispered, hugging her arms around her. "Come back soon."

With her right hand closed over the gun, she descended the stairs.

"Fan." Paul Breckenridge rose from the table where he had waited, a cup of Mrs. Dittman's coffee untouched before him.

"Your name is Paul?" she said uncertainly.

"Yes, Paul. Your husband's brother. Rex was my little brother."

He seemed perfectly in control, much more than she. She drew away stiffly when he tried to take her arm and seated herself.

"What's wrong, Fan?" He took a seat across the table from her. His eyes above the dark beard and mustache seemed genuinely concerned.

"I'm sure you know that I can't remember anything."

"So I've been told."

"Are you really my family?"

"Yes."

"Then why haven't you come for me before today?"

He took a swallow of the coffee before he answered. "I couldn't believe that you were here."

"Why not? Where else would I be?"

"Both your beds were empty. I was sure . . ."

"Both our beds?"

"You and he didn't get along."

"Because of Eufemia Carlton?"

He looked at her shamefacedly. "Partly. And partly because of other things."

"She was here today, asking me if I remembered her."

"Ah. And did you remember her?"

Fan shook her head sadly. "Not at all." She leaned forward to stare at him intently. He lowered his eyes, uncomfortable beneath such scrutiny. At last she sank back sighing. "And I don't remember you."

He heaved a deep sigh before sinking back in his own chair. "That's too bad."

Her head had begun to ache again. Her temple beneath the scab throbbed dully. "It's terrible. You can't imagine." She looked at him. "Are you really my brother-in-law?"

He clapped his hand to his chest. "I swear . . ."

She shook her head. "I can't remember. I can't remember anything. And instead of feeling better day by day, I seem to be getting worse. Today I went for a ride and . . ." She leaned forward, her hands thrust down tight in the pockets of Irons' coat. ". . . today I imagined someone was after me."

He looked alarmed.

"Oh, I know. I was so silly. But I was so scared." She could feel her mouth quivering weakly. She had cried in front of Irons and wet the front of his shirt on several occasions. But this man was a stranger to her. She bit down hard on her lower lip and took a deep controlling breath.

Paul Breckenridge waited until she released it. Then he stood up buttoning his coat briskly. "Come with me, Fancy. I'll take care of you."

She looked up at him hopefully. "I would so like to return to my family. My mother and father. I do have a mother and father, don't I?"

"Yes, of course."

"And their names?"

He cleared his throat. "Gillard."

"Gillard." She turned the name over and over, trying in vain to match it with something in her mind. "Gillard. Could they send someone for me?"

Breckenridge shrugged. "Why, yes, I suppose so. But they don't live in this part of the state."

He leaned forward to try and take her hands, but she thrust them under the table. He scowled. "The fact is that they didn't approve of your marriage. Very high in society. Old aristocratic family from back east originally. They wouldn't be inclined to help at this point."

"But surely if they knew that I was widowed, left without . . ."

He came round the table to drop his hand on her shoulder. "Fancy, I'll take care of everything. Just come with me."

She rose. "I'll have to wait until Irons comes in from work."

"Of course you don't have to wait." Breckenridge's face darkened. His mouth twitched beneath the heavy black mustache as he led her toward the door. "That barbarian. I'm sure he was mixed up in Rex's death some way. I told the sheriff to arrest him."

Fan stopped short. "Oh, no. Irons saved my life. He's taken care of me like a brother. I'd have died if not for him."

"I'm sure you exaggerate."

"No. I have to wait and thank him. You must offer some kind of repayment. He's paid for my stay here. He bought me this dress."

"I'll take care of him later." He had his hand under

her arm and led her firmly to the front door. Mrs. Dittman hovered in the background, a sour expression on her face. ''Another reason you mustn't stay here with him is if your family should get wind of it, all hope of returning to them would be gone. Your father himself told me that your ancestor was an English lord. Your family still owns a huge plantation in South Carolina. You don't want to disgrace them.''

She wavered, Mrs. Dittman's expression daunting. ''At least let me write him a note.''

''We need to be on our way.'' He pushed open the screen door.

As it swung back, Irons walked up the front stoop. ''Well, Breckenridge. Did you finally get around to coming for her?''

Chapter 7

"Irons!"

Fan's breath whooshed out as she cried his name; her taut muscles relaxed. As he stalked across the front porch, she reached for him eagerly.

His arms went around her and pulled her in close against him. "Why, Jane . . ." He could feel her trembling. "Whoa, baby. What's going on?"

She tipped her head back. Her eyes misty, she looked up into Irons' familiar face. Again she thought how quickly he had become the rock and anchor, the most important thing in her life.

He did not think how he could read her feelings. His hands tightened. His gray eyes narrowed as he searched her face for the cause of her concern.

Black beard bristling, Paul Breckenridge closed his hand over her shoulder. "Take your damned hands off her," he growled. "I'll take care of her from now on."

Instinctively, she pressed closer to Irons. "This is Paul Breckenridge. My brother-in-law. He's come to take me home."

"Oh, he has?" Irons' fingers flexed in the wool garment he recognized as his own coat. His lips thinned beneath his mustache.

"I sure have. Come on, Fan. You can let go of her." Breckenridge exerted more pressure on her shoulder.

Wincing as his fingers dug in, Fan let him turn her. As she pivoted, her right hand slid around Irons' waist. Her eyes never left his face. "I wanted to wait for you."

"What the hell . . . ?" Through the pocket of his coat, Irons felt the heavy metal swing against his belly. "Well, I'll be damned." She was wearing it, to conceal a weapon. He tightened his grip. His eyes darkened as he looked past her.

"I've come to take her home."

"You took your own sweet time getting here."

Breckenridge flushed. "I had to be sure."

"And how'd you make sure?" Irons asked coldly.

"Why I . . ." He began to stammer. "I asked around. I sent a message to her folks."

Fan frowned. "I thought you told me they didn't know anything about any of this."

"I didn't tell them anything," Paul replied swiftly. "I didn't want them to worry."

Fan nodded slowly. "I guess you're right."

"Are you satisfied now, Fan? Say your good-byes to this roughneck and let's get out of here." Breckenridge looked around him as if the rooming house were contaminated.

"Get out of here," Irons repeated slowly.

"Yes, I'm taking her home."

"And where might home be? I've asked around this whole tent city, but nobody's ever heard of anybody named Breckenridge."

"That's because the home place is way north of here, on the other side of the county." His eyes swept the muddy street contemptuously. "No one in this sty could possibly have heard of Rosemeade."

Across the way in the saloon, the player piano began

a music roll of "Camptown Races." The noise increased as more men finished their tours and came in to drink and gamble.

A trio of riders galloped down the street spattering mud onto the edge of the porch. Swinging off their mounts, they punched each other playfully. The race's winner collected his bets and they stomped in laughing. Their voices added to the din as they shouted for whiskey.

"Come on, Fan," Paul murmured in her ear. "Let me take you away from all this."

"Where're you going to take her?" Irons repeated inexorably.

"To Rex's place. It's her place now."

"And where's that?"

"Up north of here a couple of miles. He's got a house. Come on, Fan. You can ride in style." Paul pointed to the phaeton.

"Irons," Fan caught at his hand. "Please come with us."

Her brother-in-law scowled at the gesture. "You don't need him."

Irons' grin was a masterpiece of mischief. "Be glad to."

The two sentences were uttered simultaneously. Then Irons put Fan aside and tugged his hat brim down more firmly. "My pleasure, baby. I'll just get my slicker—and saddle my horse."

"She's been ridden today," Fan told him.

He shot her a quick look. "Did you borrow her?"

"Yes. I wanted to see if I could find anyone who knew me." She looked at Paul. "Instead you found me."

He scowled as Irons vanished into the house. "You don't need him with you."

"Maybe I don't need him, but I haven't really had a chance to thank him. He's such a kind man."

Breckenridge shook his head, but Fan hurried on. "He's taken such good care of me. He'll feel better if he sees that I'm all right. Then I can thank him and he can ride on."

"I tell you . . ."

"Please. I really need Irons with me."

"What was he to you?" Paul's expression turned ugly. He caught her by the arm. "Did Rex know about him? Were you sneaking around behind his back?"

His grip was harsh enough to bruise her bruises. She twisted and pushed at him. "No. Let go. What are you getting so excited about? Rex didn't know about him because I just met him. He came riding along the night Rex was killed."

"You're lying. You were playing around on my brother."

Fan's eyes flashed angrily. "How dare you! I swear I've never met him before."

"How can you be sure?"

"Well . . ."

"You see," Breckenridge snapped. "You don't know who's got you. You're treading a dangerous path. He could be the murderer."

"I know he's not. Remember I don't know you either."

"My God. Of course, you do. I told you who I was. Why would I lie?"

She would not capitulate. "You could have a reason. I don't know who to trust, but I do know that Irons could have killed me any time before he got me to town."

"Maybe he just didn't want to kill a woman. A lot of men are funny about that."

"Then he could have dropped me off on these steps and ridden on. Instead he took care of me."

"And what's he getting out of all this? What's his angle? Does he think you might have some money?"

"No, not money." Fan dropped her head to hide the burning blush rising in her cheeks.

He stared at her incredulously as the answer to his question dawned on him. Then he drove his fist against the pillar. "Goddamn it! My brother's wife. And him not cold in his grave."

"I'd be dead without him," she insisted stubbornly.

Nursing his bruised hand, Paul swung back around and stepped close to her. "Has he threatened you?" he muttered. "Is that why you're afraid to leave him? I can get that good-for-nothing sheriff back over here."

"No."

"Let me send for him. He'll be here in a couple of hours or I'll have his damned job."

"It'll take a lot longer than that. He's all the way over in Batson. He won't be back. Irons said . . ."

"Damn him!" Breckenridge's voice grated with anger. "Who the hell is he that you can't open your mouth without mentioning him?"

Fan crossed her arms about her chest. Her reply was adamant. "He's the man who saved my life."

Fancy clutched at her brother-in-law's arm as the black phaeton turned off the road. The horse trotted down a narrow wagon path with weeds grown up in the center. "Where are you taking me?"

"To your home," her brother-in-law insisted.

"I saw this today," she whispered half to herself. "I've stumbled onto this place today."

He looked at her quizzically. "You came here today?"

"Yes. There was someone else here. At least I think there was." She looked fearfully around the edge of the clearing. The hair prickled on the back of her neck. Chill bumps rose on her arms.

The phaeton drew around in front of the cabin. Small and unpainted, it hardly blocked the view of the empty corral and barn and behind that—the derrick.

Long shadows filled the clearing as the western sun sank lower. The pines stood on all sides like dark walls, with underbrush rising up to tangle with their lower branches. Crickets chirped above the gently soughing wind. From the depths of the woods, a screech owl hooted eerily. Fan's teeth began to chatter. She pressed her hands together between her knees and tried to still their trembling. "Irons?"

"Here, Jane."

"Irons, I was here today, and—"

"Her name's Fan," Paul Breckenridge interrupted irritably.

"What's her full name?"

"Caroline Fancy Breckenridge. Her maiden name was Gillard."

"Where did you say she was from?"

Breckenridge hesitated for a fraction of a second. "Out of state."

"Where?" Irons insisted.

"Damn it. I won't be bullied by a roughneck. When Fan wants to know, I'll tell her." He tied the reins around the brake and climbed down.

"Looks like nobody's lived here in quite a while," Irons remarked. "Are you sure this is the right place?"

"I'm sure." Paul gritted his teeth.

"I don't remember anything like this," Fan whispered. Her hands were ice cold when she put them into Irons' to let him help her down.

"If you don't remember your family . . ."—Paul

gingerly climbed onto the rickety porch—". . . how could you be expected to remember a house?" He pushed against the door. It stuck, resisting his efforts. He grunted and threw his shoulders into it.

"Maybe it's locked?"

"No. It's giving." He pulled up on the knob. Corner dragging across the floor, it scraped inward. "The damp must have got to it."

Fan huddled against Irons as they mounted the porch together.

"I'll light the lamp," Paul volunteered.

The dim light from the filthy chimney revealed a few poor sticks of furniture all under a layer of dust.

Fan huddled against Irons' side as a huge spider scuttled across the scarred table.

Paul pulled out a pocket handkerchief and wiped his hands. "Rex never had much," he remarked offhandedly.

"How long had they been married?" Irons wanted to know.

"A couple of years."

"Two years!" Fan gasped. "And we lived in this place in this condition for two years?"

Irons left her side and strolled across the warped floor. Pushing open the inner door, he looked inside. "The bed's got sheets on it."

"They're clean," Paul said hastily. "And the mattress was aired."

"But the filth." Fan touched her fingertips to the table. They came away thick with gritty black dirt.

"Well, I . . ."

Irons positioned himself at the table so that the two of them faced Paul. "I think you'd better tell the truth, Breckenridge. Nobody's lived in this house for months."

"You don't know how fast things deteriorate around here," the smaller man accused belligerently.

"It's been just two weeks since I found Fan. Two weeks since her husband died. This dust is months old. Those weeds out front didn't grow up that fast."

"Rex never did keep the place up."

Fan opened the cupboard. "The food that's here looks fresh," she murmured, taking down a can of coffee.

"I stocked the place," Paul admitted.

"So this is where I'm supposed to live."

"If you want to."

"I'll think about it."

"If not, I'm getting rid of it," he added.

"Not likely," Irons put in. "If this place was Rex's, then she's Rex's widow. The place belongs to her."

"Now just a minute." Breckenridge's face darkened. "This was my brother's."

"It belongs to his widow now. That's the law in Texas. And to any children they may have had."

"Children?" Fan pressed her hands against her belly.

"They didn't have any children," Paul sneered. "She couldn't get pregnant."

A small silence followed. Fan moved the cans, boxes, and bags around in the cupboard. The food was scanty. Someone had purchased the smallest amounts possible of staples. In a flash of memory she saw a huge pantry with shelves and shelves of Mason jars filled with vegetables. On a marble slab beneath them were pans of milk to separate and rounds of cheese and butter.

Only a flash. Then she was left staring at the couple of narrow shelves. She rubbed her hand across her eyes. Her fingers touched the crescent-shaped scab at her temple.

"I can't stay here for the night," she decided at last. "It's too late to clean it properly."

"We've got the bed paid for back there at Waldrow," Irons suggested. "Let's go back and sleep on it."

Paul Breckenridge looked as if he would burst with anger. "You're not going to spend another night with him."

"What difference does one more night make?" Irons asked with a straight face. "Or for that matter where it's spent?"

The smaller man turned to Fan. "You're my brother's widow. I expect you to behave yourself."

"Nobody knows who she is," Irons reminded him smoothly. "What did you tell Mrs. Dittman, baby?"

"I don't understand."

"Who'd you tell her you were?"

"Oh. Jane . . . Irons."

Breckenridge backed toward the door. "You killed him," he accused wildly. "The two of you plotted against him and killed him. The sheriff will be mighty interested to hear this."

Irons followed, his shoulders hunched, his chin thrust forward. "Why don't you just go get him, Breckenridge?"

"I'll just do that. You're in this together."

Irons laughed. "Sure we are. The two of us together hanged him. I held him while she pulled the rope. And then I beat her up so badly that her brains were bruised. And after I'd done that I moved her into a boardinghouse and asked everybody I could find who she was."

"I'm going to the sheriff."

"You go right ahead. You go roust Barfield out and see if you can get him to come from Batson again on a wild-goose chase. He asked us all he knew to ask and then he left. He won't come back unless you've got something new to tell him."

Sweeping the room with a fulminating stare, Breckenridge jerked open the door. "You killed my brother," he accused. "I'll see you both in hell."

Fancy snuggled tight against Irons' shoulder. The sheets were clean and fresh, but the bed beneath them was terribly musty. If Paul Breckenridge had paid someone to air it, he had paid for labor not done.

Morning light ventured through the four small dirty panes. Irons held her easily, his lips less than an inch from her forehead. He wished he did not have to get up, wished he did not have to leave her side and thus disturb her. In the bright light the bedroom was much more depressing than it had been in the dim light cast through the smoky lamp chimney. Mrs. Dittman's bedroom would look luxurious by comparison.

Fan stirred, murmured something, and snuggled more deeply beneath the covers.

He closed his eyes and rested his chin on the top of her head. Her hair caressed him like black silk. She moved again. Her palm slid down the side of his chest. The innocent sensuousness made him draw a sharp deep breath.

How important she had become to him! He was used to her. He could only think in terms of her being with him today and tomorrow and the next.

He opened his eyes. Through the window he could see the derrick. Suddenly, his pulse beat a little faster. The tower stood unfinished, bare of the heavy hoist equipment that would have set a drill in place to spin and drive out the thick Texas earth until the oil beneath it was released to come spouting into the air. Black gold. A fortune waiting in deep pools.

Suddenly he could stay by her side no longer. Eyes fixed on the rig, he gently extricated himself from her arms. Pulling on his pants and shirt, he tiptoed from the bedroom and out of the cabin. The morning was brisk; every weed, every branch, every wild grass dripped with dew.

Barefooted he hopped off the rickety porch and walked around to the back. The derrick stood on the apex of a gentle mound. Only a slight rise in the earth, not nearly enough to be called a hill.

The grass grew thinly at the foot of it and as the earth sloped upward, the coastal rye gave way to a thin scattering of sandburs.

They stuck to Irons' soles by the dozens, but he walked on, oblivious to the small pains, uncaring how he placed his feet. The ground around the derrick was almost bare. Down on one knee, he clawed at the soil, scraping down an inch or two below the surface. He lifted his fingertips to his mouth and tasted.

Salt.

He tasted it again. Scooped up another handful and held it under his nose. Faintly, but unmistakably he scented the odor of rotten eggs.

Sulfur.

"What are you doing?"

He clenched his fist over the soil. "Taking a walk." He started up and was suddenly aware of the pain in his feet. "Goddamn!" He hopped to the edge of the rig platform and sat down where he began to pluck out the burs.

"Oh, Irons." Fan's voice was rich with pity as she bent over his feet to help him.

He could not meet her eyes. Instead he looked away toward the woods. "I guess I wasn't watching where I was walking."

She straightened slowly, her face searching his harsh profile. "I guess you weren't."

"It's sure a mighty pretty morning."

She stepped back, hugging her arms about her. She had donned both her dress and his coat. She looked down at the ground noticing that he had been digging. "I guess I'm going to have to get a pair of boots, if I'm going to live out here. These nice shoes won't last."

He looked back at her, surreptitiously letting the soil trickle between his fingers. "You've got a lot of clothes somewhere, baby. Good clothes. Remember that nightgown. I don't for one minute believe that this is where you actually lived with your husband."

She pretended not to notice when he stood up and wiped his hand on the side of his leg. "I don't either. There isn't any clothing, either of his or mine. Not a single memento nor an ornament. I would have certainly kept house better than that."

He grinned at the tone of disgust in her voice. "Do I gather that you're ready for a ride back to town then, Caroline Fancy Breckenridge?"

She turned away and walked back down to the corral. Her voice floated up to him. "I had begun to get used to the idea of Jane Irons."

He stabbed his fists into his hips and stared upward at the derrick. The morning sun limned it in fire. His heart took up the drilling rhythm.

Reluctantly, he shook himself free of the spell and started down the decline. The slope of the damned hill was covered with grass burs, a sure sign of the soil's high salt and sulfur content. Only the most determined of plants would grow on it. This time he felt everyone of them because they were impossible to avoid.

Their barbs stuck in the arches of his feet. They clung between his toes and lashed at his ankles. Still wet with dew they were inescapable torture. He could not believe he had walked through them oblivious, his gaze fixed sixty feet in the air.

At the corral he leaned against a post and brushed them out again. A multitude of their tiny barbs remained stuck in his skin. In disgust he looked at the scratches and the stiples of blood. Each sticker would fester in a couple of days and set his feet on fire.

He was a damn fool, but a pool of oil lay somewhere down beneath that derrick. He could taste it and smell it.

"I've made you some coffee," Fan said as he limped in the door.

"Good. Thanks." He accepted a tin cup from her.

"It's black, but you could have some sugar and some condensed milk if you wanted."

"No. This is fine." He took a swallow. "Have you drunk yours?"

"Yes. I've drunk some." She looked at him, a watchful expression on her face.

He downed it not quite meeting her eyes. "I'll get dressed and we'll go."

When he came out of the bedroom, she had rinsed the cup and was sitting bolt upright in the half barrel that had been made to serve for a chair. She had pulled his coat tight around her. Her jaw was set as if she were trying to keep her teeth from chattering.

He put his hand on her shoulder. "Cold?"

"Yes."

"Let's get out in the sunshine."

Outside he mounted Pet and then held down a hand.

"Can she carry double?"

"Sure. Just so long as we don't run her uphill." He set her behind him, sidesaddle, her arms around his waist. "Now we'll take it slow and easy."

The sun was warm on his wool jacket. She rested

her head on his shoulder. "I was afraid yesterday. I was afraid he was going to drag me right out of there."

"I know. I felt the gun where you'd put it in the pocket."

"I rode up this trail yesterday by mistake. Someone was here."

"Where?"

"Over in the brush." She nodded in the direction. "I could hear him. I don't know why I was scared, but I was."

"Any woman alone near a rag town has a good reason to be scared," he told her. "Oil strikes attract lots of mean sons of bitches. Any one of them probably wouldn't hurt you with other people around, but alone . . ." He shook his head.

"I think this was different," she murmured after a pause. "I think he knew who I was. I whipped Pet into a gallop and when I'd cleared the trail I looked back. He was standing out in the middle of the wagon path."

He looked back over his shoulder. "You could be right. Somebody killed your husband. Maybe he thinks you could identify him."

She shuddered.

"Or it could have been somebody that your dear brother-in-law sent to change the sheets on the bed. He could have been scared and hid when you came riding up. A man's not all that safe alone either."

"This is a great place," she said sarcastically.

"The greatest." He patted her cold hands where they encircled his waist. "Where there's a fortune to be made, men lose every bit of Christian charity their mother's ever tried to teach them. That is, if some of them were lucky enough to have mothers. Don't worry, baby. I'll take care of you."

They rode on in silence. Clusters of tents began to appear on either side of the road.

"Will you really take care of me?" she asked as the boardinghouse appeared through the trees.

"I said I would."

"We could live at that cabin," she suggested softly.

He pulled Pet to a halt and twisted in the saddle. "You and me?" He strained to look over his shoulder into her eyes. "But you know who you are now. You don't have any excuse for shacking up with me."

She swallowed hard. "I don't think of it as shacking up exactly. I just don't see that I have any choice."

He spoke to Pet. The sorrel moved on reluctantly. "Your brother-in-law'll have a running fit."

"If I ever see him again. He dumped me in that cabin like a bundle of dirty laundry. If you hadn't been there, he wouldn't even have gotten out of his buggy."

"He sure wasn't eager to tell you where the home place—what was it? Rose something-or-other."

"Rosemeade."

"Did you remember what he said, or did you remember?"

She stiffened. "I don't know. The name certainly came fast enough."

"What's your name, baby?"

She opened her mouth. Then shook her head. "Someone told me it was Fan or Caroline Fancy. But I can't remember before that." She rolled her forehead against his shoulders. "Oh, Irons, what am I going to do?"

He halted the sorrel and swung down on the filthy straw in front of the boardinghouse. "Well, I guess for starters, we'll get down and eat some of Mrs. Dittman's breakfast. Then I'll go work a tour at the Boomin' Bessie while you pack our clothes and buy whatever you need to take out there to your place. When I get finished, we'll go out there together."

"All right."

He held up his arms to help her down. "And listen, baby. If you change you mind about me going with you, I'll understand."

She put her hands on his shoulders and leaned forward. Naturally as if she had been doing it for years, she slid down the length of his body. She felt him suck in his breath sharply as her soft parts rubbed against him.

"I'm not going to change my mind about you," she promised.

He grinned as he clapped her to his side. "Let's go eat."

Chapter 8

"Something isn't right about this whole deal. No one would have murdered anybody for this." Fancy stared around her in disgust.

The cabin's walls were rough boards nailed crossways to a frame of two-by-fours. The light of noon revealed dust thick on the floor and furniture. Ancient cobwebs, long deserted by their spinners, dipped between the rafters and festooned the corners. A rickety table, scarred and stained, a couple of stools made from turned-over nail kegs, a half-barrel chair with a board fitted across it for the seat, a potbellied stove, and a cupboard with chipped and peeling paint comprised the furniture in the front room.

A square had been crudely sawed out of the boards between two wall studs. Four panes of glass, one cracked, had been stuck into the square to form a window. It was filthy.

Irons leaned against the stud next to it, his arms crossed over his chest. "Sorta seems like a waste of time and effort," he drawled. "Probably if they'd asked him nicely, he'd 've been glad to get rid of it."

"I may not remember Rex nor Paul nor the big house Paul talked about, but I can tell you here and now that I would never, never have lived in a house in this condition. I know''—she pointed to the fading bruise on her temple—''I *know* that I did not live in this house two weeks ago.''

Irons smiled. ''Course you didn't, baby, but where did you live? I'd sure like to take a ride up to that place. What did he call it?''

''Rosemeade. We weren't invited,'' Fan reminded him bitterly.

''Think you might have been married to the black sheep.''

She took a deep breath, tilting her head back to keep the tears from falling from her eyes. ''How do I know? I can't even remember what my husband looked like. If I could just remember something—anything—at all.''

He straightened quickly and came to put his arm around her shoulders. ''Hey, baby, don't let this get you down. You'll remember.''

Her head remained tipped except now it rested on his upper arm. He stared into her eyes. Gold shimmered under the clear water of her tears. She gulped. ''I guess so.''

''I know so.''

They stood together for a minute while a slow ache began in her lower body. He was so very close and his masculinity was so very potent. Gently, he lowered his head to brush her lips. She quivered beneath him, desperately trying to resist the tug of his body.

To her surprise he stepped back. Reaching for the hat he had carelessly tossed on the table, he strode to the door. ''Got to get back to the Boomin' Bessie,'' he grated, his voice unnaturally hoarse.

Instantly she inclined her head, so he would not see the blush that rose in her face. ''Will you''—she cleared her throat and reached up to open the cupboard—"will you be coming back here for . . . uh . . . supper?"

"Do you want me to?"

She clutched a chipped plate. "Yes." She turned to face him, her color high, but not unnaturally so. She swallowed painfully. "Yes. I want to make up for all the money you spent on me. I'd like you to consider this your home while you're here in Waldrow."

He raised one black eyebrow. Under his mustache his mouth curved upward in mockery. "I'd sure like to do that, Miz Breckenridge, ma'am. I'm much obliged. But I don't need to be paid back."

Her face twisted. "I didn't mean that I could pay you back. I can't pay you back for my life. I simply meant that *mi casa es su casa.* I hope you'll feel that way about it."

"Very gracious, baby," he sneered scornfully. How dare she take this tone with him!

She clutched the piece of crockery so tightly her fingers showed white. "I want you to come back—if you will."

He pulled on his hat and waited.

"Please, Irons, I need you to come here and be with me."

He laughed then, a little nastily. "That's more like it, baby. I'll be back in time for supper."

She followed him through the door. Face drained of color, her hands wrapped tight around one of the four-by-fours that supported the roof.

He stepped off the rickety porch into Pet's saddle. Reining the mare, he made a clicking sound with his tongue. The animal ambled forward. He turned in the saddle and tipped his hat in an imitation of old-fashioned gallantry. "Be seeing you, baby."

Fan waited until he had disappeared down the trail,

then she stepped down off the porch and walked around the side of the house.

Eyes on the lay of the land, she approached the derrick. How she knew what she was looking for, she could not tell. Yet niggling within her brain, the messages came.

The sticker burs spreading a web of spindly runners all around the platform. Whitish yellow soil beneath. Salt and sulfur. Salt dome. Salt dome!

Irons had seen it too. He had been smelling it and tasting it. The best men claimed that they could.

She hitched a hip up on the edge of the drilling platform and stared at the ground. Rex might very well have died for this. When oil made fortunes for men overnight, greedy men would kill without compunction for this drilling site.

She looked upward, turning her head so a crossbar shaded her eyes from the sun. The tower waited for the crown block and the lengths of pipe, the drill stem and the drill itself to come boring down. The platform's heavy planks extended far out to one side of the derrick where a shed could be constructed over the draw works.

Had someone told her his dreams? Or was she like most of the rest of Texas ever since Spindletop: Itching deep inside, half wild at the very thought of gushing gold.

She drew a deep shaky breath and looked around her at the land. She who did not know her own name could know that a chance at a great fortune lay at her feet. Furthermore, she could see that the chances were better than good that perhaps only a few hundred feet below her a great power was waiting to be released.

She lifted her feet onto the platform and pushed herself up. Hands on her hips she walked to the very center where the hole for the rotary table would be cut.

Tilting her head back again, she stared up and up into the blue sky between the bars. After it made her pleasurably dizzy, she looked outward and allowed the landscape to right itself.

Grimly, she mulled an unpleasant probability. This very morning Irons would most likely have gone on his merry way with a tip of his hat had he not seen the derrick. It had captured his imagination so that he had not noticed the painful burs that bloodied his bare feet. Probably coals of fire would have made no greater impression. He wanted a share of it.

Or did he want it all?

Funny how much that hurt to think about. Did he want it all? What if he had indeed been the man or one of the men who murdered Rex? What if he had been struck with an attack of conscience? Men who killed other men without compunction would stick at the cold-blooded murder of an innocent woman.

But greed would ease the most powerful conscience. A killer hired for only a few dollars could listen to his creed without much sacrifice. A man who saw a chance for millions might let nothing stop him to get them. If they drilled this well together, perhaps nothing would stop him from murdering her and taking the profits.

A crow cawed raucously in a snag at the edge of the clearing beyond the rig. Another answered. Then a jay. A squirrel began to chatter furiously. A hunter was in the forest. Like a doe she froze, every muscle, every sense alert for the approach of the enemy. A vision of the blocky figure that had stepped out into the trail flashed through her mind.

She dropped down below the edge of the platform. Keeping low, she ran for the house. Her heart pounded as her feet covered the uneven ground. Her spine tingled with the thought that someone might be training a rifle on it.

Inside the shack, she bolted the door and ran into the bedroom. Jerking the gun from Irons' saddlebags, she ran to the bedroom window. The area where the land rose up to the rig was empty. She waited, panting, leaning against the wall stud. As her breathing quieted and her heartbeat slowed, she could still hear the birds fussing.

Something was out there. Something coming closer.

Did she imagine it? She could hear the plodding of hooves. A horse. A horseman? Although still far away, they were coming closer. He must be riding forward cautiously. She thumbed the hammer back on the revolver. The cylinder turned so that a bullet came to a stop beneath the pin.

Nearer the slow, shuffling hooves came. Nearer.

Around the platform came a brown head. A big black muzzle thrust forward. Fan collapsed against the wall and allowed the heavy gun to drag her hand down. A cow. Relief made her weak and at the same time, she felt her limbs begin to tremble.

The Guernsey increased her pace as she plodded down toward the corral. At the gate she bawled loudly.

Fan laughed. Obviously the cow knew she was home. Time to go let her in the corral and milk her. Putting the gun away, she opened the door in the bottom of the cupboard. The milk pail sat bottomside up in its dark recesses. Without doubt, she knew how to milk a cow.

When she lifted it out, she found that it—like everything else—was covered with a thin coating of dust. Leaving it by the pump, she hurried out onto the porch intent on putting the cow in the corral. On the first step, her skin began to prickle, her heart stepped up its beat. Fear clawed at her brain and belly.

What would have happened if instead of a cow, a rider had come out of the woods? She could not have shot him from the cabin window. Yet how would she have known until he was close enough to kill her first? She looped her arm around the four-by-four and clung for dear life. Closing her eyes did not shut out the awful truth. Since the night Irons had rescued her, she could not shake off the idea that she was in constant danger. Fear had come to play an omnipresent part in her life.

The cow bawled again. She pushed herself away from the post. She could not huddle in the cabin under the covers until Irons returned at dusk. Back she went to the bedroom straight to his saddlebags. Her mouth set in a grim line, she drew forth, not only the gun but the holster.

The belt needed to be run past the tongue and looped over and under to keep it on her hips. Its weight swung against her thigh with heavy comfort as she walked to the corral.

The cow's udder was full. Someone must drop by this place and milk her. Perhaps that explained the presence of the man yesterday. He had come to milk the cow.

Lowing piteously, the creature headed straight for the barn and thrust her head dumbly through the stanchion. Fan forked hay into the manger and patted the broad face. "Be right back. Just be patient a few more minutes, Bossie."

When Irons returned well after dusk, he was greeted by major improvements in the cabin and a very tired Fan. He sniffed the air appreciatively. "Something sure smells good. I could smell it all the way from the road."

"Could you?" She stood at the stove stirring a pot.

"Sure could." He thought it the most natural thing in the world to come up behind her and put his arms around her. His rough chin rested on her shoulder as he stared into the pot. "What's cooking?"

"Vegetable soup, sort of." She returned his rough caress by pressing her smooth cheek against his stubbly one.

He sniffed again. "No sort of about it. It's vegetable."

"Well, mostly beans and rice flavored with bacon rind. But there were some onions and we've got corn bread. So maybe we won't starve to death."

He kissed her on the neck, a friendly peck beneath her earlobe. "Baby, you don't know starving till you've been in the army. Cooks are terrible. Food's worse. It all tastes the same, full of saltpeter."

She looked at him without understanding. "I don't think I've ever used any of that."

He grinned. "No. I'll bet you haven't." As he stepped back, he noticed the gun swung low on her hip. "Shooting rabbits?"

Flushing, she started to unbuckle it. "I didn't see any to shoot."

He put his hand over hers, his fingers warm at her waist. "Leave it on. It looks sort of dangerous. Sort of exciting. I think I like the idea of living with Belle Starr." When she did not smile, his expression became serious. "Did you see somebody that bothered you?"

She hesitated to tell him how fearful she had been. "I . . . I heard a noise, but it was only a cow."

"Better safe than sorry."

"You're not angry."

"Never. Are you sure you know how to use it?"

She nodded slowly. "I'm sure. It fit my hand." Her eyes stared into the past, trying to remember.

"Just don't shoot yourself," he cautioned. He left her to rinse his hands and face in the pan of clear water she had sitting on the enamel shelf of the cupboard.

"There's no soap," she apologized. "I don't know how we'll get clean until I can get into town."

"I don't mind." His voice was muffled in the towel—one of two she had found in the bedroom. He emerged from beneath it with most of the sweat and grime expunged. His eyes lit expectantly at the prospect of food.

"I don't think I was a very good cook," she said as she dished up the soup.

He tasted it and found it bland but not unflavorful. Spooning up a larger mouthful, he told her so. "You did a good job on this considering how little you had to work with." He eyed the milk with some surprise. "Where did the cow come from?"

"She wandered up. I'm pretty sure she belongs here. She needed to be milked, so I milked her."

"And you knew how?"

She shrugged. "A little bit."

"So you haven't milked much. And you haven't cooked much."

"Is the food bad?"

"No, it's good, but you're right. You're not used to cooking." He crumbled some corn bread in his soup. "What's your name?"

She opened her mouth. Then closed it again. "I've been told my name is Caroline Fancy. But you can call me Fan." Elbow on the table, she leaned her head into her hand.

He finished his soup in silence, ate the rest of the corn bread and drank another glass of milk. Then he looked at her. "Tired?"

"Not too bad."

"I'd be surprised if you weren't. You're still shocked." He rose and stacked the plates in the dishpan. Side by side they did up the few things and put them away.

They could do nothing thereafter but retire for the night. The two nail-keg stools and half-barrel chair made very uncomfortable sitting for longer than a meal. In the bedroom they undressed where she was stricken by an uncomfortable shyness.

Cheeks blushing, she slipped off her clothing and tucked her feet between the covers. By the glow of the dying kerosene lamp, she watched him strip and slide into bed. Immediately he reached for her.

"I'm so tired," she objected. Her very bones ached along with her head.

"Just wanted you over next to me," he reassured her. "The sheets are always dank this close to the Gulf. Too much rain."

She acquiesced, sliding over against him, and resting her head in the hollow of his shoulder.

"What are you going to do about that rig?" he asked after a minute.

Instantly, she tensed. "What should I do?"

"You might consider drilling."

"There's no equipment there. Only the derrick. Perhaps I could get something extra for it if I let it go along with the lease." She smiled wryly in the darkness as she felt him stiffen.

"Lease!"

She rushed on, pretending not to understand. "I know you're too much of a gentleman to push me, and I'm so grateful. But there it stands. Evidently someone must have thought it might be worth something. And I certainly can't do anything with it. For one thing there's no money to buy equipment."

"You don't want to lease to anyone."

"Why not? It's worth a try. I've got to find some means of bringing in some money. You can't go on supporting me indefinitely with your job at the Boomin' Bessie."

He cursed furiously. "You're not going to sign a lease to some boomer who'd cheat you blind. Or some goon from Standard Oil, who'd do away with you if they struck anything but salt water."

They lay side by side in bed, only a thin cotton nightgown between their stiff bodies. The silence grew into something almost tangible. She could feel her heart beating in anticipation, could feel a quivering deep in her belly.

Beside her, he sucked in a deep breath and let it out very slowly. "I could lay my hands on equipment."

She shuddered. His hands closed over her, held her tightly as if she might run away from him. His hands touched her waist and her belly. His wrist warmed the underside of her breasts. Sensual response sharpened by fear tortured her, sucked her into a maelstrom.

What if her hot excitement, her melting desire, were blinding her to truth? What if he was a killer? What if she would open her thighs and welcome the man whose hands would close around her neck . . . ? Nausea churned in her belly. Her head began to whirl. Suddenly, she could not stand to be beside him any longer.

With a low moan she tore herself out of his arms and rushed headlong from the bedroom.

"Fan, baby!"

In the darkness she crashed into the table, banging her toes against the table leg and falling to her knees. Still she scrambled to escape.

"Fan!" He blundered after her, his knee crashed against her semiprone body.

The blow sent her reeling into blackness deeper than the darkness of the cabin. Her eyes, the windows of her mind, suddenly saw no longer. Blinded in some strange unknown way, she fled from a massive shape that came out of her inner world. Crawling across the floor, she found the door and wrenched it open.

"For God's sake . . ."

White moonlight and a gust of cold wet air flooded

the room. They did not sweep away the blackness from her mind. The massive shape became several. Shadows of white-hooded men rose out of her darkness.

She screamed piercingly.

Irons caught her by the shoulders as she pitched herself out the door.

She screamed again, a sound to wake the dead. *"No! For mercy's sake!"*

"Fan." Irons dropped down beside her and pulled her back against him.

"He'll go. I swear, he'll go."

"Fancy!"

"He's choking. He can't breathe. He's strangling!" She tried to turn in Irons' arms. Her fingernails lanced toward his cheeks, but he reared back, cupped her head, and pressed her face in against his chest. "Caroline Fancy. Jane."

As suddenly as the fit had begun, it ended. Or seemed to. She collapsed, all resistance gone. A terrible sob burst from her throat. "They hanged him."

"Yes, baby. Yes."

"They hanged him." Her words were scarcely intelligible because of the desperate sobbing. "Hooded men."

"Poor baby. Poor baby."

The fine mist that had begun to fall on him on his way home was turning to rain. It splattered against his naked skin. He shivered and gathered her up in his arms. "Let's get back in the house, baby. And you can tell me all about it."

"It's cold. So cold," she mourned. "And I'm so afraid."

"You don't have to be afraid." He hugged her tight against his chest. "I'm here, baby. Irons is here. You just come on back in with me. I'll keep you warm. I'll take care of you."

"They hanged him," she murmured again.

Teeth chattering, he carried her back into the house and into the bedroom. There he slid her between the covers and climbed in himself. The sheets were clammy and they were both shivering. He pulled her tight against him. "Now tell me all about it."

"That's all." She wept. Gone were the twisted fearful thoughts that had driven her from the bed in the first place. Irons had resumed his role as savior as once again she clung to him. "That's all I can r—remember. They wore h—hoods. They hanged him. I couldn't stop them."

"Well, of course, you couldn't, Fan. A little baby child like you. You did all you could." He pulled her on top of him and rubbed his hands up and down her back.

She clutched at his shoulders. Her tears wet his neck. "Oh, Irons. Help me. I wasn't strong enough."

"Easy. Easy. You're all right now. I'll help you now." Even as he spoke, he felt helpless in the face of her terror. "Listen, baby. You've got to forget about this. Of course, you weren't strong enough. You couldn't fight them off and get him down after they'd already strung him up."

She lay quietly sobbing, sprawled on top of him, clinging like a limpet to a rock.

He rubbed her with his hands, careless of what part of her body he touched, so long as her terrible desolate sobbing abated and she relaxed.

At last she laughed a little through her tears. "It's pretty bad when you can't remember anything except the stuff you ought to forget."

Sudden intense pity threatened to overwhelm him. He hugged her tighter and pressed his mouth against her forehead.

She murmured softly, unintelligibly against his throat.

"Don't worry about anything. I'll take care of you," he promised.

Gradually she relaxed against him, her body accommodating itself to his shape, huddling on top of him. Finally, when they were both warmer and she was calmer, he shifted her to his side.

"Now, tell me," he whispered.

"I was afraid."

"I know that. Christ. I could tell that. I didn't have any idea what was going on when you jumped out of this bed."

Suddenly she stiffened. Her voice was a hoarse croak when she said, "I was afraid."

"Of me?"

Her answer was cautious, coming after a long pause. "Maybe."

"Fancy," he chided.

She pulled herself out of his arms and lay staring at the ceiling. When she spoke, her voice trembled slightly as if she were maintaining her control only with great effort. "How can I know?"

"My God, baby. If I'd been going to hurt you, I'd have done it long ago."

"Maybe," she repeated. "And then maybe not."

He rolled up on one elbow, to hang over her. His breath fanned her cheek. His rough hand tenderly stroked her shoulder. "The hell you say." His voice had the suspicion of a chuckle in it. "Did you or did you not beg me to come here with you?"

She pressed herself back into the pillow. The springs creaked. "I did. Because you had been so kind to me. And you were the only one who was."

"But you still don't trust me?"

He was so close. She could feel the heat of his body.

He could bend down and kiss her, make love to her as he had done so many times. Or he could kill her—practically with a blow. Breathing a silent prayer, she closed her eyes. Then opened them. The darkness was the same either way.

"Jane," he prodded softly. "Why don't you trust me?"

She sighed. "I probably should. You're the one person I should trust. But I've told you. You don't know what it's like to have no memory. I'm terrified. I think everybody's out to get me. I can't help it. I don't know—anything. I don't know who I am. I don't know what I own or don't own. I don't remember what my home looks like."

He cursed softly and smoothed her hair from her hot forehead. Her brow was wrinkled. She must have a beaut of a headache.

"Oh, Irons, what if I die without ever getting my memory back?"

"Don't say that. It'll come back."

"If I never get it back, I'll go to my grave swearing that I have never lived here. But until I can remember, I'm helpless."

He was silent for a minute. Holding her breath, she could hear the sound of his watch ticking in the still room. Ticking. Ticking in the heavy silence between them. At last he spoke, his voice deep as if his throat were thick. "I'll never hurt you."

"No."

He waited a minute. "And I don't want to see you hurt. Or cheated." He let the last word hang in the air.

She wanted to cry. She wanted to tell him that she had seen him looking at the derrick, had seen him smell and taste the soil. She wanted to tell him that despite her loss of memory, she knew what he had been doing, knew what he knew about that derrick.

She wanted to tell him, but she did not dare. She dared not speak about oil. For oil and its promise of great wealth, men died swiftly and violently. A pervasive chill spread from her belly outward to all her limbs. Her voice trembled. "Do whatever you want to do with that derrick. But for heaven's sake, be careful. I'm so afraid of it."

A small sigh escaped him as if he were holding his breath. "You won't be sorry," he promised, rolling over to her and taking her in his arms again.

She allowed his kisses and his embrace, felt his warmth. She tried to relax as he stroked her breast. His mustache brushed her neck.

Prickles coursed down her spine. His kiss changed from tender to importunate. His knee nudged at her thighs, parted them. His fingers pulled up her nightgown and then dived into the warm nest of hair at the bottom of her belly.

She gritted her teeth as his fingers stroked downward, slipping into the soft openings, teasing their warm, clasping depths. Her flesh tingled as nerves jumped in instant female response to the male.

But questions ran through her mind in a steady stream. Who was Irons? Who was this man making love to her? Kissing her? Running his hands over her body? What did he want from her besides this obvious and elemental thing?

His lips nibbled at her breast, then closed sucking hard on the nipple. The nub of flesh turned diamond hard, but inside she was cold as ice.

What if he succeeded in striking oil? What would happen to her then? Would she suffer the same fate as the man who had been her husband, whose face she could not remember? Who was Irons?

The stream of questions began to recirculate. She could barely feel his hands. Fear made her stiff.

Irons kissed her other breast as he moved over her. Spreading her legs, he knelt between them, caressing the silken skin of her inner thighs.

She shivered again. Out here in this tiny cabin at the end of the road, she would have no one to turn to for help. Surely her family would help her. Her mother. Her father. Why had she not insisted that her brother-in-law help her get in contact with them?

Irons trailed a line of kisses down to her navel and below. At the same time his insistent fingers parted the black curls and the moist lips that lay beneath. With his thumb he felt for and found the tiny mass of nerves sheltered there. "Baby," he whispered. "Oh, baby."

Her body heard him. It could feel him, but she felt no desire. Memory of death, guilt over her own failure to prevent it had numbed her. And with it came a sort of submission to the inevitable. Her mind screamed at her that she was helpless.

"Jane," he whispered. "Are you ready?"

Her throat was dry. She cleared it, tried to speak, and failed.

"Baby?"

"W—whenever you are." Her voice was a thread of sound.

"Then let's do it now." He guided himself to the opening of her body and pushed himself inside.

She was not ready for him. The walls of her passage were dry as her throat.

He felt the resistance. Hesitated, then pulled back. "Jane?"

The tears were pouring from her eyes. Pain, fear, shame made her double her fist over her mouth.

In the darkness he could not see, but he knew everything was not all right. ''Baby,'' he whispered softly. ''What's wrong?''

A tiny sob escaped her. She struggled to cover it up. Somehow he must not know that she was crying. ''Nothing,'' she managed. ''I guess I'm still upset.''

He cursed as he pulled back out of her. ''Well, why in hell didn't you say so?''

Chapter 9

Irons cuddled Fan's soft body in his arms, spoon fashion. Her long mane of hair curled softly against his lips. Her buttocks fitted perfectly into the curve made by his thighs and belly. When he had first turned her into this position, she had huddled stiff as a board, her breathing so shallow that her ribs barely rose against his arm.

Gradually she had relaxed. As her lungs began to expand with an even rhythm, her body slipped back against his. Now she lay pliantly against him from shoulders to knees. Teeth set, he contemplated slipping away from her.

For his peace of mind and soul, the pleasure of lying with her warm and cozy within the cocoon of covers was a delicious one. Unfortunately, his loins ached with a dull throbbing. Her body was so small—delicate, really—and formed for a man to lust after. The curve of her hip above the indentation of her waist made his fingers itch. Gently, he trailed them across her smooth skin from shoulder to thigh.

She sighed faintly. Her hand lying curled on the pillow twitched. He shifted his leg against the underside of her thigh. Slender, firm, and smooth as silk, she lay, trusting him implicitly within the circle of his arms.

He barely managed to stifle a groan. With each beat of his heart, his manhood swelled and fitted into the valley between her buttocks. To slide inside her would be so easy. He stood hard, ready, the tip of his shaft only an inch or two away from her soft, yielding opening.

She moved again, shifting her buttocks, pressing back against him seeking his warmth in her sleep. This time he did not bother to try to stifle the groan. It came out from the very depths of his body. He wanted her, but he could not take her while she lay helpless and trusting beside him. He heaved a sigh as he removed his hand from the splendid curve of her hip.

The feeling his body was experiencing was not new to him. It was lust, pure and simple. Whenever he had known it, he had satisfied it, quickly, handily, forgettably.

Yet this time his lust was not untempered. Other feelings whispered and nudged at him, feelings new to him, feelings of responsibility and deference for a woman.

Since he had set her upon his horse and taken her away with him, she had made him break rule after rule that he had lived by for almost the whole of his life. With one part of him, he hated what was happening to him. With the other . . . He shivered and stirred restlessly. Renouncing his own wants in favor of hers was becoming more uncomfortable by the minute.

Sternly, he turned his thoughts from his own problems to her panic. Had her fear of him and what he might do brought that on? He had been so certain that she trusted him. Now he was not sure at all. In any event she had little choice. The whole problem was her memory. As it returned, she would realize that what he did, he did for her own good.

She stirred in her sleep, pressing back against him, rolling half over, her arm slid back along his waist. Her hand came to rest on his flank. She murmured softly.

He listened intently, then groaned as she curled back into her ball. That talking in her sleep was driving him crazy. He couldn't understand a word of it. If they were going to sleep together for the rest of their lives . . .

He rolled over on his back so fast that he fanned the covers. Where was he getting those kinds of thoughts? They must be coming from between his legs where most men's crazy thoughts came from.

In the morning he would have a long talk with Jane—Fan. In daylight things would look differently. He would be able to think rationally in the light of day.

"I've got a friend who'll come and work it with me. He had a rig and a boiler and maybe a couple of hundred feet of pipe last time I heard."

Fan blew a long slow breath over the top of the coffee in her cup. "A couple of hundred feet are a waste of time."

"I know that." Irons shot her an irritated glance. Slapping the table with his hand, he started up. The nail keg toppled over and rolled drunkenly around in a half circle. "But I've got some money. Not a lot, but I'm getting more every week from the Boomin' Bessie."

"I thought you said she was a dry hole. If she is, they could decide to stop drilling any day."

He began to prowl the cabin. "If I have to, I'll get another job somewhere until Clell gets here. I'll have to keep one anyway. We've got to have money coming in until we strike."

"Clell?"

"R. D. McClelland. He was with me in Cuba."

"And he works in the oil field too."

Iron stopped his pacing. He shot her a defiant look. "Yeah. He works in the oil fields. He works hard. He'll try to do just about anything you ask him. He's all heart."

"He must be something if you give him that kind of recommendation."

Irons looked at her suspiciously but her expression held no hint of mockery. "He's been down on his luck since he got back from Cuba. He's got a small pension, but it's not enough. His wife left him." Suddenly, Irons spoke with a razor edge in his voice. "She keeps in touch though, so he can send all the money he can spare and a lot he can't for his kid."

"That's too bad."

"Too bad." Irons cursed viciously. "Damn woman. He fought for her. And for his country. And she left him. Probably had already left him when he went. Probably didn't even give his side of the bed a chance to cool off. And when he came back hurt and needed her, she pulled up stakes."

Unwilling to argue with him, Fan rose and took the coffee cup to the dishpan. "You're going to be late."

"All of a sudden I'm going to be late," Irons sneered. "You don't like to hear what one of your sex did to a buddy of mine."

She did not raise her head but washed the cup with extraordinary care. "And what did one do to you?"

Her question stopped him. His skin darkened, stained by an angry flush. "Nothing," he denied sullenly. "I've just seen too much. Anyway I've got to get to work. Don't fix me anything to eat this evening.

I'll have to ride over to Batson to send a telegram to Clell."

She called to him as he pulled open the door. "We need some more coffee. And some soap. I can't clean this place properly without it."

He swung around and strode back, towering over her as she pressed back against the cupboard. Roughly, his hands went around her waist and dragged her in against him. His voice was deep and gruff, a mockery of anger. "Do you know why I'm so mad this morning?" He squeezed her waist hard. "Do you?"

Dumbly, she shook her head. Her hands caught at his wrists. Her eyes widened in alarm.

"Because I spent the night holding you after I got you calmed down enough to go to sleep."

"I . . . I'm sorry. I couldn't . . ."

"I know." His eyebrows drew together threateningly. "I know. I don't want to hear any apologies. I pulled out because it was the right thing to do, and so I ended up holding you all night long with your little rear pressed right up tight against me." He moved his hips suggestively making sure she knew just what part of him she had pressed against. "You're just like I said. A lot of trouble. And this morning you've already started nagging."

"Nagging! I just said that we needed coffee and soap."

He kissed her hard on her mouth stifling her protest. When he pulled back, his face was angrier than before. "Nagging. Don't nag me about why we need coffee and soap. I know why. Hear me. Don't nag. Don't say another word. I'll get your soap and your coffee. And when I get home with them, I expect to be thanked properly." He kissed her hard again. Then raised his head. "This works better when you kiss back."

She could feel her lips tingling, swelling where he

had bruised them. The skin around her mouth was abraded where his mustache had prickled. He was a rough crude man. But his hard-muscled body called to her own, exciting her, warming her. She lifted her arms and put them around his neck.

"That's right, baby." He found her mouth again. This time his tongue slid along her lips, assuaging the hurt. Like wet velvet, he kissed her, his mouth opening to take her lips between his and lave them.

She shivered. The kiss stepped up the tempo of her heart and started a tingle in her belly. Unconsciously, she pushed her hips forward.

When he finally drew back, the mock anger in his face had been replaced by a dazed look. He took his hands from her waist and spread them wide. She slipped away from him. Unconsciously seductive, she lowered her eyelids to hide the passion he had aroused.

The silence stretched in the cabin.

"I'll see if I can find someone who's going to Batson." His voice had a breathless quality. "I'll pay him to send the telegram for me."

"It's pretty important," she said softly, touching her hand to his cheek. "You probably ought to go yourself."

"Not so important as getting back to here is."

An unfamiliar grin spread across the lower half of Irons' face. He set the burlap bag on the table with a thud. Untieing the string around the neck, he opened the bag to reveal in addition to the soap and coffee, a bottle of whiskey.

Fan tilted her head to one side. "Why'd you buy a bottle that was only three-quarters full?"

"Jiggers. You're right. You're pretty observant." His gray eyes gleamed from beneath black eyebrows raised in mock innocence. "I thought we'd better have it around in case of snakebite."

"I haven't seen a snake."

"Not at this time of year. They're all hibernating. But let the weather warm up, and you'll see cottonmouths and rattlers by the dozens. By the dozens." He came around the table toward the cupboard. His voice dropped a nótch or two as if to impart a warning of life or death. "And they're *dangerous*. So—o—o . . . A person can't be too careful when they're crawling around."

"I can't believe that snakes are as dangerous as the men."

He nodded as with a judicious air he opened the pantry. "You're right about that. But we still need something to use for snakebite." He swung around, the whiskey bottle in one hand, two cups dangling by their handles from the other. "Now's the time to put it to the test. This stuff'll not only cure it, it'll prevent it."

His breath reached her clear across the room. She grimaced slightly. "You're sure about this?"

As irritated as he had been at breakfast, he was now euphoric. "Listen, I've known guys who've been drinking this stuff for years. Seen lots of snakes, but never had a snakebite. Never." He chuckled as he pulled the cork from the bottle with his teeth and splashed a generous amount into their cups. He pressed hers into her hands. "Drink up."

The cup was about half full and she saw that the level in the bottle was down considerably. The whiskey bit at her nostrils as she held the cup to her mouth. She barely took enough of it to wet her lips.

Irons turned up his cup and tossed its contents down his throat. His eyes watered slightly, but his grin was undiminished. "Good stuff. Best stuff in the world."

Her smile was firmly in place as she held her drink between both hands. "You rode to Batson."

"Right. Couldn't find anybody that was going over there. And Pet needed a good run anyway. She's getting too fat and lazy." He took another swallow, somewhat smaller than the last but generous nevertheless.

"The telegraph operator got the message right out too. Said I could wait around for an answer if I wanted to, but . . ." His voice lowered suggestively. "I didn't have time to wait." He tipped to the side, until his shoulder was braced against the wall. From there he hooked a thumb in his belt. His eyes slid frankly up and down her figure.

In anticipation of his return, she had put on the dress he had bought for her. Now she wished she had kept on his pants and shirt. Obviously, Irons' preventive swigs had come pretty regularly on the ride back from Batson.

Maybe some food would help. "Would you like some supper? It won't take a minute to heat up the stew. There's still plenty of heat in the stove."

He wagged his head back and forth. "I had a big lunch." He poured another splash of whiskey into the cup and toasted her with it. "Drink up, Fan. We've got to make up for last night."

She lifted the cup to her lips and pretended to drink. At the same time the thought crossed her mind that she probably ought to get herself drunk too. As drunk as Irons was, his lovemaking might not be very pleasant. On the other hand, perhaps . . .

She stared at him speculatively as she raised her cup again and sipped. So raw that it had probably been made yesterday, it burned the linings of her mouth and throat. Instantly, she tilted the cup so that the contents no longer touched her lips, but still held it to her mouth and tipped her head back.

He nodded approvingly. "Good girl. Thash it. Drink up."

When she lowered the cup, she flashed him a bright, false smile. No wonder he was reeling. "Do you think Clell will come?"

"Who?" He blinked owlishly. "Oh, Clell. Shure. Shure. He'll be here in two shakesh of a lamb'sh tail."

Cup in hand, she moved around to the other side of the table and sat. "Why don't you sit down and tell me about the adventures you two had in Cuba? I'm just dying to hear."

He hesitated, his grin softening as he remembered Cuba.

She smiled sweetly and indicated the nail keg across the table.

The sweet smile made him remember his objective. His grin widened again. "Not tonight, baby. Not tonight." He put his arms around her and hugged her tight, pulling her up and pushing her toward the bedroom. His mustache scraped her neck as he nuzzled her earlobe. "Umm-mm. You smell good. And you feel better. You're sho shoft. Sho shoft." He squeezed her breast. "Shoft," he repeated.

"Irons," she protested, pushing at his hand.

"Hey. Don't get mad. Did I hurt you? Didn't mean to." He kept one arm around her shoulder as he herded her toward the bedroom. "Jus' wanted to warm you up."

In the dark bedroom he stumbled and swayed away from her to drop down on the bed. "Get the light, baby," he muttered, his tone irritated. "I want to watch you get undreshed. Always like to watch a woman get undreshed."

"I'll get it, Irons," she murmured. "I'll get it in just a minute." Firmly, she pushed him back until his knees hit the edge of the bed. "Lie down so I can pull off your boots. I do hate for a man to wear his boots to bed. The disrespect that shows makes me so mad. You can lie up in bed all comfortable and waiting for me while I get undressed.''

''That shounds good,'' he mumbled, dropping down on the thin mattress.

''Oh, it'll be good,'' she promised as she knelt and tugged at the leather laces. ''I really hate it that you're so tired.'' She pulled off the boot and caught his foot between her hands. Through the heavy sock she began to massage the arch. ''Does that feel good?''

He had been leaning back on his elbows, but within a couple of minutes he dropped his head onto the pillow with a sigh. ''God! Does it ever!''

''You've worked too hard today,'' she told him, her voice gentle and chiding as if she were a mother and he, her little boy. ''Working all day on the rig in the hot sun. Then riding all the way over to Batson to send that telegram.'' Here she changed to the other foot. ''And then you had to ride all the way back here. In the dark.''

He mumbled something.

Gently, she lifted his feet to the bed and tucked them beneath the covers. Feeling her way up his body, she found his belt and unbuckled it, loosened the trousers so that they fell away from his waist. He did not move when she unbuttoned his shirt.

As she pulled the covers up to his neck, he gave a muffled grunt and tried to turn over. Quickly, she eased his way, moving the covers so they would not tangle, rearranging his clothing so it would not bind his skin.

Back in the other room, she dressed in her nightgown. She could not sleep in here. Cold draughts blew through cracks between the floorboards. She turned down the lamp and, squaring her shoulders, entered the bedroom. He lay as she had left him, breathing heavily. Carefully, so as not to jar the bed, she crawled in on her side and stretched out on the edge.

For a long time they lay side by side. Then his breathing was interrupted by a snort. He roused, fumbled the covers off his arms and patted the bed. "Jane."

She could not be sure if he were asleep or awake.

"Jane." The voice was imperative.

The patting hand found her arm, her breast.

"Jane." This time he pronounced her name with relieved warmth.

"Yes, Irons," she whispered.

"Jane. Baby, come on. Scoot over here." His voice was hoarse with sleep and irritation.

"Irons . . ." Reluctantly, she edged in his direction.

His big hand slid around her waist and hauled her in. "That's right." As if she were a doll, he arranged her beside him. His arm lay heavy across her waist. His warm breath fanned her cheek.

She lay stiffly against him, waiting for his next move, but none came. In amazement she realized that he had never really awakened. In his sleep he had wanted her and simply reached out and hauled her in.

Warm and protected, she nevertheless lay staring upward into the darkness. Sleep would come soon, but until then her thoughts whirled. Irons was a stranger, a temporary person who had come into her life at a crucial time. Yet daily their relationship strengthened. Not knowing who she was, she struggled to maintain distance, guarding against the hurt that would almost inevitably come when her memory returned.

Irons, on the other hand, seemed to assume more and more. Like a child clutching a treasured toy, he held her against him. But she was not a toy. She was a woman—hurt, wounded, almost killed if the bruises fading on her body were any indication.

Now she clung to him as to a life preserver. But would she still? When her memory returned, would she need him any longer? Want him no longer?

Her mother? From out of the whirling thoughts came a face, smiling. For only a second, then nothingness snatched it away as if it were a jealously guarded secret.

Tears started in her eyes unaware. They seeped from the corners of her eyes so slowly she could not feel them. They slid down her temples and into her hair. Yes, somewhere she had a mother. And she would see the face again and again until suddenly she would remember.

She clenched her hands tightly together and turned her face into Irons' shoulder.

The thud of hooves brought her to the door of the cabin. Irons had left only an hour or so ago. He would not be returning unless something was wrong. Her heart pounding unaccountably, she hurried out onto the porch.

A well-dressed man in a dark suit hauled a buggy to a stop in front of her. Two men on horseback split away from behind him. One rode to the right of the cabin, the other to the left. Then they turned their horses to face the porch.

The sight of the men surrounding her, their faces grim, their eyes watchful, brought her to an instant halt. Seeking protection instinctively, she backed against the door, her hand on the knob behind her. Silently, she chided herself for not buckling on the gunbelt.

Without being asked, the man climbed down and put his foot on the first step. "Good morning, Mrs. Breckenridge."

Her eyes dropped to the steps, then flicked upward to his face. "You have the advantage of me."

He gave a small artificial smile. His two front teeth had been partially crowned with gold that rimmed their edges. "My name is Weisberg, Mrs. Breckenridge. Alvin Weisberg." He came up another two steps and held out his hand.

She did not take it. However, she did move forward to the middle of the narrow porch and fold her arms across her chest. The position effectively blocked his entry. Unless he was prepared to shoulder her aside, he would get the message.

His smile never faltered. Clearly, he was used to hostility. "Mrs. Breckenridge, I'm here to make an offer that could make you rich."

She could feel tension tightening the muscles and ligaments of her body. She folded her arms tighter.

He waited a minute, measuring her attitude. Then he threw a quick glance both right and left at the men on horseback. At his look they moved their horses forward.

"Keep them right there," she warned, struggling to keep her voice even.

"Of course." He held up his hand. They halted and he smiled pleasantly. "May I come in?"

She took a deep breath. "No."

"I think you should reconsider. What I'm offering is the chance of a lifetime." He stepped onto the porch. Even though he was under average height, he was still taller than she.

She moved back to the door. "I think I should tell you," she said hastily, "if you want to discuss an offer that will make me rich, you should discuss it with Mr. Irons. He'll return in the evening."

"But I was given to understand that you are a widow, Mrs. Breckenridge. And that this is your property,'' Weisberg protested smoothly. From the left side of the porch, the rider moved closer. His right hand opened his coat and pushed the edge back over the butt of a six-gun strapped to his hip.

Fan could feel the color draining from her face. Were they going to shoot her? ''I am very recently widowed.'' She complimented herself mentally for the steadiness of her voice. ''That's why Mr. Irons is assisting me in making important decisions.''

Weisberg frowned. ''Who is this Mr. Irons?''

She could feel herself trembling inwardly, her stomach muscles jumping, her heart pounding. The man on the right swung off his horse. *Hooded figures in the fog.* ''Get out of here,'' she croaked.

''Mrs. Breckenridge . . .''

''If you want to talk to Irons, come back this evening.'' Blindly, she caught at the door facing. Her knees knocked together so she could barely stand.

Weisberg stared at her. ''Now there's no need to get excited.''

''I want you to leave.''

''My dear lady . . .''

''Leave,'' she repeated.

Perhaps alarmed by something in her face, he backed down the steps one at a time. ''Let me just show you what I have.''

''I tell you . . .''

''Please.'' He turned to the buggy and pulled out a grip. ''Mrs. Breckenridge, if you'll just look at these papers I have to show you . . .''

''No!'' She stepped back. ''No! Climb back in that buggy and leave.''

''Wha' d'ya want us t' do, Mr. Weisberg?'' The man with the gun spoke for the first time.

She could feel her head swimming as pain throbbed in her temples. How could she think with such pain?

Yet she must bluff them. They could do whatever they wanted to her. Alone and weaponless, she opened the door. "I cannot discuss anything with you without Irons."

Weisberg replaced the bag with a shrug. "If that's the way you feel about it, Mrs. Breckenridge, I'll abide by your wishes. But you'll be sorry when you hear what I have to say. You could have a nice surprise for your 'friend' when he gets back this evening."

She ignored the nasty emphasis on the word *friend*. "I don't think Irons likes surprises," she rejoined. "Most men don't."

Weisberg looked at his cohort. His tone was jovial as if she had greeted him with open arms. "Looks like the lady doesn't want to do business right now, boys. That's okay by us, right?"

The two looked at each other. The armed man scratched his prickly chin. "Sure, if you say so."

Weisberg nodded. He put his hand on the buggy's dashboard, then turned back. "Would you mind if we took a look around, Mrs. Breckenridge? I hate to think we've made this long ride for nothing."

Fan hesitated. Above all, she wanted them off the place. She did not want them near the derrick, but she was afraid to refuse. What if she angered them? Perhaps if she gave them a little, they would leave peaceably. "There's really nothing to see. But go ahead."

With that she backed into the house and swung the door to before her. Her knees were trembling so hard that they would not hold her. Once inside she doubled over. On all fours, she pressed her forehead to the floor at the foot of the door. Tears flowed from her eyes and her head throbbed blindingly.

The fear combined with fearful memories were making her life miserable. When would this awful time be passed? When would she regain her courage? How much longer would she cringe away from everything and everybody?

Wearily, she pulled herself to her feet and watched through the small window as the two men guided their horses around the side of the house. Weisberg walked between them. She could hear the unintelligible rumble of his voice.

By the time she had hurried to the small window in the bedroom, one man had already ridden his horse around the opposite side of the small corral to disappear out of her line of vision around the barn. Weisberg and the other man climbed the small hill to the derrick. Together they stared upward at the framework.

Weisberg kicked at the soil with his heel but did not touch it. He stood there for only a minute, then turned abruptly.

As quick as she drew back, she was sure he had seen her face at the window. Still, he should not have been surprised that she was watching. Her supervision was to be expected so long as they were on her property. She should have been walking with them.

Again she castigated herself for being such a coward. Now that she was inside the house, her trembling had abated and the headache had lessened.

Weisberg led the way down the hill past the corral. She opened the front door a crack to watch him as he climbed into the buggy. He drove slowly down the road. One man rode beside him, his horse even with the buggy's horse.

She hurried back to the bedroom window. Even as she turned, she heard the thunder of a horse being ridden at a gallop.

The back of Weisberg's buggy was disappearing into

the trees when the second man lashed his horse down the trail and passed him raising the dust.

Cautiously, she stepped outside onto the porch, staring in puzzlement as the pine forest swallowed them up. Why had the second man ridden off in such a hurry?

Then she knew the answer. And the answer terrified her at the same time that a fierce spurt of anger galvanized her into action.

The cow bawled desperately from the barn as gray smoke began to roil from the structure.

Chapter 10

"Damn! Oh, damn them."

Fan leaped from the porch and ran toward the corral. Whitish gray smoked curled out through the door of the old barn. The cow bawled again. Fan heard the thud of the heavy body as the animal lunged against the single two-by-four that barred the stall. Wood cracked and splintered. As Fan stooped low to dash into the smoke, the ordinarily docile creature came lumbering out, her halter rope trailing behind her.

"Good girl!" Fan slapped the bony hip as the cow trotted by. With her no longer in danger of burning to death, Fan dashed around to the back of the barn. There a pile of leaves, hay, and trash had been piled up against the weathered boards and set ablaze.

Calling down curses on Weisberg's head, she swiped her foot at the base of the fire.

Bits of flaming debris sprayed in all directions. Sparks burned tiny holes in her pant's leg, but she ignored them. One lighted on her arm, but she brushed it away. They wouldn't burn her barn.

Cursing methodically, she kicked again, sending the glowing ashes in a shower across the corral. Again.

One large piece arced flaming through the air and lighted in weeds and grasses clumped around one of the posts. She raced to it and stamped it out. Others looked as if they would go out of their own accord. Whirling, she inspected the wood at the base of the barn wall. Black smoke stained it to the eaves and low down it glowed cherry red. Tiny flames licked upward along the tracks that termites had reduced to the thinness of paper.

Water!

She dashed back to the well and dropped the bucket. Turning the crank faster than she had ever turned it in her life, she had it at the top within seconds and tipped into another bucket. Back into the well went the first while she ran with the second. This time drawing a deep breath she dashed into the smoke. If she could just wet down the wall inside the barn before it spread to the hay, she might have a chance of saving the old structure.

No longer did she curse. She had no breath for curses. With eyes and throat stinging, she ducked low and ran straight. The cherry red tongues led her through the smoke.

Flinging the water at the wall with all the force she could muster, she jumped back as steam hissed and smoke billowed up more fiercely than before. Nearly blinded and strangled for breath, she dropped to her knees and scrambled away on all fours, dragging the bucket behind her. She dared not enter the barn again with that much fire in the wall.

Weeping, coughing, she hurried back to the well. Again she drew the bucket up and tipped it in. The smoke billowed up above the trees. She spared it a glance as well as taking in the clear blue Texas sky. Where was the rain when she needed it?

Her heart had begun to pound by the time she got around to the back of the barn with the heavy bucket. This time she leaned closer and stretched her arms over her head, risking scorched clothing and skin to pour the water down the wall. Maybe she could save it after all?

Back she dashed. Again. And again.

She had made a half-dozen trips before she could see no more sign of fire. Drawing a deep breath, she hurried again into the barn. The smoke was so deep that she staggered blindly from side to side unable to find the source.

A terrible fear clawed at her. The boards must be smoldering on the inside. The fire would break out again. If only she had some piece of equipment. An axe. If only she had an axe. Before her eyes a living flame sprang out from the wall and threaded its way across the barn floor, catching at the dry, moldy hay. Toward her it wound its way. She stamped it out.

Another followed it. And another. The heat rose through Irons' work boots as the fire scorched the soles. Ripping the shirt off her back, she began to slap at the living flames. Between stamping and slapping, surely she could win.

A cinder dropped on her bare shoulder. As she brushed it off, she glanced upward. Through the tears and the smoke, she saw that tongues of flame had reached the loft.

Another sprig of burning hay dropped onto her arm. With a cry of pain she backed out. Helplessly, she looked around her. Four-by-fours smoldered and smoked. Flames limned the planks in the floor of the loft. Tears streaming, Fan turned and dashed from the building.

Suddenly, flames burst through a hole burned in the roof. Shielding her face with her hand as burning hay rained down, Fan ran back to open the gate. The cow ducked through it and lumbered toward the woods.

Within minutes the updraft turned the structure into a pile of kindling.

Fan's biggest job was to run around the perimeter of the corral and stamp and slap out flying sparks. At last the old timbers collapsed on themselves. A shower of sparks and flame rose into the sky. Fan dropped down under the edge of the rig platform, too drained to weep.

Irons rode in just at sundown. Smoke hung around the shack like bands of fog, its odor strong. Fearing the worst, he slapped his reins across Pet's withers and dug his heels into her sides. She sprang forward into a gallop.

"Fan! Jane!"

She heard him coming. Choking with relief, she slid down from the derrick floor and stumbled down the hill. "Irons."

He sprang from Pet's back before the mare had stopped and ran and caught her in his arms. "For God's sake! Are you all right, baby?"

She had not thought to wash her face, nor even to do more than drape his scorched shirt over her shoulders. "I'm all right. But they burned the barn. Oh, Irons. It's all my fault."

"What in hell are you talking about?"

"I told him it was all right if they looked around."

"Who?"

"Weisberg. His name was Weisberg." The words tumbled out as she clutched at his shoulders desperate to make him understand. "And then one of them set fire to the barn."

"One of them? How many were there, for God's sake?" His fingers threaded through the singed hair at her temples. "Come on in the house, baby. When did this happen?"

She tried to remember. "I don't know. Before noon."

"My God. And you've been fighting this ever since."

She looked around her. "I guess so. I couldn't save the barn. I tried. But the fire ran up into the hayloft."

"Oh, God." He hugged her hard against him, assuring himself of her presence. "God. God." He kissed her again and again.

"Oh, Irons. I tried, but it got away from me."

"You shouldn't even have tried to fight it," he groaned. "You might have been burned alive."

His concern reassured her. Somehow she had expected that he would be angry. "No chance of that," she replied. "Even the cow got herself out. Knocked down the stall and just came loping out as proud as you please."

He smiled, more a grimace without a trace of humor. His hands ran over her shoulders and found the swollen blistered flesh. Gently as a benediction, he placed his mouth against it. "I can see you weren't afraid."

"No. Just furious and then disgusted and then worried that I couldn't keep it under control until it burned itself out." She looked around her. "At least it didn't catch anything else. The house or the derrick. I sat up on the rig and whenever anything smoldered, I put it out."

His mouth twisted and his dark eyebrows drew together in a terrible frown as if he could not decide whether to praise or damn her. He swallowed hard. "Let's get you in the house. Your skin underneath all that smoke is cold."

She put her hand to her face. "Do I look terrible?"

"Terrible?" This time he did grin, and with a bark of laughter he swept her up in his arms. "Like an end man in a minstrel show. Let's go, Mr. Bones. You need a bath."

"I can walk," she protested. "You don't have to haul me around this time."

"Baby," he declared, planting a kiss on her forehead. "You deserve to be hauled. You've been on your feet enough today."

"Oh, well, in that case . . ." She hugged him tight around the neck happy in his praise despite the loss.

Rounding the corner of the shack, Irons stopped short and let her slide to the ground. A black buggy followed by two men on horseback came trotting into the clearing.

"I can't believe it," Fan whispered. "They're coming back."

"Believe it," Irons whispered in her ear.

"But who are they?"

"Unless I miss my guess, they're goons hired by Standard Oil. They'll do anything. Nothing's too nasty for them."

"Could they have killed Rex?"

"Might have." He put his body between her and the approaching buggy.

This time the horsemen dismounted first and pushed their coats back over the butts of their guns. As Weisberg climbed out, they flanked him closely. Their eyes raked Irons, then darted around the area looking for the least sign of trouble.

Weisberg came forward, his face displaying suitable

alarm. "My dear Mrs. Breckenridge, has there been an accident? Are you injured?"

"Yes," Irons said.

"No," Fan said simultaneously.

"My dear lady, what happened?"

"One of your goons set the barn on fire," Irons replied bluntly. "Mrs. Breckenridge was burned trying to put it out."

"Trying to put it out!" Weisberg looked at her in frank amazement. "You tried to put a fire out?"

"Which one of his men set it?" Irons asked Fan.

She looked from one of the hard faces to the other. "I don't know. I didn't pay any attention to which one rode where."

Weisberg drew himself up haughtily. "I assure you that any fire that you may have had was an accident. We had nothing to do with it."

"Don't give me that bull," Irons growled. He swung Fan up onto the porch and steadied her. "Go on in, baby, and take it easy. I'll get rid of this trash . . ."

Before Fan could move, Weisberg motioned to his men. Instantly they closed around Irons, grabbing hold of his arms on each side. Irons cursed bitterly.

"Shut your mouth, stupid," the one who had grabbed him advised. "If you want to use this arm again." He gave it an agonizing twist.

Irons' face turned white. Sweat popped out on his forehead. "Damned son of a . . ."

"Shut up!" Again the twist.

"Stop it. Stop." Fan could feel herself floating out of her body, even as the words rushed from her lips.

Weisberg looked up into her terrorized face. "I think perhaps you'd better listen to what I have to say."

"Don't give this son of a bitch the time of day," Irons panted.

Weisberg raised one eyebrow. "If I were you, sir,

I'd watch what I said. Floyd gets nervous whenever he hears bad language. Sometimes he doesn't know his own strength."

Fan could feel an icy blackness stealing in from the corners of her mind. Behind her eyes she crouched, viewing the scene from a long way off, hearing the man's words through a fog. Her lips felt numb and not her own as they moved. "Say what you have to say."

"Now, Mrs. Breckenridge, we simply want to lease your property. You have a very promising location here. Standard Oil is prepared to be all that is fair."

"Don't do it . . ."

"Shut your trap." The second man drew his gun and rammed the muzzle into the captive's solar plexus. Irons' breath whooshed out on a cry of pain.

"Oh, please . . ."

"The lease agreement, Mrs. Breckenridge"—Weisberg smiled as if nothing had interrupted their conversation—"will give us permission to drill and of course you will receive a percentage of anything we find."

She stared at the flashing gold teeth. Was she becoming acclimated to sights of horror? Somehow she must do something. She had been unable to save Rex. Somehow she must save Irons. *Think,* she commanded herself. *Think.* "How much of a percentage?"

"Er, two."

"Bastard," Irons grunted.

The saddlebags must be in the house. "But I have already leased it," Fan heard herself say. Her voice sounded clear and flutelike, like a bird calling from a long way off. "Was that what this was all about today? My goodness, you might have saved yourself all this trouble. You see, I've already leased this land."

Weisberg gaped. "What?"

Fan noted with some part of her mind that the man called Floyd fractionally eased his grip on Irons. "Some men came to talk to me about it at the hotel before I ever came out here. So when they offered me some money, I took it."

"You did?"

"Of course. I have the papers here in the house. Would you like to see them?" Without waiting for an answer, she whirled and hurried inside.

Weisberg closed his mouth. He pushed his hat back on his head scratching at his receding hairline, then shot Irons a look of disbelief. "Is she telling the truth?"

"You calling the lady a liar?"

Weisberg assumed a stern expression when Fan came out on the porch with Irons' saddlebag draped over her arm. "I'm afraid you've made a bad mistake, Mrs. Breckenridge," he began.

"Oh, there's no mistake." Her voice had a high nervous trill. "I have the papers right here, Mr. Weisberg. Come up here and see for yourself?"

Shaking his head, he mounted the step. When he reached for the saddlebag, she held out her arm to him. The muzzle of Irons' gun was aimed straight at Weisberg's breastbone. He gaped in disbelief.

Her voice quivered as she struggled to control her terror. "Order your men to let him go, or I will shoot, Mr. Weisberg."

He stared from the ominous black hole to her face and back to the gun again. He smiled mirthlessly. "That's an old trick with a piece of pipe, Mrs. Breckenridge."

Fan shook her head. Her voice was still quavery, but it had gained strength. "Look again. Pipes don't have gun sights on the end."

A slow flush crept into Weisberg's cheeks. Still he made one last try. "Is that thing cocked, Mrs. Breckenridge? I doubt if you have the strength to cock it with one hand.''

''She's got you, Weisberg,'' Irons interrupted the standoff desperately. ''Don't be a damn fool.''

Fan took a deep breath. Her fear was giving way to anger. Weisberg was calling her stupid. Her voice was stronger when she told him, ''This gun is cocked, Mr. Weisberg, and loaded.''

''Better believe her, Weisberg,'' Irons called. ''She might have lost the fight for the barn, but she saved the rig and the house. She means business.''

''Mrs. Breckenridge . . .'' The man managed a worried smile. ''I'm sure you've misinterpreted the situation.''

Fan's anger boiled over. ''Damn you. I have not misinterpreted the situation. But I have been through a lot today, and my patience is at an end. And my hand's getting tired. Unless you let Irons go and get out of here, I'm going to have to pull the trigger. Because I'm damn sure not going to put the gun down when it gets too heavy to hold.'' The saddlebags swayed as she gestured for effect. ''You know how weak and helpless we women are. Just don't have the endurance of you big, strong men. Why, my hand is beginning to tremble so bad, I just can't be responsible.''

Weisberg took a step backward, raising his hands to placate her. ''Hold on now. Calm down, Mrs. Breckenridge. Take it easy.'' To Floyd he said, ''Let him go.''

Instantly, the pressure was gone from Irons' wrist. He wrenched himself free and took their guns. ''Now get on your horses, and ride out of the clearing,'' he commanded.

''Can't we talk this over calmly?'' Weisberg began.

''Hell, no, we can't,'' Irons snarled. He swung

around and gestured to the two gunmen. "Climb on those nags and get the hell out of here."

Floyd and his companion hesitated, but their own guns were pointed at their bellies. Hastily, they swung up and galloped off.

Fan let her arm collapse. The saddlebags slid off onto the porch revealing Irons' gun cocked and ready, now pointed at the floor. Irons leaped up onto the porch in front of her with both weapons trained.

Before the pair of six-guns, Weisberg backed down a step. He mopped at his forehead with the sleeve of his coat. In a continuation of that motion, he tipped his hat. "I'll be going too."

"Not on your life." Irons collared him. "You started this whole thing. Now you're going to have to face the music. Tomorrow I'm taking you in to the sheriff in Batson. And Mrs. Breckenridge is going to file charges to the effect that you burned her barn and threatened her life."

"I never threatened her life."

Irons' teeth showed white beneath his mustache. "Who do you think Sheriff Barfield's going to believe, Mr. Standard Oil. You or her?"

Weisberg gulped. "You can't prove a thing. You're just wasting his time and yours."

"Maybe so. Maybe not. After we take you in, we can be pretty sure that if anyone comes around here and tries to bother us again, the sheriff'll know who to come looking for."

"I didn't set the barn on fire," he shrilled. "You heard her yourself. She didn't see who did it. You can't hold me responsible for what some passing vagrant might do!" Weisberg was flaming red in the face. Droplets of perspiration ran down his temples into his sideburns.

Irons laughed nastily. "That Batson sheriff is out to

find whoever strung up Mrs. Breckenridge's husband. When we get you over there, you'd better have your alibis ready."

"I didn't have anything to do with that. That's ridiculous. Standard Oil doesn't do things like that."

"No. They just come around and set fire to a lady's barn and almost get her burned to death. Tame stuff like that. Fan!"

She jumped. Her overcharged nerves had been strung so tightly that when she had lowered the saddlebag, she had collapsed back against the cabin wall. Now she stared at him in surprise, as if he had called her from a deep sleep.

"Get the rope off Pet's saddle, baby. I'm afraid we're going to have to bring this bastard inside tonight, but he'll be out at first light in the morning."

"No." Weisberg twisted around swinging his fists wildly.

"Yes." Irons let him tear himself away, then drew back his own fist. In the next moment, Weisberg tumbled off the steps and lay moaning on the ground.

"Irons," Fan gasped.

He turned and took her in his arms. "It's all right, baby. Just go in the house now and fix us something to eat. Anything'll do. I know you're almost too tired to move. But, damn, I'm hungry."

"Can we afford a horse for me?" Fan's eyes were big as she stared at the Roman-nosed buckskin.

Irons straightened from where he had been stooping to run his hands down the black forelegs. "We can't afford not to have it. You've got to have some way to get to me if you have an emergency. Besides, from now on you do the shopping."

Wiping his hands on his pants, Irons laid a red ten-dollar note and a blue five-dollar note in the stableman's hand. He fished in his pocket and pulled out a couple of silver dollars. He pointed to a tack hanging on the wall. "That's for the saddle and bridle."

The stableman looked over his shoulder. "I've got an old sidesaddle, if'n you want it."

Irons looked inquiringly at Fan. She shook her head. "All the women in my family ride astride."

"Thanks just the same." He led the buckskin out into the corral and began to strip the saddle off Pet.

"What are you doing?"

"I'm making a trade." He paused. "How'd you know you ride astride?"

She shrugged. "I just know. I've never been up on a sidesaddle."

He nodded, his hands busy switching the tack. "I would have figured you would have. A lady like you."

"How do you know I'm a lady?"

He looked at her warmly. "I know."

"How? My brother-in-law treated me like a fallen woman." She clasped her hands tightly together. "I . . . I haven't exactly behaved like a lady with you. You can't know anything about me."

He took her by the shoulders and tipped her face up to him. The bruises had faded. Only the red crescent-shaped scar on her temple remained of the terrible ordeal. He brushed his fingertip over it. "I wasn't born a plumb fool. And neither was Barfield."

"He *was* polite," Fan admitted.

"Polite. He was falling all over himself to offer you a chair and listen to your story. Weisberg won't get out of Batson's jail any time in the next few days. Barfield won't even get the papers filled out till the end of the week." Irons chuckled. "Everything about you tells me and everybody else with any eye that you're a lady."

She looked away. "Such as?"

"Fishin' for compliments?"

"No."

"Your speech for one thing. Someone's spent a lot of time and effort on your education."

"Education can be bought."

"That's true, but there's your manners. Our table's set like at a fancy hotel, even with just a plate and a cup and fork and spoon. You eat with one hand in your lap. You chew with your mouth closed."

"Still . . ."

He tapped her cheek with his forefinger. "Pay attention. You carry yourself like you've got a whole lot to be proud of. Like your mother before you and her mother before that had a whole lot to be proud of."

She looked up at him at the mention of mothers. "I hope you're right. Oh, Irons. I do so hope you're right."

"Hey. Don't start to tune up on me." He stared down into the strange gold eyes seeing them brim with tears.

"No." She shook her head. "No. I won't."

"Right. Now climb up on old Pet."

"I can't take your horse."

He gathered the reins for her. "Course, you can. She's perfect for you. Nice manners. She'll take you where you want to go, but she'll take her own sweet time getting you there."

Fan shook her head determinedly. "I'll take the buckskin. I won't need to ride him everyday the way you need to ride her. He'll do fine."

"You don't know what kind of . . ."

Before he could protest further, she thrust her foot into the stirrup and swung up into the saddle. The buckskin threw up his head, then dropped it between his legs and buck-jumped across the corral.

"Damn!" Irons made a grab for the reins, but the horse had already switched ends. "Fan!"

Like a bur she clung to his back, her mouth set grimly, her thighs gripping, her heels dug in. Both hands sawed the reins, pulling them back and back against the iron-hard mouth, dragging the head up.

With an angry grunt, the buckskin reared, sunfishing with his forelegs.

"Fan!" Irons leaped to her side. "Slide off! I'll catch you." But the buckskin jumped forward, coming down with bone-jarring force and then galloping wildly around the corral. Gradually, his speed decreased until Fan pulled him to a halt. With a grim smile, she bent over to pat the lathered neck.

The stableman gaped in the door of the livery stable. "That's shore ridin', ma'am."

Irons looked from one to the other. Then he flung his hat down in the dirt and stomped over to the other man. His curses turned the air blue while he doubled up his fists.

The man backed away. "Hey, wait a minute, fella. A fifteen-dollar horse don't come with no guarantees."

"She could've been killed."

"How was I supposed to know you were gonna put her on him? You shoulda got on him first and took the kinks out."

Irons was speechless with rage and guilt. He reared back his arm to punch the man out.

"It's all right, Irons," Fan called. She dug her heels into the buckskin's scarred flanks. "He'll do fine." Both men stared at her as she guided the gelding toward them. Her cheeks were flushed and her mouth was curved in a smile of pleasure. The fall of black hair had come loose and tumbled wildly around her shoulders and down her back.

Irons turned on her, his fear losing itself in anger at her recklessness. "Damn it, Fan. Why the hell did you get on that horse? He could have thrown you and stomped you to death."

"Hey, I don't sell no outlaws," the stableman put in.

Irons bared his teeth at him.

Fan patted the sweaty neck again. "He wasn't being mean. Why, he was just testing me? Weren't you, boy?"

The stableman nodded. Irons shook his head. "You do something like that again and I'm going to have a heart attack."

Fan grinned and swung the horse's head toward the gate. Suddenly, a kind of dizziness struck her, and then a flash of memory.

She sat on a golden sorrel. Not a buckskin. A stallion. Not a gelding. Instead of a corral, a stream, a bridge. An old house. Very old. Very Spanish. And a woman beside her with pale-streaked red hair. On a horse called San Isidro. She blinked. And the woman's face disappeared. And the blackness closed in around her.

She slipped from the saddle, took a faltering step, and Irons caught her before she hit the ground.

"Please, ma'am, wake up, ma'am," the stableman begged. His voice sounded at first a long way off, but gradually it grew nearer and more urgent. "Please, ma'am. He's gonna shoot that old horse."

"Sh—shoot the horse." She managed to open her eyes. The roof of the livery stable swung dizzily.

"Yes'm, he's mad as fire."

"Irons," she called weakly. "Irons."

Boots came at a run. "Fan." She closed her eyes, then opened them again as Irons dropped to his knees beside her. "Don't try to sit up."

Shaking her head, she got her elbows under the upper part of her body and pushed herself up. The stableman put his arm around her shoulders. "I'm all right."

"But you fainted. That damned outlaw . . ." His face contorted with anger and guilt.

"It wasn't the horse's fault," she insisted. "I passed out but not because of the horse."

". . . trying to pitch you off. Probably jarred your back teeth."

She sat all the way up and caught his hand between both of her own. "Irons. It wasn't the horse. He didn't have anything to do with it."

"Then why?"

She glanced at the stableman who instantly took the hint. "Excuse me, folks." He hurried away.

"Irons, I wasn't pitched from the horse. I had a flash of memory and then suddenly everything began to go black. I think I got down before I fell down, didn't I?"

"Maybe so," he agreed reluctantly. "But all the same . . ."

"Irons." She held out her hands to him. "Help me up and let's get out of here."

He pulled her to her feet and then lifted her into his arms. "I'm not letting you ride that thing again."

She put her arms around his neck. "I think it might be better if I rode him everyday. If it would help me to remember something every time."

Irons' arms tightened around her until she murmured a protest. "You scared hell out me falling off like that."

"Is that why you're set to haul me around again?"

He relaxed his tight grip. "Don't you like to be hauled?"

She tipped back her head to search his face. "Oh, Irons, I like being hauled."

"Then shut up." He bent his head and kissed her fiercely.

Chapter 11

"Clell! You old scalawag. Climb down off that boiler and let us get a look at you. Fan! Clell's here."

Attracted by the gladness in Irons' voice, Fan came out on the porch in time to see muleteams pulling two heavy wagons into the clearing.

The man beside the driver of the first wagon waved excitedly. "Hey, Irons. Long time no see."

"That's for damn sure." Irons leaped down off the porch and ran to meet the wagon, holding up his hand to his friend. As the driver pulled the wagon to a halt in front of the cabin, the man leaped down into Irons' embrace. "What took you so long to get here?"

"Long!" Clell pretended anger. "Long! Hell! We only got the telegram a week ago."

"So. You think this oil's going to wait around forever."

Clell scowled, then grinned as he raised his eyes to follow the derrick's structure up into the gray-blue overcast sky. "From the looks of that rig, I should have hurried. Looks like she's ready to blow."

Irons looked up too. "Nothing up there but an empty tree. They just got that far. No pump. No drill. Nothing. Just the derrick."

"That's a good start." Clell smiled politely at Fan. A network of laugh lines deepened as his eyes crinkled at the corners. "Introduce me to your lady, Irons, now that you've finally gotten lucky."

Hesitating only fractionally, Irons mounted the steps. His gray eyes stormy, daring Fan for some reason she could not fathom, he took her elbow to guide her down. "R. D. McClelland, may I present Caroline Fancy Breckenridge. Fan meet Clell."

"Mr. McClelland." She extended her hand. "Welcome."

With an affable smile McClelland twisted his left arm in a fluid motion and shook her hand. Only then did she see that the sleeve of the stiff yellow slicker hung empty. McClelland was missing his right arm.

Her face must have betrayed her surprise, for McClelland glanced from her to the slicker, then back again uncertainly. Irons tightened his grasp on her elbow. An awkward moment stretched for several seconds.

Then Fan cleared her throat. "I've got a pot of hot coffee on the front of the stove and soup cooking at the back. Please come in. You gentlemen too. Climb down and we'll see what we can do. Irons, why didn't you tell me? We've got six people and only three coffee cups."

His expression eased. "You're nagging again. I told you not to nag me."

Clell gave a chuckle of delight. "Nagging's the only way he'll ever do anything, ma'am. But this wasn't his fault. I can swear to that."

She looked expectantly.

"He probably left you in that fix 'cause he can't count." He turned to the man climbing down from the second wagon. "Hey, Brazel, grab that sack of supplies out from under the seat and bring it in with you."

Inside, the men lounged around the walls making the front room seem all the smaller and more crowded. From Brazel's pack they had fished out coffee cups for Fan to wash and fill. Now they waited, an odd tension in the air, while Irons explained the situation.

". . . so Standard Oil goons are going to be out to stop us. Plus we don't know who did it nor why Fan's husband was done away with. This nice little job could be mighty dangerous."

One man, introduced as Early, moved a chew of tobacco from one side of his mouth to the other before he spoke. "Ever' place I've been to in the past three years, S.O.B.'s been there. Hell! Things 'd be dull without 'em."

"They burned the barn," Fan interposed.

"Damned lucky they didn't burn the rig."

"The whole place would have caught fire and burned to the ground," Irons told them. "Except for Fan. Lord knows how she kept the fire from spreading without getting burned up herself. But she did, so we've got a head start."

"I s'pose this is one of them deals where you can't draw a paycheck until she blows." This dry comment came from a very short wiry man introduced as Hoke.

Irons grinned mirthlessly. " 'Fraid so. So if anybody wants out, now's the time to say something. That's a salt dome out there under that rig floor. There's bound to be oil under it, but it might be so deep that we can't get to it. Or it might be just under the surface, no more'n a couple of hundred feet."

"How deep are they running around here?" Brazel wanted to know.

"Some have struck oil sand at a hundred feet," Irons replied.

"A hundred feet." The men straightened away from the wall expectantly.

" 'Course the Boomin' Bessie down the road apiece is down to over a thousand and all we're hitting is limestone."

As if they had not heard this gloomy report, Brazel and Early looked at each other, broad grins on their faces. "A hundred feet. A hundred feet. Hell, we could dig it by hand."

Fan watched as their excitement grew. They were boomers, looking for the big strike. The salt dome might contain nothing more exciting than a blast of sulfurous gas, but they were undeterred.

"Some have gone down three thousand and come up dry."

They turned up their coffee cups, drained them, and set them down on the table. "Mind if we go take a look at that derrick, ma'am?" Early asked, his hat in his hand.

"Not at all. I'm sure you're anxious to get to work."

As a group, they smiled shyly, nodded, and left as quickly as they could. The salt dome drew them like a magnet. Fan turned to the kitchen window and watched them climbing the hill, their voices wafted back to her, cursing, joking, almost hysterical in their excitement.

"Well, Clell," Irons said. "You want to go too."

R. D. McClelland shook his head. His face was serious. "I think you should sit down, Mrs . . ."

"Breckenridge," Fan supplied.

He nodded politely. "I think, Mrs. Breckenridge, that you should sit down and we should put our heads together about the business end of all this."

Irons rose instantly and gave Fan his seat.

She seated herself and clasped her hands around her coffee cup. "Fire away, Mr. McClelland."

"Call me Clell, please. And I'll call you Fan, if I may." At her nod, he continued. "Irons, I think you'd better tell me what the real situation is here."

"Shaky. At best. We really don't know who owns this property."

Fan's head shot up in amazement.

"I didn't tell you, but I made a quick trip to the courthouse in Batson. This property wasn't owned outright by your husband Rex, but jointly by him and his brother Paul. Likewise, they, Rex and Paul, owned the house and plantation."

"Then . . ."

"But there's no will. Or if there is, it hasn't been brought in for probate yet. So Rex might have left this property to you and the plantation to his brother. A better guess is that you inherited his share. So you own this with somebody else."

Clell leaned back, whistling between his teeth. "We can't drill without clear leases."

"I'd be willing to sign the leases," Fan said helpfully.

"But the lease wouldn't be legal."

"If you accepted it in good faith, then my share of anything that was discovered would belong to Paul, not to me."

"I think there's another way. Paul will be pleased as punch to sign a lease," Irons said significantly. "Especially when he finds out that if he doesn't sign, I'll wise Fan up to the fact that she probably owns half of Rosemeade. A wife's got community property rights in Texas. Throw that line out and see which fish jumps."

Clell chuckled. "It just might work."

"It'll work. He thinks Fan's lost her mind as well as her memory."

Clell looked inquiringly at her.

She shrugged. "I was hurt a while ago. I can't remember some things."

"She was damned near killed the night her husband was murdered."

"If it weren't for Irons, I'd be dead." Fan said. She took a sip of coffee and grimaced at its bitter taste. "I owe him my life."

Clell rested his arm on the tabletop. "I see." He looked at his friend. "And so you're willing to grant him a potentially profitable lease as well as providing a place for him to live?"

"Clell." Irons' voice carried a note of warning.

"The truth hurts only if somebody's ashamed of it," came the reply. "I always like to know where I stand in a business venture."

"That's right," Fan said. She raised her head and stared into Clell's Gaelic blue eyes. They were infinitely kind despite his stern questions. "Irons has the right to drill that well if he wants to and he stays with me because I want him to."

Clell's eyebrows rose. He looked from one to the other, then shrugged. "Then let's do it. If you'll excuse me, ma'am." He pushed back his chair and strode to the door.

Irons dragged a handful of bills and some loose change from his pocket. Placing them on the table, he squeezed Fan's shoulder. "Take a ride into Batson, baby. Get as much food as that'll buy and as much more as you can charge to the Irons-McClelland account. Have it delivered."

"Irons-McClelland?"

"How about McClelland-Irons?" came the voice from the door. They both looked at Clell's grinning face.

Fan grinned in her turn. Rising, she began to sort the money by denominations. "I think I'll open the account in the name of Breckenridge-McClelland-Irons."

* * *

Stepping out of the Batson general store, Fan barely recognized Eufemia Carlton. The woman was climbing from a carriage, the skirt of an obviously new green broadcloth suit raised to reveal neat kid high-button shoes.

Fan stared down at her own garb, Irons' trousers, her feet shod in a pair of lace-up boots belonging to Hoke. She stepped back inside the door, but not before Eufemia had seen her.

A malicious grin turned up the corners of the woman's mouth. "Not so highfalutin now, are you, honey bunch." The woman flounced across the crossing boards and pushed her way in through the door.

"Good afternoon, Miss Carlton."

"Oh, it's Miss Carlton, now. Good for you." She touched a black glove to her amazing hair. No longer was it dishwater blond. Instead bleached and dyed a brassy gold it was combed over a rat that must have been four inches thick, so high did the roll stand around the top of her head. In the center of it sat a green straw hat with a bright pink dove, its glass eyes and beak bright red. "Like my hair-do, honey bunch?"

Fan nodded. "You've certainly changed it."

"Yeah." Eufemia tilted her head to one side. "You could do with some style yourself, honey bunch."

"There hasn't been time."

"Nor money." Eufemia trilled maliciously. "Too bad about old Rex. Sort of left you high and dry, didn't it?"

"I still have the farm."

"That shack." Eufemia gave a loud squawk of laughter. "And you're out there slaving away, aren't you? For a bunch of men so I hear. That's rich. Real rich."

The clerk at the cash register was listening intently.

Fan tried to hurry past her. "If you'll excuse me, I need to be getting back."

Eufemia caught her arm. "Still can't remember anything, honey bunch?"

Fan shook her head. "Bits and pieces. Flashes. That's about all."

"Tough." The woman's voice was unsympathetic. She withdrew her hand and wiped her thumb across the fingers of her glove as if she had touched something soiled. "Well, life's always ups and downs. Sometimes you're up, sometimes you're down. Right now, I'm up and you're down. See ya', honey bunch." And she snapped her fingers in Fan's face.

"Are you really going to Rosemeade? To see Paul Breckenridge?"

"First thing tomorrow," Irons replied.

"Then ask him about my clothes. I'm sure that there must be a closet full of them." She held out the skirt of the dress Irons had bought her. "This will fall apart if I have to keep washing it. And I can't go on wearing your shirt and pants and Hoke's boots."

He looked at her critically. Her skin had taken on a deep golden tan, but her dress, not of expensive material, had a washed-out limp look. Worst, he noted, was that she seemed to have lost weight. Her waist was impossibly slender; her cheeks, hollow. "Are you feeling all right?"

"I'm fine." She turned away from his scrutiny. "I just don't want to feel like a total charity case."

"Hey baby. Nobody thinks of you as a charity case."

"Then how do they think of me? As one of the boys."

"Fan." Trying to kid her into relaxing, Irons

grinned as he put his arm around her waist and patted her rear.

His actions did not have the desired effect. She slapped the tin cup down on the cabinet. "Irons," she gritted. "Just bring me some clothing so I won't feel like other women need to pull their skirts out of the way so I won't get them dirty."

He dropped his hands instantly. "What if he won't give them to me?"

She swung around on him. Her eyes flashed fire. Angry red stained her cheeks. "Then tell him that I remember everything, and I'm coming to get what's mine by rights."

He backed off, his hands shoulder-height in surrender. "I'll take care of that the first thing when I get there."

"How soon will we actually begin to drill for oil?" Fan asked Clell.

He turned from where he was supervising the roping of the pulley at the top of the rig. "Got to get the equipment in place before we can do anything."

She stared at the metal pieces. "All this stuff looks different somehow from what I've seen," she remarked doubtfully.

Clell grinned. "Probably does. We're using a rotary rig, like Curt and Al Hamill used to drill Spindletop for Captain Lucas."

"What's the difference?"

"Standard Oil and everybody else in the business uses what's called a cable-tool rig with a walking beam. All the wells in Pennsylvania used cable tool. It just pounds a hole in the ground. This is better and faster."

Fan came nearer to get a better look. "Were you there?"

"Where?"

"At Spindletop."

"Yeah. I saw it spouting. Everybody for miles around came and watched it. It shook the countryside when it came in. You could see it for miles."

Fan's eyes were big. She looked doubtfully at the equipment on the planking in front of her. "Would something like that happen here?"

Clell looked upward watching Brazel's progress with his job. "Might. But probably it won't. Usually wells'll just spout a little. They're easy to kill. Reverse the mud pump"—he indicated the piece of equipment off to one side of the rig—"and pack her in. It stops pretty quick. Curt and Al hardly knew what to do back then. They'd never seen so much oil. And nobody to this day has ever seen a well that wild."

"And then what?"

"Attach the Christmas tree, let the pressure clean the mud out, then send the oil right into the tanks."

"There's a lot of equipment," Fan observed.

"There's a lot, but it's the way they'll all be drilled some day."

She put her elbows on the drill floor.

"Better stay back off this platform, ma'am. Brazel's up there on the monkey board with grease all over his gloves. A tool or a line could slip, and you'd be brained before you knew what hit you."

She stepped back at his command, her arms crossed before her. "That might not be such a bad idea, Clell. Instead of knocking my brains out, it might knock some in."

He shook his head sternly. "You don't know what you're talking about. A wrench dropped from fifty feet would most likely kill you."

"I suppose so." She sighed. "I admit that's foolish, but I still can't help wanting something drastic to happen so I'll remember. So I'll be myself again."

His expression changed to sympathetic understanding as he helped her off the platform. Together they retreated down the hill to the corral. "It'll come," he advised her. "I've seen men so shell-shocked they couldn't even talk. All they could do was just sit and stare like old folks in a home. But little by little, they begin to notice things going on around them. They'll see something funny happen and they'll smile. They'll hear the nurse talking to them and they'll look in her direction. And then finally they answer back. You can believe me. I've been there and I've seen it. It'll come."

"So Irons keeps telling me."

"He's right." He watched the men at work hauling up the kelly. The operation was going smoothly. They worked together as a practiced team.

Fan shrugged faintly. "I guess I'll go back in the house. I don't want to keep you away from your work."

As she turned to go, Clell spoke. "You know if you need somebody to depend on, you couldn't have picked a better guy than Irons."

She laughed ruefully. "I've come to realize that. Of course, I don't want to *have* to depend on anybody. I don't know Irons very well really. Sometimes I think I don't know him at all."

"He's hard to know, but he's a good man."

"I'm sure you're right." She stared bleakly at the men moving the cumbersome pieces of equipment around the platform. Under her breath she muttered, "Being dependent's almost like being a slave."

"I know it is," he agreed meaningfully.

"No, you don't. You can't."

"Oh, yes, I can. I am. I saw the way you looked at my sleeve."

She flushed. "I was surprised. That's all."

"You wouldn't have hired me in a month of Sundays,'' he accused with a flash of acridity that she could sense was not natural to him. ''You hired me because Irons told you to.''

''I didn't hire you at all. I don't have any money to hire anybody,'' she reminded him bitterly. ''For all I know this is the sum of my possessions.'' She waved a hand in the direction of the crew at work on the rig. ''What's more, I'm at your mercy.''

He watched as Early leaned back and yelled up to Brazel. The answer that he received was punctuated with profanity.

Fan winced but raised her chin a notch.

Clell shot a fierce look at his crew, then looked back at her apologetically. ''We're not such a bad bunch. Just a little rough around the edges. I apologize for us all. No offense intended.''

''None taken.''

They stood side by side, arms crossed before their chests. Finally, Clell spoke. ''What happened in Batson?''

She studied the ongoing work as she decided what to answer. ''Nothing important.''

''Must have been something to make you so touchy.''

She shook her head, shaking away sudden tears that brimmed in her eyes. Swiftly, she changed the subject. ''Irons said you were with him in Cuba.''

''Sort of. Irons was with the quartermaster. I was with the Rough Riders.''

''The Rough Riders! Did you charge up San Juan Hill?''

He grinned, his eyes crinkling. ''Sort of. There wasn't much of a charge. I caught it in the arm in the first volley. As it turned out, I was pretty lucky. Lot of men got killed that day.''

"But it was a great victory. I've seen pictures in the papers."

"Yes. Pictures in the papers."

Fan hesitated. "Irons said your wife left you. That must be terrible."

"It is, but Irons took care of me. He took care of me when I got shot, and he took care of me when I lost this. If he'd been my blood brother, he couldn't have done more for me."

"Your blood brother?"

"He's my brother-in-law."

"Your wife's brother?"

"That's right."

"But I thought he didn't have a sister. I'm sure he said at one time that he didn't have any family."

Clell took a deep breath. "Irons'd kill me if he knew I told you this, but he's an orphan. He and his sister were raised in an orphan's home."

"Oh." Fan gave a moan of sympathy.

"But you mustn't let on that I've told you."

"Oh, no."

"He wasn't but two and a half and Gladdie five when they were put in it. And they stayed until Gladdie was eighteen. She got a job and took Irons with her. They worked and lived together, doing anything and everything they could find to keep body and soul together. She was working as a waitress when I met her. She was the prettiest woman, and honest and true, but hard as nails. You think Irons is hard. You ought to meet Gladdie. And terrified. Security is the whole show for her."

"I guess so."

"Irons isn't quite so bad off because she shielded him from a lot. Stuff that he doesn't even know about. Then the war came along. And we got married and she had Brucie. When I came back, my condition terrified her.'' He put his hand to his eyes and squeezed the bridge of his nose hard.

Fan clenched her fists sharing his pain.

''He really despises Gladdie for what she did.'' Clell kicked at a clod of the yellowish-white soil. ''He really does. But he shouldn't. Just because she couldn't stand to live with me in the condition I was in, doesn't mean she's bad.''

''He said she . . . er . . . found another man to take care of her and your baby.''

''My son. Brucie.'' The lines around Clell's eyes squinched tighter than ever. ''It's better for him. Byrd will be a better father to him than I could be.''

''Irons said . . .''

''Irons only sees one side of it and he doesn't know the whole story. He doesn't know how much I was drinking and how mad I was at the world.'' Clell swiped his hand across his mouth.

''Your wife couldn't stand your drinking?''

''And other things. I couldn't contribute a thing to making a home and she didn't have the strength to take care of me and herself and Brucie too. It was like starting over again with two orphans instead of one.''

They stared at the crew together. A piece of equipment did not fit together properly. Brazel cursed fluently from the monkey board. Fan made no comment.

''But Irons never faltered, except to get mad at her for giving up.'' Clell looked at her then. ''Irons is a tough customer with edges as rough as they come. He's not always going to treat you like you might like to be treated. But you're damn lucky, Fan. I think you'd better appreciate how lucky you are.''

She stared at him, uncertain what to say.

He nodded toward the rig. ''If we strike oil—and we've got a better than even chance considering what's been going on around here—Irons will see to it that we all have a share. All of us. From little old Hoke right on up the ladder to you, pretty lady. And probably Gladdie and little Brucie'll get a lot of it too through me."

Fan looked at Clell consideringly. He seemed so sincere, seemed to believe what he was saying, but he could be lying through his teeth. Were the stories of orphans and war heroes part of the act to win her over? After all, he would be a fool to tell her that his friend and employer was a swindler and a cheat. And Clell must know that Irons had every reason to treat her well. If something happened to her, none of them would have the slightest right to drill here.

"Do you believe me?" Clell prodded.

She could not entirely put aside suspicion. Still she could not let Clell know how she felt. She drew a deep breath. "I believe you."

His mouth curled up at the corner. "Do you? I'm glad. Irons may not have the best set of manners, but he's a man to ride the river with. And if Teddy Roosevelt himself said I had to charge up San Juan Hill again, I couldn't do it unless Irons was right behind me bringing the guns and ammunition."

Fan smiled winningly. "Does Irons have a last name or a first?"

Clell smiled back, the tense set of his shoulders relaxing. "I think there's a first name, but he doesn't like it much. And there's no last name at all that I've ever heard. Gladdie didn't have a name other than Gladdie until I gave her mine. Orphans don't have names unless someone gives them one."

"That's sad. Maybe that's why Irons started calling me Jane almost from the first minute he found me."

"He's a good man," Clell enjoined.

"I guess I'll get the supper started," Fan said.

"Thank you for telling me all this." She smiled her brightest smile and returned to the shack.

Irons turned Pet off the road. A long drive stretched before him between lines of stately oaks dripping with Spanish moss. Through the trees he could see the façade of a red brick house trimmed in white. His lips pursed in a low whistle. "Well, hello, baby."

Rosemeade looked as though it belonged in the Mississippi delta rather than stuck here in the Piney Woods of East Texas. If Fan Breckenridge had lived here for a while, she was lucky she had lost her memory. That cabin in the clearing would have driven her into hysterics.

The closer he came, the less impressed he was with the house, however. The lawn had not seen a mower in a couple of months. Weeds everywhere poked their heads above the grass. The gray enamel paint on the front porch was plastered with a confusion of muddy footprints. At the window to the right of the door, the lace curtains had been looped together.

Swinging down, Irons slid Pet's reins through the ring at the top of the hitching post. Innumerable horses had churned the sand around the post and no one had smoothed it out nor removed the piles of manure.

"Looks like this place is running to seed fast," Irons mused to himself as he avoided the worst of the mess and mounted the steps. He lifted the lion's head knocker and let it fall. The sound echoed through the house. He waited for several minutes, then tried the door.

It opened easily and he stepped into an entry hall. "Anybody home?"

No one answered. He opened the door on his right into a parlor furnished with massive horsehair sofa and chairs. The window in front of the looped curtain was open a couple of inches allowing the dampness in. The smell of must and mildew hung heavy in the air. No one had been in this room in a long time.

"Guess not."

Muddy footprints had tracked up and down the staircase at the front of the entry as well as along the hall to a door at its end. He opened the door to find himself in a sort of breakfast room. A cloth on the table was spotted and stained.

He closed the door and started up the stairs. The first bedroom on the right was elegantly furnished with wardrobe and chest of drawers in mahogany, a chair of flocked maroon velvet with footstool and a huge four-poster bed. The bed drew his eyes. It was unmade, the sheets trailing on the floor, the pillows crumpled. A man's boots coated with dust stood beside the bootjack.

Irons felt the hair rise on the back of his neck as a horrible suspicion began to dawn. Controlling a shudder, he backed out and shut it swiftly. In contrast the next room was in perfect order beneath an overlay of dust. Across the hall on the left a third room sent cold chills scudding down his spine. The bedcovers there were thrown back as well. A lace-trimmed pillow bearing the imprint of a muddy boot lay on the floor. A woman's robe trailed off the bed.

Irons lifted the garment feeling the sharp tug of recognition. Holding it up before him, he recognized the deep Irish crochet on the collar. This was Fan's robe, part of the set she had been wearing the night her husband died.

His fist clenched in the cream silk, he opened the huge mahogany closet. Dresses hung there, a woman's complete wardrobe in bright colors and rich fabrics. Leather hatboxes sat on the shelves above the rod, and the toes of kidskin shoes peeped out from underneath.

He had no doubt if he opened the drawers, he would find fine silk undergarments and accessories.

He touched the full skirt of a gold wool dress, thinking that Fan would look beautiful in it with her hair and golden eyes.

He froze at the sound of a revolver being cocked behind him.

"Turn around slowly, fella, or you're a dead man."

Chapter 12

Irons cursed under his breath as he turned, the robe still clutched in his hand. The rooms with their untouched appearance had transported him back to past horror. For long minutes he had forgotten to listen for the slightest sound, forgotten he was an intruder whose presence could be punished.

He crushed the garment in his fist, angry that it had so distracted him. Turning slowly, he stared into the face of Paul Breckenridge.

"It's loaded," Breckenridge informed Irons nastily. "And cocked."

"Have you checked?" Irons' tone was heavy with irony.

For answer Breckenridge shifted the barrel a couple of inches to the right and squeezed the trigger. The bullet plucked at the sleeve of Irons' coat as it buried itself in the wall. The sound of the shot reverberated through the empty house.

With a tight grin Breckenridge thumbed back the hammer again. "It's a six-shooter."

Irons said nothing, letting the man enjoy his moment of triumph.

"Now give me three real quick, real good reasons

why I don't just shoot you for a thief and be done with it?" Breckenridge continued.

"Because I'm not a thief and you don't have any reason to shoot me," Irons answered promptly. "I came to get your sister-in-law some clothing. You didn't send anything. And she was getting pretty tired of wearing my stuff. I don't have all that many clothes and what I did have didn't fit her."

"Everything in this house belongs to me." The man gestured with the gun toward the door. "Get out of here."

"Now take it easy," Irons cautioned, mentally damning himself for letting this man get the drop on him. "There's no need to get so hot about this."

"I could shoot you now. I should shoot you now." Breckenridge's teeth flashed in the bush of his beard. "I could tell that damn fool sheriff that you came in and tried to kill me. You weren't satisfied with killing my brother. You had to get rid of me too."

"Go ahead then. Kill me if you feel like you have to," Irons said coldly. "Don't listen to the proposition I have to make to you."

"Proposition?"

"Can I put my hands down?"

"No. Walk down the stairs with your hands up. Don't forget I saw you in action against Pyote. He's still mad at you. Maybe I ought to call him in and let him have you. You'd take a long time to die." He prodded Irons in the middle of the spine as they started down the stairs.

"I think you'd better listen to what I have to say instead of raving about killing and dying."

"What could a thief and a murderer possibly have to say that I'd need to listen to?" Breckenridge halted on the third riser up from the ground floor.

"I've come with some leases."

For the first time the six-shooter wavered. "Leases?"

"Oil leases. Standard Oil's already been nosing around that place of Mrs. Breckenridge's."

"Standard Oil's been out there!" Paul Breckenridge laughed, a high-pitched nervous sound. "God! Those vultures are everywhere."

Irons lowered his hands slowly. "Breckenridge, you need to sign that land over to your sister-in-law, so those goons won't bother her anymore."

Breckenridge's eyes narrowed; his brows drew together. "There's nothing out there under that land."

"Probably not," Irons agreed smoothly. "But they came out trying to scare her. They set the barn on fire."

"They burned the barn?"

"To the ground. Everything else would have gone up too if Mrs. Breckenridge hadn't worked like a dog putting the ground fires out."

"Is she all right?" The question had a shade too much eagerness.

"She was singed some—and scared, of course. Unfortunately, she's still pretty disoriented. But she's starting to remember some things. Eventually she'll get it all back."

"She is?" Breckenridge's gun came up again. "Keep those hands up."

Irons raised them with a show of weariness. "Look, Mr. Breckenridge, if you'll just let me do two things, I'll take care of them and then be gone."

"What?"

Irons reached in his coat pocket. "I've got the standard lease here with the tracts written in. If you'll just sign this . . ."

"Watch it. I've got a gun on you."

"I know, but you don't have to. Come on, Mr. Breckenridge. You know I didn't come to hurt you. I wouldn't have been going through a woman's closet if I had been."

"No," he agreed reluctantly. His shoulders hunched as he looked at the mess. "My brother was dragged out of his bedroom to his death."

"I'm sorry. I can understand why you don't care anything about this house anymore." Irons pulled out the papers and spread his hands wide.

Paul Breckenridge cast a quick look around him. For the first time he seemed to see the muddied state of the fine Turkish carpet under his feet. "Yes. Yes. It's been a terrible thing. I haven't been able to stay here since Rex was killed."

"Will you sign the lease?"

"Why should I? Why should I do that bitch any favors? You and she probably plotted together to kill my brother."

Irons gave his head a little shake in exasperation. "You keep on saying that, Mr. Breckenridge, but repetition won't make it so. Mrs. Breckenridge is remembering more every day. She'll be able to tell what really happened soon. When she does, we'll go to Sheriff Barfield."

"She'll lie."

Irons abandoned reason. "She's had a hard time, poor lady. It's a wonder she survived. Her clothes will help her feel better."

"Why should she have them? She . . ." Breckenridge gestured widely with the revolver.

Irons dived low and caught the man around the middle, pushing him back against the newel post. Breckenridge's squeal of panic was blasted away by the boom of the revolver. Irons threw his shoulder up into the man's armpit. At the same time he caught hold of the arm and brought it down.

The smaller man screamed in pain. His fingers flew open and the gun thudded to the floor.

"Now," Irons said evenly, scooping it up and stepping back. "Let's get a little sense into this conversation."

"My God. My wrist is broken."

"Your wrist is bruised. Slightly. Come on." Grabbing the man's coat at the shoulder, he hustled the fellow up the stairs.

"No. O—o—w!"

Irons pushed Breckenridge into Fan's room. "Now sit down at that dressing table and sign this lease." Irons stuck the gun into his belt and slapped the lease down in front of the quaking man.

"I don't have anything to write with."

"Here." Irons pulled the stub of a pencil from his vest.

Hastily, Breckenridge scrawled his signature at the bottom of the page and on the middle of the back. "This isn't legal."

"Oh, it's legal enough. You wouldn't want the courts to ask why Mrs. Breckenridge, your sister-in-law, gets a shack over south of Batson and you have a plantation house in the northern part of the county."

"My brother left everything to me."

"Unless I'm much mistaken, a woman in Texas is entitled to half of everything her husband had. It's called community property." Irons looked around him speculatively. "With the right legal counsel, Mrs. Breckenridge would get half of everything."

Silenced, Paul Breckenridge sat unmoving as Irons folded up the document and slid it into the inside pocket of his coat. "Much obliged. Now I'll take these clothes. You sure don't need them."

Breckenridge drew a deep breath and adjusted the

cuffs at his wrists. "No," he said in a normal tone. "I don't need them."

Irons threw him a quick glance, but all the fight seemed to have gone out of him. A quick look around the room revealed no trunks or boxes. Spreading a bedsheet out on the floor, he pulled the dresses out with a great sweep of his arms and dropped them on the sheet. Gathering up the corners he tied them together in a huge bundle.

Breckenridge watched him. "She looked so pretty in those," he said softly.

Irons hesitated, trying to read the changing attitude of the man. Their eyes met for a moment, and Breckenridge's slid off to the side. Irons took the other sheet from the bed and spread it also. On it he dropped the shoes and boots. He opened the drawer at the bottom of the closet and emptied its contents. From the top shelf he pulled two hatboxes. "That's about all I can carry," he announced.

"Take it all," Breckenridge advised, a slight edge returning to his voice. "I'll be getting rid of it tomorrow."

Irons hoisted the two bundles. As he walked by the dressing table, his eye fell on a woman's jewel box. "Hers?" he asked.

Breckenridge held it out.

"Much obliged."

Breckenridge followed him downstairs and watched while Irons looped the tied corners over the saddlehorn. He mounted with some difficulty and turned Pet away from the hitching post. "I'll leave your gun by the last tree on the right at the head of the lane."

"Keep it. You'll need it." Breckenridge stuck his hands into his pant's pockets. His shoulders were hunched. His face pulled down between them. "If you've got enough sense to take advice, you'll take those things by to Fan and then keep on riding. That's the only chance you've got."

Irons tipped his hat ironically and touched his heels to Pet's flanks. The mare moved into a smooth lope.

"Do you hear me?" Breckenridge's voice rose shrilly. "Do you hear me? You've just got once chance and that's to get out of this part of Texas and stay out."

Irons could still hear him yelling when he could no longer understand the words.

"Pleased, aren't you?" Irons grinned as Fan opened the sheet.

"Oh, Irons. Oh, thank you." She clapped her hands together, then threw her arms around his waist. "Oh, thank you. Thank you."

"Are they yours?" he asked, staring at her keenly.

"Of course, they're mine. Here's my riding skirt and my gold wool that Aunt Free brought me from . . ." She stopped in mid speech. "I remembered," she whispered. "I remembered a name. Aunt Free."

He sat down on the corner of the bed to face her. "Who's she?"

She stopped, trying to visualize the woman in her mind. Nothing came. Indeed the name seemed strange to her. Still it was a name. "Aunt Free. I don't know. Obviously she was my aunt, but somehow that doesn't seem quite right. I don't know."

"Could be she's no relation to you at all. Lots of people teach their children to call all adult friends aunt and uncle." He touched the gold wool. "I thought these might be yours. And that room. I'll bet you were dragged out of that bed a month ago. The sheets were still torn off onto the floor." He shivered at the memory, then reached down and held up the robe. "Recognize this?"

She took the sleeve in her hand, running her thumb over the distinctive Irish crochet. "The robe that matched the gown."

"Right."

She looked around her at the bare walls of the cabin, then back at the rich clothes. "This is all so puzzling. And the pieces don't seem to be fitting together very well." She closed her eyes. "Oh, why can't I remember?"

"You'll remember, baby. Just let it come. Keep the bed warm for me. I've got to take the evening tour at the Boomin' Bessie, otherwise we don't eat." He rose and pulled her around to give her a perfunctory kiss.

She kissed him back, fervently, trying to express her gratitude in her kiss.

"Hey, baby," he breathed as he set her from him. "Back off. Save that till I get home tonight. I'll be taking off my pants as I come in the door."

She did not move except to drop her hands from his shoulders. He walked to the door. She turned and began to lift the dresses off the pile one by one, shaking them out and smoothing at the wrinkles. Over her shoulder she asked, "Did you have any trouble getting these?"

He shrugged offhandedly. "Not enough to worry about. But let me tell you, your brother-in-law's got a loose screw somewhere."

"Perhaps his grief over the death of his brother has upset him more than he realizes."

"Not likely. He doesn't act like he's upset over his brother. And he's closed down that house. It's a big house without a sign of a servant. He looks like he might be living there by himself, tracking in mud, leaving the windows open for the rain to blow in. I swear nothing's been touched since you and your husband were dragged out of your beds."

She gathered the gold wool tight against her breast. "How macabre!"

He gaped at her. "What?"

"M—macabre."

"I heard what you said, baby. What does it mean?"

She flushed in embarrassment. "I didn't mean to . . ."

"Don't apologize," he growled opening the door. "Just talk plain English. I can't stand people putting on airs. That's almost as bad as praying." The door to the cabin slammed behind him.

Irons fell into bed beside her in the middle of the night. His body was cold and tired. All he could do was gather her in against him, cupping himself around her spoon fashion and fall instantly asleep. She patted the hard cold hand that lay inert a few inches in front of her breasts. He had been awake for twenty hours, ridden miles on an errand for her, then worked eight hours on a rig in the cold wind. Whoever he was, and whatever he wanted from her, he was not finding it easy to get.

"Fan," he whispered in her ear. "Come on, baby. Wake up."

"What?"

"Come on, baby. It's time to get up. We're going to start drilling."

"When?" She knuckled sleep from her eyes and sat up. "Now?"

"That's right. Right now. It's all set up and ready to go. Clell thought you ought to be out here too."

"Oh, I want to be." Fan tossed back the covers and bounced out of bed.

Irons grinned. "Put something warm on, baby. It's cold out there." He left her to her dressing, while he shoved wood into the stove and filled a pot with water for coffee. "Hurry," he called. "We don't have all day."

In less time than she would have thought possible, she was dressed in several layers of clothes and standing by the corral as the men moved about their tasks with practiced efficiently.

"Okay, Hoke?" Clell raised his hand to Hoke on the monkey board high above his head.

"Okay, boss."

"Okay, Brazel?"

"She's raring to go," the roughneck called from his post beside the donkey engine.

"Early?"

"Goddamn it, boss, let's do it. I'm freezing to death and I ain't seen a gusher in a month o' Sundays."

But Clell was determined to make a production out of it. "With your permission, Mrs. Breckenridge."

She smiled. This whole show was all for her benefit. "Go to it, gentlemen."

"Spud it in!" Clell called.

Brazel eased back the lever on the donkey. The huge belt engaged and the rotary table began to turn. At the top of the rig, the kelly began to turn in synchronization. Below the platform, the bit dug into the earth.

On the monkey board up at the top of the derrick, Hoke gave a hoarse rebel yell. It rose over the noise of the engine to be joined by Brazel and Early and combined into an ecstatic paean.

"There she goes," Irons breathed softly in Fan's ear. He moved until his hard chest rose and fell at her back and she was all but leaning against him. A trembling began in her belly and spread outward to her limbs.

His hands encircled her upper arms and held her hard, his own excitement building as hers did. "Listen to it." His lips brushed the shell of her ear as the rhythm of the equipment filled the air. "That's sending a message to the oil way down below. It's saying, We're coming. Coming. Coming."

She set her jaw as her trembling increased.

Another sound joined the first two. A pump engine began to pump liquid mud down inside the kelly. As she watched, the sun broke through the trees and turning the derrick into a black silhouette against early golden light. The moving parts became one dimensional and their shadows fell across Fan and Irons.

She thought she could feel the ground beneath their feet begin to vibrate, but she could not be sure. Perhaps her own heart was pushing the blood through her veins so strongly that it shook her body.

Perhaps Irons' heart was beating above and behind and around her. He was holding her against him so tightly that she felt a part of him. A heat built in her belly. Emotion flooded her, tears welled in her eyes. Why did she feel this way for a man she did not know? Powerful feelings ripped at her, clenching her muscles into knots, making her breath come fast. His masculinity filled her senses. And underlying everything was fear. Fear that she would be expendable at some time in the future when her presence was no longer required. A tiny sobbing sound escaped her.

His hands tightened, then loosened as he feared he had held her too tightly. He bent his head to see into her face. She could feel his breath on her cheek. Swiftly so he would suspect nothing, she turned her head to the side to speak to him. "I can feel your heart beating. Why is it beating so strongly? This must be a familiar sight to you."

He chuckled. "Not a man of us ever gets tired of seeing it start. Because it takes all the courage we've got to do it. It's the beginning of the biggest gamble in the world. Is it down there? Or will we break our backs and our hearts for nothing but a dry hole?"

She looked at the activity of the platform. The roughnecks had stepped back, Clell seemed to be lounging almost, watching as the drill stem came slowly, slowly down from the top of the derrick. "What's going on now?"

"We're drilling. At the bottom of that stem is the bit. It's digging into the earth."

"Oh."

Irons turned her to guide her back down the slope. "It'll go fast at first. Clell is using a fishtail bit to cut through topsoil and stuff. The hard part'll come when we hit bedrock. Sometime we hit stuff so hard that it just eats up bits."

"Are they expensive?"

He grunted. "Worth their weight in gold."

"Where's the money coming from?"

"From my wages at the Boomin' Bessie, plus some money that Clell got." He pushed open the door of the shack and guided her inside. "And I've got to go to work *muy pronto,* but first, baby . . ." He grabbed her waist and spun her around.

"Irons! What . . . ?"

Her question broke off against his mouth. With a rush he bore her back against the table. Her trembling that had never ceased increased until she was vibrating under him.

"You feel it," he grated. "You feel the same things

I do. I could feel you out there in front of that rig. It made you hot. And getting hotter.'' The heel of his hand ground hard against the bottom of her belly.

''No—oooh.'' Her whispered denial did not stop the impassioned flow of speech.

''It was like you were inside of my skin. God!'' Strong fingers hooked into the neck of her dress and tore it open. With one violent movement he bared her breasts. They were hard, swollen, their nipples distended.

''No,'' he snarled, his eyes almost black as he stared down into hers. ''No! You can lie with your mouth, but these don't lie.''

''All right,'' she snapped. ''Yes. Yes. Oh, yes!''

He splayed his cold hands around her rib cage and lifted her to him. His hot mouth closed over her breast, his teeth captured the nipple and bit it.

She cried out with pleasure. Her toes found the floor and she pushed up, pressing her loins up to his, needing the hardness of him. She threw her arms around his shoulders not needing nor wanting gentleness. She wanted the possession of this man, courageous and strong enough to take from the earth her dearest and deepest treasures. He could take what he wanted and she would give it freely, because she wanted that kind of man inside her.

''Goddamn,'' he groaned into her mouth, shocked by her fiery response. For a moment he hesitated. Feminine demanding was new to him. No woman before had ever taken the lead in lovemaking with him. He had never experienced elemental woman wanting, craving passionate release from him. ''Fan.''

''Irons,'' she cried out, panting. ''Irons.''

His hands went to the buttons over his swollen organ, but she was there before him, her hands already pulling them open. Had she had the strength, he did not doubt that his own garments would have been shredded as her dress and chemise had been.

"Irons."

"Oh, baby."

He was bare, thrust out of the openings in his clothing, steaming with the heat of his wanting, the moisture already there to slide into her.

She opened her legs. He found his way barred by the silken undergarments. One of her hands caught his wrist, the other parted the lace and guided him in. Not just in through her clothing, but into her body as well. In one movement he was welcomed at the threshold and taken into the very depths of the house.

A cry escaped him. The moisture and heat and throbbing passion were overpowering. He struggled for balance, dropping his palms flat on the table and pressing upward. His head bowed between her breasts.

The perfume of her body rose into his nostrils. She moved so that her nipple teased his mouth. Her hips rocked forward and slid him back and forth inside her. Her ankles locked together behind his hips, holding him still.

Instead of ravisher, he became ravished, a male animal that she used for her pleasure, teasing him insatiably with the taste and smell of her, driving him with little demanding cries and panting breaths that filled his ears. Her skin was hot beneath silk that slid up and down ruffling the hairs on his belly.

He was losing control. He could not stop the hot tide that seemed to boil over inside him. Throwing back his head, he shot his hips forward. She screamed, her head thrown back, her hair swirling about the surface of the table. Her legs flexed, pulling him impossibly nearer.

Her hips ground the mass of nerves at the center of her body against his pubic bone.

Then he felt her release. As if she were inside his skin, he felt the rippling of her muscles in the sheath, the convulsive shivering of her thighs, the expanding of her ribs as she drew in a deep breath.

Then she collapsed, falling away, every vertebrae in her spine touching one at a time, until her head sank to the tabletop. Her ankles released and her legs slid down over his buttocks. Her hands slipped off his shoulders and relaxed palm up on the table.

They lay still for some minutes, their breathing gradually becoming regular.

At last he pulled himself out of her and stepped back, staggered to the side and ended up against the cupboard. He passed his hands over his eyes like someone awakening from a dream. "I . . . I guess . . ."

She kept her eyes closed, but one trembling hand plucked at her skirt, tossed it weakly to cover her bare legs. "Please don't say anything."

"I . . . all right." He put his clothing to rights and turned to the stove. Opening the grate, he thrust in a couple of sticks from the firebox. The bank of coals from the night before would ignite them in a few minutes. "I'm going to be late," he remarked inconsequentially.

Fan pushed herself off the table and stood up. Most of the buttons had merely popped from the buttonholes, so her dress was easily put to rights. "Yes, I think you will be."

He crossed to the door. "Why don't you fix the boys some coffee and a big breakfast? I was going to spell them for a bit before I took off, but now I don't have the time."

A rosy flush stained her cheeks. "All right."

"Be seein' you." He tipped his hat and slid around the jam.

She stumbled across the room and flung herself against the door. Cheek against the rough wood, fist pressed against her mouth, she held it closed until she heard Pet galloping out of the yard. As the hoofbeats died, she began to tremble. No longer could her brain command her body. Her emotions demanded their release. Sinking to the floor, she wrapped her arms around her belly and rested her head on her knees.

Denial was impossible. She had demanded sexual fulfillment from Irons, and he had given her himself because he really had no choice. She was a woman who instinctively knew the power of a woman's body. Or—terrible thought—did she know it through long practice?

She shuddered. Without her precious memory, she could neither accept nor excuse what she had done. She could not shrug it away with a laugh nor apologize for it as an aberration of the moment.

Who was she? What kind of woman was she? Irons' responses had been familiar to her. She had known just how to elicit them. She had not hesitated. No shy shrinking flower, she.

And somehow this essential part of her nature had brought death.

Death.

Why did she know that?

She moaned. Her tears wet the skirt of her dress. Hooded figures swirled in the mists of her mind.

"Rex," she whispered. The name evoked nothing. It was as meaningless as Timbuktu. "Irons." Gray hair, thick and wavy, stormy gray eyes, tanned skin covering rippling muscles. Heat curled in her belly. She wiped at the tears with the hem of her dress.

Wearily, she pushed herself to her feet sliding her shoulder up the door. Her forehead rolled against the rough boards. "What's to become of me? I can't remember. I can't remember."

Chapter 13

A dry norther blew in on Christmas Eve. The temperature dropped to twenty degrees above zero according to a foot-long thermometer Hoke had nailed on the derrick next to the monkey board.

The gray sky was barred with clouds of darker gray scudding across it on a wind with teeth like a prairie wolf.

Every piece of metal was purgatory to handle. The wind flayed the skin on the men's faces until it looked like raw beefsteak.

"How can you work in that terrible cold?" Fan asked as she dished up red beans and rice and set a four-inch square of corn bread on the side of his plate.

Clell grinned cheerfully as she set it in front of him. "Thank you, ma'am. This sure looks good. As to the cold, we don't stand out in it a minute more than we have to. Most of the time we're huddled around that boiler in the draw works keeping warm."

"But Hoke . . ."

"Oh, he doesn't have to sit up on that monkey board except when we're adding a new section of pipe. He just stays up there most of the time because if he came down he'd have to climb back up again. And he figures if he's up there, he can't be put to work on the ground. He's just lazy. Too damn lazy." He looked at her sheepishly. "Pardon my language."

"Don't worry about it." She shrugged offhandedly. "I don't."

Clell frowned. "You sure are getting an earful hanging around that rig. It's not right for a lady like you to hear stuff we spout out there."

She gave him a warm smile. "My ears haven't dropped off, so I guess I'll be able to stand it. I like to be near the rig. And I want you boys to sleep on the floor in here tonight. You can't sleep out in your tent in this weather. It'll drop another five or six degrees tonight."

"Oh, we can bed down in the wagon."

"That's probably worse than the tent. The wind would be on both sides of you. You'd freeze to death. I know it whistles up between the floorboards, but at least in here we have a stove. You'll just have to shut down and come in and loaf around for a night."

"But . . ."

"Is this project part mine?" she asked with mock severity.

"Yes, ma'am," he replied meekly.

"Then tell the others that the orders come from Breckenridge."

The sounds of horse's hooves aroused her from her dream. At first she thought she was having a nightmare again. "Irons!"

"What?" He was still asleep. He batted irritably as she shook his shoulder.

"Horses. I hear horses."

He lay still on the pillow, his eyes staring into the dark. "You're right." He sprang from the bed and began pulling on his pants. "Clell! We've got company. Brazel! Come on, boys."

"Damn."

"How many?"

"Sons of bitches," Hoke snarled. "Coming at us in the dark on the coldest damn night of the year."

Shivering with dread, Fan tried to ignore the sounds in the other room, tried instead to listen to the sounds outside. The bumping and thumping went on as the men rose and put on their clothes. Unable to lie still she threw back the covers.

"Stay right there!" Irons growled.

"I might be able to help."

"Forget it, baby. If the five of us can't take care of this, then your sticking your nose in won't help."

"But . . ."

He pushed her back down and plumped the feather mattress up around her. "Stay there. Listen and let your mind work. Maybe you'll hear something that sounds familiar."

She began to tremble. "You think I've heard this before."

He leaned over and kissed her forehead. "Wouldn't be a bit surprised. Besides, baby, you're doing something important right where you are."

"I—I am."

"Sure. You're keeping the bed warm for me." In the other room she heard him speak to Clell. "How many of them?"

"Hard to tell. Maybe half dozen. Maybe more."

"Sons of bitches," Hoke snarled. "I'm gonna freeze my tail off out there."

"Might be preferable to gettin' it shot off," Early grumbled.

"That's our choices, boys," Irons told them.

" 'Course we can stay in here and they'll set us on fire. They've already burned the barn."

"Sons of bitches."

Irons stood, aligning his body with the thicker wood of the wall stud. "Come on, boys. Let's get out of here, one at a time. Out through the front door, and keep low. The longer we get them to get set up the worse it'll be."

The men hunkered down in front of the door, their weapons drawn and cocked.

Irons eased the door open. "Clell," he said softly, "go right. I'll go left. Hoke. Early."

"Yeah, boss."

"Follow us. Up the hill to the rig. We'll draw them away from the house and Fan. Brazel."

The man mumbled something unintelligible.

"Stay here and kill the first son of a bitch that comes through that door."

"My pleasure."

Huddled in the enveloping folds of the mattress she heard the room go quiet.

Then Irons muttered, "Ready."

The door jerked in his hand as a shot crashed through it and tore into the cupboard destroying a tin cup.

Instantly, Clell stuck his head around the door and fired at the flash.

"Go," Irons growled, and slithered around the edge of the door. He fired into the night and jumped from the porch.

A scream rent the darkness followed by a groan.

Clell glided out ducking low and leaped off the right side of the porch. Behind him went Brazel.

Inside the cabin, Hoke cursed fervently. "Gawd-damn, I hate to fight when it's cold. I always end up in the mud with my face frozen."

"You want me to go?" Brazel grunted.

"Hell, no. I'll go. I just don't like it." And the little man sprinted across the porch and jumped to the left.

Fan could hear the neigh of a nervous horse and then the stamping of hooves in the corral as the stock bumped into each other trying to get. The lone milk cow bawled hoarsely.

Despite Irons' order to keep to her bed, she slid out onto the floor and found her clothes. Even with Brazel in the other room, she did not feel safe enough to roll over and go back to sleep.

No more shots spanged into the cabin. Indeed, no more shots were fired. The silence broken only by the nervous sounds from the corral was all the more ominous. Fan slipped into the second room of the cabin and crouched down beside Brazel's comfortable bulk. "What's happening?"

"They're huntin'." His voice in the dimness carried a note of satisfaction.

"Hunting!"

"Right. And there's nobody better at that than Irons. I swear, he can see in the dark."

"Did you know him before?"

"Hell, yes. He saved my life in Cuba. Brought those guns and ammunition right through the Spanish line." Brazel chuckled delightedly. "Them bastards out there don't know it, but they've got a tiger by the tail."

Another exchange of shots made her jump. She clenched her fists and pressed them against her mouth to keep from screaming.

"Better get down on the floor on t'other side of the stove," Brazel advised. "That way any stray shot'll hit it and bounce right off."

Outside in the dark, Irons slipped between the bars of the corral. He had yet to see the attackers except by an occasional flash from a pistol. They were hanging back, at the edge of the clearing, most likely behind the trunks of the big pines.

He grinned mirthlessly. Unless he was badly mistaken, the leader of this expedition was probably the only one with the stomach for the work. The rest were probably recruited for a few bucks apiece from a saloon. He caught the sound of movement on his right and flung a shot in that direction.

A horse screamed in pain and began to buck.

"Goddamn!" a voice called. "Oh, Godd . . . !" The second oath ended abruptly as a heavy body hit the ground. The horse galloped off into the woods.

Another shot spanged into the woods on his left. Either Clell or Early had spotted something. Since he heard no answering commotion, their shot must have missed.

The slope up to the rig was the problem, Irons realized as he climbed through the back of the corral. The poor soil of the salt dome was pale gray in the dimness. Someone in the darkness just might be able to see them move across it.

He could hear Early coming up behind him. "Cover me."

"Right." Coolly the roughneck took aim at the woods. One round. Two. Three went in at intervals while Irons sprinted up the slope.

From the woods on the left, a rifle boomed. A fiery brand seared across his back, sending him sprawling and rolling. He could not suppress the cry of pain.

"Got one," came a deep voice. "Come on, boys. They're making for the rig."

"Yeah, but Curly's hurt," came a panicky cry.

Behind the house Clell and Hoke both got off shots almost simultaneously.

"Come on." The leader's voice came from a different place.

Ignoring the hot blood trickling over his ribs and his ears roaring with the assault on his nerves, Irons raised his head and listened. The leader, he acknowledged, was a smart man. He knew enough to keep moving.

Irons pushed himself up on all fours and then to his feet. His back burned like fire, but he did not think he was badly wounded. Probably creased was his diagnosis. Painful, but not serious. And the wound might work to his advantage. The leader might count him down and out.

Ignoring a dizziness in his head, he slithered over the edge of the platform and pulled himself up beside the mud pump.

He heard the scuffle of feet running up the slope and knew that Early too had made a dash. Immediately, he snapped a shot to the left, shooting down into the trees, hoping to hit the leader.

"Come on," came the voice from almost the top of the clearing. "Get into position. They're just shooting in the dark."

"Irons!" Clell's cry was drowned in a series of shots.

Early had climbed to his knees screened on two sides by one of the legs and the draw works. "They're after our hides," he gasped. He snapped another shot at the flash. "I'm about out of shells too."

"Save one."

"Hell. I've only got one."

Irons realized he could have no more than two left himself. "Then get into the draw works where there's metal to protect you."

Early dropped down again and eeled across the platform on his belly. Irons listened again and trying to separate the noise of his own blood pounding through his veins. He heard running footsteps. Were they Clell's? Hoke's? Or someone else's?

He crouched down beside the rotary table. "Clell?"

No answer. He could feel his skin prickling. Someone was under the platform. Scrabbling backward, he moved between the huge chain links that raised the crown block.

A dark shape popped up over the edge of the platform. Irons snapped off a shot, but the shape disappeared.

Suddenly, Early cursed wildly. Heavy boots stamped and scraped. Fists thunked solidly into flesh inside the house that sheltered the engine. Early cursed again. Then a sharp blow, a creak, a grinding of metal, and the engine started. The wheels began to rotate, the drill stem and the rotary table began to turn.

Where equipment had been still and cold, now it began to move. Stooping low, Irons started for the house to help Early. A shadowy figure leaped onto the platform and swung at him. Irons shifted his weapon and pulled the trigger, but the hammer came down on an empty chamber. Silently, he reversed the gun and used the heavy handle as a club. He connected with solid flesh and the man fell back off the platform with a groan.

Early. Early needed help. He turned toward the draw works.

"Irons! Irons!" Clell's voice came again punctuated by another shot.

"Clell? Where the hell are you?"

Another shot. And this time Irons whirled to see a figure throw up his hands in the middle of the platform and fall across the rotary table.

Irons yelled, "You got him."

"But I've got you."

The voice came from out of nowhere. A steel barrel connected with the side of his head. He was falling. Falling.

He put out his hands to stop himself and thrust them

into the chains and cables from the draw works. The pain restored his fading senses for one terrible minute as the machinery carried his arms over the pulley structure.

He shrieked at the top of his lungs. He could feel his flesh being ripped. He could feel the bones of his hands and arms being bent, snapping. Then he lost consciousness in a blinding red flash of agony.

"Irons. Oh, my God, Irons."

He could hear her voice, but he could not answer. The pain was too great. His arms. His hands. The nerves screamed for relief. He tried to flex his fingers, but the effort brought unbearable agony.

"We must have a doctor for him," Fan cried. "One of you must go for the doctor."

"There's no doctor who'd come out here in the middle of the night."

That was Clell's voice. He must have been all right. They must not have got him. He tried to remember exactly who they were fighting, but the memories were too fragmented, and the throbbing, pulsating pain was keeping him from thinking about that. Instead he concentrated on the present.

"Of course, he'll come," came Fan's voice, its tone imperious. "He'll come for a Gillard. He'll come to El Rincón."

What was she talking about? Irons wondered.

"He won't come, I tell you."

"Damn you." Fan's voice cracked with strain. Irons heard a hammer pull back with a click. "Go for the damn doctor, or I'll shoot your ear off."

"Fan," Irons protested weakly. "Fan, I don't want . . ." He could not go on. They did not appear to have heard him anyway.

"Hoke. Take the buckskin. He's tough and strong."

"Right, Miz Breckenridge." His tone was placating. "Just keep that thing pointed in somebody else's direction."

"Now the rest of you, help me clean him up. We've got to do what we can." She caught hold of his hand. She might have only touched him, but he felt as if she had jerked his arm off. He opened his mouth to scream, but before the sound could come from his throat, he lost consciousness.

"His hands," Clell's face was ghastly pale except for the greenish cast at the corners of his mouth. "Look at his hands."

Brazel took one look and stomped out the door. Through the thin walls of the cabin, Fan could hear his helpless convulsions. Her eyes flicked across the room where the other roughneck cowered against the cupboard.

I must not faint. He needs me. I'm the only one he has.

"Early," she commanded. "Tell Brazel to get back in here. He has to build a fire in the stove and so we can have hot water."

"Yes, ma'am."

"Clell. Under the dresser in the bedroom is a box with a couple of sheets in it. Bring them."

"Right."

Early stomped back in with a shaken Brazel, who hid his eyes and made a wide path around Irons' body.

"Early, can you help me? He's so bloody and torn. I can't see what I'm doing on the floor." She stared into the man's faded blue eyes shaded by heavy eyebrows. "We've got to lift him up onto the table where we can use both lamps."

"Why sure, ma'am. It's not real pretty, but it damn

sure won't make me puke." He threw a contemptuous glance at Brazel, who hunched his shoulders and busied himself building up the fire.

"Then let's do it."

Irons looked like a tall, spare man, but he was composed of whipcord muscles stretched over dense long bones. His unconscious weight was incredibly heavy. Nevertheless, the muscular roughneck slid his arms under Irons' knees and the small of his back and lifted him like a baby.

Fan supported the dangling arm, keeping it from striking the edge of the table. Irons' long legs dangled over its end. "Bring a pillow, Clell," she called. "At least his head won't lie on the hard wood."

She looked at Early who, despite his claims to imperturbability, was looking distinctly ill. The length of his sleeve was stained with fresh blood. "He's bleedin' on the back, ma'am."

"Oh, God. He must have been shot too." She could feel the tears starting from her eyes. "What if he's got a bullet in him? What if he's bleeding to death? What should we do first?"

Early rolled Irons over on his side and supported him. Fan saw the bloody, burned path horizontally across his back. With desperate fingers she tore open the back of the shirt. "It's a furrow," she whispered. "A shot must have almost missed him." She called over her shoulder to Clell. "Rip up one of those sheets. Make a pad. We'll put it under him and leave it for now. His hands and arms are so much worse."

With the pad folded on the table, they eased Irons' back down flat. "Now we'll cut away his sleeves and see what happened."

In silence the three of them labored to reveal Irons' arms. After the sleeves were cut at the shoulder and peeled off, Fan began to wash away the blood.

"Jesus," whispered Early. "I ain't never seen anybody chewed up that bad."

"Goin' to get some water." Brazel caught up a bucket and fled, his face white, tears trickling down his cheeks.

Clell's forehead creased. His eyes squinted, but still he too began to weep. He dropped down on the barrel chair at the foot of the table. His hand squeezed Irons' knee.

"That hoist chain really got him," Early continued, his voice a bit detached as if in self defense. He pointed with his index finger to the left hand while Fan sponged the right. "Looks like he's got all his fingers though. That's good."

Fan smiled whitely at the tone of the appraisal. "He's got all of them on his right hand too."

Brazel came in the door. Early grinned over his shoulder. " 'Course they're all bent outa shape and crooked."

Brazel spun around, his face red. "Goddamn you, Early Johnson. Shut your goddamn mouth."

Early chuckled. "That's the spirit, buddy. Get a little blood in your head and you'll be all right."

Brazel flushed even brighter. "Just don't press your luck. You could get a mouthful of fist." He stomped past them and poured the water into a pan to heat on top of the stove.

The piece of sheet Fan was using was already dyed crimson as blood continued to ooze sluggishly from deep cuts in Irons' forearm and wrist. But the swelling was already beginning, and the bleeding was stopping of its own accord. She looked at Clell. "I think his arm's broken."

Clell nodded glumly. "It'd be a miracle if it's just broken in one place. From the looks of them, they're both broken."

She took a strip of sheeting and wound it around the first of the terrible gouges. She bound it firmly, then took up another strip. Slowly, she worked her way down his arm, thinking of the work she was doing rather than the man she was doing it to. Thinking of closing the edges of the torn flesh neatly together rather than the pain she was causing.

Irons twitched and moaned occasionally, but for the most part he lay limp, his feet dangling.

Thinking, Fan decided, was the way to get this done. Deciding how to do it in the most efficient way possible kept her mind occupied. There were no prayers nor incantations for what she was about to do. For fire and blood and breath but none for this terrible mangling. Words came into her head. Words she had heard before. "There came an angel from the East . . ." But he was not burned. "There came an angel . . ." Vaguely, she wondered how she knew how to begin that prayer.

She blinked as she came to Irons' fingers. Two were obviously dislocated and one was cut to the bone. "What shall I do?"

"Go ahead and set them," Clell advised, swallowing hard. "He'd want you to do it."

"But . . ."

"I'm no doctor, but I've seen a mess of them work in the hospitals. You're doing a better job than most."

Her turn came to swallow. She felt along the index finger until she came to the second joint. The bones seemed to be side by side. She put his wrist under her arm and caught the tip of the finger. Her face was anguished as she pulled.

Irons screamed.

Early grabbed hold of his upper arms just in time to keep him from thrashing and throwing himself off the table. Brazel slid slowly down the wall, his face shiny with sweat. Clell dropped across Irons' knees. "Go ahead and do the other one, Fan, while we've got him."

"But I'm hurting him."

"Go ahead, ma'am," encouraged Early. "He don't know what he's feeling. He'll never remember it."

She could feel the sweat pop out on her body. How could she hurt another human being so? Doctors must be the most cruel . . . She pulled the third finger.

Irons' body convulsed on the table. He screamed again. She looked over her shoulder. Tears or sweat or both wet her cheeks. She was dizzy, about to fall.

"Wipe the sweat off her forehead, Brazel," Clell commanded.

From somewhere behind her a cold wet cloth swiped clumsily across the top half of her face. "Again," she begged. "Again."

The cloth came again, gentler this time, with more accuracy, sponging away the tears from her cheeks, replacing them with blessed coolness.

"Only one more arm to go," Clell said with false heartiness.

Fan exchanged another long look with Early, who shrugged and straightened up. Silently, they switched sides of the table and the process began again. If anything, the left hand was worse than the right.

Huge gouges in the shape of the chain ran across the upper arm, just above the elbow. In the forearm, the shape of teeth ran up over the wrist.

Early cursed dismally. "He musta stuck his hand into the gears. No wonder he's so mangled."

Fan set her teeth. Brazel swiped at her forehead again.

"Shut up, Early," Clell rasped. "Just do the best you can, Fan. He'll thank you for it. I swear he will."

Her ears were ringing as she held the first bandage

in place. She was going to pass out if she did not get another thought in her head. "How did he get his hands so scarred?"

"What?" Clell shot her a distracted look, his face drained of color.

"His hands. How did they get those burns?"

"Oil fields," came the curt reply. "Friend of his caught his shirt on fire. Kerosene sprayed all over the poor guy. Irons tried to beat it out. He got burned too."

"Did he save his friend?" She had worked down past the elbow now and was working smoothly. Her color was better as she listened fascinated to the tale of Irons' heroism.

"Yeah." Clell patted his friend's thigh. " 'Course he was burned terrible over most of his upper body, but he lived. And he didn't get any fire in his lungs thanks to Irons."

"He must be very brave."

"Brave. No, I don't think so." Clell shook his head. "I think brave is someone who's afraid of something and has to work himself all up to face it. Irons doesn't have to work himself up to anything. He just does what needs to be done."

When the entire ordeal was over, they all fell away from the table. Brazel pushed the other barrel under Fan as her legs gave out and she would have sat down on the floor.

"Fix us some coffee, why don't you?" Early growled.

"Comin' right up," Brazel answered.

Fan roused herself. "There's a bottle of whiskey in the cupboard."

Brazel pulled open the doors with unnecessary force. "Hell, why didn't you tell me that in the first place?"

" 'Cause she was busy doin' other things, you dern fool."

"Shut up, you two," Clell commanded. "Fan, we can watch him until the doctor comes. I think you ought to have a drink and then go to bed."

She looked at him vaguely. He seemed a little fuzzy. She blinked, and the vision cleared momentarily only to fade again. When Brazel handed her the drink, half coffee, half whiskey, she downed most of it in one swallow.

On the table Irons lay like a dead man. His hands placed carefully at his sides, his feet dangling inert from the end of the table. The healthy tan had turned to sallow gray, a startling contrast to his black mustache. His cheeks were hollow, his eyes sunken in his head. Beneath the ruin of the shirt, his chest barely moved.

"We really ought to get him to bed," she said hoarsely.

"Best leave him here until the doctor comes," Clell suggested.

"Then let's cover him up. We don't want him to get a chill."

At her words they all became aware of the cold wind that whistled around the cabin and blew up through the floor.

"More wood, Brazel, you dern fool," Early jibed. "Where's a quilt, ma'am? I'll get it for him."

"On the bed. Take the top one."

He was back in a minute to hand it to her.

Fan rose and draped it over Irons' upper body. She tucked it in around his shoulders and turned the sweat-soaked pillow. "He can't be very comfortable like this," she protested. "He's bound to be stiff in the morning."

Clell shook his head. "Fan," he said kindly, "he

won't feel any stiffness compared to what he'll feel when he wakes up. Those fingers are going to give him hell."

"I guess you're right, but still . . ." She straightened up and twitched the quilt down over Irons' lower body. The light began to fade. She looked up with a frown at the lamp hanging above her. It swung in a circular motion.

How strange that the wind should be so strong that it should blow the lamp. Dimly she heard Early mutter something. Then the roaring in her ears drowned everything.

Chapter 14

Fan felt the men lift and carry her to bed. Their hands were rough yet gentle as they tucked her clumsily beneath the covers. Accepting their help, her mind numbed in the wake of Irons' suffering, she welcomed their clumsy care. For just a few minutes, she could be helpless and put her trust in those stronger.

She should have sunk into a semicoma or failing that a disturbed sleep. Yet even as the covers settled over her and the door closed behind them, she found herself tensing. Exhaustion and cold, rather than acting as soporifics, drew her limbs into a tight ball. Her nerves set her muscles to cramping. Her mind began to whirl with thoughts of the future.

What would happen to them all without Irons? He was literally the heart of their enterprise, the catalyst that had brought them together. He had taken over her life when he had looked at the empty derrick and known exactly how to go about filling it. He had brought Clell and the roughnecks and their equipment to the same spot.

Every morning he, more than Clell, organized them and set their jobs for the day. He then rode off, a stern cast to his jaw, to earn the money to keep food in their mouths as well as to keep a steady stream of fuel and equipment flowing.

He had been the leader in the fight. She had heard him plan the strategy and deploy the troops. He had led the way into danger and like the best of officers had been horribly hurt himself while his men had come through without a scratch. Without him they were leaderless. If Alvin Weisberg and his goons knew Irons had gone down, they would be back tomorrow.

The thought of the lying, sneaking Weisberg with his gold rims on his front teeth made Fan furious all over. She clenched her fists and gritted her teeth, determined that none of them would give up. Somehow Clell must keep the operation going until Irons could heal and get his strength back.

Clell! A one-armed man who really only supervised the work. He could not do the work himself.

She turned over restlessly. Where was the doctor? Did she hear the galloping of hooves below the gusting wind?

What if the men were right? What if he did not come? What if the town boasted no doctor except some drunken sawbones who worked part time as a veterinarian? What if . . . ? She sat up in bed.

Above the gusts that shook the walls and set panes to rattling in their sash, she had heard the hooves of horses. "Clell!"

"I heard them too, Fan. Somebody's coming."

She slid her legs over the side of the bed. "How many?"

"I don't know."

"Two," Brazel chimed in. "I'll be damned. There's two of 'em comin'. Didn't think ol' Hoke could be so persuasive."

Fan opened the door for the roughneck and a weary, resentful man with a slicker and pants over what proved to be a nightshirt. ''You'd better be from El Rincón,'' were his first words, spoken in a slow-as-molasses drawl.

She blinked at the anger in his face. ''El Rincón?''

''That's what you told me, ma'am.'' Hoke nodded eagerly. ''And it sure did the trick. He was about to run me off with a shotgun.''

''Are you the lady from El Rincón?'' the doctor demanded. He looked beyond her, narrowly eyeing the three exhausted men and the still form lying on the tabletop.

Fan touched one hand to her disordered hair. The words *El Rincón* did not sound familiar. They must have come leaping out of her mouth of their own accord. But their magic had brought the doctor. ''Y—yes,'' she said. ''Yes. Indeed. As you see, we have a badly injured man. It's so good of you to come so far.''

The doctor cleared his throat noisily at the tone of her voice. ''Well, all right. Let's have a look at him then.'' He set his bag on the table beside Irons' head and moved the quilt aside. From his breast pocket, he drew his glasses from their case and hooked the wires over his ears.

Clell resumed his place between Irons' legs. ''He fell into the draw works,'' he supplied. ''Chains and gears chopped him up pretty bad. We got the worst of the bleeding stopped. But there's more. Mrs. Breckenridge thinks he's got several broken bones.''

The doctor nodded grimly as he began to feel along the bandages. ''Did you all wash him with clean hot water?''

''Yes.''

''And how about these sheets? Were these sheets fresh and clean?'' He looked over the top of his glasses at the woman of the house.

''Why, yes.'' Fan took umbrage at his implication.

"And all his wounds bled, I see." He nodded to the stains on the cabin floor.

At the mention of blood, Brazel threw open the door and stomped out, letting in a cold blast of fresh morning wind. Dawn light came filtering through the trees.

"He may still be bleeding," Fan suggested. She looked at Clell, who shrugged wearily. "He has a wound on his back."

"A wound?" Something in her voice made the doctor turn around.

"A gunshot."

The doctor's eyebrows rose almost to the top of his bald head. "See here, dear lady, your man didn't tell me there'd been a fight."

"It shouldn't make any difference," Fan said sternly. Her color was up. Despite the exhaustion and the terror, her back was ramrod straight.

The doctor stared at her over the top of his glasses. Then he returned to his examination of his patient. "Well, I guess it doesn't," he muttered. "I just kind of like to know these things before I walk into them. A man could get shot if he doesn't know he needs to duck. And, of course, I'll have to make a report."

"You do that, Doctor," Fan said haughtily. "March right into Sheriff Barfield's office first thing in the morning and report that we were attacked in the dark by men hired by Standard Oil."

"Well . . ."

"Be sure and give him the name of Alvin Weisberg, whose man burned my barn a few days ago."

"It's not my duty to report crimes." The doctor hung his head sullenly. "I don't want to get involved in that sort of thing. I just have to make a simple written report of gunshot wounds."

Clell nodded his approval to Fan. "Then I suggest

you get on with your doctoring so you can get it written up the sooner."

The doctor cleared his throat and began to feel along through the bandages. "His right arm's broken, both the radius and the ulna. I can feel the lumps where the ends of the bones are displaced."

Fan felt herself grow lightheaded at the pictures his description painted.

"They'll have to be set. His wrist, however, seems all right. And that's God's own miracle." The doctor flexed it up and down. "His fingers might be broken too."

"I set the index and third fingers," Fan volunteered.

He lifted the hand for closer observation, lifting the tip of each finger and straightened them out of their natural curve.

Irons groaned and rolled his head. Fan caught it between her palms and held him still.

The doctor tested the two fingers she had spoken of. "Now that's a good job, a really good job, dear lady. And it's probably a good thing you did it when you did. You see here. The swelling's already started."

Fan and Clell both leaned forward to see. Irons' hand had already turned purplish black. Every finger was strutted like a sausage.

"That's always the best time," the doctor continued. "After all that blood seeps into the tissues, it's a nasty job. Sometimes we have to let the thing heal up entirely, then break it again to get it straight."

Fan's stomach churned. Futilely, she fought to keep the faintness from overwhelming her.

"Here, Miz Breckenridge." Early poured a cup of coffee and liberally laced it with whiskey. He pressed it into her shaking hands. Her skin had lost every trace of color. She tossed it down gratefully, feeling the seering whiskey still the trembling in her stomach.

"If you are reasonably satisfied that you have done a good job, I'm not going to rebandage everything," the doctor continued. "I'll just put a splint on his forearm that will extend over his fingers. That way they'll be protected." He looked at Fan, who began to shake her head, but Clell forestalled her objections.

"Mrs. Breckenridge did a fine job, Doctor." He shifted his shoulder forward revealing his empty sleeve. "I can tell you that from experience."

The doctor looked over his glasses again. "Um-hum. Spanish American?"

"Cuba."

"That was a bad time for you brave men. I never really knew what that was all about." The doctor directed his attention to the other arm. "This is bad," he muttered. "Very bad. I'll have to strip off the bandages." In dead silence he unwrapped the sheeting, then shook his head. "Compound fracture of the radius. He might lose this one."

"Oh, no."

"But we'll give it a try," he said quickly. "I don't hold with cutting a man's arm off just because it might get infected. However, I'll have to cut to set it." He motioned to Early. "Can you help me?"

The big roughneck shrugged. "Been doing it all evening. Think I might get me a job as a nurse when I get too old for the oil fields."

Clell looked sympathetically at Fan, "Why don't you go take a walk out to the corral?" he suggested. "You can't do anything, and you'll need your strength later to nurse him."

"I . . . If you're sure."

"The very thing," the doctor agreed. "Go down to the barn. Get out of hearing. This is going to hurt, and he's not in a deep sleep."

She nodded her head, and taking her cup of coffee, fled.

Up on the rig platform, Brazel sat morosely, his hands between his knees. "I just can't help it, ma'am," he grunted.

A sharp cry came from the house.

They looked at each other in horror. Then Fan sat down beside him and handed him her cup.

He shook his head. "I just got a weak stomach or something. I can't help it. It's been a burden to me all my life. People think I'm crazy."

"I don't think you're crazy."

A scream of agony drove Fan into Brazel's muscled arms to huddle against his chest. He put his big hand over her ears and held her tightly. After a few minutes of silence, she sat up and wiped at her eyes.

"What's gonna happen now?" Brazel asked.

She wanted to throw up her hands and cry. Why should he look at her for that answer? He was a man, a big strong worker, a master of heavy machinery in a dangerous business. And yet he asked the question of her.

She looked at his dirty homely face as the sun picked out the bristles of his beard. Black and white, they were. Brazel was not a young man. His bloodshot eyes looked out from beneath the ledge of his brow further shaded by eyebrows liberally salted with white.

She drew a shuddery breath. "I don't know yet, Brazel." For the first time she addressed him by his name. "But we have to keep on drilling the well. Irons would have a fit if we didn't."

"Yeah, he would." A smile revealed stained and broken teeth. "Irons would prob'bly bust our heads if we didn't keep on the job."

He asked no more. She suspected that once his job had been explained to him, he thought no more about it. She, on the other hand, was left with even worse doubts and fears. What a group they were! Irons' arms were both broken. Clell had no arm. She had no memory. Only flashes such as the words *El Rincón*. What was *El Rincón*? And where was this *hidden valley*?

Brazel's casual acceptance of her reassurance told her that he was used to having someone do his thinking for him. Yet how could they survive as they were? The heart—the *iron* heart had been laid low.

Shivering in the early-morning chill, she looked around at the rig. Her eyes ran up the drill stem suspended from the traveling block to crown block and down the cable to the draw works.

Was there blood on the chain and on the teeth of the gears? Irons' blood. She shuddered, quelling a spurt of nausea.

Don't think about that. But what else was there to think of?

"The doc's leaving," Brazel observed. "Guess he's got Irons taken care of."

"Oh, no, he can't leave yet." She slid down off the platform. "He's got to tell me what to do to keep Irons comfortable."

The doctor was succinct. His patient would be in great pain. He would have fever as part of the healing process. But the fever must be watched and kept from going too high. It could kill the man if the wounds became infected.

Perhaps the lungs might be involved at this time of the year with dampness and cold. He had left quinine for the fever if it went too high, some laudanum for the pain to be used sparingly. She should, however, use cold compresses on his head and throat as the fever mounted.

As he rode away, Fan stared after him appalled. Even in the twentieth century, the treatment of the injured was so limited. Only when she was on the porch did she realize that she had forgotten to ask about El Rincón.

Inside the cabin Clell, Hoke, and Early sat in dismal council at the table. Fan shook the empty coffeepot. "I think we're going to need more of this," she said with forced lightness.

"Thank you, ma'am," Hoke said. "I could sure use some more to get me started."

"You're welcome. It's full daylight out there. And it's going to be a long day."

"Don't know why we need to hurry," Early grumbled. "This about tears it for now."

Fan gaped at him. Early had been her mainstay through the long night when her hands were bloody, and Irons was writhing in pain. She put her hand on his shoulder as she sat down in the seat Hoke stood up to give her.

He glanced up but looked back down again, sunk in gloom. Clell too was quiet. His good humor gone entirely in the aftermath of the night. His face was gray, the lines around the mouth deep.

She leaned forward. "What shall we do?"

Clell heaved a sigh as he lifted the cup to his mouth. "Not much we can do with Irons out for at least six weeks, maybe more if those cuts get infected."

"Damn shame." This from Hoke. "Good cuttings just beginning to show up."

"Cuttings?"

"Rock from down in the well. It was looking damn good," the little man said glumly.

"Yeah, damn shame." Clell raked his hand through his graying hair. The night had aged him. Deep lines showed in his face. He was gray around the mouth.

Fan drew a deep breath. "If the rock is good, then that's all the more reason to go on."

"How?" Early asked with just a touch of sarcasm. "We were short-handed as it was. Irons'd help us get spudded in every morning and tied down every night."

"But surely, you know the routine. You can do it yourselves."

"Well . . ."

"You added more pipe to the kelly by yourselves," Fan insisted. "I've watched you do it."

Hoke shrugged. Clell looked glummer than ever. "We'd like to keep going on, Fan, but Irons was the only one bringing in any money. That engine's got to have fuel, and we need a load of pipe. Plus, we're not going to drill too many more feet on that bit. Then we've got to pull all that pipe out of the hole. We're going to have to add some casing up at the top too."

"Who could go to work at the Boomin' Bessie in Irons' place?"

The three men exchanged glances. "I guess I could," Early said finally. "I never been a driller before, but I can dress tools pretty well. I guess they'll take me on just until he gets able to go back to work for them. That is, if they last that long."

"That just leaves the three of us to drill," Hoke whined. "Two and a half really. No offense, Clell."

"None taken," he agreed readily.

"We can't do it, ma'am. It's just not possible. There's not enough hands."

"What if I were on the monkey board?"

The three gaped at her. If she had suddenly sprouted two heads, they would not have been more amazed nor horrified.

"I could do it," she said firmly. "I've watched you, Hoke. You don't do anything that requires great strength, only competence. I could do it. And it's the perfect solution."

"No, ma'am," Early said flatly.

"I use a lot of strength," Hoke protested.

"Irons would kill the lot of us," Clell declared.

All three spoke at once, their voices rising in a storm of protest.

She waited until they subsided, then spoke again. "What other solutions do you have?"

"Well . . ." Clell began. "I could go back to Houston and see about getting some more financing."

"Do you think you'd have any luck?"

"I might."

"And what would we do while you're gone?"

"The boys could hire out around here as roughnecks."

"And what happens to Irons and me? And to the drilling that's already begun?"

"We could live here and bring in some money. We could work half a tour every evening," Hoke suggested desperately.

"A woman don't work on a rig," Early said adamantly. He thrust his hands into the pockets of his overalls with such force that the straps cut into his beefy shoulders.

"I wouldn't be out there all the time," Fan protested. "I wouldn't get in the way or anything. I could do the job on the monkey board when you needed to add more pipe. The rest of the time I could come back in here and take care of Irons."

"What about him when you're up there?" Hoke wanted to know. "Suppose he needs something."

"I admit that's a problem, but he won't do anything except rest and sleep for the first week or so," Fan pointed out reasonably. "After that he can sit and watch us."

"More likely he'll kill us," said Hoke, who had a healthy respect for Irons.

"How can he with two broken arms and hands?" Fan looked around the circle.

Clell stared into his coffee cup. Since he could do little work, her acceptance or rejection was left to the others.

Early was clearly angry, his brow knotted, his lips drawn in. He looked ready to explode. "It won't work," he snarled at last. "Everybody's got to pull his weight on a tour."

Still Clell said nothing.

Hoke looked miserably from one to the other uncertain whose side to be on. The silence grew.

"We still haven't said where we'll get the money to eat on," Clell spoke with the air of a man playing his final card.

"Early can go over and work at the Boomin' Bessie," Fan said firmly. "He'll feel better there anyway."

Clell turned half around at the table. He drummed with his fingers once then twice. "No," he murmured but with a note of uncertainty. "No. You can't do it. It's too dangerous."

"That's right," Early enjoined. "It's near fifty feet from that board down to the floor of the rig. You fall and we'll have to scrape you up."

"How does Hoke keep from falling?"

"I'm used to it. I don't fall." The little man thrust out his chin pugnaciously.

Fan looked at him seriously. "You could tell me, show me how to keep from falling, couldn't you?"

He gulped. "I guess I could rig something up there, that would tie you to the derrick. Maybe a belt or something."

She smiled her most winning smile, and Hoke melted visibly. "That's wonderful. Then we can all work together. And I'll feel like it's my well too."

Clell looked from her eager face to Hoke's bemused one. "You can come out and try, but if you get scared, or if the work's too hard for you, we'll all understand."

Early set his cup down and stomped to the door. "Since you've all gone crazy, I'll go saddle a horse and ride over to the Boomin' Bessie. I hope to God the boss'll take me on. At least over there I won't have my brains knocked out by a monkey wrench."

"Take Pet," Fan suggested generously. "She knows the way."

He closed the door behind him harder than necessary. Fan held out one hand to Clell and one to Hoke. The one-armed man took it immediately, his smile troubled. The little man hesitated, wiped his hand on his pants and then put it in hers. The palm was rough as an old corn cob and calloused over. The tip of the third finger was missing. His faded eyes met hers with a peculiar light.

They held tight to each other for a minute, then a low moan and a muffled cry came from the bedroom.

Fan rose. "I'll see to him and get him comfortable. Would you . . . Do you mind getting your own breakfast? I don't know how much care he's going to need." She stopped at the door. "Clell, for all my brave talk, I don't think I can do anything today."

As she spoke, she doubted her own reserves of strength. Exhaustion and nervous strain had drained her. She had not slept except for a couple of hours in twenty-four. Pain pounded in her temple and her stomach cramped from too much coffee and alcohol with no food.

Clell rose from the table and followed her to the door of the bedroom. He heaved a sigh. "I don't think any of us can. We'll need to go over the situation out there and see if anything was damaged. A bullet's always going to hit somewhere if it doesn't hit the target.

Sometimes the misses can be darn near as bad as the hits."

"Clell."

"Here, Irons, old man."

"Clell."

They entered the room together. By the light of day, Irons' gray eyes, bright with pain, sought them. He had managed to sit half up in bed. His eyes dropped from their faces to his hands, then back up. Horror was written in every line of his haggard face.

"Both broken," he muttered staring at the splints.

Fan came to the side of the bed and pulled the pillow from behind his head. She fluffed it and turned it over. "Lie back."

"Are they both broken?" he demanded of Clell, who came to the other side of the bed.

"I'm afraid so. But you didn't lose any fingers and your wrists weren't broken."

Fan put her hand to his forehead. It felt hotter, but also damp with perspiration. He was sweating. "Are you in pain?"

He shot her a vituperative look. "Hell, yes, I'm in pain."

"Then I'll get you some water and laudanum." She turned on her heel.

"I can stand it," he called after her. But when she left the room, he looked at Clell. "Hell of a thing. What happened?"

"You were shot."

"I remember that."

"But the doctor said it was just a crease. No permanent damage done."

"Then . . . what . . . happened?" The three words were punctuated by gasps as the pain mounted in the swollen hands and fingertips.

"You got knocked out and fell into the draw works."

"Goddamn." Irons lifted his hands a few inches off the bed. His incredulous pain-filled eyes inspected the blackish-purple fingers, swollen to half again their size. Like bloated bloodworms they curled over the ends of the splints. He gritted his teeth and tried to move the index finger of his right hand. It would not move.

Sweat broke out on his forehead. A terrible groan slipped from between his teeth.

Clell leaned forward and tried to support the left hand back to the bed. "Actually, you were pretty damned lucky. You could have lost them both. They could have been ground up for dog food."

Irons rolled his head away. The pillow so recently turned was soaked with his sweat. His gray hair looked black plastered to his forehead. If he held his hands in fire, they could not have hurt more. It made him weak, and it nauseated him. It frustrated him, and it crippled his ability to think. The tears began to slip down his cheeks.

Fan came in with a tin plate that she had turned into a tray. "I've brought coffee, water, and laudanum," she announced. "You can have any or all, but I suggest you take the laudanum." Her voice was cool.

His eyelashes swept down, then up. The motion was the nearest he could come to a nod. The pain was taking his power of movement. "I'll take whatever you say."

She put the little tin plate down on the bed beside him. She could feel the tears prickling behind her own eyes. His pain must be very great for him to have changed his attitude so quickly. Carefully, she measured out the drops and stirred them into a glass of water. "Drink this."

She slipped her hand behind his head and raised him off the pillow. When he had swallowed the mixture, she held some coffee for him. He managed only a few sips.

"The rig's all right," Clell said.

"That's good," Irons' voice had no strength.

Fan touched his mouth with a piece of clean sheeting she had ripped off. "More?"

He shook his head.

"Early's gone to take your job at the Boomin' Bessie."

"Good."

Clell exchanged a glance with Fan. "I guess I'll go get my breakfast and then spell Brazel. He's at the rig waiting to get started. But I think we'll take the day off. We're all too tired. We might get clumsy."

Irons watched his friend go. His eyes were glassy as the laudanum and shocked weakness began to take effect. "What's going to . . . ?"

"What's going to happen?" She smiled as she wiped away the perspiration from his forehead.

He nodded weakly, his eyelids sinking.

"We've made plans. Everything's going to be fine."

"I'm really a mess," he whispered, his eyes closed.

"Don't worry." She bent and touched her lips to his forehead. "Clell and I will take care of you. Everything will be all right."

Chapter 15

Irons' fever began to rise in the middle of the afternoon. Fan lay stretched out beside him on the bed. She had intended to doze only, but the mere presence of his body in bed beside her, the long warm length of him, safe for the moment, lulled her. She was deep in sleep when she heard him.

"Jane?"

Her eyes would barely open. Their lids felt weighted, the lashes stuck together.

He whimpered faintly, then ground his teeth. His voice was a little stronger when he called again. "Jane?"

She just managed to pull her head off the pillow and turn it to face him before letting it drop back again. She was so tired she could hardly move, yet move she must. She pushed up on her elbows. "I'm here, Irons."

He tried to reach for her, but pain stopped him cold. His eyes flew open, his face contorted. "Jesus God." The words escaped on a hiss. He looked down at his hands. Conscious now, his face a dull gray, except for a distinct flush across his cheekbones, he drew up his knees and pushed them back down again. ''Fan,'' he panted. ''Help me.''

She tumbled out of the bed. Pulling on her lace-trimmed robe, she lifted the tray from the floor. ''I'll mix you up some laudanum.''

He took a deep strangling breath and set his jaw. ''I . . . I hate to take that stuff.''

In the act of prying the cork from the tiny laudanum bottle, she froze, staring at him incredulously.

Irons could not lie still. Even as he denied the medicine that would give him relief, he flexed his legs again. As he closed his eyes against the pain, she looked at his hands lying on either side of him on the quilt. Every fingertip was black. The nails on several fingers and both thumbs were ripped off into the quick.

Shuddering, she poured water into the glass and held it up at eye level to measure the drops. ''Don't be a fool.''

He opened his eyes wide, then immediately closed them again. A muscle flickered in his jaw. ''I can stand it. I won't get used to that stuff. You don't know how fast it gets to you.''

''Irons . . .'' She tried to soothe him.

''I've seen fellas that can't live without it. Addicts. Don't come near me with it.''

She picked up the spoon to stir the mixture. ''I've been warned. And you won't become addicted if I give it to you as the doctor ordered over the next three or four days.''

''No.''

''Yes. Irons. Your hands and fingers were smashed. Your fingers are as sensitive as your eyes. You're in great pain. And you don't have to be. Please be sensible.''

His Adam's apple moved convulsively. ''No.''

''You're already starting to get a fever.''

"No." His voice was weaker, just a shade less adamant.

She put her palm to his forehead. He felt warm, but not dangerously so. "I guess you're all right for now. I'll fix you some coffee. When you get to hurting so badly that you can't stand it, you let me know. You ought to think though that you've got a wait in front of you when you decide to ask. You ought to take your medicine right now."

"No!"

"All right for you." She left, taking the tray with her.

When the door closed behind her, Irons managed to bend his right elbow. The pain was excruciating as tendons down the length of his forearm protested. The arm seemed to weigh a ton. Yet when he had it up, the sight of the splints and bandages frightened him. He could see dark circles of bloodstains beneath the upper layer put on by the doctor. His arm must have been chewed to pieces by the chain links and gear teeth.

The fingers sticking stiffly out from beneath the bandages were the most frightening of all. What if they became infected and he lost them? They were already swollen to almost twice their normal size and throbbing excruciatingly. He wanted to weep and call down curses, but his tongue likewise felt swollen and thick.

He looked longingly at the water on the tray beside him. The very least she could have done was to give him a drink. With a groan, he let the arm drop back. Instantly, he regretted his action as the arm hit the bed with a thump that ripped a guttural cry out of his arid throat.

Fan pushed the door open. This time she had a board rather than a tin plate. "I brought coffee and oatmeal. The men must have made it for their breakfasts."

"Don't want anything. Just water." He realized how

pitifully weak his voice sounded, but the pain was making him sick at his stomach. The organs of touch in the ends of his fingers were throbbing, throbbing, throbbing.

"Very well." She poured more water into a second glass and held his head while he drank thirstily. Then she seated herself on the end of the bed opposite him and began to eat the oatmeal.

His temper flared. "At least have the decency to clear out of here and leave me in peace."

She looked at him quietly. "Would you like a sip of coffee before I go? It's sweetened with some brown sugar, and it's just the right temperature."

His gray eyes shot steel at her. "Give it to me, damn you?"

Not by a flicker did her expression change. She rose and came around the bed with the coffee cup in her hand. He raised his head but let it fall back on the pillow. The pull of muscles across his injured back drew a groan from him.

She slipped her arm under his shoulders and lifted. With her strength he was able to sit partway up though his body trembled. She held the cup to his lips.

He took a sip, then grimaced. After a second, he looked up. "Are you doping me?"

The cup did not move. Her expression did not change. "Yes, I am. You're torturing yourself for no good reason. Tomorrow I'll let you do it. Today you need to rest."

He hesitated, then drank the coffee down swiftly. "Thanks."

She let him lie back and brought the oatmeal.

"I'm not going to eat oatmeal." His tone was one of total revulsion.

"Do you want to start vomiting all over the bed?"

"I . . . I wouldn't vomit."

"Who knows what that laudanum's going to do on an empty stomach? It's dangerous stuff."

"I wouldn't vomit." Still he allowed her to feed him several bites.

"Now drink some more coffee. It's real coffee this time," she assured him, picking up a different cup.

He shook his head wearily. "I don't think I'd better."

"Why not? It's good. You're going to need nourishment to get back on your feet in a hurry."

"Because . . ." The spots of color over his cheekbones brightened. He looked around him desperately. "Because . . . Where's Clell?"

"Clell?" She frowned. The non sequitur dropped her back on her heels. "He's out on the rig."

"I need him."

She looked at him suspiciously. "Why?"

"I need him. In a hurry."

Suddenly, she realized what he needed. She rose briskly. "Don't worry about that. I can help you."

He rolled his head from side to side. "No, damn it. You're a lady."

"And you're a gentleman. Most of the time." She put her hand on his shoulder stroking him soothingly. "Listen, Irons, I know how you work. Helping you to the pot isn't going to shock me. You didn't think anything of helping me when I was in trouble. You bathed me like a baby. And took care of everything."

"That was different."

"How? Because I'm a little girl and you're a little boy." She dragged the utensil from under the bed and pulled aside the covers. With almost impersonal efficiency, she helped him to sit up.

The flaming pain in his back was nothing compared to flaming color in his face when he realized she would have to unbutton his underwear and free him from his clothing. He closed his eyes, almost sick with shame while her hands moved impersonally on his body.

"I'll leave you alone for a few minutes," she said quietly when he was ready. "Call me when you're through. I'll help you back in bed." With a pat to his shoulder, she took up the makeshift tray and she hurried out.

Irons sat with bowed head, shivering in embarrassment. The laudanum had reduced the pain in his hands to a bearable ache, but it could do nothing to alleviate the mortification of his spirit. He was helpless. Utterly and totally helpless. Worse even than Clell. Clell at least had one arm. He had none.

A woman, a young woman who had been dependent upon him, whom he had rather matter-of-factly taken his pleasure with, would now be privy to the functions of his body. No one had even so much as touched him since he had been old enough to care for himself. No one had laid a hand upon him without his express permission. The humiliation was almost more than he could bear.

Urine streamed from his body, splashing into the jar between his feet. When he was through, he could not even move the thing back under the bed where it would be decently out of sight. She would come in, and it would be the first thing she would see. She would carry its contents away and dispose of it.

Eyes closed, he let his head fall back onto his shoulders. When he opened them the situation was unchanged.

He scooted back onto the bed and managed to thrust his feet beneath the covers. Beyond that he was helpless. He could not even pull the covers up over his exposed body. A light sweat broke out over his skin as he lay back with eyes closed and called to her.

She came in silently, adjusted his clothing, and covered him up.

He heard the handle clank as she lifted the jar to carry it away. He remained with his eyes closed, his spirit seething until the laudanum took effect and he fell asleep.

"Brazel, could you take the time to saddle the buckskin?"

"Why, sure, ma'am. Be glad to."

Fortified with two cups of coffee, Fan crossed to Clell. He looked her over from head to foot, an admiring smile curving his lips. She was dressed much better than he had ever seen her. He told her so.

Her riding habit, made of excellent quality fabric, had obviously been fitted to her body. Her feet were clad in fine leather boots. Her hair was pulled back into a knot at the nape of her neck, and she had tied a silk scarf around her head to further secure it.

Despite her pallor and the thinness of her face, she looked every inch a lady. "I'm going into Batson," she announced. "From there I'm asking directions to Rosemeade. My brother-in-law should be able to help us. Even if I have to borrow the money from him, I should still be able to get enough to tide us over."

She had expected that he would, but instead he nodded approvingly. "That's a good idea. I didn't think much of your idea of coming to work on the rig with us."

Fan smiled grimly. "Oh, I'll come to work with you. But I can't do anything for the next three or four days. Irons is helpless. He can't feed himself; he can't even lift the covers off himself."

Clell shook his head, his face grim. "For him that's torture."

She nodded. "Agony of mind and body. The second thing that I have to ask of you is will you go and sit with him while I'm gone?"

"Be glad to."

Brazel came up leading her horse. "You want I should go with you, ma'am?"

She considered his kindly offer. "I probably should take you with me, but I know how tired you are. I'll be all right. A woman is pretty safe around here."

The main street of Batson, Texas, was just as much of a mire as the main street of Waldrow. The buckskin slogged through hock-deep mud past the sheriff's office in the front of the jail. Fan could not bring herself to ask help of the taciturn Mr. Barfield except as a last resort.

Instead, she rode on to the general store where a small American flag flew from a pole beside the steps. In the open door she stopped to let her eyes accustom themselves to the dimness. The customers and the storekeeper turned to stare at her. Feeling decidedly uncomfortable under their eyes, she hurried down the single aisle between the counters and the boxes and bins of dried foodstuffs.

Before the brass cage surrounding the little post office, she stopped. "Can you tell me what route goes to Rosemeade?"

The woman looked at her over the rim of her spectacles. "Rosemeade. Never heard of it. Mail addressed like that don't come through here."

Fan sighed. "What about Breckenridge? They live there. Can you tell me where you deliver the mail addressed to Breckenridge?"

The woman shook her head. "Don't have no letters addressed to Breckenridge, so I can't tell you where we'd deliver them. Don't deliver anyways. Everybody around here comes in and picks up his stuff."

"No letters addressed to Breckenridge?"

Plainly disgusted with the conversation, the woman went back to her sorting. "Naw."

Fan turned from the window and walked back to where the storekeeper stood behind the counter beside his roll of brown paper and ball of string. "Do you happen to know how I might get to Rosemeade?"

He scratched his balding head. "I've heard tell of it. Guess if you took the road north, and kept on riding you'd get there eventually. You might ask at the hotel."

Fan sighed. She very much doubted that anyone at the hotel would know any more than these people did. She should have set her teeth and gone to the sheriff's office first thing.

As she walked out of the post office, a crowd of people had gathered at the boardinghouse.

"Whoo-ee! Lookee that."

"What you call it?"

"Heard tell of 'em but never seen the like."

The comments came thick and fast as an automobile plowed its way through the mud. Obviously brand new, it was a bright red two-seater with leather seats and black leather cover like a buggy.

Though Fan had seen pictures of automobiles, this was the first one she had ever seen up close. Curiously, she watched as the man in the canvas driving coat and goggles squeezed the brass horn on the steering column, waved to the crowd, and climbed down. With a swagger he mounted the steps of the boardinghouse.

"What you call it?" someone shouted.

The driver turned, his mouth spread in a smile. "A runabout. It's built in Detroit, Michigan. It's the first one of 'em, so it's model A."

"Here's the name on the side." A man pressed forward to read the discreet gold medallion. He sounded out the name carefully. "It says it's built by Henry Ford and Comp'ny."*

"Do tell."

A woman rushed out and threw her arms around the driver's neck. She wore a modish traveling suit of navy blue broadcloth, but Fan recognized her instantly by the brassy-bright yellow hair. Eufemia Carlton locked herself into a passionate embrace kissing his mouth and pressing herself against his body. As the crowd cheered and shouted, the couple finished with a loud smack.

The man stripped off his goggles and turned to wave again. The crowd who had begun to offer some rude advice on how he should proceed laughed uproariously.

Fan gasped. Divested of his goggles, his hand raised to the applauding people, Paul Breckenridge grinned whitely through his neatly trimmed beard.

"Hey, Breckenridge," called a man from the crowd. "How fast will she go?"

"Don't know," came the laughing reply. "The roads hereabouts are so dang muddy."

"It'll go fast enough to take us to Houston," Eufemia yelled joyfully. "And from there we've got a railroad car waiting to take us to New Orleans. Right, sweetheart?" She pressed herself against Paul's side.

He grinned a little uncomfortably at the crowd as the roughnecks whistled and cheered. "That's the way to leave town in style," remarked one man standing down in front of Fan.

"When you've got a well that's blowing in fifteen

*The first Ford car was called the Model A, built in 1903. Seventeen hundred were sold for $850 each. Not to be confused with the Model A that replaced the Model T in 1927.

hundred barrels a day, you can afford to live high on the hog,'' another reported enviously.

''Do tell. Some fellas're just too lucky to live.''

''Yeah. And oil going for four twenty-five a barrel.'' The speaker spat a stream of brown tobacco juice into the mire.

Fan moved along the other side of the street until she was directly across from Paul. Rocked back on his heels, his chest puffed out with pride, he was talking to two men who had come out onto the porch. Eufemia still clung to his side, both arms about his waist.

A series of planks caked with mud served as a boardwalk for people to cross the street. Lifting her skirts Fan stepped out onto it. The closer she came to the other side, the more she had to pick her way as men jostled about looking at the ninety-day wonder of the horseless carriage with its red spoke wheels.

Despite being nearly forced off the plank, Fan managed to make the crossing and started up the steps.

Paul Breckenridge caught sight of her just as she put her foot on the porch. His mouth dropped open. He fell back a couple of steps, dragging Eufemia with him. His eyes widened. So startling was his reaction that Fan looked over her shoulder, wondering who might be behind her that was threatening him.

When she looked again, he had ducked in the open door of the boardinghouse.

''Paul.''

He stopped and swung around, his eyes wary. ''Fan.''

''Paul, I need to talk to you.''

He shook his head. His hands waved nervously as he backed into the lobby. ''I'm sorry, but I don't have time. We were just leaving. The bags have to be loaded and tied on. We have a train to catch.''

''I must talk to you,'' Fan insisted.

"Look, honey bunch." Eufemia came toward her, barring her way and pulling her aside. "Can't you be a good loser about this?"

"I have no reason to be a loser at all," Fan insisted. "I wasn't trying to win anything. Paul, wait. You've got to give me a few minutes. I need help."

But her brother-in-law all but ran up the stairs to the second floor. From there he leaned over the railing. "What do you want?"

She looked around her, aware that some people had followed her into the lobby and others outside were listening avidly to their exchange. "I have to talk to you about a private matter."

Shaking his head desperately, he called to the desk clerk. "Send up a porter for the bags immediately."

"Sure thing."

"Paul." Fan could feel her color rising. People were staring at her. She was being forced to stand in the middle of a lobby in a boardinghouse and yell up the stairs. Suddenly fury shook her. How dare he treat her this way? His own sister-in-law. She took a deep breath and yelled. "Paul Breckenridge. Come down here this minute. I must speak to you."

The man at the desk gaped. Out on the porch the pregnant silence was followed by a low hum of conversation. Feet shuffled as people edged closer to the door to look inside. Fan could feel their eyes on her, catch snatches of their comments.

"Who is she?"

"Where'd she come from?"

"Never seen her before."

Eufemia Carlton grabbed her by the arm. "You're not spoiling this for me, you high-toned bitch."

Before Fan could move or respond, the brassy blonde doubled up her fist and swung. The blow hit Fan's temple on the tender crescent-shaped scar. Uttering a cry of pain, she staggered sideways, spots whirling in her vision.

"Nobody wants you around here," Eufemia snarled, "so get the hell out."

Fan reeled away, coming up short against the reception desk. The top of it caught her across the back of the waist and knocked the wind out of her. As her head and upper body slumped forward, Eufemia came at her again. This time she drove her fist to the pit of Fan's stomach.

"Hey! Lookee here," cried a voice from the doorway. "There's two gals a-fightin'."

More of the onlookers crowded into the lobby and others peered over their shoulders. "What's it all about?" yelped one shrilly.

"That gent upstairs." A third pointed. "With the fancy auto-mo-bile."

"Don't that beat all."

"Some fellas're just too lucky to live."

They looked upward, but Paul Breckenridge had already vanished into the upstairs room.

"Here now. That'll be enough." The desk clerk dived around the desk and put himself between the two women as Fan slid to the side and collapsed to her knees.

"You're right about that, sure enough." Eufemia made a show of blowing on her knuckles. Her breathing was harsh, her color high. She grinned cockily at the crowd. "She ain't gonna get my man." She pushed her fingers into the desk clerk's shoulder. "Send that porter up for my bags and keep this bitch outa my way."

"Yes'm. Right away."

She leaned down to look into Fan's contorted face. "You try to queer this, honey bunch, and I'll tear every hair outa your head.'' With that admonition and another grin at the crowd, Eufemia flounced up the stairs.

Fancy had no breath to reply. The blow to the pit of her stomach had doubled her over in pain and nausea with the wind out of her. The first blow had opened up the cut on her cheek. Blood oozed from the wound.

She stayed there, crumpled in a ball, until the desk clerk helped her to her feet. ''Come with me,'' he said in a soothing voice as he led her into the parlor and seated her on the sofa.

''No,'' she managed to gasp. ''You don't understand. That man is my brother-in-law. I've got to talk to him. Please.''

''I'm not going to let you go back there, ma'am. That little fly-up-the-creek'll tear you apart.''

''Not now. I'm ready for her now.'' Fan tried to stand up by herself, but the pain in her belly still left her weak. Unprepared as she had been, the blow had knocked the wind out of her and shocked her. Her body, exhausted after the night's events, had begun to shake and would not stop. Even as she spoke, she closed her eyes. Her head lolled on the high-backed sofa.

The desk clerk hurried away but returned almost immediately. ''Ma'am,'' he murmured. ''Ma'am. You're bleeding.'' He pressed a cool wet cloth into her hand and guided it to her cheek.

In a sort of hollow dimness, she could hear footsteps hurrying down the stairs and out onto the porch. Someone cranked the car, once, twice, again. It started, at last. With another cheer and a barking of a couple of dogs, it drove off.

A faint smell of exhaust fumes wafted in through the open window.

The clerk straightened up. His face was sympathetic. ''You can wait here until you get your strength back, ma'am.''

Fan nodded. Her hand still clasped her bruised diaphragm.

He stepped out into the lobby, then looked back in. "Can I get you something to drink? Perhaps a cup of coffee?"

She pushed herself painfully to her feet. "No, thank you. I have to be going. Thank you."

"She played you for sucker."

Clell daubed gently at the crescent-shaped scar, now surrounded by a livid pinkish, purplish bruise. It had swollen out in a pump knot the size of a hen's egg by the time Fan had made the ride back to the shack.

"I just never expected . . . Ow!"

"Sorry."

". . . that a woman would hit another woman."

"Whores like her do it all the time." Clell managed a faintly reflective grin. "You're just damn lucky she didn't take a hat pin to you, or knock you down and jump on top."

"She did," Fan murmured.

"What?"

"She knocked me down. She would probably have done more if the desk clerk hadn't gotten between us."

"Oh, Fan."

"I didn't know what to do," she confessed humbly. "I couldn't think."

He patted her shoulder. "Well, of course, you couldn't."

"All I wanted to do was talk to Paul about a loan. He has plenty of money now. You should have seen the automobile."

"I've seen one."

"You have?"

"They've got a few over in Houston."

"He could have lent us a little just until Irons' hands heal," Fan continued, her voice stronger with righteousness. "He's got a well blowing in fifteen hundred barrels a day."

Clell whistled through his teeth. "And he wouldn't even talk to you?"

"N—no."

Clell put his arm around her shoulders and rocked her from side to side. "Your first brush with fair-weather friends, Fan, is always the hardest. Let someone get a little money, have a little good fortune, and suddenly he doesn't know the people he grew up with. His friends, relatives, sometimes his mother and father. He won't even speak to them.

"It works the other way too." He picked up the pan of water and cloth and walked to the cupboard. "You get down on your luck, and people don't know you, don't want your problems, cross the street to keep from meeting you face-to-face."

"Leave you?"

He seemed to shrink as from a blow, then nodded. "Yes. That too. But it was the right thing to do. What kind of father would I have made for a kid?"

"A very good one."

He tossed the rag down beside the pan and turned around, his face carefully blank. "We've got to rig up some place for you to spend the night in comfort. A good night's sleep is what we all need. In daylight everything looks brighter."

"Unless it looks worse."

He grinned. "You're getting to be worse than old Irons in there. No hope for the future at all. Just gloom and doom."

She smiled in return. "I'll try to do better."

"Fan?" Irons was awake.

They looked at each other. Her hand flew to her cheek.

"Fan!" came the irritable voice. "Fan, come to bed."

"Solved the problem of where to bed you down," Clell said softly.

"But he'll see my face."

"He'll see it sooner or later anyway."

"Fan!"

"Coming!" She rose, her fingertips still pressed against the wound. "Thank you, Clell, for everything."

"My pleasure. Don't often get to hug a beautiful girl."

She smiled, thinking how deeply wounded he must be beneath that smiling exterior. Deliberately, she crossed the room to him. Gently, she kissed him on the cheek. "Good night, Clell."

She picked up the makeshift tray to carry into the bedroom.

"Good night, Fan."

Chapter 16

"Where've you been?"

"To Batson." The room was almost dark. The lamp she carried in was turned so low that it illuminated only a small aura around the tray. "How are you feeling?"

"Awful."

"I'm sorry. Is the pain bad?"

"Not so bad as this morning." His voice had a strained panting quality.

"Take another dose before you try to sleep. You'll get a good night's sleep and feel even better tomorrow."

"You're nagging again," he muttered savagely.

"At least you have someone who cares enough about you to nag," she pointed out gently as she measured the drops. "Drink this."

He could not object with the lip of the cup in his mouth. She thought her bruises had escaped his notice, but as she straightened, his gray eyes narrowed. "What the hell happened to you?"

She grinned in what she hoped was a cheeky manner. "I got in a fight."

"Who with?"

Clell had labeled Eufemia Carlton. She would accept his estimation. "A whore."

He tried to sit up, but she pushed him gently back down, her fingertips splayed across his chest. He frowned darkly, then acceded with a weary groan. "Tell me about it."

"It's not important. It won't happen again."

"You're damn right it won't happen again. You're in danger just like the rest of us. They left you for dead before." He rolled his head on the pillow, his frustration and helplessness tangible. "You won't go into Batson again by yourself. Clell ought to be shot for letting you go alone."

"Irons." She bent over him. "Irons. Stay calm. It's all right. I'm all right."

He raised his splinted hands off the bed and tried to flex the broken fingers. The effort drained all the color from his face and wrung a groan from him.

"Irons," she whispered. The tears started then—the tears she had not shed in pain and embarrassment.

He heard the quaver in her voice and looked up. "Fan." Despite the pain, he spread his arms. She slid down onto his chest, fitting herself alongside his body, tucking her hands underneath his shoulders, holding him when he could not hold her.

She was so tired. So tired. And so hurt. And so frightened. She had ridden a couple dozen miles on horseback only to be attacked for no other reason than she wanted to speak to the man who claimed to be her brother-in-law. Murder had almost been done to Irons. And she had not slept in twenty-four hours.

The tears were over very quickly. She was too tired to weep.

"Fan." Irons' deep voice rumbled out of his chest. "Get under the covers, baby." His lips brushed the top of her head. "You'll catch cold."

"What?" She realized she had drifted off to sleep.

"Get under the covers," he repeated softly.

She roused. Pushing herself off the bed, she just managed to pull off her outer clothing and walk around the bed to her side. When she climbed in, Irons was looking at her. "Come on," he invited. "Crawl back in my arms. You keep me warm."

"I'll hurt you."

He shook his head slowly, grogginess from the laudanum overtaking him. His own face was just as pale as her own. "Baby, I'm hurting as bad as I'm going to hurt. You can't do a thing except make me feel better."

She shook her head. "I might roll over on one of your hands."

"Come on."

Reluctantly, then thankfully, she edged closer to him, putting her hands around his upper arm and her forehead against the side of his shoulder. "There. Now you'll be protected and we can share the warmth. You need to sleep undisturbed."

He cursed sleepily. "Nagging again." The words trailed away as the drug overcame him.

She lay pressed against him. Her own side of the bed was cold and damp, but his was warm. She moved her feet over against his legs and kissed the point of his shoulder. Wounded as he was, he was still the source of warmth and safety.

The thirty-five feet to the floor of the rig looked like a hundred. Around her waist Fan fastened the safety belt that Hoke had rigged for her. She leaned against it testing its strength and looked almost straight down at the cold steel surface of the rotary table.

Hoke patted her shoulder. "Hey! Don't think about

falling. You won't fall. I've got you rigged, so you can't even slip off. Falling's the least of your worries."

"If you say so."

"I say so." He grinned a little and patted her again. "You can do this. Now. What you've got to do is attach this drill pipe to the kelly"—he pointed to the heavy piece at the end of the traveling block—"at the same time we'll attach it to the drill collar at the bottom. Now don't worry about making it tight. You don't have the strength in your hands to do it. We'll check it at the bottom before it goes into the hole."

"What if it comes loose? Will it fall into the hole?"

Hoke looked disgusted. "Not likely. Down at the end of all that pipe is the drill bit and it's imbedded in rock or mud or whatever it's going through right now. Believe me, it's not going to fall in."

She looked doubtfully at the half-dozen thirty-foot lengths of pipe leaning against the inside of the derrick. "I don't think I can move those over to attach."

"Of course, you can't. That's our job on the floor. All you have to do is move the end of the pipe around until you get it into a position so you can attach it. You just work it in. The whole thing swings. The block swings from the crown." He pointed up at the top of the derrick. "The kelly's hooked into a swivel. It's real simple."

"If you say so," she repeated.

"I say so."

"Ready up there," Clell called.

"Ready."

"Then let's spud her in."

The piece of pipe came swaying within reach of her heavily gloved hands. The kelly was heavy, but she leaned into Hoke's harness and managed it. As Hoke said, it swung easily. At the bottom above the rotary table, Brazel and Clell worked as a team to attach the pipe to the drill collar. Hoke helped her clamp it in, then hurried down the ladder to help them.

When the process was complete, the three of them looked up at her. "You did it," Clell called. "Ready to put another thirty feet down."

"That's all there is to it?" she cried.

"For now."

"I can't believe it. It was so fast."

"Fast!" Hoke laughed and slapped his thigh. "That was slow as cold molasses. It oughtn't to take us but about a minute to do that whole thing."

"Oh." She sat back disappointed. "Well, I'll get faster."

Brazel eased the engine into life. The mud pump and the rotary table started turning together, and the derrick began to vibrate as the drill bit into the dark earth far below.

Fan leaned back letting her eyes rove over the countryside. She was wet with perspiration, so afraid that she would ruin something that she had worked herself into a nervous lather. But she had done it.

She took a deep breath, then looking down, she caught sight of Irons leaning against the corral. His expression shocked her almost as much as did his presence. His face was white and drawn; his eyes, stormy.

As she met his eyes, he shifted his weight. The movement made her aware that his body was clad only in his long underwear. He had not been able to dress himself. He shifted again and she saw that his feet were bare.

The sight of those feet angered her. He was courting disaster if he caught a cold or pneumonia. Never mind that the day was still, with a fitful sun breaking occasionally through gray clouds. The temperature was still low and the ground beneath his soles was damp.

Angrily, she waved to him and unbuckled the belt.

Down the ladder she came, prepared to do battle. "What are you doing out of bed? If you catch a cold, it could turn into pneumonia."

As she stormed up to him, he grinned weakly. She made a ludicrous figure, dressed as she was in a combination of garments belonging to him, her, and Hoke. He waited until she was almost to him, before muttering, "Never seen a woman like you for nagging."

Ignoring his accusation, she put both arms around his waist to support him and to force him back to the shack. "You're out here barefooted."

He balked like a mule, dead in his tracks. She pushed, but he would not move. "I came to see if you could do it."

She looked up into his face with a gamine grin. "And I did."

"You did it once with Hoke helping you. What are you going to do when they go down another thirty feet, and it's time to get up there again?"

"I'll do the best I can," she maintained stoutly. "The next time I'll ask Hoke to tell me how to do it. Then I'll go up and do it."

He cursed softly. "I don't want you up there. You could crush your fingers. You could fall off that monkey board and break your neck."

She grinned up at him. "Now who's nagging?"

He had no choice but to allow her to lead him to the house. The throbbing in his hands, hanging limp and heavy at his sides, increased with each beat of his heart. The wound across his back burned like a brand as sweat broke out on his body. His head ached.

Fan had to put her shoulder under his arm and push to get him up the steps. He barely made the bed before collapsing completely.

Anxiously, Fan wiped the perspiration from neck and chest and covered him. Tears welled in her eyes as she gently sponged the gray-white skin of his face. He had suffered great pain and risked further injury to watch her. If she had started to fall, she had no doubt he would have run forward and caught her, despite his own injuries.

He cared more than just a little about her. And she could think of no one she cared about more, nor admired more. Stooping, she pressed her lips to his forehead. As she drew back, his eyes opened wearily.

"Kiss me again," he commanded.

"All right." She bent and brushed his cheek.

His mouth curled upward on one side. "You can do better than that, baby."

"You're too weak," she whispered.

"You make me feel better."

"I'm supposed to be working. They're going to need me."

"Just kiss me."

She sat down on the edge of the bed and kissed his other cheek and the corner of his mouth.

He turned his head to catch her lips, but she drew back too quickly. He scowled. "You missed. Kiss me on the right place."

She put her hands on his cheeks and held his face still. "If I do, will you promise to stay in bed?"

"No. I'm already going crazy in here by myself."

"Just for another forty-eight hours. Just until we're sure that you're not going to have an infection."

"If I'd been going to get an infection, I'd have shown some sign of it," he said reasonably. "There's no swelling. No fever. I can get up." He tried to push himself upward in the bed but failed because she held him down. "Besides there must be something I can do out there to help."

"With two broken arms and an assortment of broken and dislocated fingers?" she scoffed.

He lifted his right hand which was slightly less swollen than his left. "Look at that." He moved his index finger up and down and side to side.

She put her hand on the splint and pressed gently. The pain made him catch his breath. He lowered his arm.

"Give yourself a rest," she murmured as she leaned forward and kissed him long and lingeringly on the mouth. When she finished, his eyes were closed and his breathing had accelerated. She left the room and came back with water. "How about a drink?"

"How about another kiss?"

"You need water to drink. Then I'm going back out on the rig and be useful."

"Damn it."

"Drink." She held it firmly to his mouth.

He drank.

She kissed him again, and then smiled lovingly. "That should keep you sweet for an hour or two."

He lay back staring at the ceiling, a scowl on his face. "The next time you think you might come in, send Hoke instead."

"You like his kisses better than mine?"

"No. But I'm going to need to take a leak before too much longer."

On that bit of information she fled.

From her perch on the monkey board, Fan saw the top of a black buggy approaching among the trees. A thrill of apprehension ran through her. Her stomach tightened. "Clell!"

He looked up instantly.

"We've got visitors."

Her words galvanized her crew into action. Hoke dived inside the draw works. As she came down the ladder, he came out with a pair of long pistols. One he pitched to Brazel, who caught it and slipped it down into the pocket of his overalls. Hoke stuffed his into his belt and pulled his coat to cover it.

Clell pushed back his coat to reveal a pistol already strapped to his right hip, ready for a cross draw. At the foot of the ladder, he met her. "Get in the house."

She shook her head. The rig platform vibrated under her feet as the bit tunneled through the earth. The mud pump and the donkey engine kept up their rhythmic churning. Like a live thing, her rig's heart beat. She owned it. And she would not give it up. "I'll do no such thing."

"Don't be a fool. They could come shooting."

The thought intimidated her for a minute, but then she shook her head. "But not at me. Too many people have had a chance to kill me and haven't. For some reason they want me alive."

Clell cursed roundly. He threw a glance over his shoulder. The black buggy with its accompanying outriders cleared the trees and came down the lane. "You don't know that. They could have just been squeamish about killing a woman. Probably were. You could have just been standing on the sidelines. But if you get in the way, they'll smash you too quick to talk about."

"I don't think so. They need my signature. And something else. I may be someone they need." She stripped off the heavy gloves and adjusted her clothing. Proudly, she walked toward the buggy. When its occupant saw her, he drove on past the shack and pulled up at the corral.

The two outriders split. One rode around the shack, the other circled the corral. The driver climbed down from the buggy. His smile was affable. "I've come to speak with Mrs. Breckenridge."

"I'm Mrs. Breckenridge."

His smile never faltered. In fact it broadened as he took in her dress. "I'm Harry Glennville, Mrs. Breckenridge."

He waited, but she did not extend her hand. "What have you come for, Mr. Glennville?"

He hesitated, his smile fading fractionally. "I like a woman who gets right to the point." He made an effort to exchange a knowing look with Clell. "Women are going to be a force in the business world in the twentieth century."

Neither Clell nor Fan responded to his remarks. Hoke climbed the ladder until he could see the outrider who had circled the shack. He hooked an elbow over one of the rungs and hung there. His coat fell open so the sun glinted off the hammer of the pistol stuck in his belt.

The visitor cleared his throat. "I understand you've had some trouble. A man injured seriously." He waited, but Fan neither denied nor confirmed his statement. His eyes narrowed speculatively. "Greed makes men do violent things. Because there's so much money—as it were—enough for all, the business attracts the most reprehensible kind of man. It's not a business for a lady."

The man beyond the corral halted his horse and started to climb down. Brazel came around the edge of the mud pit, his hand in his overalls. "Better stay up there, mister, until you're asked to step down."

"Mrs. Breckenridge, I'll get right to the point since you seem a very practical lady. First, I'd like to say how sorry my employers are that Mr. Weisberg was so abrupt with you. You can rest assured that we have recalled him to our main office where he'll be dealt with most severely."

Fan looked at her three men. They were all in place.

She pushed back her own coat to reveal Irons' weapon strapped to her waist. "Too bad," she said succinctly.

He raised his eyebrows in surprise. "How so?"

"You should have talked to Mr. Weisberg before you sent him away."

"He had gotten greedy, Mrs. Breckenridge. He used strong-arm tactics to try to secure your land for a lesser price than we had authorized. He was going to pocket the rest. We are appalled at the reports of his behavior and are here to make reparation."

Frowning heavily, Clell reached out for Fan, but she smiled reassuringly at him. "So you're going to pay me for the damage he did?"

Glennville frowned slightly, then nodded enthusiastically. "That's right. You're a very lucky woman, Mrs. Breckenridge. I've come to offer you a very generous deal. I've been authorized to offer more than twice as much as Mr. Weisberg was going to offer. The difference should make up for whatever damage he has caused. We feel that something is owed to you for all the trouble that he caused."

"Something is owed," she agreed. "I'll be happy to take the money . . ."

"You'll be able to turn a handsome profit without turning a hand. You won't have to work. Think of it." He reached behind him and lifted a black leather portmanteau from the buggy seat. "Shall we go in the house and let me explain what I have here?"

Fan shook her head. ". . . but I won't lease the land."

"Come now, Mrs. Breckenridge, you don't want to be foolish. You're turning down the opportunity to be rich."

Despite her outward coolness, her heart was beating in her throat. What she was about to say might cause men to shoot at each other, to be killed. She took a deep breath. "Mr. Glennville, I'm going to be as quick and as direct as I think you would want me to be. No matter how generous your offer, I'm not interested in leasing this land. We have a promising operation here that has a good chance of success."

"My dear lady, wait until you hear . . ."

Her voice shook, but she managed to go on. Her fingertips were cold and her lungs felt starved for air as if she could not get enough through her nose. "I have no interest in anything you might say. And now I want you to leave. We're working peacefully on land that I have the right to. We're bothering no one. We're drilling this oil well ourselves, and we don't wish to lease it to anyone."

"You aren't being smart, Mrs. Breckenridge." Glennville put on a stern face. He might have been a father talking to a particularly recalcitrant daughter. "The large majority of wildcat wells are dry. If you lease, we would still pay you a handsome amount whether the well came in or not. We would even pay for acreage that we were not drilling on."

"But the lease money would be a very small amount."

"If we struck oil, the royalties would make you rich beyond your wildest dreams. And you could have your profits sooner with around-the-clock crews."

"And be cheated faster by having the oil drained off," Clell broke in.

"I represent a reputable company."

"Standard Oil is a bunch of crooks."

"I'm addressing Mrs. Breckenridge."

"That's all right, Clell." Fan put her fists on her hips, her right one remained only inches from the revolver. "Mr. Glennville, I don't want to sign a lease."

"Mrs. Breckenridge, you're making a big mistake. We can't pay you a separate amount for the damages.

After all, Mr. Weisberg acted without authorization. You'll just have to suffer that loss."

"I somehow thought that was how it would be."

"I have a suggestion. How about taking a drive with me? I can show you some of the fields we are developing and you can talk with some of the satisfied people who are living well off the money we're paying them."

Fan took a deep breath. "And if they don't sign, they're injured and their barns burned."

The smile became wolfish. "My dear lady, I've heard of such things happening."

"And sometimes you don't even bother to make them look like accidents. Sometimes you kidnap people out of their beds at night and take them miles from their homes and murder them."

Glennville managed to look shocked and angry at the same time. "I can assure you that we would never do such a thing. It's gotten so we get blamed for every crime of passion, every robbery, every assassination that takes place around here. If somebody's horse stumbles and throws him, Standard Oil did it. They're the ones to blame."

"Perhaps because you are to blame."

He spread his hands wide. "We're not. Listen to me, Mrs. Breckenridge. There's no question that this business is a highly competitive one. People want the leases that they know we're interested in. They get there ahead of us and threaten and bully. All the more reason for you to sign with us. Then we take the risks."

"And if we don't sign, you create the risks."

"Of course not. What happened to Mr. Irons was exactly what I'm talking about. People knew we were coming. They wanted to scare you all off first. And now instead of being scared, you're being foolish. You're a small, weak woman and worse—you're inexperienced. For weak, inexperienced people working around potentially dangerous heavy equipment, the chance of accidents is very high. And accidents will happen around rigs. I repeat. They're incredibly dangerous. You never know when something tragic will happen."

His threats couched in hypocritical words of warning angered Fan. Her sense of grievance exacerbated by Eufemia's attack yesterday boiled over. She dropped her hand back onto the butt of Irons' gun. "Mr. Glennville, I'm of the opinion that you don't believe me when I tell you you're wasting your time."

"My dear Mrs. Breckenridge. Women are famous for changing their minds."

"Maybe women are, but I'm not going to. I have been dragged from my bed and beaten while my husband was hanged. My barn has been burned and my partner in this venture has been seriously hurt. Frankly, Mr. Glennville, if I never brought this well in, I still wouldn't sign with Standard Oil."

He raised his hand like a witness about to give testimony. "I swear to you that neither I nor the company I represent had anything to do with that hanging, Mrs. Breckenridge. We are a legal leasing operation. We don't believe in violence."

"I didn't expect you to admit to anything. I'm just telling you the reasons that I want you to get off my land."

"My dear lady, be reasonable. You can't make this work. You'll only run the risk of being hurt yourself. Some of your crew might be killed working shorthanded as they are."

Deliberately, Fan drew her gun and pointed it at her visitor's ample girth. "Mr. Glennville, I'm going to give you till the count of ten to get back in your buggy and drive off. And take your riders with you."

"There's no need for this." The man turned red,

then white. "Mrs. Breckenridge, I think you'd better think again."

"One."

"You're behaving foolishly."

"Two."

Hoke swung around behind the ladder. Brazel eased his gun out of his overalls.

"Mrs. Breckenridge, no need to get nasty. I'm offering you an opportunity. You have a choice."

"Three, Mr. Glennville. I don't have any choice. My husband died for this piece of land. And Mr. Irons has been badly hurt. None of that has been my choice." She thumbed the hammer back. It gave a satisfying click, and the man threw his hands in front of him.

"Hey, watch out. Don't point that thing at me. I don't know anything about your husband's death. I swear."

"Four."

Glennville pulled a handkerchief from his pocket. He looked at Clell. "You're her driller. Make her see sense."

Clell's lips peeled back in grin. "What do you suggest that I do? I've only got one arm."

"Damn you . . ."

"Five."

Glennville waved his handkerchief.

The man at the corral rode back to the buggy. "Boss?"

"Six."

"We're going," Glennville said. "Round up Clem and let's get out of here." The man touched his hat and cantered away.

"Seven."

Glennville tossed his portmanteau into the buggy. "You'll regret this. You haven't heard the last of this."

"Eight."

He unlooped the reins from the brake and turned the buggy around. His men were already loping their horses down the road.

Fan walked behind the buggy to the porch of the shack where she stopped. With her left hand she eased the hammer forward. She was conscious of a ringing in her ears and a weakness in her knees but at the same time of a sense of exultation.

"That took guts." Clell had come up behind her grinning his irrepressible grin. "He sure didn't expect to get ordered off with a gun."

Fan listened until the hoofbeats died away. "I think he did. He had his men with him."

"That was just to handle us in case we objected. He expected you to greet him with open arms and sign those leases with tears in your eyes. That's the way they operate. One goes in first, makes threats, causes a few accidents. Then another comes in and makes another offer."

"They must have been the ones who killed Rex. They got Rosemeade. Why did they follow me here?"

Clell shrugged. "Greed. Like the fella says, Greed makes men do terrible things."

"Poor Rex."

"What would you have done if you'd counted to ten?" Clell asked curiously.

Fan hesitated. Her voice was sober when she answered. "Shot him."

"Is that a fact?"

"My mother shot Yankees. My great-grandmother shot pirates. I guess I can do the same with land grabbers."

"You're remembering," he told her softly.

She shrugged. "I must be. I didn't have to think about them. They just popped out. I know what I said is true." She grinned humorlessly. "You're right. I'm remembering. A few more times where I'm scared to death and I'll know it all.''

She looked around at their smiling faces. ''Thank you all for backing my play. Without you, Brazel, out on my flank and you, Clell, at my back and Hoke up on the rig, that man wouldn't have paid any attention to me.'' She shook each man's hand gravely in turn.

''Pleased to be of service,'' Clell assured her gallantly.

Then her lips twitched again and her grin burst wide. ''You know I feel great about this. For the first time in a long time, I feel like *I'm* doing something instead of somebody doing something for me. And, you know what? It feels great.''

They grinned back at her. She ran a hand through her hair. ''So, since we're all down here at the cabin, let's go in and have some food. No sense getting back on the rig until we've eaten. Is that all right with everybody?''

Clell looked to Brazel and Hoke. Both were worshiping her with their eyes. ''Whatever you say,'' he drawled. ''You're the boss.''

Chapter 17

"You should have signed."

"Irons!" Fan could not believe her ears. The crew had returned to the rig after a joyous lunch. Each of the three had told his own version of her facedown of the Standard Oil goons. Her audacity, her coolness, her bravery had been lauded to the skies. She had never felt so wonderful.

"I should never have gotten you into this. Now you're a target. So long as I could protect you, you were all right, but now . . ." Irons shook his head. Frustration rode him hard. Unable to sit still, he rose shakily to prowl around the cabin.

Fan swung around on the nail-keg stool. "Irons, they came in here expecting me to roll over for them and sign the lease. They were flabbergasted when I refused. I was scared, but I was determined to protect what we'd built. So the men and I ran them off. I thought you'd be proud."

He stared down into her upturned face. "You're a damn fool," he said softly. His own face contorted. With some difficulty he bent his injured arms at the elbow. His bandaged hands and swollen, discolored fingers were inches from her eyes. "Look here. You want this to happen to you? They play rough, baby. Damn rough."

"I know that. The man who came today had riders with him just like Weisberg did. They wore guns."

"Damn right."

"But we drove them off," she insisted stoutly.

He cursed and stalked away, swinging his arms, looking for something to hit, frustrated because he dared not hit anything. "As long as I could protect you. As long as I was whole, I could be pretty sure everything was going to turn out all right, but now . . ."

"Irons . . ." She rose and came after him.

He gave a wordless growl as he lifted his hands again and stared at them with agonized eyes. In his helplessness he could not even clench his fists. Furiously determined to prove his point, he reached for his gun strapped to her waist. He could not close his fingers around the butt.

Pain made him curse. His storm-gray eyes were dark and filled with fury and despair. "I got you into this. When this all started, I wouldn't let you sign because I thought I could fight them. I never imagined I'd be crippled like this. Why I can't even get out of this cabin without kicking the door down. What happens if they come tonight and set the place on fire?"

She grinned at him, the light of battle in her eyes. "Then we fight. Hoke and Clell and Brazel and Early and me. That's five of us. We can hold them off."

He cursed again. The words were groans uttered deep in his throat, pain in every syllable. "You baby. You damned stupid baby child. I'm helpless. Don't you understand? I'm totally helpless. I can't feed myself. I can't dress myself. Nor undress myself to take a leak. I can't protect myself. And worse than that I can't protect you."

She caught him by the shoulders and held him still. "Irons. Stop this. Stop it."

"But goddamn it . . ."

"Stop it!" She slapped his face.

He drew back with a snarl, then relaxed, his face white except for the slight pinkening on his cheek. "You see," he said with quiet fury, "I can't stop a little bit of a thing like you from slapping me around."

She snorted. "If you think that was a slap, you don't know much."

His lips curled back from his teeth. "You're enjoying this, aren't you? Turnabout's fair play, I guess."

"Irons!" She clenched her fists struggling for control. Her own anger built to meet his. How could he be so difficult? "Stop carrying on like a crazy man," she said calmly, though her jaw ached with the effort. "I just sort of tapped you. I certainly didn't slap you around. I had to get your attention because you've worked yourself into a frenzy. You weren't thinking straight."

He pressed his lips tight together. A muscle leaped in the corner of his jaw, but he waited.

She took a deep breath. "Now listen to me. You're going to be all right. Another month and you'll be back to taking care of me. Until then I'll take care of you. No one's going to take what's ours."

"You don't understand." His storm-gray eyes concentrated on a spot beyond her shoulder.

"Yes, I do." She put her hand against the spot where she had struck him and turned his head until he was looking at her. "Yes, I do," she repeated. Liquid gold swam in her eyes. "I understand perfectly. Because I felt the same way just a few weeks ago. I was helpless. So helpless that I couldn't remember my own name. I *was* like a baby. And you took care of me. But I'm not a baby anymore, even though you seem to think so. And I'm not going to abandon you now that you're my baby."

Her tender confession was lost on him. He shook his head, belligerence in every line of his body. "I tell you, you don't understand. And when you hear, you won't want to stay." He twisted away from the comfort she offered. Quick, deliberate strides took him across the cabin until his back was to the door. The expression in his eyes was that of a man about to ascend the gallows.

She smiled with no humor. "You don't have to tell me."

"Yes, I do." He swallowed hard. "And you have to listen. I didn't do this for you. I did it for me. Hell! You were just a poor dumb baby. You were easy, so easy for me to set up. You didn't know a thing. I only had to touch you and you were hot for it."

Instant color rose in her face at his crude words. She ducked her head.

"You don't like to hear that, but it's the truth. Even half dead you were ready, willing, and able. And after you woke up, you were hot as a two-dollar pistol." He broke off to stare mulishly at the floor. His chest heaved as he drew in a shuddering breath.

"Go on," she said tonelessly. "I'm learning things I didn't know. Let me hear the rest of it."

He looked at her doubtfully as if perhaps he wished he could take back some of what he had said. Then he shrugged and went on. "All right. I used you because I could. You were so scared, you'd do anything to keep from being thrown out into the street. And I could tell you anything I wanted to and you'd believe me."

The silence grew between them. Neither could look at the other. Embarrassment flamed in Fan's cheeks. She put a shaky hand to her mouth pressing back a sob, then asked in a quavery voice, "Are you through?"

"No," he growled.

"I think you've said enough."

"I haven't even got started. Let's get this out in the open so you can at least have a fair chance to decide whether or not you want to get yourself killed. I didn't do anything out of the goodness of my heart except bring you into town. After that, I took everything that came my way."

She shook her head. "You didn't."

"The hell I didn't. Why didn't I take you to some nice ladies and let them take care of you? Why didn't I take you to the Methodist Church in Batson? It wasn't much of a ride."

"You were trying to find out who I was. And I was afraid to leave you. I begged to let me stay with you."

"And I'd have been a fool not to. I was getting laid every night I wanted it. My clothes were clean and mended. Hell, I didn't even have to pay room and board for you. You scrubbed floors for the two dollars a week."

"I chose to."

"No!" He rocked back on his heels. "No. Don't you see? You didn't have a choice. Because of who you were. I had you figured out from almost the first moment I laid eyes on you. Silk and lace nightgown and all.

"I had a few bad minutes when that brother-in-law of yours turned up, but he'd hardly opened his mouth before I'd figured he wasn't a damn bit better than I was."

"Irons." Fan begged. "Please . . ."

"No." He leaned forward again. "No. I went to Rosemeade. I saw that place. Your clothes were in a bedroom at the head of stairs. Right next to the one with a man's clothes in it. You were the wife of that man. I'd swear to it. That was your house. And your brother-in-law had taken it over."

"Oh, Irons."

"But did I tell you? Did I go get that dumb sheriff and the two of us go over there and find out who really inherited that plantation that was going to rack and ruin? No, I bundled up your clothes in a couple of bedsheets. Your sheets. And brought them back to you, to this shack and let you live in it and cook and clean for five men."

She looked at him then with understanding in her eyes. "For an oil well?"

"Damn right."

"I see."

"Finally." His forehead was beaded with sweat. He lifted his splinted hand to his mouth but let it drop in disgust. He took a deep breath.

She wrapped her arms across her chest. "Irons, I'm glad you told me all this, but I had already figured out most of it for myself."

"What?"

"My mother didn't raise any stupid girls," she told him flippantly. "I had even become suspicious of you, thinking that you might mean to do me some real harm when the well came in. Now I know you aren't going to hurt me. I feel better."

He shook his head as if he doubted his hearing. Silence fell between them. At last he spoke. "Well, I'm glad you're glad. But it doesn't change anything. I'm still crippled."

"So what?"

"So what you need to do is climb on that buckskin tomorrow and ride into Batson and find Weisberg or Glennville or whoever they're working for and sign that lease quick."

"And then what?"

"Get out of the way."

"What will happen then?"

"We'll clear out and they'll come in."

"And what will happen to you and all the pipe and the equipment?"

"We'll pick it up and move somewhere else."

"What about all the fuel and the drill bit and . . ."

"Damn it, woman!" He waved his bandaged hands in front of his face. The tendons in his neck strutted in his anger and frustration. "I've told you. We've cheated you."

"I don't see how you've cheated me, if you're drilling a well for me."

He reached for her, but could do no more than clap her shoulders between the splints on each wrist. He loomed above her, his mustache fairly bristly. "I should have taken you over to that plantation. You'd have stood up for your rights."

Fan lifted her chin. "If you feel so strongly about that, you can take me over there next month."

"If you live that long?"

"I'll live that long," she assured him. "We'll all take care of ourselves. Then next month after those bandages come off, you and I will ride over to the plantation house and see this room that you claim was mine. My esteemed brother-in-law and his friend have left town. I imagine the house is still standing."

He shook his head, but she put her hand on his cheek again. Emotion welled within her. Her eyes were moist as she kissed him softly on the corner of his mouth. "Until then," she whispered, lifting her lips away an inch, "you'll just have to let me baby you."

Two weeks later Irons stopped his friend on his way out of the cabin after lunch. "Take these damn things off."

Clell stared at the splinted hands. "You're not healed yet."

"I don't give a damn. Take 'em off."

"Why, for God's sake? You'll just hurt yourself. Even with them off you can't use broken arms and fingers."

"The hell I can't."

Clell moved to put the table between him and Irons. "I'm not going to do it. Fan'd kill me."

"Rather her kill you than someone kill her. Take 'em off. I want to be ready for them when they come back."

Clell shook his head.

"Clell, damn it. Do I have to call in someone else to do this for me?"

Reluctantly, the one-armed man leaned forward eyeing the bandages critically. "I'm not sure I can untie everything."

"Bullshit. You can dress and undress yourself including tieing your neckerchief." Irons' scowl was pure acid.

Silently, his ears listening for footfalls that might signal Fan's return from her stint on the rig. Clell plucked at the knotted strips of gauze. In minutes they fell away, the splint clattered to the table.

"You're sure about this?" Clell asked. The under bandages were a sorry sight, stained with blood and matter that had seeped from the wounds in the skin. Clell wrinkled his nose.

Irons clamped his teeth. "Get on with it."

When at last the hand was exposed, it was terrible to see. Fingers and thumb were still swollen, the broken ones exceptionally so. Blood had seeped into the hands from the broken tissue leaving the skin dark purple.

Irons dropped down at the table, his face pale.

"Want me to go on?" Clell wanted to pointedly. He reached for the knot at the wrist.

"Leave that. Tie it off there."

A little clumsily, Clell tucked the gauze. "You'll have to get her to tie it tight."

"Now the other."

The left hand was less broken than the right. It looked a little better, but only by comparison.

Clell shot his friend a quick look, but Irons' face was rigid. With a sigh Clell leaned back against the wall of the cabin.

Irons sat forward, his elbows on the table. With teeth set he forced the fingers of his right hand to clench. Sweat stood out on his forehead. Almost half a minute elapsed before the four fingers could bend sufficiently to touch the center of the palm and straighten again. Then Irons looked at his friend. "God."

"Want me to put the splints back on 'em?"

"No."

"Fan'll kill me."

"She's not so tough," Irons sneered. The pain was making him nauseated. "You're just soft." With blind stubbornness, he repeated the bending with his left hand. Perspiration dripped down the side of his face. He ducked and wiped it on the sleeve of his shirt.

"Better take it easy," Clell advised at last. "You'll do more harm than good."

"Damn it. I've got to get these limbered up. At least if I can use my hands, I can shoot." He rotated his wrist and tried to form his fingers and thumb into the configuration necessary to grip a gun butt and pull a trigger. The index finger refused to work independently. He cursed.

Unable to bear more, Clell edged to the door. "I'd better get back out there. I don't want to be here when she finds out. She'll have a fit."

Irons grinned raggedly. "She'll get over it."

"You're braver than I am. Or a bigger fool. You haven't seen her on that rig. She's figured it all out. And now she's all over it. Just as cheerful as you please. Sweat and grease don't phase her. She swipes it away and goes on."

"She's not going to be doing it but a few more weeks," Irons promised direly.

Clell grinned. "Don't make book on it. She never slowed us down a time. Hoke was a lazy so-and-so and she shows him up bad. We can put in another pipe in less than a minute."

Irons shook his head. "She's a fool to be out there in the first place. I told her so. She's got to be protected from herself." He clenched both hands at the same time. His lips pulled back from his teeth. His anguished breath hissed between them.

Clell came back to his side. "Don't be a damn fool, Irons. You can't help us until those breaks heal. You'll just slow 'em down if you keep doing that."

"I'll be all right. I know what I'm doing."

Clell patted his friend's shoulder. Talking to Irons was like talking to the wind. "We've got things pretty much under control, ever since she ran off Glennville. I don't expect that they'll be back any time soon. They've tried everything short of actually sending a dozen men out here for a shoot down. And we're too small for them to want to try that. I think it's about over. They've got bigger fish to fry than us."

"You sound like she's been talking to you," Irons snorted angrily.

"Well, we do talk a lot. She wants to know everything. And she's easy to talk to because she doesn't forget what she's been told. She's one of the best roughnecks I've ever had. If she were a man, she'd be a driller in six months. Just naturally."

"For God's sake, Clell. She's a woman," Irons exploded, flinging himself out of the chair. "Don't forget that. She's in danger every day she's out there. She might fall. She might get mangled. She might get shot."

Clell looked at his friend, a slow smile spreading across his face. "She's sure important to you, isn't she?"

Irons gaped at him, then looked away. "Hell, no. She's not important to me. Not at all except that this is her property. Something happens to her, we don't have a leg to stand on. I just don't believe in killing the goose that lays the golden egg."

"Sure." Clell chuckled. "You're right. I'd better get back out there. Take it easy on those hands, Irons. We're doing okay." Pulling his hat forward off the back of his head, Clell walked out, leaving Irons to fret.

Wagon ruts crisscrossed the lane leading up to Rosemeade's stately portico. A section of whitewashed fence had been torn down, its boards thrown aside. In the center of the pasture a rig rose eighty feet into the air. For a radius of twenty-five yards the grass was gone, replaced by mud pit, draw works, and miscellaneous equipment.

Fan frowned and pressed her fingertips to her temple where the throbbing began faintly.

"Any of this look familiar?" Irons asked cynically.

"Where are the horses?"

"Were there horses there?"

"Of course. Beautiful ones. Fine horses." She paused, her mouth framing the word "my."

The wagon bumped across the ruts and executed a neat circle before the portico of Rosemeade. The same window was up that had been up when Irons had come before. He did not comment but watched her closely as she fastened the reins around the brake and climbed down. He jumped down himself and came around to walk with her up the steps.

The same mud only deeper caked the steps.

"This isn't right," Fan muttered.

"Do you remember this?"

"Yes . . . Yes, I do."

She reached for the doorknob, but he put his hand on her wrist. "Better let me go first." His teeth set, he managed to pull his gun.

"For heaven's sake," she said irritably. "I told you. I watched them leave town."

"We're breaking into a house," he reminded her. "Who knows what we might find? Or who?"

She opened the door and stepped inside. He followed her, slid around the transom and stood back to the wall, listening.

She looked down at the floor, then gasped. "The carpet!"

"Looks like your brother-in-law didn't care about this place."

"Mrs. Gonzales would never let this happen."

"Oh. Mrs. Gonzales."

"The housekeeper. She's been with Paul's family for years. She and her husband . . ." She stopped, her breath catching in her throat.

A burly man leaped to his feet from where he had been snoozing on the horsehair sofa in the living room. He swayed slightly as he pulled himself out of sleep, then came toward them gesturing angrily. "What the hell you doin' in here? This here's private property."

Stepping in front of Fan, Irons pulled his gun and swung it in a quarter arc to train it on the man's belly. "Pyote," he grated, "as I live and breathe. Right on top of the situation as usual."

Pyote swayed, shaking sleep from his eyes and swiping a hand across his jaw where he had drooled while he snored. "What the hell you doin' in here?" he repeated.

"Mrs. Breckenridge came to inspect the property."

"Oh, she did." The burly man blinked owlishly as Fan stepped out from behind Irons. Light from the open doorway shone on her features.

Pyote staggered back a step. "Miz Breckenridge!" He looked accusingly at Irons. "Why'd you bring her here?"

"I asked him to come to help me carry some of my things," Fan said easily.

"This house don't belong to you no more."

"But it doesn't belong to you either. So what are you doing here?"

"Mr. Breckenridge left me in charge. I'm the caretaker."

"I can see what care you're taking." She gestured toward the mud on the carpet.

Pyote did not act as if he knew what she was talking about.

"What do you want me to do with him, Mrs. Breckenridge?" Irons asked.

Sensing himself about to be trapped, Pyote scooted out of the parlor and around beneath the staircase. "You're not gonna do nothin' with me. I'm gettin' some of the boys."

"I didn't see any of the boys as I rode up. Only roughnecks. They wouldn't be interested in leaving their jobs to come and help the caretaker," Fan said silkily.

The man shook his head. He stretched one shaking hand out before him to ward off trouble. "You done lost your mind. Mr. Breckenridge tol' me so."

"But I'm remembering more and more every minute," Fan told him.

Nervous because he was unarmed, Pyote backed away. "Damn."

Irons laughed nastily. He gestured with his own gun from its holster and aimed directly at Pyote's chest.

"Shee—utt!" Pyote flung his heavy body against the door at the back of the entry hall. It cracked open, and he thundered through a short hall and through a swinging door at the end. They could hear his progress as another door banged and then his footsteps died away.

"Why did you scare him like that?" Fan demanded angrily. "He might have told us something important."

Irons shrugged. "We can always pick him up later. If he's got anything to spill, it'll fester. The longer he has to worry, the easier he'll be to crack."

"I'm not so sure of that." She tilted her head to the side to look at Irons. Why had he let Pyote escape?

Irons let his gun slide into his holster and came back to her. "See anything that looks familiar?"

She looked around her. Despite the mud and oil that stained the filthy carpet, the house looked very familiar. She crossed slowly to the archway. "Parlor. Beyond that the dining room. Bedrooms upstairs. Kitchen down that hall behind the swinging doors. I think that's right, but I could be just imagining what any house would be like." She shook her head. "It's hard for me to tell whether I'm remembering or just knowing stuff."

"Think hard," he suggested. "Surely there's something you can remember that's one of a kind. Something so ugly or so beautiful that it's the only one of its kind."

She rubbed the heels of her hands in a circular motion over her temples. "Something ugly. The only one of its kind. Suddenly she burst out laughing. "I think . . ." She pointed to the parlor. "There's the most hideous table in there. It's a piece of wood riding on the back of a stuffed alligator."

Irons chuckled. "If that thing's there then we know this is your house. Nobody could make something like that up."

He opened the door. Together they walked into the room. No sunlight filtered through the drawn draperies. The room was dim and smelled musty.

"Can you see it?" She brushed past him, found the pulls and drew the draperies open with a dusty swish. In front of the horsehair sofa was a large, low, dusty table. The two of them stared at it together.

Irons whistled in amazement. "I'm here to tell you that I've been from San Francisco to Habana, and I've never seen anything that ugly before."

She laughed richly. "And you're sure that you've never seen another one like it?"

"Lord, no."

"Then I remember this house." She patted the top of the table. "And this is the proof."

"If this is a sample of the rest of the furniture, I'm not sure you want to remember." Irons went down on his haunches to stare at the monstrosity. The body of a six-foot alligator, stuffed and glistening with many coats of varnish, was curved in a circle, its tail almost touching its right front claw. A six-inch-thick slab of cypress, also highly varnished rode its back and head. Its wide mouth gaped open, displaying rows and rows of yellow teeth lining a leather maw. Its marble eyes gleamed malevolently from the shadows.

"Rex would never let me get rid of it. His grandfather bought it for his grandmother in New Orleans."

"He must have hated her."

She nodded. "Beyond the parlor is a small room that

Rex used for an office.'' She looked at Irons uncertainly.

He sketched a bow. ''After you, Mrs. Breckenridge. The caretaker's deserted his post. You've won the first battle without firing a shot.''

Everything in the parlor had a thick coating of dust. ''I can't imagine where Mrs. Gonzales is. She would never let this happen.''

''Maybe she was too concerned about you to suit your brother-in-law.''

''Maybe, but she was loyal to the family. Not to me. I come from . . . San Antonio,'' she murmured. ''And from time to time I visited on a ranch. I remember a ranch. A place called El Rincón.''

''The hidden valley,'' Irons translated for her.

''Yes, an old Spanish land grant. Of course, I only spent summers on it. My parents live in San Antonio.''

She said the words slowly as if they were a tale told by someone not sure of the language.

''And their name?'' he prompted.

''Gillard.'' She clasped her hands tight around her body. ''My name is Caroline Fancy Gillard. My mother's name is Fair-Eleanor Christine Gillard and my father is a lawyer. E. C. Gillard. Have you heard of him? E. C. His friends call him Cash. That's his real name.'' She was laughing now. ''My father's real name is Edward Cash Gillard. I remember. I remember.'' She put her hands on Irons' shoulders and hugged him hard. ''I remember. I remember.''

Chapter 18

His mouth split in a grin as he closed his aching arms around her and kissed her hard. His tongue slid into her mouth tasting the pleasure after so many weeks of fearful uncertainty.

"I remember," she cried at last, throwing her head back. "It's like waking up after a long sleep. I'm awake and free. I remember."

"Sure you do, baby. I always knew you'd get it back. A little patience, a little time to heal . . ." He kissed her again, unwilling to let her go, sharing her joy, reveling in the passionate length of her pressed against him. He could feel himself quickening.

Like a child desperate to recite before it forgot its piece, bits of her lost identity came tumbling out of her. "My name is Caroline Fancy Gillard. I married Rex Breckenridge three years ago. He came to San Antonio for a fiesta. My father didn't like him. My mother had bad dreams about him. But I married him and came here to Rosemeade. I have two brothers and a sister. I'm the youngest."

She broke away from him and hurried to the window. "My Uncle Rand, my father's cousin, and my Aunt Free—I have an aunt named Free—came to the wedding and brought me a horse. They raise some of the best horses in Texas. My horse should be out there in that pasture. But now the pasture is just a mud pit for that damned oil well."

He grinned at her passion and excitement. Gone were the last traces of cowering uncertainty. "We'll find it."

"Her. A mare."

"We'll find her."

Her eyes drifted to the ceiling. "My room is directly above us."

He nodded. "Right. Leastwise that's where I found your clothes. The bed was kind of a mess."

She shuddered, looking around her helplessly. "I don't know where to start."

"Why don't you look in the office first?" he suggested, reaching out to take her hand. It was cold, the palm moist. "Come on. If there's a will, or some sort of deeds of entitlement, they'll be in there."

"You're right. Of course. First things first."

The desk was a disappointment. A couple of drawers hung open. Papers overflowed them and were stacked untidily on the floor. A couple of file boxes lay open, their contents divided between the box and the lid. "Looks like your esteemed brother-in-law's made a mess in here."

She lowered herself tentatively into the leather chair behind the desk. "This place always looked this way. Believe it or not, it hardly looks touched. It used to drive me wild. Rex didn't care anything about office work. When I dared, I'd come in and try to straighten things up, but Rex always got angry. He'd get furious when I'd suggest that he pay bills."

"It's a hell of a way to run a railroad."

She sifted through a stack of unopened envelopes. "These are all unpaid, and they're mostly Rex's.

Personal stuff. Tailors, haberdashers, hatters. From all over the country.'' She looked at some of the return addresses. ''Here's one from New York and another from Michigan. And these would get paid sooner than the bills for the plantation. Rosemeade was just running along, getting farther and farther into debt. Rex was good at avoiding bill collectors, but people had gotten to laying in wait for him on the road.''

Irons grunted. ''I wonder if some of them could have been mad enough to lynch him.''

Her mouth tightened. ''What a twist that would be. If they'd only known, they could have gotten their money from the oil. I don't suppose there's any use to look in the 'bank.' ''

Irons looked at her inquiringly. She grinned as she slipped out of sight behind the desk. On her knees, she pulled open the bottom drawer and released a spring at its back. The drawer came out completely, and she dropped down on her knees to feel inside the foot of the pedestal. ''It's gone,'' she reported. ''I guess you can never be too rich.'' With a sigh she sat back on her heels and dusted off her hands.

While she was out of sight, Irons dropped his head and sank shakily into a chair. With exquisite care he placed his hands on his knees. From shoulder to fingertips, he ached like thunder, but he dared not admit his helplessness. Most in need of his skills with a gun, he had bluffed his way through a terrifying encounter. If Pyote had not run, Irons knew he could not have cocked the .45.

Moreover, his fear had been doubled when he had caught sight of the ring flashing on Pyote's little finger. The shape of a crescent moon was hammered into the gold on top of the bezel. Slim chance of another like it anywhere around.

The scar on Fan's cheek was the same shape. Of course, it might be a coincidence. The cut might have been made by almost any kind of circular object including the muzzle of a gun. Still he had looked at it and the cold sweat had broken out on his body. If Pyote attacked, if he tried to correct his mistake, Irons would have been virtually helpless to defend her.

Coming here today had been a mistake, for she had told Pyote that she had regained her memory. The gunman might decide to ensure his own safety by killing her. Irons gritted his teeth and flexed his hands. He must regain their strength. He must.

Meanwhile, Fan sifted through another stack of unopened mail. "Feed bill. Tax statement. Farm and ranch equipment. Houston. San Antonio. Waco." She shuffled through them noting the return addresses. "I would have thought Paul would have taken care of these before he left." Suddenly, she picked up a letter again. "This one's addressed to me. And this one. And this. These are my letters. Why do you suppose Paul didn't send them to me?"

Irons' sigh was almost a groan. "Probably didn't give a damn." He looked nervously at the sunlight moving across the faded carpet. "It's getting on toward the end of the afternoon. We need to get a move on."

Nodding Fan quickened her pace. Carelessly she tossed correspondence of all kinds into an open drawer, keeping out only ones addressed to her. Finally, she reached the bare desktop. With a sigh she tucked her letters into the pocket of her jacket. "Let's go upstairs."

"You go," he said through set teeth. "I'll wait down here."

"Irons, are you all right?"

"Sure, I'm fine. Just don't think we both ought to be upstairs, in case Pyote comes back."

Fan stood in the center of what had been her room. Memories uncomfortably clear and sad came tripping back. Some of her unhappiest moments had been spent here. Here she had lost her illusions about love and caring. Here she had discovered that all Rex Breckenridge really wanted from his wife was a compliant body on which to visit his lust.

In this very bed she had awakened to terror. From it she had been dragged screaming and fighting. In pitch darkness she had been abducted with her husband. The two of them had been taken away to die. Somehow she had been spared.

Shudders began to course through her. With her restored memory came terrifying pictures. The masked faces. The terrible cold. The bruising ride. The stench of their unwashed bodies heightened by their perverse excitement.

And pain. Memory re-created the pain in her chest when she tried to hoist Rex by the knees. She lifted her finger to her cheek, tracing the crescent-shaped scar. It would mar her face for the rest of her life. She hurried to the mirror over the chest of drawers. The fading red mark seemed to blaze like a brand on her white skin. She gritted her teeth in silent rage.

Then she dropped her face into her hands. At least she could feel the scar. Rex would never feel anything again. Turning away, she stared at the stripped bed, at the feather pillows still in their cotton and lace cases. She tried to summon up a memory of Rex and his lovemaking. None of it was very clear.

Irons. She could remember Irons and his strong thighs and wide chest. And how he made her feel.

Bracing herself, she walked across the hall to Rex's room. It was bare. The wardrobe stood open. The expensive suits and boots and hats were gone. When she opened the chest of drawers, she found it empty too. The starched shirts so carefully tended by Mrs. Gonzales, the linen handkerchiefs, the fine-loomed cotton underwear—everything was gone.

Poor Paul. The memory of his older brother must have preyed upon him. He must have given the fine clothing away?

She slid the mahogany drawer closed and walked out of the room. With the sense that she left nothing of herself behind, she closed the door and walked swiftly down the stairs.

"Irons?"

The chair creaked in the office and he came slowly in to meet her. "About ready?"

"Just a minute." Back into the parlor she went. On a mahogany table before the window she stopped before a collection of photographs in silver frames.

Eyes misty with tears, she lifted the picture of her mother and father. The sight of their dear familiar faces was like pain. Her mother so small, her dark hair piled on top of her head in the latest style, the high collar of her dress trimmed with Chantilly lace. Her father, handsome, strong, deep lines at the corner of his mouth and eyes, his age only beginning to tell on him in the camera's relentless eye. She pressed them to her heart.

Another photograph caught her eyes. Another silver frame. The picture of Rex and her on their wedding day. She sat in her virginal white, the appliquéd white lace flowers decorating the train, with her sister's veil billowing around her. Did her expression look a little strained?

Hand proprietarily placed on her shoulder, Rex stood beside her in his morning suit, his handsome face unsmiling. His mouth thinned, his eyes narrowed, anticipating the flash powder. Of course they had posed for the photographer until both were tired.

Poor Rex! Smooth-shaven, a handsome man, a year younger than she. She concentrated on his face. He was so much like Paul. The resemblance would have been more striking had not Paul chosen to wear a close-clipped beard to hide the scar on his chin.

She set the photograph back on the table. The handsome young man had died horribly. The girl no longer existed. The woman that remained bore only a superficial resemblance to her. Gently, she turned the picture face down. "Rest," she whispered to them. "Rest."

"Fan?" Irons asked from the door.

"Coming."

He nodded toward her parents' picture in her hand. "Got everything?"

She smiled. "Everything except my mare. And if she's not in the stables or in one of the corrals, then Paul Breckenridge had better look out."

At the front door she paused to look back. The filth and neglect were even more apparent at a second glance. Spiderwebs festooned the chandelier. She took a last look through the open door into the parlor. The alligator table caught her eye. "I suppose I ought to take that," she said with a perfectly straight face. "We could use it back at the cabin to give the place a little feeling of home. And after all, it did make me remember."

Irons' mouth dropped open. He was already shaking his head when he caught the gleam in her eye. He took a step toward the thing and nodded sagely. "I sure am glad you thought of it because I'm real taken with it myself. It's got to be worth a lot of money sometime down the road. I've been studying about how to get it back there."

"You mean we can't just carry it home between us?" She thrust out her lower lip.

"Now don't get upset. We'll get it tomorrow. We'll ask Early to ride by on his way home from the Boomin' Bessie." He held the door for her. "It can go in our bedroom."

"Her name is Santa Justina," she told Irons, "but I call her Tina. Poor baby," she crooned. "I'll bet nobody's even so much as exercised you since I've been gone." The sorrel whickered softly in recognition and put her nose into Fan's hand. Her dark mahogany hide was rough and dirty with neglect. Even ungroomed, the color was a startling contrast to the pale blond mane and tail.

Irons put his hand along the arched neck. "She's a beauty," he admitted. "Sure makes Pet look plain. That's some wedding gift."

"Oh, the MacPhersons and the Gillards of El Rincón are famous horsebreeders. All their horses are named for saints."

Irons looked blank.

"I can surely tell you're not a Texan born and bred. Everyone's heard of them. The 'sainted horses of El Rincón.' They've been famous in ranching since before Texas became a Republic. The ranch was a land grant from the King of Spain. It'll stand so long as Texas stands."

She opened the gate and led the mare through by her hackamore.

"Here! What y' doin'?" A lanky man came hurrying across from one of the cabins. "You leave that horse alone."

"Who are you?" Fan countered.

"I'm in charge, that's who."

"I don't remember you. Where is Addams?"

The man's eyes shifted to the ground, to the sky, to left and right. "He quit."

"Addams! Surely not. He's been here for thirty years. Why he taught both Paul and Rex Breckenridge to ride."

The man wavered, then straightened, setting his shoulders belligerently. "Well, to tell the truth, he was let go."

Fan exchanged an amazed glance with Irons. "Why?"

"We didn't need so many hands anymore, what with the oil and everything." He pointed to a couple of derricks rising above the stable. "This place is settin' right square on top of a lake of oil. No more farmin' and runnin' cattle. Just drillin'."

Fan became aware of the donkey engines, a drone that filled the air. No doubt several crews of men were bunked down in the cabins where once farm workers and their families lived. "But who takes care of the horses?"

"I guess I do. I've always liked 'em."

She smiled sweetly at him. "I'm obliged to you then because this is my horse. My mare Tina. I'm taking her."

The man studied the sorrel, whose nose rested on the woman's shoulder. "I guess she's your'n all right. She's spooky around everybody else."

"Thank you. Would you saddle her for me, please?"

"What? Oh, I guess."

"I'll show you the tack."

In a minute she and Irons were walking their horses down the lane. "This is awful," she declared. "I know oil makes lots of money, but so does farming and ranching if they're done right."

"I'm thinking your brother-in-law thought he'd never need Rosemeade again except as an oil pool."

"But to let all the old people go. Mr. and Mrs. Gonzales and Mr. Addams. Those people had known him since he was a child."

"He let you stay with me," Irons reminded her. "He didn't give a damn about his own brother's wife. Why should he care about a housekeeper or a wrangler?"

"It's tragic."

"It's the way of the world."

"My mother and sister Faireine are both worried about me because I haven't written," Fan announced, looking up from the letters spread open on the kitchen table. "If I don't write by the end of the month, they're coming for a visit to find out what's wrong."

"Maybe you'd better write to them." Irons paused, looking directly at her. "On the other hand, maybe you'd better get the rest of your clothes packed and take the next train back to . . ."

"San Antonio."

"Damn right."

"With my tail between my legs."

"It's better to tuck it than get it whacked off." He put his arm around her and squeezed her rear. "Besides it's a nice tail. Chalk this up to experience. You learned a lot. And you didn't lose anything except a couple of months of your life."

"Three years of my life and my husband."

"I can see your grief," he remarked dryly. "You sure didn't care anything about that farm back there.

You walked out of there without a backward glance. What are you hanging around here for?''

She shook her head. The question was a valid one. Why did she want to stay here in this cabin with five men? She hated to think she wanted to stay because of Irons. But the truth was clear in her mind, if hidden on pain of death from him. She loved Irons. Loved the way he made her feel. Loved the strong will, the uncomplaining strength. Loved the gentle way he treated her. Loved the strange sense of ethics by which he operated. Loved the earthy sexuality that made her blood sizzle.

She loved even as she doubted him.

Why had he let Pyote escape out the back door? Irons' confession a couple of weeks ago had rid her of her doubts. Then today a new one had arisen. She shivered suddenly.

Irons felt the vibration. He put his other arm around and pulled her against his chest. ''Rabbit run across your grave?''

She looked up into his storm-gray eyes. The look out of them was piercing as he tried to read her thoughts. Nervously, she looked away. ''I don't know what you mean?''

''It's an old expression,'' he explained patiently. ''You broke out in goose bumps. Why?''

She fumbled for an answer, found one that no one could doubt. ''I . . . I was just thinking about the hanging. Even though I can remember a lot, I can't remember much about that night.''

He put his hand under her chin to keep her from ducking away from him. ''Sometimes if you have a choice between dark and light, dark's better.''

Annoyed, she lifted her chin higher. ''I was thinking about Pyote and what he might have said if he hadn't run away." She searched Irons' face trying to judge his reaction.

"You think I let him get away on purpose?"

"Did you?"

He caught his breath in the thick silence. Finally, he dropped his hand and slowly released her. A backward step, another. Then he turned on his heel and headed for the door.

"Irons! For God's sake. I'm trying to understand."

He hesitated. "Then understand this. That *hombre* had a ring on his pinky with a crescent moon on it."

"A crescent moon?"

He strode back to her. His hand slid around the back of her neck, his thumb sliding over the scar on her cheekbone. "It might—I'm just saying 'might'—have caused this."

She fell back away from him appalled. "And you did nothing?"

"What did you want me to do? Risk a gunfight with you the target?"

"But . . ."

"You think what you like, baby. I think you'd better get on reading your mail. The boys need me out there on the rig. They've probably added two or three lengths of pipe while we've been riding all over the countryside."

She jumped to her feet and caught up with him. "Irons, I only thought it for a second."

He twitched his shoulder violently, getting away from her hand, but she shifted her grip. Her hand closed over his forearm. He cursed.

"Irons."

"Damn it. That's mighty sore."

She pulled her hand away instantly. "I forgot."

He reached for the doorknob. She watched the bruised, scabbed hand try to close. It was badly swollen across the back, the fingers strutted. They could not form the necessary shape. He hissed a fierce, foul word.

She stared at the pitiful effort. Her hand flew to her mouth. "Oh, Irons, I'm sorry. I didn't realize. I didn't understand."

"Don't make a big deal out of it."

"You can't bend your fingers," she accused. "You couldn't have squeezed a trigger if you'd wanted to."

"It's the end of the day," he snapped. "It begins to stiffen up and swell some." She put her arm across his shoulders, but he shrugged her off. Putting both hands on the knob, he managed to turn it. "I'll be back later."

She returned to the table furious with herself. She could have come nearer to stopping Pyote than Irons could have done. Yet he had never complained of the pain. He had spoken the truth when he said she would have been in danger there in the house. But she knew he would have gone after Pyote and brought the man back if he had been able.

What strange twisted pride that would have him let her think ill of him rather than admitting that he could not use his crippled hands! That same pride would have driven him out into the night hurting. She would never had known had she not been close enough to see with her own eyes.

"Oh, Irons," she whispered. "Irons. You fool."

She shook her head. Whatever he was, she felt a wave of love so potent that it shook her. This man whom she hardly knew had taken her heart. Besides her very life, she owed him the flowering of her womanhood. With returning memory had come the realities of the less than wonderful days of her marriage bed. She had never learned such joy with Rex Breckenridge's inept lovemaking.

The thought of Breckenridge made her quiver. What

dark secrets did Pyote keep? Desperately she plumbed her memory for the relationship between the brothers. Pyote had worked for them both. She had hardly noticed him among the half score others employed at Rosemeade, now all inexplicably dismissed.

Her fingertips traced the raised pink skin. A crescent moon? She shook her head. It was a common shape. Other things might have made it, the sight of a gun barrel for one. Yet she remembered him more often talking to Rex than to Paul. Could others have noticed him? Could he have been paid to . . . ?

She shuddered. So much money to be made and so many greedy men anxious to make it. Even Irons. Even the man who made her love him with every fiber of her being.

When Irons made love to her, he caressed her body and turned it molten. He had once accused her of going up in flames. And she did, dissolving in crystal flames and springing from them triumphant as a phoenix.

". . . take the next train back to San Antonio," he had said. But she could not leave him now. She owed him too much, loved him too much. And he did not love her at all. Still he was worth staying with to discover his feelings. She smiled faintly. Perhaps she never would, but to go away now would leave a void in her heart that she would perhaps never fill.

In the early hours of the morning, Irons eased himself down on his side of the bed to pull off his boots. Placing them neatly together on the floor, he sat for a moment, slumped, his chin on his chest.

Behind him Fan sat up and put her arms around him. His shoulders and neck were cold and damp with dew. His cheek was bristly and he smelled of kerosene and hard-worked man. The heavy deltoids flexed beneath the smooth skin. She ran her palms over them, trembling inwardly as she did so. A slow delicious ache mounted in her thighs and belly.

"I thought you were asleep," he said huskily.

"I've been waiting for you." She stroked his cheek and ran her hand across his chest.

"Fan . . ."

In the cool darkness her lips found the corner of his. Her hands slid through the hair on his chest to his nipples, shaping and pinching them gently. They erected as he sighed and arched his back.

"Lie down," she whispered.

He flinched, moving his shoulders uneasily. "Now, listen, I came in here to sleep. I've got to take another tour in eight hours."

Her tongue traced the shape of his ear. She covered the opening with her lips and blew gently, hotly. Her fingernails flicked imperatively across his taut flesh.

He gasped, then tried again. "I'm tired . . ."

"When I'm through, you'll sleep like a log," she promised. Muffling his complaints with her mouth, she rose above him on her knees and wrapped herself around his shoulders. "I promise."

"You don't owe me anything," he protested.

"Shut up." The words entered his open mouth. She pushed him back against the pillow. Her hair fell around them like a curtain. Her nipples rubbed against the cold skin of his chest. "Just put your arms and hands out of the way."

"Fan . . ."

She began by kissing him on the face and swiftly moved down the column of his throat that pulsed and moved convulsively. His sweat tasted cold and salty. She ran her hands across his chest, finding his nipples easily and pinching the erect flesh. They were hard, their aureolas slightly swollen and pebbly. His chest rose and fell with his rapid breathing.

Her own excitement built with a curling pain in her belly. She could not keep still, but slid her knee between his thighs, loving the satin feel of his hair.

He groaned and lifted his hips as her knee pressed against the massed nerves between his legs.

"You like that, don't you?" she murmured.

"Yes." He groaned again, this time into her descending mouth as her tongue drove between his lips.

He lifted his arms, but she pulled her mouth from his. "No touching. Your hands are hurt. Remember."

Obediently, he let his arms fall back. She kissed him again, feeling the grin that spread his mouth. Straddling him, she placed the hot, moist opening of her body against his turgid manhood.

"God, Fan . . ."

"Sssh." She kissed him into silence, all the time sliding her hips over him. Her fingernails scored and pinched his nipples.

"I can't stand this," he groaned. He lifted his arms again, but she raised her head.

"Put 'em down," she growled. The pleasure points of her body, her nipples, her belly, the masses of nerves between her thighs throbbed and swelled. Every minute she tormented him was equal torment to herself.

The minutes passed in the heated darkness where she moved by instinct in the most ancient of dances.

At last his voice began to plead with her. "What do you want?" He kissed her. "I can't stand any more. Tell me what you want. I'll do whatever you want. I'll give you whatever you want. Whatever you ask."

His words tore at her, uttered as they were from the heights of passion and longing. Tears slid down her cheeks. She set her mouth against his. "Then don't hold back,'' she told him between kisses. ''Trust me. I'll take care of you.''

''No!''

''Why not?'' Her question was muffled. Her lips trailed down his neck nipping at the skin that was no longer cold, but warm and dry.

''You don't trust me.''

''I trust you.''

''You thought I let that bastard go because I didn't want him caught.''

''I'm sorry for that.'' She did not still her hands, nor stop her mouth from caressing his chest and belly. She did not stop her hips from undulating. ''I can't help my doubts. But I do trust you. And, Irons . . .'' She let her mouth touch his swollen member, let her tongue slide over it to taste the first drop of moisture on its tip. ''Irons, I love you.''

He stiffened. His hands found her hair, scarred fingers slipping through the silken strands. He would have torn her away from him if he had been able.

She sat up suddenly. Her hand closed over his iron-hard member and guided it to her entrance, hot, wet with her own desire. With a cry she slid down over him. He answered her with a hoarse shout. His hips arched upward, lifted her with him.

The size of him hurt her. At the height of his penetration, she cried out again, afraid that she could not take him all.

One moment only and then they were locked together, vibrating in unison, their bodies one body. They were one magnificent beast that undulated and breathed a white-hot breath.

Chapter 19

Fan latched her fingers over the headboard, a rough-hewn slab of pine knocked into slots in the bedposts. Stretched above him, she had the leverage to fight back as Irons' violence, his deep resentment, his entrenched hostility toward all women erupted beneath her. He wanted to throw her off. He hated to need her, to want her so much that he would beg.

The words he had uttered tormented him. He heard her cry of pain, felt the muscles contract around him. He opened his eyes then to her white arms stretched above him.

"Let go," he sneered. Even as he commanded her, his hips lifted. His body acted blindly, refusing to deny itself the pleasure that she offered.

Her eyes were closed, her teeth set, her lips pulled back in a tortured smile. They were duelling. She knew it. Knew that he resented her demand, knew that he could not help wanting her.

He could not tear his eyes away from her white arms, her white throat and face, her white breasts so close to him. "Let go," he commanded.

"Trust me." The words slid out between her teeth. "You have to trust me."

He shifted from side to side, his whole body moving in negation. The movement brushed the mass of nerves at the base of her belly throbbing and swollen, the thin skin distended, stretched unbearably thinner. It drove her over the edge. Her body convulsed, then shattered into a million pieces.

Irons gritted his teeth and lunged up. Male called to female demanding to share the ecstasy, demanding not to be left behind. His heels dug into the mattress, his spine arched. And he followed her. Followed in a series of convulsions that all but stopped his breath, shook his limbs, left him lying beneath her, his breath coming shallowly from his dry throat.

A curl of black hair tickled her lips. The rhythm of the pillow of hard muscle slowed. Fan pushed herself up wearily on her elbows. "Did you enjoy yourself?"

In the dimness she could not see whether or not he was looking beneath his eyelashes. "Bitch."

As if his body had become a hot stove, she sprang up to hands and knees and tilted herself off him. With a dexterity she did not know she possessed, she avoided his sprawled arm and rolled onto her back, sliding her cramped legs under the covers. The only sound in the night was her harsh breathing as she stretched out and pulled the quilt up to her chin.

"Listen, baby." After long minutes his voice fairly grated out of his throat. "I don't trust anybody. Not anybody. Get me?"

"You're welcome," was her only reply.

"Hell. I don't thank people for getting what they want."

"You think the only reason I made love to you was because I wanted it?"

"Damn right, rich woman."

"Not that it matters, but I'm not rich."

"You don't know that."

"I do. Oh, my family would help me if I were in desperate need . . ."

"You don't call this desperate?" he sneered.

". . . but I don't intend to ask them for help to drill an oil well."

"What do you want an oil well for? Just go home to San Antonio. If you don't trust me, don't ride with me."

Suddenly, she could take no more. "Listen, baby," she stormed, her tone a mocking imitation of his own. "You're upset because I doubted you, but you've never believed in me."

"I believe in what I see with my own eyes. Nothing more," he grated. "You've stuck with me because you've needed me. Now you don't need me anymore. I'm no fool."

The injustice of his accusations wounded her. She could feel the tears starting in her eyes. Her whole body clenched as she willed no sound to come from between her clenched teeth. Stiff as a board she lay beside him, conscious that he lay stiff too.

Neither said another word. The dark cold hours stretched interminably.

The letter mailed from a lawyer's office in Charleston, South Carolina, and forwarded from San Antonio was the last one Fan opened. It was addressed to Mistress Caroline Fancy Gillard in a spidery old-fashioned hand. Steeling herself for a bill for some service for which she had no knowledge, she unfolded it.

My dear Miss Gillard,

As you are the direct lineal descendant of Caroline Fancy Gillard nee England (deceased) and bearer of the name of

Caroline Fancy, I, as executor of her estate, am desirous of meeting you and making you the heir to a sizable bequest.

It is with regret that I beg you to make the arduous journey from Texas to South Carolina, but my own declining health will not allow me to travel more than a few miles at a time. Likewise, its precarious state impels me to request that you make the trip without undue delay. I promise you it will be well worth your time and effort.

I enclose a train ticket and a letter of credit to defray your expenses incurred over the journey.

I remain your great-uncle,
Richard Gillard

She had to read the letter through twice before she could come to grips with its contents. Because of her name, a name she had never really liked, she was to receive an inheritance from a man whom she had never met.

She looked at the envelope again, studied the train ticket and letter of credit drawn on a Charleston bank. They were unquestionably authentic as was the letter which she turned over in her hand. Nowhere on the back was written "April Fool." She shook her head in wonder, a slow smile spreading across her face.

She had taken for granted that her father had relatives, knew they lived somewhere on the Atlantic Coast, but she had never met them. He had never visited. When his own father had died, he had not attended the funeral.

But the elder Gillard had died in Boston. Why was she receiving a letter from Charleston, South Carolina?

An inheritance. She sprang to her feet and twirled around the table. An inheritance from a relative she did not know. Would she be rich?

The idea made her hug herself hard. She was most

desperately in need of money, and here it fell into her lap. She sobered. She must not get her hopes up. It might be little or nothing at all.

She looked again at the ticket and letter of credit. More was involved here than a small bequest. The thought stirred her to activity. Pulling her grip from under the bed, she began to sort through her clothing, deciding which garments would be suitable for travel, which for meeting a long-lost uncle who wanted to leave her a bequest.

"I'm leaving in the morning," she announced at the supper table when Clell and Irons were both present. "Which of you will take me into Batson?"

Clell's fork clattered out of his hand; his smiling mouth drooped at the corners. "Fan," was all he said.

Irons' mouth, on the other hand, flicked upward in a sardonic smile. "Taking my advice about San Antonio, Miz Breckenridge? Good."

"Actually, I'm going to South Carolina, but I ought to be back in a couple of weeks."

Clell's smile appeared magically. "Taking a vacation?"

"No." Hands laced together, she leaned forward like a child with a secret she was anxious to share. "I've received an inheritance."

Both men stared at her openmouthed.

"Look." She sprang up from her chair and got the letter. She spread the three pieces out on the table before them. "Look. And look. And look."

Clell shook his head in wonderment. "I'll be damned. What do you know about that? Hey!" He slapped the table in delight. "I've never met anybody that ever did before. Can I touch you?"

With a gleeful chuckle she held out her wrist. "Just do it now. After I'm rich, I'll have to think about it."

He put his index finger on the back of her hand, then jerked it away as if she had burned him. "Whoo—e—e—e! Wow! That's great. Our troubles are over."

She nodded happily. "Of course. It's wonderful."

Like the skeleton at the feast, Irons tilted his chair back away from the table. His voice cut through their gaiety like a skinning knife. "Always supposing that Mrs. Breckenridge will be back with her money. Not likely, I'm thinking."

Clell swung around frowning at his friend. "Irons. Come on."

Fan's smile was saccharine sweet. "Why, of course, Mr. Irons. How nice that you understand me so well. I certainly should go on I suppose. I could leave this shack behind, get a new start. After all, why should I stay here where no one wants me?"

"Everyone wants you, Mrs. Breckenridge," Clell interposed. "Irons, don't be a bigger fool than you already are. She's needed here like nobody else in this whole crew."

"Mrs. Breckenridge doesn't need to be a roughneck anymore, Clell," Irons sneered contemptuously. His eyes never left Fan's face where bright red spots of anger rose on his cheekbones. "With money she can go anywhere, do anything. Why should she hang around here in this shack with the likes of us? After all, she doesn't know anything about us. We could be desperate criminals just waiting for a chance to kill her."

"Irons . . ."

"I suppose if it were left up to Mr. Irons, I'd go whether I have any money or not," Fan interrupted. "He's been trying to get me to go ever since he got those bandages off."

Clell rose, his face serious. "I think you both ought to calm down."

Fan leaned forward across the table, her eyes shooting yellow flames. "I think Mr. Irons wants me out of here at a crucial time."

"You don't belong here. You're liable to get your head shot off."

"You don't like women and you don't want me around."

"I'm not denying it."

"Irons!" Clell thundered. "Shut up!"

Fan rose too. Irons rocked forward in his chair. "I'm coming back!" she shouted. "You won't send me away from here. You tell me to make a new start for my life. But what better place to make a start than in an oil field with my own oil well in my own backyard?"

"That could be a dry hole."

"Pull the other one. We're getting good cuttings. Better and better each day." She put her hands on her hips, jeering at him. "You can't fool me about that. I've been out there on the monkey board more than you have."

Irons turned on his heel and stomped to the door.

Fan caught up the ticket and letters. "Clell, I'll need someone to take me into Batson tomorrow. While I'm gone, I expect you to keep the operation going. If any of the goons from Standard Oil come around, tell them they'll just have to wait until I come back. Tell them that I've gone to Houston to get fresh financing."

"Yes, ma'am."

"That'll hold 'em for a while."

Clell caught up with Irons at the corral. "What in hell do you mean laying into her like that?"

"She needs to go on down the road," Irons declared doggedly. "She's in danger here."

"We look after her." Clell defended her obstinately. "She's a grown woman. She doesn't have to lift a finger if she doesn't want to. She's got a right to stay here if she wants to. You practically booted her out the door."

"I was only thinking of her."

"As she says, pull the other one." Clell felt his own anger build. "Irons, I've never known you to be greedy."

The gray-haired man swung around, fists clenched. "My God, not you too."

"What?"

"She doesn't trust me either. I could expect something like that from her. Especially after all she's been through. But you and I have known each other for seven years."

Clell waited silently.

Irons vaulted over the corral fence.

"Where're you going?"

"I'm going to get drunk."

"Irons!" Clell climbed to the top and perched there watching as Irons caught Pet. "Maybe you'd better tell me what you're so upset about."

"She's in danger. She needs to get the hell out of this part of the country."

"Hell, yes, but she knows about the danger. And this is her place after all."

"It's not her place to act like a damn fool." Irons threw the saddle on Pet and reached under her belly for the girth.

Clell sat silent for a minute. "She didn't seem like a fool to me."

"That's all you know about it."

"Maybe you'd better tell me."

Irons turned, one hand cupped around the horn, the other doubled into a fist at his side. "She knows that Pyote character probably tried to kill her the night her husband died."

"Pyote? The one who didn't have sense enough to know whether his gun was loaded or not."

Irons shrugged. "That's the *hombre.* And just for your information, his gun was loaded. No one'll pull that bluff on him again. Paul Breckenridge is using him for a bodyguard now."

"How'd you figure out he tried to kill her? I didn't think she could remember anything about what happened that night."

"She can't. And that's probably God's mercy. But Pyote was in that house when Fan and I walked in on him. He started threatening and ordering us around, waving his arms and trying to bully. When we bluffed him into running, he told her she was crazy. I got a good look at a gold ring that he had on his left hand. It had a moon on top of it."

"A moon?" Clell was clearly puzzled.

"The same shape and size as the scar on Fan's cheek."

Clell let out a long low whistle between his teeth.

"Exactly. She got that the night her husband was killed. It was still bleeding when I found her."

"Then you think that her husband wasn't killed by Standard Oil?"

"I think his own brother had him done away with."

Clell shook his head. "Irons, that's coming on pretty strong."

"It all fits together. Pyote had to be working for someone. Standard Oil might have hired him as an outrider, but nothing else. He's too dumb. It had to be someone who stood to gain by Rex Breckenridge and his wife Fan being dead."

"But Fan wasn't killed."

"But she was beaten and left for dead. And that, Clell, sounds like something Pyote would do. He's too dumb to do a job right. Probably thought he'd killed her. She would have been, if she'd been any other woman. But she was just too stubborn to die." Irons laughed a little, then swore softly. "She's in danger, deadly danger. But she won't leave. And she's got a big mouth. Before I could get her attention about the ring, she started telling Pyote all about how her memory was coming back and she remembered everything. He lit out of there like a bat out of hell."

"You figure he ran to his boss with the news?"

"Had to've."

"She said a whore beat her up in Batson. It was the woman who left town with her brother-in-law." Clell volunteered the information in a troubled voice. "The hotel clerk broke it up before the other woman could stab or shoot Fan. That could have been because someone's mighty afraid that she's got her memory back."

"I don't doubt it." Irons swung up into the saddle. "I've got to get her out of this part of the country." He waved his injured right hand under Clell's nose. "I can't even make a fist with this, much less squeeze a trigger."

"God, Irons, I'm sorry."

"Now you're sorry." Irons leaned out of the saddle to slip the bar of the corral gate. As it swung open he guided Pet through. "I've got to get her to leave. And I'm not getting much help from any of my so-called friends." He turned the mare down the corral fence until he was even with Clell. "My friends," he said pointedly, "think I'm trying to cheat her."

"Irons . . ."

"Forget it, Clell. Just get her out of here tomorrow."

"I will."

"And don't be slow on the road. Pyote might take it into his head to try again."

"I can't tell you how delighted I am to make your acquaintance." The man sitting behind the huge mahogany desk held out his hand. "I do hope you'll forgive me, but it's such a struggle for me to hoist myself up onto my feet that I save it for times when it's absolutely necessary."

His voice was warm and wonderful, honey-tongued, as Fan had always imagined a gentleman of the Old South should sound. She smiled as she took the extended hand. It was dry, like paper, the veins gnarled. "Please keep your seat. I don't require a show of gallantry."

He smiled. His eyes were faded blue, his hair thin and white. He studied the woman across the desk from him minutely. The masses of black hair piled under a stylish bonnet, the delicate face, the great gold-colored eyes surrounded by black lashes. "You don't look very much like her," he observed regretfully.

Fan lifted her gloved hand to her cheek. "I'm sorry. My coloring is very much like my mother's. We have the same color eyes and hair."

"Your eyes are her color. Unusual to have that coming from both sides of your family. Unusual color. That same bright yellow gold. But she had red hair did my mother. Beautiful long red hair." The old man's eyes misted as the thought of his mother long dead hurt him. His head sank forward on his chest.

"My father has black hair too," Fan hurried to add.

"But you know that, don't you?" She looked at him anxiously.

He raised his head, his smile in place again. "Ah, yes. Your father. Cash. How is the boy doing? I think of him every so often. He had a fine mind for the law. A fine mind. Does he practice?"

"Yes. He's quite successful. People want him to enter politics in San Antonio."

"Councilman?" Richard Gillard suggested. "Representative?"

"Perhaps," Fan shrugged.

"Governor?" the old man chuckled wickedly. "That would certainly be a first for us."

"I suppose so." Fan looked at him curiously.

"Do you know that your great-great-great-grandfather was a pirate?" he asked point-blank.

"I heard that story once. I didn't know whether to believe it or not."

"Oh, you can believe it. It's true. We have a long and checkered family history. He was the gentleman pirate—Edward England." His eyes sought the map on the wall behind him. The fine white skin was drawn tightly across his cheek and jaw. Despite his fragility, he managed to look fierce and prideful. "The Scourge of the Madagascar Coast in the eighteenth century."

"Sounds like a cutthroat."

"The Scourge of the Madagascar Coast," Richard Gillard repeated, satisfaction and pride ringing in his voice. "His ship . . ." Here he caught Fan with a blue stare, one white eyebrow rising. "His ship was called the *Fancy*."

She started. "Is that where I get my name?"

"Yes. That's where you get your name," he said gently.

"I've always wondered. It was different. I've met some girls named Fanny, but never Fancy."

"It's the name of the plantation." Here his voice broke and wavered. His eyes watered, then his face became stern again. "England's Fancy. She's being sold. Broken up into parcels for small farms."

Fancy sat silent, not knowing what to say as he struggled with his pain.

He cleared his throat. "So I have a bequest for you."

"But surely there are heirs closer than I." Fancy looked doubtful. "Your own children. My father. I'm the youngest in my family."

"Oh, all the cousins will get their shares of the sale." Richard Gillard waved his hand as if they were of no consequence. "I'm writing myself out of the proceedings. By the time it's settled, I'll probably be pushing up the daisies anyway."

"My father?" she asked politely.

"To be sure. He'll get a share. And his sister, your Aunt Dulcy."

"My uncle Rand?"

A shadow passed across the old man's face. A bit of color brushed the high pale cheekbones. "My son will get a share," he repeated sternly.

Fancy took a deep breath. "You know I'm the youngest of four."

He leaned forward then, his hands steepled on his desk. "I know, my dear. I know that for a fact, for I know all about everyone in the family. I've made it my business to know. Everyone remembers that he's a Gillard. No one seems to remember that he was once an England."

"But . . ."

His old face was alight with admiration. "Your concern for the others does you credit, my dear. Your unselfishness is seldom seen in this day and time."

"I just want to be fair."

He raised his hand. "Humor me, my dear. I'm an old man. I have a gift for you from your great-grandmother, if you will accept it. It may even be important to you if you have a need."

The word "need" broke down her resistance immediately. "Oh, I need it. I need it desperately. My need is so great."

He smiled. "You must be very tired. You've spent four days on trains. I have made arrangements for you to stay in a friend's home. My own home, I'm afraid, is strictly an old bachelor's den. No women allowed."

She would have come around the desk to help him, but he waved her away. He rocked forward in his chair, gripped the arms tightly, and pushed himself up. His paper-thin nostrils dilated with the effort of sucking in enough oxygen. His back seemed to straighten one vertebrae at a time each requiring a painful adjustment. He chuckled a little breathlessly. "Being eighty-seven is much harder than being eighty-six."

A black man came behind them with a flatbed wagon. A second black man rode a horse and carried a shotgun.

In the old-fashioned carriage, Fancy sat beside Richard Gillard. The old man wore a topcoat and stovepipe hat. His hands were gloved in fine gray suede. He clasped them over the top of a gold-headed cane. The interior of the vehicle was warm despite the chilliness of the day, for the sun beat down on the black top. "I must apologize for the stuffiness," Gillard muttered. "Unfortunately, they tell me I don't have any bones anywhere that have any padding left in between them.

I positively creak when I walk. And when they get cold they stiffen."

"I'm fine," Fan assured him, surreptitiously patting her neck with her handkerchief. She looked out across the steam rising from the rich earth at the bend of the Edisto River.

Richard sighed again. "You're a very kind young lady. Young bodies need fresh air and sunshine no matter how cold the day. In my youth we would have ridden in a landau with the top down to the open air. Or more likely ridden horseback. We used to raise some wonderful horses on England's Fancy. Heavy hunters. Incredible stamina. Your father rode one to war. An iron-necked brute named—er—Shaitan." He glanced at her apologetically. "I'm afraid I'm boring the life out of you."

"No, no. You're not. My father had that horse for years. He rides a descendant of his to this day."

Her companion looked pleased. "You're not like so many of the young people in this twentieth century. You don't seem to mind hearing stories of how life was back then forty years ago."

She thought of her months without her memory. Was she different as a result of it? Had she been as accommodating before the ordeal? "Of course, I don't. It's important that I know where I come from."

"Then look," he said. He tapped on the top of the carriage with his cane. The driver pulled the horses to a stop. "Climb down," he commanded. "Climb down, so you can see it all. I can see it from the window, but I really don't need to see it. I'll carry the sight of it to my grave."

With the help of the driver, Fan stood down and looked around her. She stood at the top of a gentle slope down to the Edisto River on three sides.

"This is the spot where the great house stood,"

Richard's voice quavered then thickened with tears. "Those few water oaks that we passed between are the last remaining sentinels of a veritable colonnade of trees that used to shade the road. And all around was the tobacco and the rice. Over one hundred people worked this plantation in her day." He waited for a minute while Fan tried to visualize what it had been like.

"Over there in that small grove is where they're all buried. Edward England, the pirate, with Holy Dulcibella, his wife, a royal princess of Madagascar, beside him. Richard England, his son. Fancy's little baby that was born dead. And Fancy England herself, my mother."

Fan scanned the grove but could see nothing among the trees. She glanced inquiringly at him.

"I had the tombstones moved to the cemetery in Charleston. But I didn't even think about moving the bodies. They belong here in the earth they loved." The curtains had been rolled up so that the view was good. Richard leaned forward. "The docks and drying sheds were down there by the river."

"What happened?"

"Oh, the usual things that happen to a house after a hundred and fifty years. Wood doesn't last forever, especially not in this climate. Several hurricanes didn't help. Then some Yankees came through in sixty-six. Looted and set some fires. We managed to put them out, but they did considerable damage. If Alex hadn't been more of a Northerner than Southerner, they'd have burned us to the ground." He looked disgusted.

"My father fought for the North," Fancy reminded him.

"I know. I know. But your mother was a Southerner."

"She was a mountain woman from the hills of Tennessee. She didn't believe in the southern cause either. Her own father was killed at Shiloh."

He looked sympathetic. "A tragic loss I'm sure."

"It was all a very long time ago."

"I suppose it seems so." He sat silent again in the carriage.

Fan looked around her at the fields, a mass of broken ground and rotting stalks, the remains of harvested crops. A small brown rabbit hopped from the cemetery grove. At its edge he sat up on his hindquarters to rub his forepaws over his nose and ears. A buzzard swung in the sky above. Its shadow passed over the rabbit. Instantly, it leaped to one side and dived for the thicket.

Richard Gillard cleared his throat. "So we must get on with the work. No use sitting around all day. Benjamin, help me down."

"Oh, should you?"

"Yes, my dear, I should. I have a distinct feeling that I shall not pass this way again. That I am come to pay my last respects, or perhaps to let them know that I am coming."

"Mr. Gillard."

"Sorry . . ." He allowed the driver to help him down from the carriage. "Now the house faced the river." He tapped with his stick on the foundation stones, then pointed in a semicircle. "It faced the river. And there were the sheds for curing tobacco, the stables, the overseer's house, the servants quarters, slaves at first, then later free workers."

Gesturing to the men to follow, he walked around where the house had been and down the slope a couple of dozen yards. He sighted from the corner of the foundation to the river, moved a couple of long steps to the left, and tapped with his stick on the damp earth. "Dig here. The gazebo was built on this spot."

Fan looked at him in surprise. "Gazebo! Dig?"

He chuckled softly as the black men came forward and began to throw the earth aside in great shovelfuls. "Naturally, Fancy, what else would you expect us to do but dig?"

"But I thought we came here for a bequest."

"We did. My mother was the most prudent of women. She didn't trust banks entirely. Indeed she did not really trust anyone else in the world once Holy Dulcibella died. She buried this for you."

"Buried. Like a treasure." Fan laughed. "I can't believe I'm hearing this. In the twentieth century."

"It is indeed a buried treasure." He laughed in his turn. "It belonged to a famous pirate. It was buried by his granddaughter."

Chapter 20

"A pirate's treasure?"

"The treasure of Edward England." The old man nodded. His eyes were bright with tears that he did not shed. "Brought from the island of Madagascar in white oak boxes and buried again in the earth of England's Fancy to await the time of need. And do you need it, my dear child?"

"Oh, yes. My need is so great." She still could not believe her good fortune. The entire expedition was taking on the quality of a fairy tale. She cast a wary glance around her. Was Richard Gillard in his right mind? Could this be some sort of trick or trap? Experiences in her recent past sent chills scudding down her spine.

"Benjamin." Richard turned to the driver. "We'll take luncheon in the grove." He held out his arm in an antique gesture of gallantry. "Shall we stroll down to the shade together?"

She chided herself inwardly for her unfounded suspicions. "Why thank you, Mr. Gillard."

Fan had never been on such a picnic before. Accustomed in Texas to rough-and-ready barbecues and church socials on long tables spread with every woman's favorite recipe, she could only stare with delight at a totally different way of life. From another century it bespoke the manners of gracious landed gentry entertaining themselves, their wants attended to assiduously by a retinue of loyal servants.

While they had strolled arm in arm down the gentle slope to the grove, Benjamin had driven the carriage around by the road. There he had unloaded a folding table and two chairs. By the time they arrived, he had spread a linen cloth elaborately embroidered in hardanger work, had placed linen napkins beside china plates and silver, and was pouring cold water into crystal glasses.

Fan seated herself while Benjamin held the chair for Richard. When he was seated, the servant opened a picnic hamper and began to serve. First came a light salad of greens with fresh hard rolls and butter. It was followed by cold fried chicken, green peas and carrots pickled with fresh dill, and new potatoes.

Benjamin produced a second pair of stemmed glasses and poured a pale French wine. A board of cheese with both candied and fresh fruits and nuts finished the repast. When Fan commented on the luxury, Richard smiled.

"We are a family of merchant traders after all. My brother Alex inherited the Shepperton Lines of Boston. Before he died, Dulcy's husband took over the line, so Sheppertons still sails the seas. Of course, now the ships are iron and the power is steam."

"Generated by oil," Fan told him with a touch of triumph in her voice. "That's what we're drilling for right now in Texas. The oil I find will help the ships to sail. It gives me a strange feeling to think of it."

"And you're doing it yourself?" he inquired politely.

She shrugged. "I helped out when Irons was hurt.

It takes four or five men to add a length of pipe to a drill stem."

Richard nodded reminiscently. "And I'm sure you made the fourth man with enthusiasm."

She shot him a quick look. "You surprise me. Irons was furious with me and with Clell for letting me."

"Is Irons your husband?"

"My husband was killed. Murdered. I've formed a partnership with Irons, a man who knows all about the oil business. Things were going fine. Then we were attacked and he was injured, probably by the same men who killed my husband. It's the roughest business in the world. They want the oil that's under our land, and they don't care how they get it."

Richard looked alarmed. "It sounds a great deal like piracy, my dear. Does my nephew know you're in this situation?"

She shook her head. "I've been ill," she told him confidentially. "I was beaten the night Rex was killed. I didn't know who I was for the longest time. I couldn't tell anyone anything."

"My dear child . . ."

"Oh, I'm all right now. And there really hasn't been time to contact anyone since I remembered who I am. If I hadn't remembered and found your letter, I probably wouldn't be here now because the well's about to come in. That is if we can get some more money to finance it. When I read that you had something for me, I thought you were my patron saint. So that's why I hopped on the next train."

Richard shook his head deprecatingly. "My dear, you owe me nothing. The person you should thank lies beneath the clover and sweet grasses in this grove. Your great-grandmother Fancy England."

"My great-grandmother." Fan smiled and lifted her glass. "To Fancy England."

"To Fancy England," Richard said reverently.

They drank and sat in silence. The wind soughed through the trees, swaying the Spanish moss above their heads. The temperature was at least twenty degrees cooler in the grove. Fan could pity the men laboring in the hot sun.

Richard held his full wineglass aside and poured the contents on the earth, then held it out to Benjamin. "Permit me my fantasies." He smiled at Fan's startled expression. "Is everything the way you like it?"

"Oh, it's wonderful." She smiled a little shyly.

He nodded and took a sip from his refilled glass. At last he touched the linen napkin to his mouth and leaned back in his chair. "My father's not buried here."

She looked at him in some surprise. "I didn't think of that."

"No. He was lost at sea, a terrible storm in the North Atlantic. One lifeboat made it back to England to tell the tale. He refused to abandon his ship."

"How terrible!"

"Not really. It was the way he wanted to go. He loved the sea. Mother loved the land. They were ill-suited for each other. The only thing they had in common was their love and we boys."

She thought of herself and Rex. "It's probably pretty common for a couple to be ill-suited to one another. At least they had their love. It made the marriage work."

"Not necessarily," Richard observed drily. "I'm his son, but not hers."

She lifted her hand to her mouth, then dropped it quickly back in her lap. A stillness filled the grove as if others listened to his words.

"The woman who bore me gave me up when she returned to her husband. I never saw her. Only heard her name spoken once. I never cared. My mother—*my mother* made sure that I was the happiest of children, the best-loved of boys."

"How did you find out?" Fan asked. Instinctively, she knew that Richard Gillard had not been told by her namesake.

"Oh, Alex, my older brother, told me who I was, what I was. I tried to kill him. But she stopped us. Father was away, of course."

"How terrible for you!"

"Yes, really. I should have tried to kill my father."

"Those things don't mean so much anymore."

He took another sip of wine. "They shouldn't mean anything to me, a man at my age, but here I am with a woman who looks at me out of the dear golden eyes of my mother and I want to lay my burdens on her. Being old is a terrible thing, Caroline Fancy, because there's no one left to tell your troubles to. Everyone wants your advice, so everyone tells you his troubles."

"Did she know who you were from the very beginning?"

"Oh, yes. She knew exactly where I came from when she brought me home, but nobody else did. At least not in South Carolina. It was a family secret. She took another woman's child and gave it a beautiful home." He stared at the men laboring in the sun over on the shoulder of the slope. "But she never trusted my father again."

Fan nodded slowly. "I can certainly see how she would feel betrayed. She must have had incredible strength of character to take you in. I guess to forgive him would be too much."

"Oh, she forgave him. She just didn't trust him. She knew him too well."

They sat in silence. Benjamin, who had watched out

of hearing, came forward and emptied the bottle of wine into their glasses.

"So when she got the treasure," Richard Gillard continued, "she never told him about it."

Fan looked over her shoulder at the men. "Good for her."

"She worked the plantation. He sailed the seas and came home three or four times a year for short stays. He really preferred Boston, especially after Alex went to Harvard and moved up there."

"And you became a lawyer?"

Richard Gillard smiled sadly. "I couldn't take the plantation. It didn't belong to me you see. It belonged to the blood of Edward England. And I was none of that. It really should be given to you. It belongs to you. You're her namesake. But it's too late now and you're too far away. Your father and the others have decided to sell it."

Fan felt the tears starting in her eyes. Melancholy feelings stole over her as the significance of his words sank into the silence. They had lived and died here on this land. They had loved it with all their hearts and sacrificed so much for it, and now their descendants would let it fall into the hands of others. She wiped her cheek.

"Probably it's for the best. My father and my half brother were cut from the same cloth. A certain talent for alienation, even their own children didn't like them very much."

"Mr. Gillard! We've found something."

He smiled as he leaned forward to pat her hand. "Shall we go and see your treasure, Caroline Fancy? It's the first time it has seen the light of the sun in eighty-seven years."

With Richard leaning heavily on her arm, they made their way across the slope. One man dropped down into the hole and tried to lift the lid off a box. The ancient trunk disintegrated beneath his hands. Inside were boxes, wrapped in oilskin. He looked up at Richard for direction.

"Tear the covering, man. Be quick."

A quick rip and then the box was lifted up and into Fan's hands. Its weight dragged her down to her knees as she all but dropped it on the edge of the hole.

"Open it," the old man said excitedly.

She looked up at him. "Don't you want to?"

"Me! No. Not at all. This is your treasure. From your great-grandmother. And from your great-great-great-grandfather." He looked over his shoulder toward the grove. A fair breeze blew across the shoulder of the hill, the Spanish moss swayed. "I wish they could be here. I wish we could all be here together." He turned back, his withered cheeks wet. "Open it, Caroline Fancy."

The lid slid out smoothly in its groove revealing black metal discs.

She looked up quickly, then threw up her hand as she looked directly into the bright afternoon sun. Richard moved so his head and shoulders shaded her. She held up the disc.

"Tarnish," he assured her. "Silver tarnishes. Solomon, your knife."

The black man fished his penknife from his overall pocket and handed it to Fan. She scraped the surface of the metal. Silver white and pure showed beneath. She tilted the piece in the sunlight. *"Dei 1733 Philipus V."*

"Pieces of eight," Richard said reverently. "And I have lived to see them. After hearing about them so many years ago and thinking and dreaming about them. I have lived to see them."

"These are yours by rights." His words struck Fan

with such force that her fingers began to tremble. The heavy silver pieces fell to the ground.

"No. This is the treasure from the *Fancy,* Edward England's ship. It was buried on the island of Madagascar in the Indian ocean until his granddaughter needed it. When she brought it home, she found her troubles were ameliorated. She buried it again to await the time of need. It's a pirate's stash. And it belongs to you, Caroline Fancy." He took an unsteady step backward.

The sun's light blinded her eyes. Out of the sun, figures seemed to move for only a second—a man and a woman, their silhouettes separating and merging in the spot where Richard Gillard had been standing. Then she blinked, dropping her head. The wind gusted then died completely.

When she opened her eyes, everything was as it should have been. And the figures might have been a trick of the eyes.

The banker in Houston stared bug-eyed as the coins slid out of the leather pouch onto his desk. Fan had selected a bag at random and polished the contents so they gleamed mint-bright. When two dozen of them lay before him, she stepped back and sat down. A cat-like smile lit her face.

He picked up one, stared at it, held it up to the light, put it down, picked up another. "What's this?"

"That," she replied, "is an eighteenth-century Spanish coin. And these are its mates. They're called Pieces of Eight and they've been buried in the ground for a hundred and fifty years."

He looked doubtfully at her. "I don't think these are negotiable in this bank, Miss . . ."

"Mrs. Breckenridge. Possibly not, but they can be

placed in a safety deposit vault and used as collateral on a bank loan, can they not?"

"Well, that would depend on how many and, of course, we would want to check their authenticity."

"Oh, I can assure you as to their authenticity. I have letters to that effect from two numismatists. Their value is much more than the value of the silver content because of their age and condition. They're of a quality the numismatists called very fine. Since they've never been circulated, he placed their value at between twenty and twenty-five dollars apiece."

The man looked down at the coins. He put down the one he was holding and picked up another. His thumb slid over and over the silver fascinated by its crude stamping of crown and heraldic shield. His thumbnail picked at the Arabic number eight. "And how many do you want to deposit?"

"Thirty-six boxes of two hundred to two hundred and fifty coins each."

He dropped the coin from his shaking fingers. "What's this? What's this?"

"A pirate treasure. I want to deposit it in the bank, a portion of which will be set aside as security against a loan."

He pushed his chair back and came to his feet. His voice rose in agitation. "We've never done anything like this before."

She just managed to suppress a smile. "I shouldn't imagine that you have."

He looked at her narrowly. "Is this stolen?"

She shrugged. "Once upon a time it was. But the people from whom it was stolen as well as the people who stole it are long dead. According to international law, treasure of this kind belongs to the one who finds it."

He rubbed his hand around the back of his neck. "I don't think there's any precedent for this . . ."

But Fan had been prepared by Richard's careful advice. "People frequently deposit valuables in bank vaults and use them as collateral on loans. Silver, jewelry, paintings."

"But . . . We've never done anything like this before."

She shrugged. Rising, she swept the coins back into the pouch. "If you can't accommodate us, I'm sure there will be one who can among the many other banks in Houston."

His face contorted as he watched the heavy pieces disappear. "I'm sure you won't find better service anywhere else, ma'am." He came around the desk making little deprecatory motions with his hands. "Please be seated. I'm sure we can do business, Mrs. Breckenridge. If you'll just make yourself comfortable, I'll have my secretary bring you refreshments while I begin the necessary arrangements."

Shading her eyes from the sun's bright glare, Fan stepped off the train in Beaumont. The porter came behind her carrying two bags. She had started into the depot when she caught sight of Irons standing on the platform. His lean face was shaded by his hat; his arms, folded at ease across his chest.

Before she remembered the circumstances under which she had left, she waved enthusiastically. Her face split in a smile of greeting.

He nodded soberly and strode forward, his heavy brogans thwacking the platform. With a tip of his hat, he reached for her bags.

Though she remembered how heavy they were, his expression forbade her to interfere. Instead she handed a quarter to the porter and followed Irons down the platform to the waiting team.

"Is everything all right at home?"

"The drilling's stopped. We ran out of pipe and can't buy anymore. The Boomin' Bessie shut down so Early's out of a job."

She smiled to herself. "That's all right. I've got enough money to buy pipe. So long as we're here, let's go ahead and buy as much as we need, plus supplies."

He cast her a sidewise glance. "So you got something?"

She nodded, her lips twitching. "Something."

He hesitated, looked as if he were going to speak, then stopped. "Are you hungry?"

"Not yet. I had some breakfast in Houston."

"Houston?"

"I had to deposit my inheritance in the bank."

"You shouldn't spend it on this well," he said gruffly.

"Why not?"

"Why not! For starters, you shouldn't have come back here at all. For seconds, you shouldn't pour your inheritance that ought to be setting you up for a secure future on an oil well. Oil's a gamble anyway you look at it. Don't you realize? The chances of our bringing that well in are slim to none."

She looked at him in amazement. "But when I left the cuttings were good. Clell told me so."

"Clell's a damned optimist. Any sand in the mud pit is oil sand."

"Irons," she scolded. "He's your best friend."

"I don't give a damn . . ."

"Don't!" she all but shouted at him. "Don't say another word. I want to buy this pipe and these supplies. I have the money to do it. It's my land and my cabin and my derrick. I'm not a helpless baby anymore. I know who I am and where I came from." She hugged that thought to her.

"But . . ."

She looked him squarely in the eye. His objection died on his lips. "When it comes right down to it, I'm your boss, Irons. And I'm giving you an order."

Dark color rose in his cheeks. The dark brows pulled together and the jaw jutted out.

She returned his stare unwaveringly, then lifted her chin. "Let's order the pipe first and pick up the supplies on the way out of town."

The man lounging across the street from the oil field supply warehouse studied the two as they went in. When they left, he crossed the street. For four bits the clerk gave him a look at the last purchase order in the book.

A low whistle slid from between his lips at the amount of the cash transaction. He left the office on the run.

"We don't need all this stuff," Irons protested as Fan bought whole cases of tin-canned peaches and pears.

"They'll taste good at the end of the meal."

"But they're too expensive. Good God, you'll spend it all."

"It's mine."

He cursed virulently. Behind the counter the clerk's mouth dropped open. He stepped back against the shelves.

Fan's mouth tightened as she looked around in embarrassment. She put her arm through his and tugged. "Irons."

"What, damn it?"

"Step outside with me."

On the sidewalk outside the general store, they confronted each other nose to nose. "What are you so upset about?" Her jaw was clenched so tightly that she could barely speak.

"Women," he spat angrily. "Give 'em a little bit of money. Just a little and they fritter it away. Waste it. Just like throwin' it down a rat hole to give it to a woman."

"And how do you know that I just have a little?"

"You came back," he accused, as if that fact were proof incontrovertible that she had only received a pittance. "And your money's going so fast you'd think you'd got a hole in your pocket."

She searched his flushed face. Her own softened. "Is that why you're angry? You think I ought to save it for myself?"

"Damn right," he growled. "You're making a fool of yourself."

"And could it also be that you don't like to take money from a woman?" she continued, a silky tone sliding into her voice.

He took a backward step. "I'm no fool. I'll take money from anybody, if he's got it to give."

"Then you just don't like taking money from me?"

"I don't want your money," he stormed. "You don't have a husband. You need that money to take care of yourself. You don't want to have to go to work in some penny-ante job to pay the rent and buy beans. That money is your security. Damn it. Take care of it."

"I'm trying to take care of it. I'm trying to make it grow. An oil well is a good investment. I could make millions," she continued in a more reasonable voice.

"Only if you've got millions to lose," he argued.

"It's a good investment," she insisted.

"Did I hear the word investment?"

They both looked around, startled. The world suddenly swam into focus. The heavyset man tipped his hat. "Mrs. Breckenridge, do you remember me? Harry Glennville. We spoke under rather different circumstances. May I take this opportunity to say how remarkably lovely you look."

Irons made a rude noise, but Fan smiled graciously. "I certainly do remember you, Mr. Glennville. My circumstances are different now, but yours are the same."

"Get the hell out of here, Glennville," Irons snapped.

"I think not," Glennville looked pointedly over Irons' shoulder.

Fan saw an armed rider climb down off his horse and move toward them. "Mr. Glennville," she interposed hastily. "Let's please save us both an unpleasant confrontation. The property was not for lease when we talked a couple of weeks ago. It is certainly not for lease now that I have come into some money."

He raised his eyebrows. "But you shouldn't invest your money, Mrs. Breckenridge, as I overheard your man tell you. Pay him heed. Let your money grow where it is safe in a bank. Let those with plentiful capital and a head for the business risk theirs."

Irons struggled between his disgust and dislike of the man and his concern for Fan's safety. Concern won. "Better listen to the son of a bitch. He's making something that sounds like sense."

"Thank you, sir." Glennville touched his hat ironically.

Fan glared at them both. Her anger focused on Glennville. "Sir, I insist that you leave us in peace to get on with our business. We need to get started back toward Waldrow. If we don't get these supplies bought, we'll have to spend the night in Batson."

"Fan."

"Mrs. Breckenridge, I'm prepared to make an offer that will make the trip unnecessary." Glennville was grinning, his eyes already totaling up the dollars.

Irons clenched his half-healed hands, unable to stand the thought of all their hard work pouring into the pockets of Standard Oil.

She stamped her foot. "Irons, are we in this together or not?"

"Damn right." He pivoted halfway around. His action froze the rider who had dismounted and was gravitating to Irons' back. "You want to try something?"

"You're making a big mistake," Glennville insisted. "It takes big money to finance a well. That's where leasing comes in. You let us spend the money and take the risk. You get a share of the profits."

"But if you already have the money to finance, then when the well comes in you don't have to divide the profits," Fan insisted softly.

"A large majority of the wells drilled are dry holes. For most people it's a heartbreaking not to say financially ruinous experience."

Fan placed her gloved hand to her temple. This man was making a damned nuisance of himself. "Mr. Glennville, I have the money to spend and I intend to spend it."

His unctuous expression turned nasty. "You could be very sorry. Accidents do happen around oil wells." He looked contemptuously at Irons' scarred, bruised hands. "Can you use that gun you're packing?"

"You want to find out?"

"Turk."

The man who had dismounted walked to the end of the sidewalk.

Fan planted herself in front of Glennville. "Stop this

right now. This is the twentieth century in Beaumont, Texas. Not eighteen eighty in Dodge City."

"Get out of the way," Irons snarled.

"I will not. What I will do is start screaming bloody murder in about ten seconds. People will come out of their stores and shops. Someone will run for the police. In fact, I believe I see some kind of law officer coming right now. At least he's wearing some kind of silver metal shield on his vest. And if I remember correctly, Standard Oil is not all that popular in Texas right now. He might take it into his head to hold you in jail over night, just for the sake of annoyance."

Glennville glanced over his shoulder. A burly man had indeed strolled out of a feed and grain store down the street. He pulled his watch from his pocket, then stared pointedly in their direction.

"I'll scream," Fan said sweetly. She opened her mouth and sucked in a deep breath.

"That won't be necessary," Glennville said. "We'll let this go for now. That'll do, Turk."

Irons relaxed. Fan put her hands around his arm and tugged him toward the door. "Let's go buy those things right now. It'll be dark before we get to the city limits."

"You've had your chance, Mrs. Breckenridge," Glennville called.

She gave him a fulminating look. "I think you might have had yours, Mr. Glennville. I'm serving notice right now. Don't come near my place."

Chapter 21

"When we get to Waldrow, I want to hire another crew." Fan kept her eyes directed straight ahead, her tone conversational.

Irons hunched his head between his shoulders. "Yes, boss."

"You'll have to hire them with the understanding that they probably will have trouble with Mr. Glennville and his goons."

"Sure thing, boss."

She gritted her teeth and shot him a baleful glance. Men were so stupid about women having a little money. "I'd hate to be responsible for getting somebody into something that he didn't bargain for."

He slapped the reins on the backs of the horses and moved them from a walk into a brisk trot.

Fan gripped the edge of the seat more tightly. They jounced along in uncomfortable silence for a few more minutes. "You do expect that we'll have to fight, don't you?"

His teeth were tightly clenched. "Hell, yes, we'll have to fight. You just waved a red flag in front of Glennville's face. We'll be lucky if we get home without being bushwhacked."

"Is that why you're pushing the horses so hard?"

He shot her a glance just as the front wheels dropped into a washout. It threw her forward and then snapped her head back as the wagon jounced back up again. He eased back on the reins, slowing the horses to a brisk walk. "That and the fact that we don't want to be caught in the open tonight. It's been hot and still all day. A norther's bound to blow in."

Fan looked about her for the first time. No wind soughed through the trees that lined the road. The field grass was still, but to the northwest Fan could see a line of white high clouds creeping toward them.

Cold wet winds were slapping Fan in the face when they pulled up to the boardinghouse in Waldrow. Mrs. Dittman scowled heavily at the sight of them, but the roll of bills Fan pulled from her purse cleared the housekeeper's face miraculously.

Irons carried her bags up to the room then turned to leave.

"Where are you going?"

He stood in the door, his shoulders squared, the muscles in his jaw like granite. "I'll bed down with the horses in the stable."

His stubbornness infuriated her. "You'll do no such thing."

He compressed his lips into a thin line. "Somebody's liable to make off with that wagon load of supplies you paid so much for."

Snarling his name, she caught him by the coat lapels and dragged him into the room. Her foot shot out and kicked the door too with a resounding bang. "Now, you stop this."

"Hey!"

"Just stop it."

"Stop what?"

"Stop treating me as if everything I do is the wrong thing. Stop acting as if you hate and despise me."

"I don't hate you." He ducked his head. "I just don't . . . I just can't stand . . ."

She tugged sharply on the unfortunate lapels. "You just can't stand for me to stand on my own two feet. Is that it? So long as I was crazy and helpless as a baby, everything was fine. I could stay in the cabin with bullets flying everywhere."

"Damn it. That isn't so." His righteous anger vanished as if it had never been. He looked astonished that she should have even thought such a thing.

"That's the way it looks to me."

He closed his scarred, discolored hands around her wrists. For the first time in over a week, she saw them up close. They had never been beautiful, the skin all rippled and drawn from burns. Now with the remains of bruises and the fresh scabs, they made her ache with the pain he had endured. Something of her feelings must have shown in her face, for he dropped her wrists and stepped back. He thrust his hands deep into the pocket of his khaki work pants. "It's not so," he said lamely. "I just didn't realize what we were up against until now."

"Irons," she groaned. "Oh, Irons. If there's something going on that I need to know about, just tell me."

He stood silent, his jaw granite, his shoulders hunched.

She took his face between her hands. The obdurate pride in the gray eyes wrenched her heart. Hurt by his attitude, afraid for them all, she knew that understanding was a long way off.

She smiled sadly. "Then just don't say anything at all."

"I . . . You . . ."

She kissed him. Her lips brushed his. He stiffened, pulled back halfheartedly. She followed him, kissing him still, her breasts leaning against his chest. Her tongue slid back and forth across the seam formed by his defiant lips. "Irons," she whispered. "Irons. It's been so long."

He capitulated with a groan. His arms went around her. "Fan. Oh, Fan." His tongue followed hers back into her mouth, locking with it. His hands slid over the curve of her spine and cupped her buttocks.

She arched against him, heat bursting inside her, an ache growing at the bottom of her belly. She pushed up on tiptoe trying to get closer to him, to feel his hardness through their clothing. She was desperate to rub herself against it. Her nerves prickled as she twisted futilely. "Irons."

"Fan." With one arm he bolted her to him, his hand splayed at the base of her spine, holding her with shocking familiarity. The other hand dived between the facings of the traveling suit to find her breast. She was so aroused that he found the nipple instantly, hard, shaped, waiting for him. When he touched her, she felt her legs go weak.

"Irons," she gasped. "Irons, this is terrible. I can't stand this."

He raised his head, looking into her eyes. They were dilated so that the iris was a narrow ring of gold. Her whole body was vibrating against him, its tension rendering her powerless. "Fan," he whispered. He kissed her again. "Oh, Fan, you're as hungry as I am?"

Sensual pressure inside her grew. Wild with seeking, she slid her thigh up over his hip, opening her more to his hardness. She could feel the tip probing through the thicknesses of material. "Irons, please."

His hand slid under her thigh and lifted. She groaned as he spread her exquisitely and pulled her tight against him. Her head fell back, her black hair tugging at its pins. She groaned again as tender swollen openings were bruised against the seams and fastenings of their clothing. Still she struggled impossibly closer.

"Hold on, baby," he murmured, his mouth against her throat. "This way is no good." He took a couple of quick strides and dumped her rather unceremoniously on the bed.

Her eyes flew open and she glimpsed the thrust of his jaw, the luminous desire in his eyes as he fell on top of her. "Irons."

"Yes, baby. Oh, yes." He kissed her forehead, her temple, her cheeks, her lips.

She moaned and arched her throat for him to kiss that too, writhed beneath him in an agony of desire. Her body ached from breasts to thighs. "Irons," she begged. "Irons."

Reluctantly, he stood, his mouth lingering on hers, reluctant to break the contact. Then never taking his eyes from hers, he pulled at the buttons of his shirt.

Fan unbuttoned her suit and the blouse beneath. With impatient fingers she tugged at the ribbons of the camisole and bared her breasts. Boldly she cupped them and arched up, entreating him, challenging him.

He grinned, his eyes promising her retribution. "You even nag when you're making love," he grumbled as he pulled off his own trousers and boots. Then he straddled her, knees holding her thighs together while he bent above her to kiss and suckle her nipples.

She reached down to find him velvet-hard, pushing and leaping in her hand.

"Fan," he warned. "Don't . . ."

"Don't," she whispered, laughing. "I never expected to hear you say those words."

"You don't know what that feels like. Your hand. I . . . Ah, Fan . . ."

She pulled him down into her nest, rubbed him against the mass of nerves hidden there.

"Fan. That feels . . ."

He edged farther apart, split himself. She spread her legs, guided him into the warm welcoming center of her being, and closed her thighs around him. "Irons," she whispered triumphantly. "You're trapped."

He closed his eyes, her words stirring him so that he leaped inside her. His hands closed over her breasts squeezing until she arched and twisted. Her sheath convulsed, locking around the root of him. Her body twisted from side to side, caressing him in ways he had not known.

"I've missed you so," she groaned as tears slid into the hair at her temples. "I've missed you so."

"Fan." He rocked his hips forward, lifting her half off the bed. "Fan, it's been hell."

The last word rose in an ecstatic cry mingled with hers as they shattered into a thousand pieces mixing, comingling, fusing into one exquisite sensate being.

She was under his skin but good. Irons rolled over on his back, his head turned away from the woman beside him. Mrs. Dittman's bed was narrow and the old springs and mattress sagged inward tilting them together so that their bodies had adjusted to each other's curves. Even now her cheek was pressed against his shoulder, and—until he had moved—her knee had been drawn up, intimately high, between his legs.

When she had stepped off that train in Beaumont, he had wanted to cheer and shout, to run and grab her and swing her around and around and kiss her until she cried for mercy. He had cursed himself a thousand times during the long days and longer nights while she was gone. He had all but driven her off and when she was gone, he had needed her badly. He could barely eat, much less sleep. His behavior the night before she left had been a calculated insult from beginning to end.

But—hell—she should go away somewhere safe. Even were there not very real threats to her life, a drill site was no place for a tender, well-bred woman. And she was certainly that. Even with her memory gone and her body clothed in rags, she was every inch a lady. Education, culture, manners revealed in every movement she made, every word she uttered.

He had known she would come back. Known it in his heart and bones, and bet against himself. He would flip that twenty-dollar gold piece out of his pocket and slip it to Clell with a scowl, but on the inside he would be grinning.

He rolled his head back to stare at her. Despite a hint of shadow under her eyes, he could see that her color was better than when she left. The train trip and the visit had given her a break from the unremitting tension and bone-tiring work. Her cheeks had a touch of color. The last traces of bruising had faded. Only the pink crescent-shaped scar remained beside her right eye. The color would fade in time and no one but he would even notice.

Fixing his eyes on the ceiling, he blew his breath slowly out from between his lips in a silent whistle. He expected to stay around while the scar faded. He expected to come home to her, to eat with her, to sleep beside her, to make love to her, to extend his life with her into the unknown future.

Women were more trouble than they were worth.

The well would come in, or it would prove a dry hole and they would part. Foolish to think that she would remain with him. She would take her money and her full measure of pride and go back to her family in San Antonio. She should have gone before. He should have forced her to go. She was in more danger now than ever.

He closed his eyes. His hand blindly slid across the narrow space between them to touch her belly just below the indentation of her navel. His index finger traced down through the invisible hairs of her linea alba to the nest of soft black curls. He sucked in his breath, knowing the heat and pleasure that waited for him there.

When he would have pulled his hand away, he felt her hand gently circle his wrist. "What a lovely way to wake up."

He opened his eyes and looked deep into her own. The golden eyes were smiling, the curved lips bewitching. "Go back to sleep. I apologize," he said softly. "It's too early to wake up."

"Umm-hmm." She closed her eyes and burrowed deeper into the pillow, but she did not let his hand go away. Instead she guided it lower until his hand cupped her sex, his fingers in the hot moist space between her thighs.

He steeled himself to keep his voice normal when he wanted nothing so much as to roll her over on her back and shove himself into her.

Her gentle acceptance of his right to touch her angered him too. She should be resentful. She should be angry at the things he had said to her. She should not be eager to make love again. Hell, he was going crazy.

"When are we going to get started?" she asked him with eyes closed. Her voice was husky with sleep.

He cleared his throat. "Not for a while."

She nodded and said no more. In a moment her breathing evened.

Satisfied she had drifted back to sleep he slowly pulled his hand from between her legs. He stared at it, his mouth curling in distaste. The old burn scars made the skin look as if it had melted. Two fingers were misshapen, their knuckles still swollen grotesquely. What a monstrosity to stick between two silken white thighs. His very ugliness was another reason why she needed to get the hell out of here.

He looked at her again. Her breasts were pushed together by her arm. A deep cleavage where ordinarily there was none. He wanted to . . . *Shut up,* he told himself. *Just shut up.*

The least he could do was insist that she stay here in Waldrow. She had no business out there in the shack, especially not with extra men coming. Especially not with . . . He made a hard fist and pressed it against his mouth.

And yet, his spirit cried out for her. In his secretest heart he acknowledged that he wanted more than life itself to lie beside her every night. At this minute the present was enough. He wanted no future.

"I'm gonna need that room tonight." Mrs. Dittman planted herself at the head of the breakfast table and glared down at Fan. The rat was coming loose on one side, she needed a new henna job, and her hair looked as if it had not been combed in a week.

Fan frowned over the second cup of coffee regretting now that she had lingered while Irons hired a crew from among the unemployed men hanging around the muddy rag town. Less than an inch from her lips, the rising steam told her that it was really too hot to drink. She set the cup down and stirred it gently.

"I said, I'm gonna need that room tonight."

"And you shall have it, Mrs. Dittman," Fan replied. "In fact, you can go up right now and begin cleaning and scouring the way you usually do."

The woman's cheeks flushed as the dart went home.

"I run a decent house here," she huffed. "The sheriff never had no need to come around here before. And he ain't gonna come around again because of you."

"The sheriff will never be back because of me, Mrs. Dittman. He hasn't, to my knowledge, looked any further for the men who murdered my husband. He'll go way wide to keep from crossing my path."

Dittman sniffed. "Maybe so. Maybe not. I told that Irons fella that was sleepin' with you last night that I run a decent house and you couldn't stay here."

For the first time Fan looked directly at the landlady. "He asked you if I could stay here?"

"Wanted me to put you up, he did, but I told him that I run a decent house . . ."

"Yes, I know. And I couldn't stay here. But why did he think that I would want to?"

"How'd I know! I only know that you can't do it. I won't have it."

Fan finished her coffee. "Not even for money?"

"Money." Floreine Dittman snorted. "It'd take a damn sight more than ten dollars a week for me to put you up here."

"Mrs. Dittman, please don't concern yourself. I'll be out of here as soon as Irons comes back." Fan pushed back her chair.

The woman trailed after her, her voice uncertain now. "I'd have to charge at least fifteen. And you'd be getting a bargain."

Fan could not keep from laughing. Suddenly the whole purpose of the conversation was clear. "I'm sure I would."

"At that price you could have the east room. It's bigger than the others on the quiet side of the house."

Halfway up the stairs, Fan paused. "I wouldn't think of ruining the reputation of your house, Mrs. Dittman. When Irons gets back, we'll be leaving."

The woman followed her to the foot of the stairs. "You may be back before you know it, Miss High and Mighty. You don't know what's been goin' on out there."

Fan did not even glance over her shoulder.

"You Miz Breckenridge?"

Fan stared suspiciously at the two men who peered over the rail at the end of Mrs. Dittman's porch. "Who wants to know?"

They exchanged narrow-eyed glances. One of them came around to the front steps. "I'm Billy and him's my brother Lenny Tolliver. I think you're Miz Breckenridge for a fact, and we need to have ourselves a talk."

"I'm waiting for my men to load supplies. They'll be back any minute."

"If you're talkin' about that big gray-haired feller, he ain't been gone but a few minutes. I reckon he'll be gone a spell longer."

Fan rose from the chair and backed toward the door of the rooming house. Mentally, she regretted her foolish anger at Mrs. Dittman that had driven her outside to wait.

Billy Tolliver crossed the porch in two quick strides and placed the flat of his hand firmly against the door. "Now, ma'am, don't try to run off. We ain't goin' to do you a harm. We just need to talk."

"About what?"

"Your husband. I heard tell he was that feller Breckenridge, him that got hanged a while back."

"Yes."

"Well, he died owing us a lot of money."

"That's right," the one at the end of the porch agreed. "A lot of money. Near a hundred dollars."

Fan took a deep breath, knowing well what was coming. "I'm sorry to hear that, but—"

Lenny Tolliver mounted the porch and came up beside her, effectively hemming her in between his brother and the door. Both were over six feet tall, broad-shouldered and big-bellied. The stench of their unwashed bodies pressed her back against the wall, her nose wrinkling. "I'll just bet you are," Lenny growled. "So what're you going to do about it?"

She looked up into their unshaven faces. Anger as well as frustration was written on them. She spread her hands. "I don't see how I can do anything about it. When my husband was killed, his brother took over everything. You'll have to get your money from him."

"That skunk." The two men exchanged glances. "He lit out for parts unknown after they struck oil out there."

"I know." She put her hand on the door. "I really wish I could help you, but I can't."

"Now, just a minute . . ."

Billy let his hand drop from the door. "You got left in the lurch too, huh, lady?"

"I got my clothes and my horse," she told them honestly.

"You got more than we did."

Fan slipped inside the screen. "Why don't you go out to Rosemeade and talk to a man named Pyote? He's in charge of the place while Paul Breckenridge is away."

"That pizen snake." Lenny spun around and strode to the edge of the porch. He slammed his broad fist against the column. "Damn cheatin' son of a bitch."

"Hesh up, Len," Billy tossed over his shoulder. " 'Tain't her fault and she's a lady." He tipped his hat to Fan. "Pardon us, ma'am. We done took up enough of your time."

Lenny swung back. "Well, what in hell're we gonna do about our money?"

Billy turned his brother around and led him down the steps. "Guess we'll have to get it the hard way. Catch that Pyote when he ain't lookin' some night and take it outa his hide. He's got some somewhere. He don't work for free."

"Hey, they're comin'!" Hoke yelled down from the monkey board. "Halloo, Miz Breckenridge."

"Hoke." Fan waved to him. "Hey, Hoke." Irons pulled the wagon to a halt in front of the corral. "Hey, Brazel. Clell."

The three left their positions and hurried down to greet her.

"I've ordered pipe," were the first words out of her mouth. "It's on its way from Beaumont right now."

"That's good, real good." Clell's eyes skittered over her face to Irons. An unspoken question flashed between them. "We're going to have to pull out of the hole and replace the bit."

"I've hired six more roughnecks, Clell," Irons said. "They'll be out here first thing tomorrow."

Fan looked at him inquiringly. "Why aren't they coming today?"

"Because . . ." He looked at the three grave faces. "We have some things that need to be straightened out among us."

"Like what?"

"Like who's the boss."

She smiled. "Oh, you're the boss. You didn't really think otherwise, did you? I only have one thing that I want to do."

They watched as she climbed over the back of the wagon seat and opened her big suitcase. From the top of it, she pulled a cloth-wrapped board. "From now on this well has a name," she announced from the wagon bed. She pulled off the wrapping. "Help me down."

Irons obliged her, still staring puzzled at the sign. It looked to be a piece of mahogany, varnished until the grain in the red wood shone.

"Here." She handed him the piece. "Nail her up."

He held up the sign, read it, shook his head. "I don't understand."

"Every well needs a name. Our well needs a name, so here it is. The only name it could have. It has to be this."

"This doesn't sound like a name at all."

"I suppose you'd like something like the Boomin' Bessie. Put it up."

Hoke handed a ball hammer and a spike down from the toolbox.

Irons shrugged. "Whatever you want. It's your well." And proceeded to nail the sign to the center of the first cross beam on the rig.

"England's Fancy," Fan read. She patted the leg of the derrick as if it were alive. "You're a long way from where you started, but you're still afloat."

The men stared from her to the sign and back again. She smiled at them, eager to tell them the story of the name.

"Aren't you going to introduce us?"

Irons hunched his shoulders. Clell spun around, his face alight. Fan turned to see a woman who had come up behind the wagon. She carried a child of about three on her hip. One little arm was around her neck, his head on her shoulder.

Clell hurried forward to take the little one from her.

Smiling sweetly at him, she rubbed her lower arm as if the little one's weight had bruised her. She was pretty—very pretty—and very fragile. Cornsilk hair curled wispily around her face. The child, too, had naturally curly blond hair.

Clell looked anxiously at Fan. "Mrs. Breckenridge, I'd like you to meet my wife Gladdie. And this is my son Brucie. Gladdie, this is the woman who owns this well, Mrs. Fan Breckenridge."

Startled, Fan could not help glancing in Irons' direction. He caught her eye then hastily looked away. Conscious that all eyes were on her, Fan smiled pleasantly at the woman and extended her hand. "I'm pleased to meet you, Mrs. McClellan, and you, too, Brucie."

The little boy promptly hid his face in his father's neck.

"Call me Gladdie. I'm pleased to meet you too. I've heard a lot about you. Clell just can't seem to stop talking about you." She smiled a little pouting smile at her husband.

No one seemed to be able to think of anything to say. Fan tried not to gape at the marked difference in Irons and Gladdie. She could not see the slightest resemblance between them. Hair, eyes, complexion, bone structure all were different. Gladdie might sooner have been taken for Hoke's sister. The two were at least slight in build.

Breaking the uncomfortable silence, Irons stalked around to the back of the wagon and lifted Fan's bags out. "I'll carry these up to the cabin. Brazel, you and Hoke sort through the supplies. Bring the food on up. You're going to smile when you see the canned peaches and pears that she bought for you in Beaumont."

"Canned peaches." Brazel's face split in a grin. He hurried to the side of the wagon.

Gladdie's face twisted into a petulant scowl. She caught Irons' arm and turned him half around. Although their backs were to the others, her words carried clearly. "I thought you were going to take care of everything, Sammy. The house's only got the one bed."

Irons looked annoyed. "I told you nothing of the sort. I told you that Mrs. Breckenridge might want to stay in town rather than roughing it out here, but she didn't."

"Well, then, what are we going to do?" Her voice, shrill and surprisingly strong, grated out of the diminutive body.

"Now, Gladdie, honey, I've got a nice tent," Clell said placatingly. "It's floored and everything." He tried to turn her away, but with the little boy sitting in the crook of his good arm, he could not.

"But the house . . ." she protested.

"Is not yours," Irons finished for her. "If you don't like the accommodations, I suggest you clear out and go find some other man to support you."

"Sammy!"

"Irons." Clell shook his head mildly. "Gladdie's welcome to whatever I've got. She's the mother of my son."

"That's right. Clell loves Brucie. Brucie needs his father."

Hoke backed hastily away and returned to the monkey board, while Brazel abandoned the peaches with a muttered comment about the donkey engine sounding funny. Fan turned away embarrassed by the bitterness of the family argument.

She did not catch Clell's soft-spoken attempt to placate his wife.

However, Gladdie's shrill reply startled Fan. Avoiding Clell as he tried to shepherd her toward the tent set up behind the barn, Gladdie planted herself in front of Irons and pushed out her lower lip. "A fine brother you are."

He looked down at her, his face a picture of contempt. "A fine sister you are."

"I'm just like you," she sneered, standing her ground, her tiny fists planted squarely on her slender hips. "Nobody's going to push us around." She looked over her shoulder at Clell.

"Gladdie," he called, a hint of desperation in his tone. "Let me show you the tent."

She moved so she could look Fan in the eye. "Are you going to stay here in the house?"

Fan hesitated.

"Yes, she is," Irons declared. "It's her house."

Gladdie shot him a look of pure malevolence.

"Gladdie," Clell called.

She turned on her heel and stalked away toward the tent. Her voice floated back as she jerked Brucie off Clell's arm as if the child were a doll. "Goddamn you. Why'd you get me out here if you didn't have a place for me to stay?"

Fan leaned towards Irons. "I don't know what to say. I feel terrible about putting the little boy out."

"Don't." He took her arm. "This is your place. She's not earning her keep, but she's eating your food. She says she left the guy she was living with, but I don't buy that. He probably kicked her out."

Fan shook her head, not knowing what to say.

"Clell's been short of money the last few months while we were trying to get enough together to buy the equipment. Gladdie was probably taking the money Clell was sending her and supporting the guy. When he didn't get any more money, he most likely told her to hit the road."

"But that's terrible."

Irons shrugged. "She picked him. We looked around

and there she was. Rode out here on the last load of pipe."

"She's your sister. We can fix something . . ."

"She's Clell's wife. Let him provide for her. It's what he wants to do. Poor bum. He's happier now that she's yelling at him, than I've seen him in years. And he's got Brucie."

"I'm still sorry. Maybe I could stay in town."

"Not if you don't want to. You've gone through a hell of a lot the last few weeks. If you want to be here, then here you stay." He smiled ironically. "I tried my damnedest to keep you from coming back here, but not because my sister wants to sleep in your bed. She can roll up under the platform for all I care." He picked up the bags and strode rapidly toward the cabin.

"I've run a string of barbed wire knee high around the edge of the brush," Clell told the fully assembled crew. The five new men had arrived and set up their tents on the far side of the rig where they did their own cooking and tended to their own needs. "We've got a gate up across the road coming in. It stays closed."

"Sounds like you're expecting trouble any time." The man who spoke had the heaviest jaw Fan had ever seen. It moved constantly as he shifted and chewed a huge plug of tobacco.

"Standard Oil's out to take over this lease," Irons told them honestly. "They've been here before scaring us. We ran them off, but they'll be back. And they won't be trying to scare. Anyone feeling particularly peaceable better roll up and move on."

No one moved. A couple of the roughnecks exchanged glances and shrugged unconcernedly.

The man with the big jaw moved his tobacco to one side of his mouth. "What about them ladies?"

''One's the driller's wife and my sister,'' Irons said. ''And I'd like to introduce you to Mrs. Breckenridge. This is her well. She's financing it and we're bringing it in for her.''

Fan smiled and nodded.

''You gonna post guards?'' another man wanted to know.

''I'm taking care of that,'' Irons replied.

He waited a minute to see that no other questions were forthcoming. ''We'll run two tours a day after we get the pipe pulled out of the hole and a new bit in. The cuttings are looking real good, so you might not have a job too long. But there'll be a bonus at the end. Any questions?''

''Yep,'' called one.

''Fire away.''

''Who's England? And what's he fancy?''

Chapter 22

Cans clattered and jangled. The grandfather of all cowbells set up a fearful clanging. Irons rolled out and reached for his pants. "Here we go again."

"Are we being attacked?" Fan sat up in bed, her heart pounding.

He stuffed his feet into his boots. "Sounds like it."

"Where's that noise coming from?"

"From all the junk I hung on that barbed wire I strung around the edge of the clearing." He strapped his gunbelt around his waist and reached over to give her a kiss. " 'Course it could be some animal's stumbled into it, a deer or a javelina."

"But you don't think so?"

"We'll soon know. Get dressed and get down on the floor. You don't want to take a chance on a slug coming through the wall."

"Oh, Irons. What about your sister? Send her and Brucie in here."

"Right." He drove his arms into the sleeves of his heavy coat.

The door to the cabin creaked open. They both froze until Gladdie's petulant voice came out of the darkness. "Sammy, it's me. I've brought Brucie in here where it's safe."

Irons hurried out of the bedroom. "Good girl. Keep down," he ordered. "Better spread Brucie a pallet on the floor. You'll like that, won't you, Brucie?"

"Sweepy," came the muffled reply.

"I'll take care of them," Fan said from behind him. Although the night was relatively warm, she was shivering so hard her teeth were chattering.

"Good." He hurried back to her. "Keep down low," he ordered again. Catching hold of her dim white figure, he dragged her down to her haunches to illustrate.

She pressed two folded quilts into his hands. "I brought these for Brucie."

"Good girl." He passed them to Gladdie.

With a last metallic thunk, the noise stopped. The silence hung heavy and sinister.

"Maybe no one's out there after all?" Fan whispered.

"Maybe so. Maybe not. If it's them, they'll have more men with them, and chances are they'll have rifles. It'll sound like a war out there. Bullets'll start flying everywhere and these walls won't stop a Winchester." He squeezed her arm, feeling her whole body trembling. "Hey, chin up."

She fumbled for his hands, feeling the deep scars, the crooked fingers, still swollen from the terrible wounds he had sustained.

"Why, Fan . . ."

She did not realize she was crying until the tears splashed on their joined hands. "Do be careful."

He swallowed hard. "It's probably nothing."

She squeezed his hands tighter. "Just be careful."

"Damn right." He found her face in the darkness and kissed her hard. Then he released her and slipped lithely across the cabin, opened the door, a narrow slot of gray, and scooted out onto the porch.

Fan ran her fingertips over her lips, savoring the warmth of his kiss at the same time she tasted her tears. *I'm in love. And it's painful.*

"Is there any coffee?"

She shook herself out of her daze. "I think so." Keeping low, she made her way to the stove. It was still warm to the touch. The coffeepot sitting on the back of it sloshed when she lifted it. "It's not very hot."

"Just so it's wet and strong," Gladdie said.

Fishing two cups from the cupboard, Fan crawled back.

"Thank God for coffee," Gladdie murmured.

"Amen to that."

They strained to hear the murmured conversation carried on in deep tones outside against the wall of the cabin. When the voices moved off, the silence grew between them.

"You know you've got everything, don't you?" Gladdie burst out, making no effort to conceal the envy in her voice.

Fan looked around her in the darkness. "If this is everything, then I'd hate to see less."

"Sammy cares about you. He *really* cares. I can't believe it. I didn't think I'd ever see my brother take up with another living female."

"He didn't take up with me. I was shoved off on him." Nevertheless, Fan felt a warm tingle. She wanted to believe Irons cared, wanted to believe she was more than just a convenient body and potential source of wealth.

"That probably explains it," Gladdie sniffed. "He's hated women like poison, ever since Clary."

Fan stiffened. Irons had never discussed any personal history with her. She did not think he would want her to know what Gladdie was about to reveal.

"God! I hated that bitch."

Fan could hear the click of Gladdie's teeth against the rim of the cup.

"She got her claws into Sammy but good."

How Irons would hate to hear this conversation! "Wouldn't you like some more coffee?"

"Love some if there's some more."

"If there's not, I'll make some. The men are going to want it anyway when this is over." Awkwardly, Fan moved back to the cupboard. Better to keep busy than dwell on what might be going on outside. In her mind's eye she could picture rifles trained on Irons and his men from the deep pines. She could see the man draw his breath and hold it, see the trigger finger tighten . . .

"She didn't want me around."

Fan started. "Who?"

"Clary. But I fixed her but good. Sammy was workin' nights and she was steppin' out on him with a cowboy. A cowboy, for God's sake! I sent a message that I was sick and he was needed at home. 'Course, he came on the run and found her with one of the sorriest so-and-so's in that wide place in the road." Gladdie chuckled softly. "Served her right. She cried and took on, but he just told the guy to hit the road and take her with him."

Fan dropped the lid of the coffeepot. It sounded shockingly loud in the still room. Brucie murmured a little protest from between the quilts, but Gladdie paid no notice.

"Once a saddle tramp, always a saddle tramp."

Fan pushed a piece of wood through the door of the stove and sank down on the floor. She cupped her hands around the enamel coffee cup. It gave no warmth, but she pretended that it did.

"You're no saddle tramp. Somebody brought you up right and gave you ad—van—tages." Longing strung out the syllables of the word. "You've got a lot of nice clothes," Gladdie went on shamelessly. "I went through 'em when I moved in. Too bad they were too big for me. You'd have had a time gettin' some of 'em back."

"A couple of them might be altered," Fan said generously.

"No!" Gladdie's answer was swift and angry. "No, you don't. I don't take charity. I don't take anything from anybody. And don't you feel sorry for me neither."

"I just thought—"

"Well, just unthink it." Gladdie sounded insulted.

Fan lifted her shoulders in a silent shrug as she wondered at the code of ethics that would permit someone to help herself to another woman's clothing but would flatly refuse to take a gift.

"I accept help from two people," Gladdie said more calmly, "and two people only—Sammy and Clell. They both owe it to me, so I take it."

The coffee began to boil. Fan stood up to lift it off the stove.

Gladdie held up her cup. "I like to've died when Clell came back without that arm. I said to myself, 'That's it. There goes the whole damn thing.' My whole future was shot to hell and gone. I'd had this baby and he was going to be a handful to take care of. I knew I'd never have a chance if I stayed with a one-armed man. A kind word and a pat on the head and he'd turn into a drunken bum too fast to talk about." She cursed softly.

"But surely . . ."

The shrill petulant voice went on and on. "And I was right. He was a monster. Mad at the world one minute and bawling his eyes out the next. Brucie was just a baby and I couldn't leave him. And I couldn't find anybody very choicy to take on the two of us. That damned arm ruined everything." She lapsed into morose silence.

Fan waited and hoped exhaustion had overtaken Gladdie so she would slip down on the quilts beside Brucie and go to sleep.

Instead she repeated self-pityingly, "I didn't have a chance."

"Maybe your luck's changed," Fan said softly. "England's Fancy will blow in any day now. And then we'll all be rich."

"I don't count on it," Gladdie scoffed. "A wildcat well. Don't make me laugh. Besides it's yours. Sammy told me so."

Fan started to protest, then decided against it. "Is Sammy his real name?"

His sister chuckled. "Nope. And mine isn't Gladdie. We don't have real names. We're orphans. I remember my real name, but Sammy doesn't even remember his. We were left so long ago. They called him Sammy in the home. I just call him that because it gets under his skin."

"He told me his name was Irons."

"That's a fancy name that he made up for himself while he was in the army. I hate it. It's like he's braggin' that he's better than me."

They sat in silence. The wind gusted around the cabin carrying the faintest of metallic sounds to their ears.

They both started, then Fan said hopefully, "I don't think there's anything out there."

"Damn, I wish they'd never gone." Gladdie's voice quavered, then strengthened. "Goddamn stinkin' place. Cuba. Why? Whoever heard of it? Whoever cared?'' She leaned toward Fan, her breathing rapid. ''I loved Clell. So much. I loved everything about him. He was going to take care of me. I could be a little girl for him. He carried me around in his arms half the time.''

Fan laced her hands around the cup, thinking of Irons carrying her from place to place when she was too weak and sick to walk. His arms had been the only haven in her tormented world. Her ears strained in the darkness to catch the slightest sound.

''Now he can't even carry Brucie to do any good. I had to pick the poor little kid up and carry him in here.''

''He loves you so much,'' Fan whispered, trying to offer some comfort. Gladdie swung her white face toward her. Her mouth in the dimness was contorted into an agonized grimace.

''Well, of course he does. He really don't have much choice. He's got nothin' else in the world but me.'' She sank back bitterly. ''Say, don't you have anything to sweeten this stuff?''

''I think there's some whiskey in the top of the cabinet.'' Fan rose to find the bottle.

''I don't hate Clell, but I don't love him neither. He shouldn't have gone to Cuba with me pregnant and all.''

''Did he know?''

''No, but he should have guessed it was going to happen.''

Fan pulled the cork out of the bottle and poured a bit into Gladdie's cup.

''Much obliged.'' The blond woman drank deep. Her hand sought Brucie on the pallet. ''Poor little boy. He's not a lot better off than I was at his age.''

The wind blew and buffeted the cabin, carrying tiny metallic clinks to their listening ears. Fan's overactive imagination could picture the men creeping through the darkness following the line, searching for intruders. If one came upon the other, would they recognize each other in time? Her eyes were burning. Salty tears impossible to suppress slipped down her cheeks. She was drowning trying to keep from sobbing aloud.

Gladdie took another drink. "And now you've gone and fallen in love with my brother." She waved Fan's embarrassed protest to silence. "It's all right if you want to make a fool of yourself. Just be sure you don't try to take him away from me and Brucie." Gladdie took another drink. She leaned her head on her elbow and cuddled closer to her son.

"I wouldn't take him away," Fan assured her, her voice wobbling only slightly. "Even if I could, there's enough for all if that well blows in. Oil's selling for four-fifty a barrel."

"And you'll just love to saddle yourself with a crippled man and his family?" Gladdie sneered.

"I like Clell," Fan replied coldly. "He's been a good friend and he's worked twice as hard as anybody else has."

Gladdie sat up suddenly. "Say, you're not thinkin' he might be a good bet if you can't snare Sammy? Listen. Clell's mine. And don't you forget it. I'm the mother of his son and no high-toned . . ."

Boot heels stomping up on the porch stopped her in mid-sentence.

She leaned toward Fan. "Just leave him alone," she grated. "He's mine."

Irons and Clell came in the door. "Nothing there," Irons told them. "False alarm."

"Clell, sweetheart," Gladdie exclaimed struggling to her feet and running to him. She put her arms tight around his middle. "Are you all right?"

"Right as rain, Gladdie." Clell's arm closed around her. His voice reflected his surprise.

"I was so worried. I just sat here and waited and worried. Now I'm just exhausted. Can we get back to our tent?"

Fan lit the lamp and took down two more clean cups. "There's hot coffee fresh made," she suggested softly. "Don't you want some?"

"I want to go to bed right now," Gladdie pleaded.

With the look of a man in a dream, Clell gazed down into her pretty face upturned to his, her chin only inches from his chest. "If that's what you want to do, darlin', we'll do it."

Gladdie threw Fan a triumphant look. "Why don't we just leave Brucie here on the floor where he's comfortable?"

"Probably a good idea," Irons said. He looked at Fan for confirmation. She was busily engaged in opening the stove door to poke at the coals. Her face was very red.

Irons' eyebrows rose then drew together as he stared after the departing couple. What had Gladdie said? "Fan?"

She turned to him, her face twisted.

Without thinking he held out his arms. She went into them, with a muffled exclamation. Her hands latched together in the small of his back. She hid her face against his chest. He hugged her. "What happened?"

"Oh, Irons."

"What did she say? If she hurt you—"

"No. No." She pulled back, shaking her head. Tears began to trickle down her cheeks. Why this evening of all evenings was she unable to control herself?

He frowned. "What's wrong?"

"It's just that I—I'm sorry. I shouldn't be crying

like this, but I can't seem to stop." She let her head sink forward until it rested against his broad chest.

He rubbed her back. "What did she say? Damn her. She's got a tongue like a file."

"Nothing. Believe me. Please. She's so frightened. And unhappy."

He heaved a deep sigh of relief. "Oh, is that all? Did she give you her story about how Clell should never have gone to war."

"Yes. But I can't say that I don't agree with her. I don't care anything about Cuba either."

He was silent. Her tears wet his shirt. He rubbed her back and rested his chin on top of her head. Finally, he heaved a great sigh. "Tell me what this is all about."

She waited a minute. He thought she might not tell him what was wrong, but she finally turned her cheek to his chest. "It might have been you."

He went still. His breathing stopped, his heart skipped a beat, then thrummed erratically.

"You might have l—lost your hand in the draw works. Or both your hands." She shuddered convulsively. Her teeth clicked together when she tried to clench her jaw.

"Fan!" He pressed his fingers—all eight of them and his thumbs—against her back, feeling the fragile cage of ribs, the slenderness of her waist.

"I can't stand this," she whispered. Her arms hugged him so tight that her grip was almost painful. "You could have gone out there and died. And I'd have never told you again. Never."

"Told me?"

"I love you, Irons."

He sucked in a deep breath. "Fan, you don't know what you're saying."

"I do. I love you." She tipped back her head and

looked into his face. The light was still too dim to see the expression in his eyes. His mouth was closed, his jaw clenched. His body felt stiff and hard as he withheld himself from her.

Slowly, she released him. His arms loosened allowing her to step back out of them. "I'm sorry if you didn't want to hear that."

He rubbed his hand around the back of his neck and turned away. Crossing to the stove, he poured himself a cup of hot coffee. Suddenly he was conscious that his hands pained him. The fingers that had been broken, the trigger finger particularly throbbed.

She stared at his forbidding back. Without his arms the cabin felt cold as ice. "I guess I'll say good night."

He set the cup down. "No." He caught her, turned her in his arms. Her face was pale, in contrast to the high spots of color that set on her cheekbones. "Don't go."

"I need to go to bed." She tried to twist out of his hands. When her efforts failed, she turned her face away.

"No, we'll both go to bed in a little bit." His voice shook, then gathered strength. "You didn't mean what you said."

She looked at him then. "I wouldn't have said it if I hadn't meant it."

"But you know who you are now. And you know who I am."

"What difference does that make?"

He shook her gently. "Look at me." When she complied, he went on. "What do you see?" He revolved their bodies so that the lamplight fell on his face, not hers. "What do you see?"

She tried to conceal her emotions since he did not want them. Composing her face, she raised her eyes. The jaw might have been granite so tightly was it set.

Blue-black shadow covered it completely except for a tiny white scar near the corner of his mouth. The nose was straight and finely modeled, not hawkish or flattened as it might have been if he had had Indian blood. The black eyebrows were drawn tightly together above the storm-gray eyes. Silver gray hair, incongruous over a face so young, flopped over his forehead.

His eyes looked levelly into her own. His eyes tore at her heart.

She raised her hand to touch the scar on his cheek. "I see Irons."

His face contorted. "That isn't my name. I made it up."

"It's a wonderful name."

"Listen, before you say anything more. When you've heard the story, you may want to change your opinion." She shook her head, but he put his hand over her mouth. When he spoke the bitterness was thick in his voice. "Listen. My name is Sammy. At least that's what my sister Gladdie says it is. If she is my sister."

"How can you say that?"

"Oh, very easily. My earliest memories are of her taking my hand and leading me away from the other children, teaching me to call her 'Sister,' telling me I was her brother. Maybe when she was a child, she needed someone to be her brother. Maybe she just picked me."

"Oh, Irons, I can't believe . . ."

"No, you can't," he interrupted. "Because you're just lately come to hard times. You lost your memory and it almost drove you crazy. But you never gave up hope that you'd regain it. Your past would all come back to you. Your mother, father, grandparents, sisters, and brother. You'd get them all back. You'd be whole again and everything would be wonderful. What if there were no memory to regain?''

She felt the tears again in her eyes. Until that very minute, she had never understood his obdurate pride. Her fingertips caressed his cheek. He caught her hand and turned his lips into her palm. She swayed toward him her very bones melting, but he clasped her hand and sternly moved it away from his mouth.

''I'm nothing,'' he grated. ''I'm sure you understand. I'm nobody. You say you feel sorry for Clell, but you wouldn't if you knew who he is? He's R. D. McClelland. His folks came to Texas while she was still part of Spain. That's the kind of a family he's got. His father and mother stand behind him one hundred percent.''

''Families are wonderful, but they're not *that* important.''

His beautiful mouth curled up at the corner. ''You say that when you've just had your whole future secured by yours,'' he jeered. ''You take off for South Carolina and come back with a damned fortune. You don't need this well. You come back to buy pipe for it, put a fancy name on it, and suddenly it's just a damned hobby for you.''

''That's not fair. If I hadn't wanted it to succeed, to make our fortunes, I wouldn't have come back.'' Clenching her hands in frustration, she turned away. ''You have this idea about yourself being unworthy because you were brought up in an orphanage.''

''My folks could have been anything. They probably were the worst kind of scum.''

She swung around to face him. ''That's ridiculous. This is the twentieth century. Nobody—but nobody—believes that stuff anymore. You're as good a man as I've ever known.''

''But—''

" 'But' nothing." She flung herself across the room, caught him by the shoulders, and planted a hard kiss on his mouth. "I love you. Irons. Not somebody's son or grandson. I don't care about anything else."

"But—"

She put her hand over his mouth. "Don't say it."

His gray eyes glinted silver above her hand. The black mustache tickled her palm.

"Oh, Irons." She pressed herself against him. "I love you. If you don't love me, if you can't love me because I nag or because I argue with you or because I've been somebody else's wife then say so and I'll never mention it again. But don't turn away from me because you don't think you're good enough for me."

Their eyes locked—gold and silver glinting in the dying lamplight. Slowly, trembling, she removed her hand.

He hesitated. His whole soul torn with longing, his mouth twisted in anguish. Then he caught her to him, wrapped his arms around her. As though he were drinking after a long thirst, he kissed her mouth, her cheeks, her forehead, her eyes, her mouth again. "I do love you. I do. I do."

She clasped her arms tight around his neck and hung on laughing, glorying in his declaration. "Oh, Irons. Irons."

"I love you. And right or wrong, I can't keep it a secret any longer."

She was weeping with joy. His lips traced her tears and caught them. "Don't cry. Please don't cry again."

"Oh, I know. I've been doing it all night long. Like a watering pot. I can't help it. But I'm so happy."

"I hope to heaven I never make you sorry for this." He kissed her on the lips, drinking from her. When he lifted his head, they were both reeling.

"I'll never be sorry."

He stared down into her face, taking in her high color, her lips bruised red with his kisses. "You're the best thing that ever happened to me," he mused. "Somehow back last winter my luck changed. I found you under a tree. I almost rode away and left you, but you looked at me." He touched the side of her cheek. "You looked at me just like you're looking at me now. And I couldn't leave you."

"And now you'll never have to." He kissed her long and lovingly, taking his time, drinking from her lips. Their eyes closed, all other senses alert to taste, touch, and scent.

The lamp guttered out, its fount empty of kerosene.

She spoke out of the gloom. "It's morning. We've been awake the entire night."

"No wonder I feel like I've been knocked into a mud hole and tromped dry."

She kissed him. "Suddenly I'm so tired I can barely stand."

"We've still got a good hour before full daylight." He put his arm around her waist. "Hop aboard."

"You don't have to carry me."

"Damn right, I do."

Giggling a little, she slid her arms around his neck and kicked up her feet. He caught her beneath the knees and lifted her into his arms. Stepping over Brucie, who had been asleep on the pallet the whole time, he carried her into the bedroom.

Chapter 23

"Take the day off tomorrow?" Clell stared at Irons' smiling face. "What for? It's not Christmas."

"Fan and I are going to get married."

At those words Clell's smile matched Irons'. "Well, I'll be. Put 'er there, pard."

Irons grinned idiotically as he pumped Clell's hand. Wiping their hands on their overalls, Brazel and Early also came forward to shake with him and clap him on the back.

"You're gettin' a wonderful girl," Brazel declared, carefully pronouncing a word he had almost never had occasion to use. "Miz Breckenridge is wonderful. Just wonderful."

"Congratulations, boss," Early added.

"We'll knock off the first tour tomorrow," Irons said, "Get cleaned up, have a party."

Hoke came leaping down the ladder from the monkey board. "What did I hear?"

"Fan and I are going to get married."

"No!" Hoke made a show of distress. "Well dang my luck. Missed again. Found the girl of my dreams and then she ups and marries my boss."

Brazel scratched his head in astonishment. "She

warn't gonna marry you anyway, Hoke,'' he said slowly.

Early hooted and slapped Brazel on the back. ''You may not catch everything, buddy, but you're sure right about that.''

''Hey,'' Hoke protested in mock anger. ''Don't you guys have any feelings at all. My heart's broken.''

''It'll mend the next time you get to town,'' Early jeered. ''Hey, Hoke, face it. She wanted someone smart and good-lookin'.''

''Yeah, but she picked me.'' Irons ended the conversation. ''Brazel, I'd like you to hitch up the wagon and ride with Fan into Batson. She needs a new dress, new shoes, everything. We're getting married in style.''

''Don't you need a new suit?'' Clell asked staring pointedly at Irons' disreputable gear.

''We've decided that I'll get one the day the well comes in. It's so close now that I'd probably get a new one all dirty when she blows.''

They all exchanged fatuous grins. Irons tilted his head up at the rig and inhaled deeply. The sharp rotten-egg odor of hydrogen sulfide gas filled his nostrils. With it came the knowledge that he was in all probability also inhaling natural gas, colorless and odorless, but a likely precursor of oil. ''Come on, black gold,'' he called to the towering structure. ''I got me a wife to cover in diamonds.''

Clell threw his arm over his friend's shoulders and hugged him hard. ''I hope she appreciates who she's getting.''

''I guess you heard who's back in town?'' The woman at the post office window leaned forward to whisper to Fan.

"No. I can't say that I have." Fan remained at the window, sorting through the mail.

The postmistress waited, searching the cool features avidly for some sign of curiosity from her customer. When none was forthcoming, she sniffed. "All I can say is, you'd better find out before you go out in the street after what happened to you the last time."

Fan froze. "What do you mean?"

"I heard all about what happened between you and that huzzy Eufemia Carlton."

Fan flushed. "Oh."

The postmistress nodded eagerly. "Yes, ma'am." She leaned forward until her face was only inches from the bronze bars of her cage. "She came back into town a couple of days ago. Her and that man she rode off with. And no wedding ring on her finger either." Her mouth lifted at the corners, then drooped again so quickly that Fan could not have sworn she had smiled. "Her kind never does get one."

"Did she come back with Paul Breckenridge?" Fan looked at the addresses skeptically. "All the mail for Rosemeade is still here."

"She came back in a wagon with the man she left with," the postmistress said with a note of satisfaction.

"But they were so rich. Their wells had come in flowing hundreds of barrels a day at four-fifty a barrel," Fan objected. "They must have come back for a visit."

"Well, maybe so. Maybe not. My husband says that nobody's smart enough to read those Standard Oil contracts. You can go over them with a magnifying glass and read every comma and still get cheated."

Fan remembered her own happiness. "For their sakes, I hope you're wrong." She handed the Rosemeade mail back to the woman. "Paul will probably get around to this soon."

She and Brazel left the store, loaded with packages. The dress was not what her first one had been. She could remember it clearly. White satin with lace appliquéd in seed pearls. A magnificent veil also hand-appliquéd by the church ladies at Nuestra Señora de la Concepcion in San Antonio. It had been a dress for another woman.

Then she had been a baby, a virgin bride, stupid and eager to run out into danger. Now she was a woman whom danger had found. Now she knew enough to make a clear choice.

She would wear a tailored suit in navy broadcloth. The jacket was severe, buttoned down the front, nipped in at the waist. The skirt was gored and fit her quite well considering it was bought from the rack. It represented the new practical woman. Among all the clothes Irons had brought her from Rosemeade, not one looked anything like it at all.

Its plainness was offset by the soft white blouse. It tied around the neck with a bow edged in lace. To wear underneath it, she had bought white satin knickers and a camisole edged in lace two inches wide. She grinned at her own calculated sensuality. No longer innocent, the thought of Irons' expression when he took off her clothes made her feel hot all over.

Happiness swept through her, raising the skin on her arms. As the faithful Brazel held the door for her, she realized she was still grinning—like an idiot. And why not? She was getting married to the man she loved. The horror of the previous year seemed dim and far away. Irons was her future.

She would be Mrs. Irons. Mrs. Samuel Irons. Mrs. Sammy Irons. Mrs. Caroline Fancy Irons. Oblivious to the passing faces, she led the way to the wagon to deposit their purchases.

Suddenly, she was shocked out of her revery by the

face of Eufemia Carlton thrust into her own. "You'll never get him back."

Brazel dropped the packages on the boardwalk. Fan had never seen him move so fast. He shouldered his way between her and the other woman before either one of them could draw a breath.

"Don't you touch me, you stinkin' roughneck," Eufemia screeched, jostled backward by the burly figure.

Brazel hunched in a stance that a wrestler might take facing an opponent in a ring. "Just back off there, lady."

"Get the hell out of my way. I'm gonna speak my piece." Eufemia tried to go around him. Brazel shifted with her, keeping his body between hers and Fan's. He cast an embarrassed look over his shoulder as Eufemia let fly with a string of curses. Yelled at the top of her lungs, her tirade turned heads all along Batson's main street.

Hastily, Fan dropped her packages into the wagon bed and turned to face Eufemia. With her hands free she could defend herself if the woman tried to attack again. "It's all right, Brazel. I can take care of this."

Reluctantly, the big roughneck moved out of the way. Instead of meeting Fan head on, Eufemia shifted sideways to face them both. "Think yer smart, don't yuh, honey bunch? With yer big bodyguard."

"We were minding our own business," Fan told her calmly.

"Oh, la-de-da," Eufemia sneered. "Well, you just keep right on mindin' yer own business. 'Cause you ain't never gonna get him back." She pushed without success at the brassy blond hair. Her ducking and dodging had canted it to the left where it hung over her ear. On her right side, the roots around her ear and across her forehead were an inch long and very dark brown. Her waist was wrinkled, the hem of her skirt soiled and stained.

Why she's pathetic, Fan thought, she doesn't even know how to take care of herself. But dangerous. She remembered what Clell warned her of. A hat pin in the ribs as easily as a fist. "Miss Carlton, you seem to be operating under some sort of misunderstanding. I don't want Paul Breckenridge. He's always been yours, if you can get him." Fan stared pointedly at the woman's left hand.

Eufemia snatched her hand back, then laughed shakily. "Oh, I'll get him. We've worked it all out."

"Then good for you." Fan kept her voice carefully cordial. "I congratulate you."

The blond woman seemed at a loss. "That's all you got to say?"

Fan smiled coolly. "I didn't begin the conversation in the first place."

Eufemia shrugged. "That's right, you didn't. But you been warned. I'll get him. He'll come up to snuff. You just keep that in mind, honey bunch."

"I will. Good day, Miss Carlton."

Fan motioned to Brazel, who hurried to untie her mare from the hitching post. He held her stirrup while she mounted, then climbed to the wagon seat himself.

As she reined the sorrel, a man stepped out onto the steps of the hotel across the street. His hands were thrust deep in his pockets, his shoulders hunched; his hat brim shaded his face. He glanced up as the mare danced nervously. Across the width of the muddy street, their eyes met.

Fan swayed in the saddle. "R—rex!" The world swayed around her. The mare pivoted beneath her and unbalanced her, so that she slipped sideways.

"Miz Breckenridge." Brazel tumbled off the wagon box reaching out his big hands to catch her. She was barely conscious of his moving her back to sit on the steps of the general store. "Miz Breckenridge?"

He knelt beside her, his hands under her arms.

"Brazel?" She looked up at him vaguely. "Brazel? Did you see that man?"

"What man, Miz Breckenridge?"

"The man on the steps." She pointed but the wagon was between them and the hotel.

Brazel raised up. "There ain't nobody there."

"I saw him." She looked suspiciously around her.

Eufemia Carlton was beating a hasty retreat down the street.

"Catch her," she commanded Brazel. "Catch her and bring her back. I have to talk to her. I have to."

"Yes'm. Just let me get you up in the wagon or in the store where you can sit down and rest a spell."

"No. Don't mind me. Go after her. She's getting away." Even as she spoke, Eufemia rounded the corner of the building and disappeared from view.

Brazel looked after her in alarm, then stubbornly persisted in helping Fan to her feet. Only when she had wrapped her arm over the sideboard of the wagon and assured him that she was going to be all right, did he loop the horse's reins over the hitching post and lumber off in the direction Eufemia had taken.

Fan stared at the porch of the hotel. No one was there. The door itself was open, but the interior was dark.

She must have been mistaken. Rex Breckenridge, her husband, was dead. Hanged more than half a year ago. A lifetime ago.

She was as sure of his death as she was that she was standing in the street, the hot sun beaming down on her so hot it cracked the mud. That was it! The sun! The sun was too hot. A dose of it must have caused her eyes to play tricks on her. She had stayed too long in the street talking to Eufemia.

She took her own pulse. It raced and jumped erratically, but it proved nothing. She shivered. With all her heart, she wished she could climb onto the sorrel's bright back and gallop away, leaving Brazel to follow at a more dignified pace in the wagon.

Even as she made the wish, it died aborning. She could not. Curious as Pandora, she put her booted foot on the boardwalk.

Step by step she crossed the street and climbed the steps to the porch. The shade of the hotel lobby dropped over her head, a difference of twenty degrees in temperature. The pupils of her eyes reduced to pinpoints by the bright sun reacted slowly in the new darkness.

Momentarily blind, she waited, shudders running down her spine. When she could see, she licked her dry lips. By that desk Eufemia had attacked her, punched her and driven her to her knees. If the hotel clerk had not intervened . . .

She nodded to the same clerk who regarded her warily.

"May I help you, ma'am?"

"Do you have a Mr. Breckenridge staying here?"

"Not really, ma'am. He's checked out and already left. You probably saw him. He just walked out the door."

"I saw a man on the porch, but he ducked back into the hotel."

The clerk looked puzzled. "Did he, ma'am? I was back in the office for a minute."

"Is there a back door?"

"Yes, ma'am, but—"

She hurried to the back of the lobby behind the stairs and tried the door. It was locked.

"That's not it, ma'am. It's a guestroom. The only back door is behind this desk and through the office and out. We nailed all the others. Had to. We had guests trying to sneak out without paying their bills."

"Then Mr. Breckenridge must have gone back upstairs."

"He might have. But his bags are gone."

"Was Miss Carlton with him?"

The clerk grimaced, then nodded. "She stayed with him in the room for one night, ma'am. I believe he said they were checking out and going back home today."

"Did he have a horse in the livery stable?"

"Yes, ma'am. And a wagon." As he spoke, they heard the rumbling of a wagon pulled by a galloping horse.

She ran to the door. It flashed by, Eufemia Carlton on the seat beside the driver, her body between Fan and the man who whipped the horses into even greater speed.

More determined than ever to have the truth, Fan hurried across the street. "Come on, Brazel!"

"Miz Breckenridge! Wait!"

"Come on!" Pulling the reins from the hitching post, she swung up on Tina's back and laid her heels to the sorrel's ribs. The mare leaped forward.

"Miz Breckenridge, don't go ridin' off by yourself." Nearly frantic, Brazel clambered into the wagon and struggled to turn the balky team around. By the time he had gotten them through the deep mud, the road ahead was empty.

For Fan the chase was over almost before it had begun. The old livery horse that pulled the wagon could do no more than a couple of hundred yards at a gallop before it began to heave and pant. Before the couple were completely out of sight of town, the creature was already slowing down to a trot that no amount of laying on with the whip could increase.

Eufemia looked back over her shoulder, her lips pulled back from her teeth in a sneer. "Looks like we've got company."

The man beside her threw a glance over his shoulder and cursed. He slashed the whip twice. The old horse whickered in pain and tossed its head. It galloped heavily for a couple of rods, then stumbled to a trot again.

The sorrel's smooth flowing stride ate up the intervening space.

"Rex!"

The man pulled back on the lines. The old horse stopped instantly, sides heaving in and out, neck beneath the collar white with foam.

"Rex! My God. What? How?"

He smiled a sickly smile. "Hello, Fan. How are you?"

"I'm alive," she whispered. "But just barely." Pain lanced through her head as she stared at him unbelieving. And Rex Breckenridge—not the shadow shape that remained in her mind after the beating, nor the face in the black and white photograph—stared back at her. Her husband's face.

Despite the beard and mustache it was he—not Paul.

Paul! His brother!

She steeled herself to ask the question to set the record straight. "Rex, I thought you were dead. I thought—everyone thought you were hanged. If you didn't die that night, who did?"

Rex hesitated.

"Paul?" She answered her own question.

"Yes."

"Dear God!" She could feel the tears starting in her eyes. The memory of the night swept over her. The terror, the pain, the brutality. "Oh, Rex. It was awful."

He hung his head. His jaw set.

"I tried to hold him up." The tears streamed down her face. Oblivious to the sun and the dust of the road and the dark green pines on either side, she tried to make him understand why she had not been able to save his brother. "I did lift him, Rex. But they just pulled the r—rope tighter."

His body shuddered convulsively. The reins fell from his hands.

"Then they beat me down and one of them grabbed hold of his knees . . ."

"For God's sake, Fan!" Rex's voice was a groan of agony.

"I tried to save him, Rex. I t—tried. But I wasn't strong enough."

"Please, Fan . . ." He thrust out a shaking hand in her direction.

"I couldn't do anything against them."

"Surely to God, you don't blame yourself." He managed to meet her eyes for the first time. His cheeks were white, the black beard a startling contrast.

With a tormented nod, she whispered again, "I wasn't strong enough."

They stared at each other, nausea and pain heavy in the air between them.

Into the silence Eufemia's voice cut like the swipe of a cleaver. "Let's get out of here," she complained. "It's damned hot out here in the sun."

Although he did not move, Fan watched the play of expression over Rex's face. The moment of union with her was over. The corner of his mouth curled in distaste as his eyes slid sideways at the other woman. He hunched his shoulders, pulling his head down between them.

Suddenly, Fan remembered why she had ridden after him. "Why didn't you help me?" she demanded, guilt giving way to resentment and outrage. "Why didn't you tell me who I was?"

At her tone he thrust out his jaw. "I did tell you who you were," he reminded her self-righteously. "I just didn't tell who I was."

"For heaven's sake, why not?"

"Well, I—I should think that would be perfectly clear to anybody with half a mind. It was me they came for. I'm the older brother, for heaven's sake. They got Paul by mistake." He looked around restlessly. "Don't you see? They'd have come back if they'd found out they hanged the wrong man. If I took you home with me, they'd have another clue to figuring it out."

Fan stared at him in disbelief. "Rex, for heaven's sake, that's the flimsiest excuse I've ever heard. Everybody thought I was your sister-in-law. I wouldn't have told them. I was almost beaten to death. I didn't know who I was. You left me at the mercy of strangers."

"When I saw you, you looked like you were doing all right," he sneered. "That big roughneck was giving you plenty of what you've always wanted."

She tightened her grip on the reins, knowing that if she had a whip she would have struck him. The sorrel danced under her. "That's perfectly ridiculous. You didn't even leave any money for my care. I scrubbed floors at that boardinghouse in Waldrow to keep Irons from having to pay out of his own pocket."

Rex made a second plea for understanding. "I figured you were all right and I was all right. If I'd helped you too much, someone might have gotten suspicious. Until I got everything worked out, I wasn't going to take any chances."

She stared at him narrowly. "And how long was it going to take you to get everything worked out? You left town in a fancy motor car after Eufemia punched me out."

The blonde laughed, but Rex threw her an angry look. "She didn't hurt you. I—I was afraid you'd spill the beans and—and then they'd come after me again."

"Who? Who might have come after you?"

He lowered his voice. "Why—er—goons, yes, goons. That's who. Goons from Standard Oil—"

Fan interrupted his fumbling speech. "Rex, you leased Rosemeade to Standard Oil. They wouldn't have sent goons to try to kill you."

"I hadn't done it when I was—that is—when Paul was—"

"If you knew goons had tried to kill you, why did you tell Sheriff Barfield that Irons had done it?"

Rex hunched his shoulder against her. His gaze flicked away to the space between his horse's ears. "Well, he could have been guilty. I'm still not sure that he wasn't. He might have been one of the one's who did it."

"That's ridiculous. I told you that. Why would he have saved me if he'd been hired to kill me?"

"Do we have to sit here in the middle of the road and straighten this out?" Eufemia complained shrilly.

"Why, Rex?" Fan insisted.

"I—I—"

"Let's go on to Rosemeade." Eufemia made a great show of fanning herself. "At least there we can sit down in the shade and have a cool drink."

Not without a faint sense of satisfaction, Fan shook her head. "You won't like what you see when you get there. It's horrible. Everything is ruined. The land, the house. A wreck. The servants who worked for the Breckenridge's for years are gone."

Eufemia shot Rex an accusing look. "You mean that your house is gone to rack and ruin? You promised me—"

"Shut up!" he snarled.

Fan nodded coldly. "It's a wreck," she repeated. "Oil and dirt all over everything."

"Rex!"

"Shut up, I tell you. After Paul was killed, I wanted to get away as fast as I could. I let everybody go."

"You let Mrs. Gonzales go," Fan accused, "and Addams. Why he taught both you boys to ride. You told me so. You told me he was like a father to you."

Rex's ears beneath the brim of his hat turned scarlet. "I—It was safer."

"Safer maybe for you," Fan scoffed. "That's why you did it, wasn't it? They knew who you were. They knew you weren't Paul."

"They might have been beaten up, killed," he protested. "I did it to protect them. You don't understand. I was terrified."

"So terrified you pretended to be your own brother. This doesn't make any sense. If the goons from Standard Oil had killed you, then Paul would have been the next target. Why would you pretend to be your own brother?"

He jutted his chin out defiantly. "I had my reasons."

Eufemia thrust herself forward. "He did it for me."

"Eufemia," Rex cautioned.

"Tell her," she commanded suddenly. "Tell her. She's just dying to find out. Go ahead. Let curiosity kill the cat."

"Maybe you'd better tell me."

Eufemia leaned around Rex's cringing body. "Paul was a damn fool, honey bunch. He wanted everything to stay just the way it was. He went on and on about how that place had been in the family for so long. And how they could make a go of farmin'. Farmin', huh!" she sneered. "Farmin' ain't nothin' but grubbin' in the dirt and gettin' farther and farther in the hole."

"Standard Oil offered thousands of dollars in royalties if we'd lease the land to them," Rex added. "And he wanted to turn it down." One narrow hand clenched around the handle of the whip. He leaned toward her, his dark eyes intent. "I knew it was a mistake. I begged him. But he wouldn't listen. I warned him."

"Are you saying they came for Paul?" Fan shook her head. Her confusion grew. "None of this makes sense."

"Well—"

"Then why me? Why take me? I didn't even know this was being discussed."

"I was the one in danger," Rex said calmly and patiently. "I was the one doing the negotiating."

"Then they thought you turned them down?"

"Yes!" he exclaimed eagerly. "Yes! They came for me but got him by mistake. Poor Paul."

"What are you saying?" Fan felt the cold knot of nausea form in her stomach. "You held out for more, but you didn't try to fight them. You didn't organize guards."

"I—I couldn't afford to," he whined. "You remember how things were. I didn't have any money."

"Oh, no, Rex." Suddenly it was all clear. His admission slipped the last piece into place. "That's why you took his name. Paul didn't owe all those debts. You did."

He hung his head. "It was a chance for a fresh start."

"I can see how well you've started." Fan said drily remembering the Tollivers. "I still don't see why they took me."

"Er—you must have seen their faces."

"No. I'm sure I didn't. They came for me. But where were you? You were supposed to be in the room across from me. Paul was down the hall. Where were you?"

"I—I thought—I—I didn't think—"

"You ran." Fan closed her eyes against the pain. When she opened them, she had turned her head to stare into the depths of the cool dark piney woods. "You left us there to die." In her head boots thudded. Her door burst open. Yellow light from the hallway silhouetted a blocky figure with features hooded. It darted toward her, another following close behind. She blinked and heard Rex speaking.

"I—I went for help."

"With us dead you could be Paul and be free and clear of your debts."

"Damn you, you don't know what you're talking about."

"Tell her the truth," Eufemia interrupted.

"Shut up." He whirled on her. "What the hell are you talking about?"

"He wasn't there that night."

"Eufemia."

"He was with me. You hear that, honey bunch? He's alive because he was with me. I saved his life."

Fan tightened the reins on Tina's neck. "You're welcome to it. You both deserve each other. There's just one other thing, Rex."

"What?"

"One of the men who did the job was your man Pyote."

"What?!"

"Pyote."

He gaped, then licked his lips. "Impossible."

"Irons is sure."

"Impossible," he repeated. All the color drained from his face. "He's crazy."

"Rex, he's not. Pyote wears a ring that made the scar on my face."

"A ring." Rex scanned her cheek, then threw back his head and managed a false bark of laughter. "That's crazy. He's crazy. You're crazy."

She straightened in the saddle. "Believe what you want. If it makes you feel better to think that a murdering goon couldn't possibly be riding behind you, it's your funeral. Just remember. You were warned." She reined Tina around.

"Wait." Rex made a swipe for the horse's head. The mare shied and danced out of his reach. "What about that piece of property of Paul's?"

She hesitated, while Tina half rose and came down, champing at the bit. "What about it?"

"Did you ever get drilling started?"

"It's started."

"Lease it?"

"No."

His dark eyes narrowed. "Is it looking pretty good? Is it close to coming in?"

Fan gave him the truth of all oil men. "Nothing is ever close on a wildcat well."

They stared at each other across the roadbed. "You're my wife," he reminded her.

Eufemia uttered a shrill cry of protest.

"Shut up!" Rex snarled. "Half of what's hers is mine. That's Texas law. I want my share of that well."

"You got your share of everything," Fan reminded him. "You and Eufemia left town in a motor car. I never got my share of that."

"You're my wife," he repeated doggedly. "If you know what's good for you, you'll look around for your wedding ring and put it back on."

"I'll never put it back on. I gave it back to you."

"Rex," Eufemia protested. "You promised me."

"Don't get pushy," he retorted nastily.

"Listen, you promised me, you son of a . . ."

He cuffed her brutally across the side of the head. The blow knocked her backward off the seat. She fell into the back of the wagon in a tangle of skirts, petticoats, high-button shoes, and naked legs. Fan stared at the pinwheeling confusion as Eufemia screeched curses and threats like a banshee.

"She's not going to come between me and my lawful loving wife." Rex made a show of dusting his hands of her. "Now, Fan—"

"You're a monster. And I'm not your wife."

"You'll give me my share of that well."

"Never. You don't have a share."

He looked at her speculatively, then shrugged. "What's it worth to you to get rid of me?"

"That well is mine. It belongs to me and to the men who drilled it for me. You'll never get your hands on a penny from it."

Eufemia had righted herself and crouched on all fours in the wagon. Her hair streamed around her shoulders. A huge sausagelike rat dangled from the side of her crown. Her eyes looked daggers at Rex's back. Her teeth were bared in an expression so malevolent that Fan felt cold chills down her spine.

Rex's own expression constituted no less a threat. His eyes flicked right and left along the road. He dropped the lines of the hired wagon and stood up in the box.

Fan's hand tightened on the reins. Tina backed. At that moment the heavy trot of a horse reached their ears. Brazel rounded the turn astride one of the wagon horses, the long reins trailing in the ground. At the sight of her, he whipped the beast. It buck-jumped then galloped toward them.

Brazel pulled it to a halt only when he had guided it

in between her and Rex's wagon. "Miz Breckenridge, are you all right?"

"I'm fine, Brazel. What happened to the wagon?"

"It got bogged down to the axles in that damned mud. I was afraid I couldn't get it out fast enough. So I just unhitched him and came on."

"Lucky this time, honey bunch," Eufemia sneered.

Rex shot her a murderous look which she returned. "Just don't forget," he flung at Fan. "Your property is my property."

"I'm filing suit just as soon as I can get a telegram to Houston."

"Houston?" His smile was less sure.

"That's a wildcat well out there," she reminded him. "It might come in. It might not. But I promise you this. You'll never get your hands on one penny that it makes. I'll hire the best lawyer in Houston. If I have to prove reason, there's always her"—she pointed to Eufemia—"with a dozen witnesses including the sheriff."

"Damn you, Fan."

"No, Rex. Damn you." She swung her horse around. "Let's go, Brazel."

"Yes, ma'am." His voice cracked with relief as he reigned his horse and drove between her and the angry couple in the wagon.

Chapter 24

Fan clasped her hands together so tightly the knuckles showed white. "We can't get married until I get a divorce."

She felt her heart turn over inside her as the warm and welcoming smile disappeared from Irons' face and the closed wariness replaced it. "What's the story?"

"Those goons didn't hang Rex. They hanged Paul by mistake." She clasped her arms around her waist, feeling the trembling start deep in the pit of her stomach. "Rex heard them and—ran. He says—for help."

"He's a liar."

She shrugged. "Probably. But he never was a fighter."

"This makes everything different, doesn't it?"

"Well, yes. We'll have to wait until a divorce is granted. I'll have to file. But I'll file immediately. I'll get a Houston lawyer."

His lip curled under his mustache. "Maybe you don't want a divorce?"

She searched his face. "Of course, I do."

"He's rich."

"He's a swine."

He blinked at her vehement retort but insisted doggedly. "He's rich."

"He isn't," she denied instantly. "He's in debt up to his eyebrows. And if he were the richest man in the world, I wouldn't want him. He left me with you there at that boardinghouse because he was afraid someone might figure out that he wasn't his brother and try to collect some money he owed them. He fired all those poor old people who had worked for him for years for the same reason. He owed money and he saw a way to get out of paying it. And then he struck oil and still he didn't pay his debts. He's a coward. And I don't want any part of him."

Irons appeared to be gnawing at something. His eyes slid over her and studied the bare walls of the cabin with unusual intensity. "You could get a lot of money by this divorce."

Her eyes flashed angrily. She stabbed her fingers into his chest, rocking him backward. "Irons, I ought to be furious with you. You're implying that I'm a fortune hunter."

He shrugged. "I just thought—"

She pushed again. "Then don't think. Listen! I'll pretend you didn't say what you said. And forgive you because you don't know what the situation is. *He* could get a lot of money by this divorce."

He nodded slowly. "The treasure."

"He doesn't know about the treasure. He knows about this well." She gestured toward England's Fancy, its engine throbbing away in the late evening sun. "He wants his share."

"What about your share of what he made on Rosemeade?"

"That's gone. I told you he didn't have any sense about money. He's spent every penny that Standard Oil gave him for the leases. He and his girlfriend have come home poor as church mice.'' She made a face. ''A stupid comparison if I ever made one.''

''So you want a divorce before the well comes in.'' His face was still closed, his mouth tight beneath the black mustache.

She pushed him again. This time with both hands. Her cheeks flushed bright pink. ''No, you big fool. That isn't why I want the divorce. I want the divorce because I want to marry the man I love. He is a man who loves and trusts me. He believes what I say. He doesn't question everything as if he were a prosecuting lawyer. I want to marry that man, if that man exists.''

Shamed color also darkened Irons' face. ''I'm sorry,'' he muttered. ''I guess I just let my hopes get too high.''

Instantly, she forgave him. Putting her arms around his neck, she drew his head down for a kiss. ''Our hopes were both high as that rig out there, but we'll just have to wait. It won't take too long. After all, he deserted me and denied me in front of Sheriff Barfield. And he left town with Eufemia Carlton. I should be able to get my divorce quite easily charging desertion and adultery.''

Irons raised his black eyebrows. ''I think I'd stick to desertion. Adultery might be kind of a problem since we've been living together.''

She sucked in her breath. ''But that's different.''

''Not much.'' He lowered his head and kissed her. Long and deep. His tongue caressing, sliding down the super-sensitive interior of her mouth while she squirmed in pleasure against him.

When they both came up for air, she looked up at him, her eyes liquid gold. ''Are you going to take me to bed and work your wicked, adulterous ways on me one more time?''

He gulped. ''Sorry. I've got to take the next tower.

The hard work will do me good.'' He pressed his body against hers, leaving her in no doubt that he wanted her every bit as much as she wanted him.

''Irons, I do love you.''

''I love you too.''

Slowly, he put her from him, kissing her lips first, stepping back, then leaning over and kissing her forehead. She swayed with eyes closed.

With a sigh he stepped back and smiled. ''I love the look on your face right now. I could eat you alive for breakfast, dinner, and supper.''

She opened her eyes and smiled. ''Greedy man.''

''Damn right.''

He pulled his hat down tight on his head and managed to walk to the door without actually strutting. ''There's just one thing I want you to promise me.''

''What's that?''

''Don't leave this site without at least two men. Brazel's a good hand, but he's not quick enough. Take Hoke with you too. He's too lazy to work the well anyhow. And he'd love to ride around with you.''

''Rex would never hurt me. I'm the goose that laid the golden egg.''

He frowned. ''You're not usually slow. My kiss must be more powerful than I suspected.''

She made a fist and brandished it at him.

''Seriously. He'd kill you in a minute. All this would be his just so long as the two of you are still married.''

''Surely not. Rex is a coward and a philanderer, but he's no murderer.''

Irons came back. The scarred, misshapen hands dropped down on her shoulders. ''I didn't want to mention this possibility because I didn't think you needed to carry any more around with you than you're already carrying.'' He looked down into her eyes. His own hands began to tremble. He kissed her again, hard. "Oh, God, Fan."

"Tell me," she breathed when her blood had stopped pounding in her ears so she could hear his answer.

He touched the crescent-shaped scar on her temple. "You remember when we talked about that goon Pyote?"

"Yes, Pyote. I warned Rex about him."

He grinned a sharp, mirthless grin. "Oh, you did." Irons cupped his hand under her chin, holding her face as if it were something infinitely precious. His thumb rubbed back and forth gently across the slightly raised skin. "The chances of Pyote working for Standard Oil are next to none."

She stared at him in growing horror. "No. You're mistaken. You've got to be mistaken."

"How did it happen that he took you too? Standard Oil wouldn't have bothered with a woman."

She drew a deep shuddering breath. "I can't believe this."

Irons' smile was quietly ironic. "Think just a little bit harder, baby."

She stood silently with eyes closed. When she opened them, they were hazy with tears. "But Paul was his own brother. He couldn't have . . . That's hideous . . . horrible. I won't believe it. S—Standard Oil . . ."

"Standard Oil gets blamed for a lot because they do a lot. They're a crooked bunch. They probably would have come after Rex. But in this case I don't think they did."

She swayed weakly. "I think I'm going to be sick."

He put his arm around her and drew her in against his shoulder as if hiding her eyes would somehow shield her from the truth. He could feel the dampness of her body through her clothes. She had broken out in a cold sweat.

Gently, he stroked her hair. When her shuddering stopped, he spoke again. "My guess is that Rex told Pyote to hang you both. But Pyote made a bad job of it, though to give him credit, you'd have been dead by daylight if I hadn't come along. Chances are the others were just roughnecks he'd hired to do the job. They didn't mind stringing up Paul Breckenridge, but Fan Breckenridge was a horse of a different color. They might even have kept him from finishing the job. Not many men from around here'll hurt a woman."

"Standard Oil hires people like that all the time," she protested feebly.

"Why kill you? You'd be the bereaved widow, willing to sell up for a song and a ticket home to mother."

She raised her head and leaned back against his arm. "I never knew he hated me so much."

Irons shrugged, his mouth tight. "Probably didn't. He got to sounding right jealous there in the boardinghouse when he found out I'd been taking everything I could get."

She flushed. "But he ordered Pyote to kill me."

"Probably didn't think anything about it like that. He saw what he saw: a chance to make a lot of money and get his creditors off his back. He tried to get Paul to go along with leasing the land, but Paul wouldn't move. So the easiest thing would be to have him re—moved."

Silent tears began to fall. "He said that Paul wanted to farm the land."

He nodded. "Can't run cattle or raise cotton with an oil well every few yards. It's a filthy business. It ruins the land for anything else."

She wiped the back of her hand across her cheeks. "I was—am—married to a monster."

His fingers slid down her spine, rubbing the bunched muscles. "Relax. It's not the end of the world. Remember all the people who love you. Your family. Your friends. We'll protect you." His hand trailed away from her body. "I'll knock off early."

Fan was the first to smell the smoke. Its acridity penetrated the delicate membranes of her throat and set her coughing even as it woke her. She sat up in bed, eyes smarting, conscious of a gray haze in the darkness. "Irons." She reached over and shook his shoulder. "Irons."

He was breathing heavily beside her.

"Irons." He rolled over on his back, mumbling unintelligibly. "*Irons!* Something's burning."

He roused. Coughed heavily. "Damn."

She felt him begin to tremble. She threw back the covers and stumbled across the floor to the door. The nearer she came the thicker the smoke became. The planks were hot to the touch. "Oh, Irons, hurry. The fire's on the other side of it."

Closing his eyes, Irons tossed his covers back and thrust his feet into his boots. Even as he bent over to tie the leather laces, he could feel the terrible fear rising within him. Fire. His fingers fumbled. He clenched his hands into tight fists. Instantly, he remembered the flames licking around them. He gasped and flexed them, trying to bring them back to reality. More than anything in the world, he hated and feared fire.

"Irons."

He kept his head bent, his eyes focused on the floor. Someone had set this. He tried to whip up fierce anger. No need to ask who. No time to wonder how a marauder had gotten through his alarm system. No time.

Fan staggered back and caught at his arm. "Irons."

Sucking in the lungful of smoke-filled air sent her into a paroxym of coughing. "Irons!" The tears were streaming from her burning eyes. "For God's sake!"

Irons could feel nothing, hear nothing except that Fan was calling to him. He knew he was in deadly danger, but the fear of the fire held him paralyzed. He could not rise and open that door and go into the face of it.

Frantically, she wrapped her arms around his arm and tugged, but he sat like a stone. "We've got to get out of here! Stand up! Stand up! Irons! We'll be burned alive!"

The very blood retreated from his skin to the center of his body. There it buried itself to escape the agonizing torture it had experienced before. Without oxygen his brain no longer received and transmitted messages. He began to lose consciousness.

"Irons!" She slapped his face. Twice.

His head rolled on his shoulders. He did not feel the blows. Only one thought flashed over and over. The fire would burn him. Would burn his hands. His hands. He could not go to face it. He coughed, but the struggle for air was nothing to fear.

Fan looked frantically toward the door. Grayish-white smoke was pouring between the cracks. Where were the crews? Three gangs of men had been working and sleeping only a couple of hundred feet from where they were trapped. Why did they not come to the rescue?

Her eyes began to stream. She coughed again. The heat was already building in the upper air. She dropped to the floor where the air was still cool and relatively fresh. As though he were a huge limp doll, she dragged him with her. One glance at his terrorized face and she knew her course. She must think for them both. Get them both out. There could be only one reason why the men on the tower had not come to their rescue. They must not know of the fire. It must be contained in that room. Someone had set the cabin on fire to kill her. And Irons with her.

A surge of adrenaline tightened all her muscles. She must not fail this time. She had not been strong enough when Paul had died. This time she would be smart enough to save them both.

A glance at the door told her that no one would go out of the bedroom through there. The planks were beginning to glow red-hot through the blinding smoke pouring between them. She and Irons had bare seconds left before the whole thing crumbled. When that happened, the blast of heat would probably knock them unconscious.

Crawling to the head of the bed, she pulled Irons' gun from its holster. Dropping back flat, her cheek to the floor, she took a deep breath of the clearest air in the room and held it. Then springing to her feet she smashed the butt of the revolver through the windowpane five feet above the cabin floor. The six-inch square of glass fell away, making only a faint tinkling sound in the darkness.

"Clell! *Clell!* Fire! Fire! Help! Help!"

Her air was gone. She broke out the other three panes, then reversing the pistol, she fired it out the window.

As if the shot were a signal, the area suddenly seemed to come alive with movement. The cowbells on the alarm system set up a terrific clamor. Questions, exclamations, orders echoed and re-echoed. The kerosene lanterns hanging from the legs of the derrick were instantly doused.

The invaders had waited for an alarm before beginning their assault. The blaze had gone unnoticed longer than anyone had expected because Irons had frozen, unable to act.

"Miz Breckenridge!"

"Brazel! Oh, Brazel!"

"Mother o' God! The cabin's on fire." A bullet whizzed past his head. "Hell and damn. We're gettin' shot at."

"Brazel, get a crowbar and tear out the window."

"Yes'm." He spun away, almost crashing into Clell, who had come on the run.

"Fan, get the hell out of there. Jump." Clell held up his arm to the window, his nightshirt a white target in the darkness.

"I can't. The window's too small and too high."

He looked around him desperately. A volley of shots came from the woods on the other side of the rig. A man cursed. Then the blast of a shotgun was followed by screams and a terrific din of jangling metal.

Clell's teeth flashed white in the darkness. "That's Early. Where's Irons?"

"Here. With me." She was coughing. The smashed window served as a flue to suck the smoke from the cabin. She could not breathe in it. "He can't move."

Clell cursed again. "Come on. You're small enough to wiggle through that window."

"No. I won't leave him."

"I'm comin'. I'm comin'." Brazel came running with the crowbar. He hooked it over the top of the vertical planking at the edge of the window. Setting his foot against the side of the house, he jerked back with all his strength and weight.

The nails squealed in protest. The board gave a couple of inches. Brazel stepped back, spit on his hands and set foot against the very bottom of the board. A deep groan slid out between his clenched teeth. Clell slid his fingers into the crack that began to open and added his weight to the effort.

The shotgun boomed again, this time to the right. The cowbells jangled again. A man screeched in agony.

"Get that son of a bitch!" a strange voice yelled. A couple of seconds later the shotgun boomed in his direction. Early had broken the gun and reloaded with lightning speed.

The vertical one-by-twelve spanged loose.

"Come on, Fan."

"Irons." She crawled back to his side and crouched above him. "Irons, we can get out without burning now. Come on, Irons. Clell and Brazel have rescued us. You're not going to burn."

His eyes were closed. He barely seemed to breathe. Thrusting her hands under his armpits, she began to drag him across the floor.

"Pull off another one," Clell shouted to Brazel. The crowbar hooked again. At that instant the inner door collapsed. Tongues of flame leaped through the space. Borne on the firestorm they headed upward through the window into the night. The blast drove Fan backward, but she did not lose her grip on Irons.

If they died, her hands would be locked to his body, dragging him in the direction of safety.

"Fan."

"Miz Breckenridge." Brazel wedged his own thick body in through the gaping hole and grabbed Irons' shoulder. His strength pulled the body swiftly across the floor.

"Come on, Fan. We've got you now." Clell's arm was around her legs.

"Irons," she protested, but he swung her through the opening and set her on the ground.

"Get down flat." He pushed her off her feet. "A stray bullet could take the top of your head off."

Brazel had maneuvered Irons' head and upper body through the hole. Clell sprang to help him. Suddenly, he seemed to stumble. Fan saw him throw up his arm, arch his back, and turn halfway around.

"Clell!"

"I—I'm hit." He staggered a step. Dropped to his knees. "I'll be damned."

"Clell!"

He fell face downward. His hand struck her cheek. Brazel pulled Irons through the hole and stretched his body on the ground. Then he knelt beside Clell. His hand fumbled for the heartbeat.

"Clell." Fan caught his wrist between her fingers and thumb searching for the pulse. She could not find it.

"He's dead, Miz Breckenridge," Brazel groaned. "Lord, he went quick."

Irons stirred in the cold air. "Fan, baby."

She began to tremble. Her whole body shook with her effort to deny the awful reality. "Clell." She leaned over and pushed Brazel's hand aside. "We've got to be wrong. In this confusion—"

The shotgun boomed again. The cabin roof caught fire and blazed into the sky illuminating the scene, bathing it to the edges of the clearing in garish red-orange light. Now the men of England's Fancy had targets. Crouched behind the feet of the derrick and the draw works, they could suddenly see their enemies advancing toward them from the trees.

"Get 'em boys," Early yelled. "Make every shot count."

"What's happening?" Irons sat up. His face was drawn with strain.

"We're under attack. They've hurt Clell," Fan sobbed.

"Hell!" He rolled his head back staring at the fire. "Hell!" He climbed to his feet.

"Be careful."

"Damn right." Bending low, he sprinted toward the tents.

Fan realized with a guilty start that she had not even thought of Gladdie or little Brucie. Breathing a fervent prayer, she pressed her ear to Clell's chest. Then clutched at his shoulders. He was dead.

The fire cast macabre shadows through the rig's skeleton. The drill still moved, like the heartbeat of a giant, oblivious to the struggles of the little creatures around its legs. A shot came from the monkey board. She grinned. Hoke crouched there, taking careful aim, picking his targets, protected by the rig.

As she stared, a movement at the base caught her eye. Something strange, foreign, moved on the rotary table. In the leaping light it glistened, then bubbled. She blinked, rubbed her eyes, stared again.

"Clell," she whispered to the dead man. "Clell. Oh, look. Is that what I think it is?"

It seemed to grow in height, like a little bubbling fountain of water in a park. Glistening black, it flowed across the floor of the rig. Higher the fountain climbed and higher still.

Hoke saw it too. "My Gawd!" he screamed. Thrusting his gun into his pants, he leaped for the ladder. "Gawd Almighty. Watch it, Early. She's comin' in."

Early glanced behind him. The firelight picked out the whites of his eyes. He plugged another shell into the shotgun. Turning toward the woods, he leaped from the rig floor. Firing the shotgun to clear a path, he yelled, "Run for it, boys! She's comin' in."

With a roar that shook the entire dome of earth, oil shot up through the joints of the derrick.

It hit Hoke in the face, blinding him completely. Rocks and pieces of equipment blew by his head. He dared not take a breath. His lungs burned as he hugged the ladder and struggled doggedly down. Its force threatened to tear him away with each step he counted off.

"Miz Breckenridge. Miz Breckenridge! Get away from the cabin," Brazel shouted. "If the oil hits that fire, we'll be burned alive." He lumbered up to her and pulled her to her feet.

"But—" She reached out toward Clell. The leaping flames illuminated his still face giving it the illusion of movement. His dead eyes glittered from between the slitted lids.

"He's dead." Brazel's face was covered with shiny black. His shirt and overalls were soaked.

Pulling her with him, they ran for the woods. Behind them rocks, mud, and pieces of the rig exploded into the air. No more shots were fired as both sides fled for the comparative shelter of the trees. From behind the thick bole of a pine, she watched the stuff spouting into the air, streaming down in a great fall of black liquid.

"The good Lord's put out his hand," Brazel muttered beside her. "It's spoutin' north."

"The cabin's about gone out anyway."

He shook his head. "It'd start over again if that stuff was to hit it. And then that fire'd run right up and back into the hole. We'd have a wild well for sure."

"Come on, boys." Irons' voice thundered above the roaring of the well. With a feeling of relief, she recognized it. He was all right. "Let's get her capped off."

"What about the goons?" somebody yelled.

"They're runnin' for their lives," Early shouted. "I'm pretty sure I got their boss."

"Come on. Show's over." Irons yelled again. He strode through the debris toward the roaring, spouting torrent. "Let's kill it. We don't want to waste any of it."

In fascination and disbelief, Fan stared at the well. England's Fancy a hundred feet high, a torrent of power. At that moment she could not believe any force on earth, even the strength of Irons could control that force.

Seemingly oblivious to the black rain coating him, he directed the men. Brazel reversed the pumps and the heavy mud that had been filling the mud pit for weeks was forced back into the hole. At first the pressure from beneath blew it out almost as fast as it was pumped in, but slowly at first, then swiftly the spouting stopped. Oil welled above the floor, then mud from the pit closed it off.

One man threw back his head and let loose a rebel yell. They clapped each other on the back, congratulating each other. Frenzied, with oil coating them, looking like actors in a minstrel show, they danced and shouted.

Irons drew in a deep breath and looked around.

Fan stood at the foot of the salt dome, her heart in her eyes. Like a man in a dream, he stepped down and came toward her. A yard from her he stopped. "I'll get you all dirty," he warned.

"That's not dirt," she whispered, and went into his arms.

Chapter 25

"Clell. Clell!" Gladdie moaned his name at the sight of the still figure on the ground.

Irons tried to intercept her, but she dodged around him and skidded to a halt beside her husband. Her face contorted as her tears began to flow. Stiff as an old woman she dropped down on her knees. Her trembling hands reached for him, then clenched into fists.

"Clell, Goddamn you. Why'd you have to stop another damn bullet?" Gladdie pounded the ground beside his shoulder. "Clell!"

"Sister." Irons spoke with more gentleness than Fan had ever heard. A pair of white furrows tracked through the oil and grime on his cheeks as he put his hands on his sister's thin shoulders and tried to lift her to her feet. "Come on, baby. That's not going to do any good."

"No!" She twisted and clawed at his hand. "Let me go. Clell, damn you." The men on the drilling crew shook their heads as she caught the body by the shoulders and shook it. "Clell. Clell. For mercy's sake, snap out of it. Talk. Don't leave me. Don't you dare die and leave me."

"Gladdie!" Irons caught her wrists and pulled her up by them. "Gladdie, calm down."

She stopped crying instantly. From under swollen lids she glared at him. The first rays of morning sun lit her fierce eyes. "He did it again," she rasped. "I'll never forgive him for this. Never. Never. Never. This time he got himself killed." Her face crumpled. "Oh, my God, what's going to become of me?"

"Gladdie, come away from here." Irons pulled her toward the trees.

"Where?" she screeched. She tore herself out of his arms. "Where? To the cabin?" She gestured toward it. Nothing but the foundation of rocks and a corner of the bedroom remained. It had burned completely to the ground. "Oh, sorry, can't go there. It's gone." She put her hands to her cheeks in mock dismay. "But there's always the tent?"

She pointed to it, her voice wobbling crazily. "Brucie and I can just go right back in there and be snug as a bug in a rug."

The spouting oil and mud had flattened it. The pieces of furniture—the table, chairs, cots—remained upright, but the black viscous liquid covered it. Where it sagged among their shapes, pools of the stuff had collected in its hollows.

Forcing her voice under control deepened it to a rasp. "Where am I going to go, little brother? Where are Brucie and I going to go?"

Fan tried to put her arms around the smaller woman. "We'll get in the wagon and go into town right now," she said. "Brazel, hitch it up. We need to get into town and give Brucie a place to lie down. Listen, Gladdie, we'll rent Mrs. Dittman's whole boardinghouse. We've got money now. You can have a bath and rest."

"And then what?" Gladdie whirled out her arms.

"What do I do then? Go back to Beaumont. Try to find someone else to take me on."

"You'll have Clell's share," Irons promised, "and everything I can spare."

"And live on charity," she snarled.

"It's not charity. Clell worked hard for his share. It's yours."

One of the new men came over to them. "Ma'am, our tent wasn't slapped down. Wouldn't you and the little boy like to lie down in it?"

She stepped back and looked him up and down. One hand went to her hip, the other to her hair. She pushed the blond locks back from her forehead. "Have you got a sip of whiskey in that tent?"

His eyes shifted from her to Irons standing like a statue, an ominous expression on his face. "I—I—just thought the lady would like to lie down."

"Don't worry about what he thinks." Her usually shrill voice was a hoarse rasp from the sobbing and crying. "He don't have a thing to do with this. Have you got a sip of whiskey?"

He swallowed hard. "Yes, ma'am."

"Then let's go." She swept Brucie up in her arms. "Let's go, sweetheart. This nice man is going to give us a place to lie down and rest."

Remembering his manners belatedly, he extended his invitation to Fan. "We can find room for you, too, ma'am."

"Don't bother about me," Fan said.

Gladdie carefully refused to meet Irons' eyes. As she walked away, she managed to shift Brucie into the roughneck's arms.

Irons swayed back and dropped down on his haunches. Clad only in his boots and long-handled underwear, his filthy, scarred hands drooping between his knees, he made a pathetic figure.

When his sister had disappeared into the roughneck's tent, he looked down at the body of his friend, now stiff and cold on the ground. Sudden tears followed the path of the two that had already washed his cheeks. He drew in a shuddering breath that racked his entire body. "Ah, God, Clell."

Fan came up behind him and put her arms around his shoulders. "Please, Irons, don't think about it anymore." She kissed his temple and cheek. "She didn't know what she was doing. She'll feel better after she's had time to think. Now she's terrified. She really loved Clell. I don't think even she knew how much."

"He's dead because of me," Irons' voice broke. "I froze."

Fan knelt in front of him and took his hands between her own. They were ice cold. She began to chafe them. "Don't be ridiculous," she said nervously. No light seemed to enter his eyes. The gray irises were opaque as winter ponds. "Irons. Listen to me."

"I froze." His voice, sick with exhaustion and pain, pronounced judgment on himself. "I went off in a funk when I should have put that fire out."

"I don't believe it could have been put out," Fan argued. "That shack went up like tinder."

He shook his head. His eyes drifted to Clell's still face. Again he had to swallow a sob.

"I woke up first," Fan argued, bringing her face only inches from his. "When I got to the door, it was already hot. Smoke was pouring through it. I never even opened it."

He closed his eyes, refusing her comfort. "If I'd gotten right up and charged in there the way I should have—"

"You'd probably have been burned alive."

He shook his head. "You don't understand. I had all that training in the army. I could have—"

"You couldn't have put it out," Fan insisted flatly. "Believe me. It was out of control before we ever woke up. We were almost overcome by the smoke. We were lucky to have had Brazel and Clell on the outside to pull the wall down. Otherwise, we'd have burned alive. You in a funk and me wishing I was in one."

He would not answer.

She took his face between her hands. His jaw, unshaven for more than twenty-four hours, was blue-black and prickly. With her thumbs she scrubbed at the tears, only succeeding in smearing the oil and grime on his face. "You've got to stop this. Just stop it."

He jerked her head back away from her rough ministrations. "My best friend is dead."

"But you didn't shoot him."

"No, but if I'd done what I was supposed to do, he wouldn't have needed to be out there. He came to help me."

She rocked back on her heels. "That's not the way of it, I'll have you know. He might have been coming to help you, but he was helping me when he died."

Irons pressed the heel of his hand hard between his eyes. "Clell," he groaned. "Damn it, Clell."

She felt his pain within her, but his assumption of guilt made her angry. She put her hands on his knees. "Irons. I love you more than anything else in the world. And I've seen you work miracles. The fact that I'm here right now is one of your greatest feats. But you are not God Almighty. Every once in a while you have to remember that you're only human."

"Damn it. Clell is dead. Because I—"

"No. He's dead because someone—probably my husband—wanted to kill us both. The fire was set to kill you and me. The men who were shooting weren't shooting to kill. No one else was even hurt."

"I can't—"

"Yes, you can," she declared. "If you want to, but I'm not going to blame myself for his death. I want to find the person who did it. And when I do, I'm going to see that he hangs." Her voice was low and deadly. The words were a vow. With her hands on his knees she pushed herself wearily to her feet. The rising sun limned her body through the thin nightgown, her only garment.

Irons rose, too, suddenly embarrassed at the sight of her. He was conscious, too, that he wore nothing but his underwear. Everyone who saw them could be in no doubt of their relationship. He glanced around. The roughnecks were going about their business, carefully ignoring them.

He sighed. Nothing about his own state could have penetrated the depths of his despair. Her state of undress, her provocative near-nudity, acted on his fierce male possessiveness to jar him out of his self-pity. "I need to find you some clothes," he muttered.

She nodded. "So you finally noticed."

He looked in the direction of the cabin. Nothing remained. Her clothes—every garment she had brought with her from Rosemeade—were gone forever. His own practicality enabled him to put aside the grief and guilt and concentrate on solving her problem. "You don't have anything to wear."

The morning sun had bathed the whole dismal scene in its bright light. Fan grinned down at herself. "I'm in my nightgown again."

He returned her smile, his own so weary he could barely lift the corners of his mouth. "And I'm in my long handles. Come on. We'll rustle us up some clothes from the undamaged tents."

As she started off beside him, he noticed she was limping. Going down on one knee, he lifted her foot. The sole of her bare foot was coated with oil and mud.

He touched it with his thumb. "Are you cut somewhere?"

"I don't think so. My feet are just tender. I've been running around barefoot all night. Also I think they were scorched while I was getting out of the cabin."

"I have to thank you," he said. "Brazel told me how you wouldn't get out through the hole when he got the first board off. He said you ran back into the smoke to drag me out. You saved my life."

She smiled. "Not really. I probably didn't really do much more than get in the way. If I'd gone ahead and jumped out, Brazel could have gotten in and dragged you out quicker."

He hugged her tightly against his side. "You stayed with me."

Her heart was in her eyes. "That's what a wife is supposed to do for her husband."

He touched her lips in a tender kiss. ". . . 'to find you and save you or perish there too.' "

She drew back searching his face. "Poetry, Mr. Irons?"

He flushed. "I can't say for myself what I want to say."

"I've always thought you did very well."

He lifted her into his arms. "If we weren't in the middle of an oil camp, you'd be in trouble right now, baby."

Pyote could not feel his feet. He lay on his back blinking at the patch of blue sky fringed by black pine needles. He had lain so for several hours while the sky turned from black to gray to pink to blue. A couple of times, he had tried to move his head, but it was wedged in some rocks and his neck would not work properly.

He could hear the sounds of the oil camp. People walked and talked and went about work not too far from where he lay. They would not help him. He did not shout for them to come to his aid.

The night had been long. With the cabin burning to light the clearing, they had been sitting ducks. After the fight, he had had to lie low and rest for a while longer, then creep away. Breckenridge would pay plenty for this job. He would pay, or else—

He was damned tired of doing the dirty work and getting paid little or nothing. This time the boss would pay.

He was thirsty. He tried to lick his lips, but his tongue was dry.

A fly buzzed around his head and lighted on his cheek. He lifted his hand to bat it away. A splash of brighter color drew his eyes from the patch of blue. His fingers were stained with blood. As he stared, a trickle of blood slid down into his palm.

His hand had been lying in blood. He tried to raise his head. His neck hurt like hell, but he managed. Finally he managed. Grimacing in pain, fighting the stiffness, he stared down the length of his body. His belly rose in a mound that prevented him from seeing his feet. He looked all right from here. No sign of blood. No torn clothing.

He looked again at his hand. His vision faded in and out, the image splitting and coming back together. The blood had to come from somewhere. Where had his hand been lying? At his side. He let it fall wearily back. Beneath his fingertips the ground felt wet. He patted at it making a sticky, splattering sound. Blood was on the ground beside his body. He felt with his other hand. It too was lying in a wet spot.

Then he remembered. He had been shot. That damned shotgun. He had been shot!

His face screwed up tight. He began to whimper.

* * *

Dressed in Hoke's clothing again, Fan rode beside Brazel in the wagon. "Won't be no trouble at all, replacing your stuff," he assured her cheerfully. "Storekeepers'll fall all over themselves givin' you credit for whatever you want."

"I had just bought my wedding dress," she mourned. "I didn't even get to wear it."

He clucked sympathetically. "You can have a prettier dress than that. Now that you're rich, you can send all the way to Houston or even New Orleans for it."

The wagon jolted over a bump and she sighed. She was bone-weary and her shoulders ached. What she needed most was a bath and place to lie down—for a week. "Will we have any problem getting tankers to come out?"

"No, ma'am. They're just like the storekeepers. Just let 'em hear there's oil and they come like ants in a line."

"We've found one of 'em, boss, but he looks like he's pretty bad hurt."

Irons leaned the swab against the leg of the derrick. "Can you bring him in?"

"Not likely. I think he'll die where he fell."

"What happened to him?"

"Looks like Early got him with the twelve-gauge. I think his back's busted."

Irons exchanged a quick glance with his tool dresser.

"Nothing like one of them babies for givin' a man the edge," Early said without a trace of regret.

Clad in Clell's garments fished out of the chest from under the tent, Irons led the men to the wounded man's side. The terrible limpness of the porcine body confirmed the roughneck's diagnosis. Still, Irons went down on his knee. "Pyote?"

"Goddamn. Mighta know'd you'd find me." The man's breath was wheezing in his throat. He lay in a mess of blood and body wastes. His bladder and bowels had emptied when his spine had been shot in two.

Used to sights like this and worse in Cuba, Irons showed no emotion, but one of the younger men paled and hurried away. "Are you willing to say who put you up to this?"

The wounded man's beady eyes slid around the circle of faces that blocked out the fringes of pines. He closed his eyes and sent a message to his feet and legs. Nothing happened. He could not even feel the muscles that should be moving them. He opened his eyes again. "Am I hit bad?"

Another one of the men, one with a youngish face beneath the streaks of oil, pulled back out of the circle.

Irons' expression did not change. "I'm no doc, but I'd say that shotgun did a lot of damage to your backbone."

Pyote closed his eyes swallowing hard. "Shee—utt!"

In the silence that followed, Irons put his hand on the man's bloody thigh. Dispassionately, he pinched up a piece of the loose flesh. "Can you feel that?"

"Naw."

Irons looked up at Early. The roughneck shrugged. "A twelve-gauge can do a hell of a lot of damage."

Pyote opened his eyes. "Got a drink?"

"Water or whiskey?"

"Whiskey."

"I'll get some." Another man loped away and the circle closed again.

Pyote concentrated on the tiny patch of blue that their faces had not quite closed off. Again he tried to move his lower body. A great groan tore out of his throat. Blood spread into the pool beneath him.

Irons leaned forward. "Don't try to push it. Something might still be together. We'll get a piece of plywood and move you onto it."

Pyote shook his head. His eyes filled with tears. "Shee—utt," he said again. "Moving me ain't gonna do no good. I can't feel a damn thing. I can't see a whole heap of a lot neither." He blinked, but the edges of his vision remained cloudy.

The man returned with the flask. Irons held it to Pyote's lips. He drank eagerly and lay back. A little color returned to his lips. "Again," he begged.

Irons turned the whiskey up and Pyote gulped the fiery stuff. When the flask was empty, he dropped his head back onto the rocks. "Breckenridge hired me," he said in a clear, strong voice. "That damned son of a bitch has had me ridin' all over the county doing his dirty work and never payin' me a tenth of what it's worth."

"Rex Breckenridge?"

"Yeah. That gal's husband. He sure likes money, and he don't much care who he hurts to get it."

"What was the first job he hired you to do?"

Pyote concentrated on the patch of blue sky. It faded to black then became blue again. He coughed fretfully. His chest felt heavier as if a weight rested on it. He tried unsuccessfully to draw a deep breath. "Damn son of a bitch. He had me get a gang together to kill his wife and his brother. We dressed up like Ku Kluxers and hanged him. But when it came to her, them fools balked. Said they wasn't paid enough. They was sure right about that."

"So you tried to beat her to death."

"I wasn't going to beat her to death," Pyote denied

querulously. "She just kept on screamin' and fightin'. Just wouldn't shut up."

"You left her for dead."

"She come to all right, didn't she?"

"You're a liar," Irons growled. "You thought she was dead when you left her."

The men around the circle muttered among themselves.

"You men need to remember all this," Irons prompted. "You're hearing a murderer confess to a crime."

Pyote tried to roll his head from side to side in negation, but his neck was too stiff. He closed his eyes, then opened them immediately. A peculiar drifting feeling seemed about to carry him away with his eyes closed.

"When Breckenridge found she was still alive, he was mad, wasn't he?" Irons prodded. The ground beneath Pyote's body was soaked. His blood was trickling away in little rills down a gentle slope. No one could lose that much blood and live for very long.

Pyote licked his dry lips. The whiskey hadn't done that much good. He wanted water, but he could not hold the thought long enough to ask for it. Irons was asking for something. He wished Irons would go away and leave him to die in peace.

"Wasn't he?"

"T—told me to hang around and wait until she left the hotel. Then to finish the job."

"But you couldn't get her alone."

"Never found her alone but the once. She came out here. I'd left my horse in the trees, or I'd have got her."

"And then Breckenridge left town, so you stopped working."

"Hell, he wasn't payin' me enough to keep on tryin'. Figured it didn't make no difference anyhow."

"Until last night."

"Figured I'd get yuh both with one shot." He coughed shallowly. His belly seemed to settle. More blood trickled away. "We set the fire at the front door, then keep the crews pinned down so's they couldn't do nothin'. It shoulda worked."

Irons nodded. "Except for Clell." He could feel his own tears starting again. Listening to this mound of offal tell how he had mercilessly plotted and planned their deaths brought the terrible loss of a good man, a good friend flooding back to him.

"Breckenridge," Pyote coughed. His breathing began to rattle a little. "It was Breckenridge. Said he was broke. Wouldn't have no money to pay less'n he could get ahold of this place." His eyes closed. His hands twitched.

"You boys heard it all." Irons looked at the men leaning above them.

"Every word," Early said.

"Yeah, boss."

"Right."

Suddenly, Pyote's eyes flew wide. He coughed again, deeply. A tiny froth bubbled at the corners of his mouth. "Goddamn son of a bitch," he whispered. "He's gonna get outa payin' me again."

He looked for sympathy to Irons. A tiny shrug was his last movement. He concentrated on the patch of blue, until it faded from his sight forever.

On her way into the hotel for a bath, Fan met Harry Glennville. His eyes took in her men's clothing and the oily condition of her hair and skin. "So you've struck it," he said mildly.

"Last night. Blew in sky-high."

He shrugged. "My congratulations. Of course, it's not good for us. I'm afraid more and more of you Texans are doing that."

"We intend to continue to drill," she added, suddenly enjoying herself thoroughly. "My driller tells me there are several promising salt domes in the woods not far from our present site."

"Ah, but finding it and getting it out of the ground are not the whole of the business. You still have to get the product to market," he said, playing his last card. "Expenses can pile up, absorbing your profit."

"I've been informed that tankers will troop out to the well like lines of ants to get a fee for transporting oil. And I've enough capital at my disposal," she assured him, "to defray expenses over the short haul."

He bowed and smiled thinly. "Then we have nothing more to discuss."

She did not smile. "There is one more thing, Mr. Glennville. As soon as I've cleaned some of this off and made myself presentable, I'm on my way to see Sheriff Barfield about a fire that destroyed my cabin last night and almost killed me and my husband-to-be."

He looked at her with distaste. "We are not criminals, Mrs. Breckenridge. Everything we do is strictly legal. We would do nothing to endanger someone's life."

She looked at him narrowly. "Nevertheless, I intend to give Sheriff Barfield your name and remind him that one of your men set fire to my barn months ago."

"I've already told you. That was a mistake for which my immediate successor, Mr. Weisberg, has been removed. What's more, he has said over and over that his man did not deliberately set the fire. It was an accident. A careless match thrown into dry grass."

"Then there was the night attack when Mr. Irons was so badly hurt."

"You say he was attacked in the night. I heard that he fell into a piece of machinery. Are you sure he wasn't merely careless and trying to cover up his clumsiness by making up the story?"

"I was there. I heard the shots."

"Anyone may fire shots," Glennville insisted smoothly.

"We'll let the law decide."

"Let the sheriff come and bring that damned Texas Ranger that he's sent for. Neither I nor anyone who works for Standard Oil had anything to do with anything dishonest. Good day, Mrs. Breckenridge." He clapped his hat on his head and strode up the street.

"You sure ticked that fella off, Miz Breckenridge," Brazel remarked.

"I sure did, didn't I? And good enough for him."

Chapter 26

"Early, I've brought the sheriff. Where's Irons?"

The roughneck-turned-driller stubbed his boot at a clod of oil-stained earth. "He's gone, ma'am."

"Gone?"

"Yes ma'am. He lit out of here on that mare of his right after that *hombre* died."

"What man died?" Fan looked uncertainly at the sheriff, who was taking in the entire conversation. Behind him the Texas Ranger's shoulders seemed to swell as he took in the information.

"That bastard Pyote—beggin' your pardon, ma'am. Him that worked for your husband. Least that's what Irons said. He's the one that killed Clell. Confessed with his dyin' breath that he set the fire to try to kill you."

"How'd he come to be dyin'?" the Texas Ranger wanted to know.

Hoke hurried up behind Early and edged his way into the conversation. "Your husband's been the one all along, Miz Breckenridge."

Paschall Barfield fastened sleepy eyes on Early. "You say you got a dead man lyin' around here somewheres?"

Early shifted his bulk with just a touch of defiance and jerked a thumb in the direction of the lean-to that served as a barn. Booted feet and legs stuck out from under oily pieces of tarpaulin. "Got two. Our driller was shot and killed. And then the man that killed him was found—before he died."

"And who killed the man that killed him?" the Ranger wanted to know.

Early hesitated, but Hoke burst in. "Hey! Nobody knows for sure. Must have been a dozen people shootin'." Hoke gestured toward the remains of the burned-out cabin. "Just take a look at that mess. It was goin' like blazes when that well blew in. It's a wonder we weren't all blown sky-high."

Neither lawman seemed as interested in the charred remains of the cabin as they were in the bodies. The Ranger knelt and pulled the tarp back from the face of one.

"That's the fella that spilled the beans before he died," Early repeated stubbornly. "He was the one in charge."

Fan gasped. "It's Pyote."

"Yes'm. The bastard done cashed in his chips," Hoke said with satisfaction.

The lawman flipped the corner of the tarp back and walked around to the other side. Fan steeled herself as he revealed Clell's face. The skin had already gone to gray and sagged away. The bones of the face—nose, cheeks, and forehead—stood out in unnatural prominence as if her beloved friend were turning into a skeleton before her eyes. The teeth showed between the thinned lips as if the corpse were grinning.

"Oh, Clell." Fan could not help herself. Tears started in her eyes. She turned her face into Brazel's strong shoulder.

The sheriff stopped and covered the face up immediately. "Sorry, ma'am."

"He was such a good friend," she murmured, wiping her cheeks with her fingers. "And he'd suffered so much."

"Yes, ma'am." Paschall Barfield looked genuinely sorry.

"That skunk shot him in the back," Early said.

"And what happened to the skunk?" asked the Ranger.

"He got in the way of a twelve-gauge."

The Ranger rose, his hand moving back to the butt of his Colt, but Barfield intervened. "Looks like you folks have had a heap of trouble."

Fan smiled at the sheriff. She kept her hand through Brazel's arm accepting his support as she had come to do as a matter of course. "We've had nothing but trouble. This should be the happiest day of our lives. And we're looking at a burned-out cabin and two dead men."

Barfield hung his head. "Yes, ma'am. I'm already thinkin' that this twentieth century ain't gonna be all it's cracked up to be. To tell you the truth, I'm glad I'm close to the end of the trail."

The Texas Ranger cleared his throat. "Did somebody say something about a man having rode out of here?"

His question startled Fan. She turned to Early. "Did you say Irons has gone to Rosemeade?"

"I don't know whether he's gone to Rosemeade or not, but, yes, ma'am. He tore out of here more'n a hour ago."

Fan clenched her fists trying to stem the rising panic. "Sheriff, we don't have any time to look at dead men. We have to get to Rosemeade as fast as we can get there. Hoke, saddle Tina for me. I'll need a good horse."

"Hold it, ma'am," the Texas Ranger said. "We'll ride over to this place and find out what's going on. You can't come along with us."

Fan motioned Hoke on about his business. "Of course, I can. It's my home."

"From the sound of this there might be trouble," he protested. "A bullet can't tell whether it's gonna hit a man or a woman."

"I'm fully aware of that. I was within arm's length of poor Clell last night when he was hit."

The Ranger looked to Barfield for confirmation, but the sheriff merely shrugged and started for his own horse. "We'll be riding fast."

At that moment Hoke led up Santa Justina. The Ranger gaped at the elegant sorrel. The red hide was splotched with oil as was everything in the clearing, but the mare's conformation made his eyes glow. He came forward almost reverently. "Where'd you get that animal?"

"She was a wedding gift."

"Glory be. That looks like one of them Spanish horses that they breed over west of here."

"That's what she is." Fan put her toe into the stirrup that Hoke held for her. "She's was born and bred on El Rincón."

He snapped his fingers. "Sure thing. What's her name?"

"Santa Justina."

He put out his hand to stroke the pretty dish face. The mare accepted his touch as if it were her due. With a sigh he shook himself. "I don't suppose I could talk you out of coming with us."

For answer she set her heels to the sorrel and cantered away to join the sheriff, who was already through the gate.

Rosemeade looked infinitely worse than the last time she had seen it. Its paint had begun to weather and peel away. More and deeper ruts crisscrossed the lane to the house. A tanker wagon stood on the overgrown lawn. Its axle had broken and the oil had spilled. Evidently, no one had considered the old wagon worth the trouble to fix, so it had been abandoned there.

Fan shook her head. The criminal neglect of a once fine home brought tears to her eyes. What had Eufemia said? Paul was a damn fool. He had wanted the place to stay just the way it was.

Poor Paul. The place would never be the way it was. At least he did not have to see its desecration.

A rawboned sorrel stepped into the road ahead of them. "Took you long enough?"

"Irons!" She urged Tina forward until she could clasp his hand. "I was so afraid."

"Afraid I'd shoot him, Fan? I thought about it, but on the way over here, I did some thinking. I'm going to be a married man. I've got responsibilities to think straight."

"Oh, Irons." She lifted his hand to her cheek.

"I decided I'd rather see the guilty bastard swing. Dying quick and easy's too good for him."

He leaned over in the saddle and kissed her lightly. His grim expression belied his light words. "Howdy, Sheriff Barfield. Didn't know whether you'd bother to come this far."

Barfield flushed, then shrugged. "I come when I can do some good."

The Ranger pulled his mount to a halt. "I take it you're Irons."

"That's right. Samuel Irons."

The two men stared at each other taking each other's measure. "Pleased to meet you." The Ranger spurred his horse forward and held out his hand. "I'm Ord Coxey. Was you the one I've heard tell about who brought them boys the guns and ammunition?"

Irons looked surprised. "I was one of the ones."

Ord Coxey nodded enthusiastically. "Right glad to make your acquaintance. What's going on here?"

"Mrs. Breckenridge's husband is in that house. He paid that gang of roughnecks to raid our lease last night and set fire to the cabin. Mrs. Breckenridge was almost burned to death."

"Then let's go get him," the Ranger said. "Sheriff, why don't you stay back here with Mrs. Breckenridge." He drew his revolver and checked its chambers. "I'd appreciate your ridin' in at my back, Mr. Irons."

"Glad to do it."

The interior of the house was worse than the exterior. Cobwebs thick with dust stretched between the corners and webbed the banisters. Mud and oil had completely covered the hall carpet.

With gun drawn, Irons pushed open the door into the parlor. It was empty as was the office beyond and the downstairs. He and Coxey exchanged glances. The Texas Ranger pulled his hat lower on his head and started up the stairs.

Fan twisted fretfully in the saddle. "They're taking such a long time."

"Got to go slow," Barfield advised her. "They can't

just go bustin' in and hoorawin' the place. Liable to get their heads shot off that way."

"I can't stand this." She clapped her heels to the mare's sides and galloped up the lane.

"Miz Breckenridge. Wait! Don't do that. You don't know what you're walkin' into." He cursed under his breath and urged his own horse after her.

Eufemia Carlton came out of the room at the head of the stairs. She had dressed herself with care and pinned up her hair so that it looked as nice as it ever had. She had applied just the right amount of makeup. Not as much as she usually did and not nearly enough to cover up the bruises.

Her dress had been bought in New Orleans. It was buttercup yellow broadcloth. The gored skirt was slim to the knees then opened like a flower around the hem. The modiste who had made it swore that it was seven yards around the bottom.

She knew she looked exceptionally good in yellow. It was her best color. If she had had enough time she could have bleached the roots of her hair, but she did not have enough time.

The taffeta petticoat with the pleated tiers rustled as she walked to the head of the stairs to wait.

The Texas Ranger with his silver star on his chest climbed toward her, his gun drawn. "Ma'am?"

He was polite to her, she noted with approval. Clothes really did make the woman. Her smile flashed. "It's miss. Miss Carlton."

"Miss Carlton." He noted the swelling on the side of her mouth, the bruises on the cheekbone and temple. She kept on smiling.

"Miss Carlton." Irons had waited at the bottom of

the stairs. "Miss Carlton. We're looking for Rex Breckenridge."

"You've found him." She chuckled a little. "He's in the bedroom." She waved her hand over her shoulder.

The Ranger came up the rest of the stairs and moved warily around her.

Fan stepped into the door behind Irons.

"Too late, honey bunch," Eufemia called. She started down the stairs. "You'll never get him back. I told you, didn't I?"

"You told me, Miss Carlton."

"Looks like neither one of us will get him." Eufemia stopped in the front door and looked back at the ruin of the house.

The Texas Ranger came thudding down the stairs. "Who shot him, miss?"

"I did." Eufemia swayed back against the door facing. "I had to. It was self-defense. He beat me." She turned her face to the light and pointed to the bruises. "See what he did to me?" She stepped closer to the Ranger, who shook his head.

His voice was gentle as he studied the smooth skin. "Sure looks like he hurt you bad, Miss Carlton."

"Just so you've seen the proof with your own eyes, Mr.—"

"Coxey, miss. Ord Coxey."

"Ord. I have a cousin named Ord. He lives in Galveston. Any chance you might know him?"

"Well, no."

"I think there's a wagon and a team out at the stable. I'm really glad you're here, Mr. Coxey. I needed help so bad. Now I want to leave here, just as quick as I can."

"I'll get the wagon, miss."

Barfield stalked up the stairs to have a look at the body.

Eufemia turned to Fan. "That's how it's done, honey bunch. Think I'll ever have to stand trial?"

Fan shook her head. "Not you, Miss Carlton. If Mr. Coxey's not married, you may not even have to go back to Batson."

Eufemia tilted back her head and laughed brassily. "It's a thought."

Fan linked her arm around Irons' waist and hugged him against her. Together they climbed the steps of Mrs. Dittman's boardinghouse in Waldrow.

"We want *our room* for the night." Irons dropped a couple of silver dollars on the table that served her for the desk.

She stared at the dollars longingly, then shook her head. "I don't hold with that kind of truck."

"What kind of truck might that be, Mrs. Dittman?" Fan asked, her happiness gurgling in her throat.

She rose defiantly. "You just come back here over and over 'cause I'll let you in. I'm poor, but I'm proud. I just won't have it any longer."

"But we're married, Mrs. Dittman," Fan said. "See." She held out her left hand. Her plain gold band gleamed in the lamplight.

The woman bent over, lifting her spectacles to scrutinize it. "Is this some kind of joke?"

"No, ma'am." Irons' own happiness matched his wife's. He chuckled as he plunked down another couple of dollars and pulled the wedding license from his vest pocket. "We're married."

"Come to spend our wedding night in the best bed in Waldrow."

She raised up suspiciously. "I—I don't know exactly quite what to say."

"You could congratulate me," he replied, hugging Fan until she squeaked. "It looked like I wasn't going to be able to pull it off for a while."

Floreine Dittman, her face blank with surprise, handed over the key to their room.

Irons swept Fan up into his arms and started for the stairs.

She put her arms around his neck and took his earlobe between her teeth. "What do you mean, you didn't think you could pull it off," she whispered. "I never had the slightest doubt. Never the slightest."

Epilogue

England's Fancy pierced the blue Texas sky like a mast. The big horsehead on the pump rose and dipped, rose and dipped with the same unbroken rhythm as the ceaseless rolling of the ocean waves.

And the name of the rhythm was Power.

Caroline Fancy Irons lifted her eyes to the top of the tower and swayed back lightly on her heels, swayed back against her husband's broad chest. He put his big scarred hands on her shoulders to steady her and dropped a light kiss on her temple.

Edward England Irons popped his chubby fist from his mouth and waved it around in the warm air. Waved it and stared fuzzily up at the giant framework that waited for his hand.